Penguin Books

# UNABLE BY REASON OF DEATH

Catherine Lewis and Judith Guerin completed their formal education in a variety of Antipodean tertiary educational institutions. Despite this experience, they then went on to take up teaching careers, where their informal education in the School of Life continues daily.

This courageous pair have now entered the world of the literary arts. This is their first novel and they are currently working on a sequel.

FOR HARRY AND JOHN

Both the College and the characters are entirely fictitious and no resemblance to or identification with any institution or persons is intended or should be inferred.

# UNABLE BY REASON OF DEATH

★

CATHERINE LEWIS
& JUDITH GUERIN

Penguin Books

Penguin Books Australia Ltd
487 Maroondah Highway, PO Box 257
Ringwood, Victoria, 3134, Australia
Penguin Books Ltd
Harmondsworth, Middlesex, England
Viking Penguin Inc.
40 West 23rd Street, New York, NY 10010, USA
Penguin Books Canada Limited
2801 John Street, Markham, Ontario, Canada, L3R 1B4
Penguin Books (N.Z.) Ltd
182-190 Wairau Road, Auckland 10, New Zealand

First published by Penguin Books Australia, 1989

Copyright © Colin Golvan in trust for the authors, 1989.

All Rights Reserved. Without limiting the rights under copyright reserved above, no part of this publication may be reproduced, stored in or introduced into a retrieval system, or transmitted, in any form or by any means (electronic, mechanical, photocopying, recording or otherwise), without the prior written permission of both the copyright owner and the above publisher of this book.

Typeset in Palatino by Southern Cross Typesetting
Made and printed in Australia by The Book Printer, Maryborough, Victoria

CIP

  Lewis, Catherine.
    Unable By Reason Of Death.

  ISBN 0 14 012219 2.

  I. Guerin, Judith. II. Title.

A823'.3

# 1

It was another wet Monday morning. Great cold raindrops fell on Sam Klusky as he stood at the back entrance of Building 1956. He shifted his bundle of books and papers awkwardly from side to side, trying to keep them dry, as he scrabbled in various pockets for his keys. They weren't there. Sighing, he resorted to the tried and true expedient of jumping up and down on the spot. His ears were rewarded with a faint metallic jingle. Thank Christ for that, he thought, at least I don't have to drive all the way back to Elsternwick.

All the same, he still had to solve the problem of freeing both hands from the books and papers so that he could track down the keys, wherever they lurked in the lining of his vast coat, and persuade them to reappear through the hole in his left-hand pocket.

The lane where he stood offered no protection from the elements, and Maintenance seemed to have forgotten about it some years ago. The century-old bluestone paving was just discernible through the mud and litter. Sam considered asking one of the derelicts who graced the laneway whether he would mind holding the papers for a minute, but quickly dismissed the idea, realising that their level of consciousness probably wouldn't be up to the job. Hard to know why Campus Security let those guys hang around. They were usually so fussy about giving a nice middle-class impression.

Perhaps someone was using them for experiments? You'd never know, would you?

The rain was pelting down now. There was nothing for it but the old feet trick. He reorganised his belongings so that they rested on a large folder, and balanced the whole pile precariously on top of his feet. Then he scrabbled through his coat, easing the keys back into his pocket and, finally, into his hand. At last, he thought, stepping forward eagerly. The rusty old lock gave under a determined twist of Sam's powerful wrists. He performed the athletic marvel of holding the heavy door open with one foot while rapidly hauling his belongings off the filthy wet bluestones where he had scattered them with the effort, and diving inside.

The door banged shut behind him, and Sam was left in pitch darkness at the bottom of the stairwell. Muttering, he scrabbled about until he found the light switch. He could have sworn it had been somewhere else last week. Bloody Maintenance, warped sense of humour those guys had. Sighing, he reassembled the books and notes, preparatory to the long haul upstairs. There was a lift, but not even Sam Klusky would use it. Patience he had, but sitting about waiting to be rescued on a regular basis would have demanded tendencies to martyrdom. He moved gloomily towards the stairs at the precise moment that the lights automatically switched themselves off again. Sam's resigned muttering changed to audible cursing as he hunted about for the light switch once more.

'Why,' he demanded of the building, 'have automatic light cut-outs on a bloody flight of stairs?'

He looked upwards again and a classically conditioned gloom descended upon him. Doggedly he trudged up the first flight. Sam was a tenured lecturer (Level III, grade 2) at the Justice Barry College of Technology, known as Bazza Tech to its inmates. Working at Bazza had never exactly been fun, but lately it had been sheer bloody murder. Puffing already, he decided to pause for a rest near the switch instead of trying to make it to the second landing before the light cut out again.

'They've timed these lights on the Olympic ski team.' He spoke aloud again, his voice echoing around queerly in the stairwell. The building creaked bad-temperedly as he stood puffing and brooding. What on earth could this week hold that would be as bad as the last one, he wondered. Iain Scott, the Department's Chairman, had confirmed that Johnston would be the Academic Co-ordinator of Sam's new course. That meant that he could kiss any hope of promotion goodbye. Johnston would take the credit, Sam would do the work. Course fucking development, he muttered, some bloody hope, the minute you develop anything around here, they're onto you like vultures. He loathed Johnston, he realised, and he was not the only one. Loathing was not a feeling that came readily to Sam; he was an easy-going person really, but there were some people that made him want to go out and crush things. The lights went out again and Sam put them back on, bracing himself to make it to the next landing.

Where had it all gone wrong, he wondered, clutching his papers to his broad chest. He distinctly remembered being promised, back in Krakow, that if he worked hard and did well at school, he would get a good job. Well so he had, worked hard and got good marks that is, but what had happened to the job bit? Of course, there had been that unpleasantness back in Poland but other people immigrated, Australia was the land of immigrants, even the bloody Aborigines had immigrated, it was all a matter of your time scale. He, it seemed, had unerringly picked the wrong moment to land. Tertiary education was all he was good for, he thought, reaching the halfway mark on the stairs. But tertiary education was in a recession. Why was life so miserable, he wondered. Of course things had been better when Becky was alive.

The lights went out again, but he had made it to the landing and he stopped in the dark for another rest. There was nothing nervous about Sam. If you were built like a tank, nothing much frightened you really. Still, he was in no hurry and he didn't want to twist his ankle and have to wait hours for the other staff to come in. Half of them would put his moans down to ghosts, he thought crossly. Called themselves logical positivists and frightened the wits out of themselves with ghost stories!

Would there be another almighty row this week, he wondered, leaning back against the second-floor fire door. He just couldn't stand those tea-room feuds. He did his best to cope by walking away, but you couldn't always manage that.

Johnston had received a publication acceptance for his blasted paper on the use of hormonally active inhalants to attain control of mood. All he had to do now, he had gloated to the assembled throng, was to purify the compound and he'd be away and heigh-ho for Stockholm and the Nobel Prize. Somebody, was it Florence, Sam couldn't quite remember, had tried to make polite conversation by asking him what he was going to call it. Sam had been expecting something like Ameronium, Richard's fanatical loyalty to his mother country was well known, but Johnston had proposed 'Civilein'. Of course, Jacinta had snorted and said 'Slavein' would be nearer the mark and it had been on for young and old.

Johnston had been very strong on the conserving properties of conformity in a complex post-industrial society, while Jacinta and a few other malcontents had pointed out that progress appeared to come from the alienated and rebellious. Thoreau, she had said, could just have done with a good dollop of your Slavein, that would have fixed him. Johnston had retorted furiously that one day Civilein would be automatically piped through plane air-conditioning systems to prevent hijacks. Funny how the neurochemists, led by Jacinta, had ranted about the social impact while the sociologists had asked about neurological side effects. No-one had spoken to anyone else since last Wednesday, Sam recalled, after the screaming about terrorists and fascists, but he hoped the weekend would have given everyone a chance to calm down.

Well, standing about on the stairs was getting nobody anywhere; besides, it was cold. He snapped on the next set of lights and made a determined rush to the fourth floor. At last, heart pounding, head swimming, he made it to the top.

He really must do something about getting fit, he thought for the umpteenth time as he puffed down the dank corridor clutching the mail from his overflowing pigeonhole. They told me the sun shone all the time in Australia, he thought ruefully. Trust me to pick Melbourne, Helsinki of the South. He paused where the end of the corridor used to be, before they had converted half the lobby into extra tutorial rooms, and reached for the light switch. Spilling memos and students' papers on the faintly squishy carpet around him, he flicked at the switch. Nothing happened.

'Fiat lux,' he muttered to himself as he grovelled for his papers, 'et bloody tenebrae erat. Typical.'

Still, it could have been worse; in fact it frequently was. Barry College's austerity budget made the Siege of Leningrad look like a summer picnic, and Maintenance was always busy somewhere else. At least this time the electricity supply had only failed on one floor. Sam stared up and down the dingy corridor. A pale stream of light filtered through about halfway down. Alan Hoxha's door was open as always, even at the comparatively early hour of – Sam dropped another memo straining to read his watch in the gloom – 9:06, but his was the only one. Looking in as he trudged past, Klusky saw a jacket carelessly flung over a chair. Gone to his other job, half his luck, he mused. How does he get away with it? I mean, the man's just about due for the Scarlet Pimpernel Award. They seek him here, they seek him there, but he's always 'at the other office' or 'just on his way' or something. Home in bed with a warm student more likely. The man could drop dead and it would be weeks before we noticed, mused Sam. Wait a minute, though, he does come in on paydays.

Why are so many academics such horrible people to deal with, he wondered. Something to do with the way a combination of hope deferred, lousy pay and poor conditions blighted naive, hopeful young thinkers? He plodded on, clutching the top-heavy heap of papers that threatened to fall onto the unsavoury carpet.

It wasn't that Maintenance missed out on Barry College of Technology's budget. Quite the opposite, they retained a small army of overalled yobs, in addition to the building programme that Sam could hear crashing into life outside. But somehow the trickledown effect hadn't quite trickled into the Department of Psychological and Sociological Inquiry. In any case it was probably a hopeless task. Building 1956 had started life as a garment factory, built on the cheap, and never maintained. Sam suspected that Barry College had only run electricity into it so that the Department of Radiocommunications could actually see television, then a new toy. Twenty years of thundering engineering students had done little for the fabric of the building by the time the psychologists had moved in to the top two floors. How Peter Harwell ran the Student Health Centre downstairs without causing a plague, Sam had no idea.

This morning the odour of decay oozed from Bennett's and Summerfield's offices. The roof had leaked again, as usual, after a wet weekend. It meant another round of tantrums from Edmund Bennett, acid comments about Australian workmanship from Summerfield, ripping up the mushroom-infested carpets, and futile claims against the College's insurance company.

Last time it had happened, over in the Department of Geography and Recreation Studies, poor old Dr Nettleship had lost a full lecture course. He'd written it all up on overhead projections and didn't have any teaching notes. His files had looked like avant-garde water colours, but he hadn't taken too kindly to the Director's suggestion that he transfer to Graphic Arts. The insurers, Beneficial Permanent Mutual or somebody, hadn't come through with a cent to replace the mouldy books, let alone compensate for the lost time and effort of the overheads. Personal effects, they had written crisply, the Barry College of Technology does not insure the personal effects of staff. Stationery supply had, to this very day, flatly refused to change over to waterproof pens. Nettleship had got his own back, though, by going off on compo for nervous exhaustion. Rumour had it that he was running an educational tours company in Bali. That was the unfairness of life, thought Sam, pale skinny people could always get away with nervous exhaustion. I'm nervously exhausted too, but who would believe it?

Those sharks at the insurance office won't part with a cent this time either, he prophesied, opening his own office door and dropping the pile of papers in his arms onto a larger pile of papers, books, stop-smoking guides, journals, and old sandwiches on his desk. The new arrivals caused some sort of geological activity further down the heap, and a layer or two slid onto the floor, revealing the minutes of the last Common First-Year Steering Committee Meeting.

Barry Institute of Technology
Department of Psychological and Sociological Inquiry

Common First Year Steering Committee

it began, and Sam read on wearily. How come nobody proofread these things? Or, worse, had somebody already done so?

*Course 13C: Proposed. Sex and Death in Sport for the Aged Report of 10th meeting*

*Present: R. Johnston (Convener), F. Lark, R. Potoch, I. Scott Apologies: A. Hoxha, S. Klusky*
  *1. Compiling submision for Government Academic Review Panel R. Johnston reported that work had begun on colation or curriculum materials developed to date into the submission format. The steering committee will be able to identify areas which require development in utilising the accreditation guidelines. It is dersirable to have a skeleton submission draft ready for the Course Develpemnt Committee meeting.*
  *2. Continued development of course structure*
*F. Lark asked for clarification of the Sex/Person/Death concepts discussed at the eighth and ninth Steering Committee meetings. Concern was expressed over the notion of separating Sex and Person. The notion of Person as object is difficult ofr people to accept.*

*There was lengthly discussion about the concepts and the following points were raised:*

  *– should a holistic or a reductionist view of the Person be taken?*
  *– Steering Committee members should read Smith, J. & Wesson, S. (1954)* The Zen of Holism: A Short Journey *in order to obtain a perspective on holism.*
  *– The terms Sex/Person/Death require rigorous definition. In identifying these concepts, the steering committee was trying to develop the underpinings for the curriculum.*

– *It was suggested that the concepts are too contraversial to be used, ie. if there is misunderstanding among the steering committee members then others will have an even more difficult time.*
– *Further to the preceeding discussion, it was agreed that a basic conceputal framework be developed that leads into the thermatic approach. The concepts Person/Death/Worldview will be used to unerpin the themes.*
– *S. Klusky be asked to formulate a descriptive statement as to the foundation concepts and interrelate the concepts and the themes in coperation with R. Johnston.*
– *I. Scott moved that the matter be rerferred to the Academic Committee meeting.*

Sam groaned. The worst thing about being an academic was the endless futile meetings. In fact, as futile meetings went, academic committees were the worst. People felt obliged to have an opinion about Academic Issues, and to air it at length. To prove they were academics, Sam supposed. The endless wrangles about paradigms and conceptual frameworks, the drafting and re-drafting of policies that nobody would abide by unless it suited them at the time, the acrimony and bitterness, and above all the agonising waste of precious time, of life itself, over trivia. Surely he could stay away. He could develop a Jewish holiday of the acute, inconvenient variety. He could claim that the mould spores in the atmosphere had given him asthma. O'Faolain got away with it all the time. He sighed and turned to the agenda for the next Academic Committee meeting. He had forgotten it was scheduled for this Thursday, and wondered if he dared miss another one. His eye lit on something familiar halfway down the page, and he read:

*3. It has been proposed that a sociological perspecive is needed in Dr Johnston's new umberella course 'Computer simulations of sex and death in sport for the aged'.*
*Moved: F. Lark, seconded R. Potoch*
*For discussion.*

Angrily he flung the paper down. It was really more than he

could stand. Why did Florence Lark insist on arguing with Johnston? She ought to know by now that it always ended in tears. At least for her anyway; Jacinta, on the other hand, scored the odd victory by being just as rude and rather more ruthless in return. There certainly was a feud between those two; Sam had no idea what had started it, but neither was the sort to forget easily. Even Scott, the Head of Department, was scared of Johnston, and that was something. But once the man got wound up he'd say anything and he was well known to dig the dirt on everyone's private life. Sam knew that to his cost. As Johnston had pointed out to him, it really wouldn't be worth Sam's while to make too much public fuss about plagiarism.

Besides, who wants a sociological perspective anyway? He stormed out into the corridor in search of a friend to listen to his righteous indignation. Computer simulation of sex and death!

'Jesus H. Fucking Christ on a raft!' he heard himself shouting. He looked up and down the corridor again, but all was still so he stamped back into his office and sat down heavily. But all I wanted, he fumed, all I wanted to do was put together a good, solid, sympathetic introduction to the physical and social changes associated with age. I just wanted to introduce the students to the notion that people over seventy don't come from outer space, that they're human beings, and that the aged have a rather different perspective on the world from the young. It could have been a good course. But no. That bloody Johnston stepped in. It wasn't paradigmatic enough, said he. Whatever that means. Okay, so I read a lot of boring silly books and put a lot of boring silly theory into it. Not good enough, says his lord bloody highness, Chairman of the Steering Committee.

Sam was well aware that if you wanted to pinch other people's courses to advance your own career, the Chairman of the Steering Committee was the ideal position to have. He had nominated himself, but was still awaiting the minutes of the meeting at which the election had been held. Funny how he'd never received notice of it either. He was a cunning bugger, that Johnston. No wonder he was always being held up as a Renaissance Man, combining research with teaching and course development. He got poor schnorrers like Sam to do the hard work and pinched things at the crucial moment. Knight of St John too, thought Klusky viciously, doesn't say much for Christianity, does it? But anyway, he thought, I let him put sex and death and computers into the course, anything to get the enrolments up. But now sociology! It's the bloody end.

Sam wished Jacinta and Lisa were there to talk to. He'd said all this, and more, to them in the tea room only last week, leaving out some of the bloodies from a totally misplaced sense of chivalry. They'd been sympathetic, in their own way. Jacinta was all right really, provided you didn't cross her, and Lisa was fun. Lisa reminded Sam of a younger version of himself. He suspected she might still believe that the education system might be intended to help people develop their powers of reason.

It was good to have a few pleasant colleagues around the place though, even if they were smartarse young shiksas. He sighed as he remembered something Jacinta had told him in confidence. It seemed she was likely to be leaving soon; she'd applied for a job as Senior Research Officer at the State Electricity Commission. Something to do with the effects of electromagnetic waves on the human brain. Well funded too. The first interview had been last week, and she'd just heard that she was on the short list.

He didn't like the thought of Jacinta leaving. Why didn't a few of the bastards who made his life so hard leave, instead of the few staff who were recognisably human? Lisa had been talking vaguely about leaving too, but then so had he for the last ten years. So had they all. But who would they find to replace Jacinta? Some absolute dead-head, he was sure of that. It would have to be a woman; most Departments swore they never got any female applicants, so that the few who admitted they did, like Psycho, got the hard word put on them by the Director to appoint women wherever possible.

'Affirmative action,' Goldwyn had said in ringing tones, 'has got to work and be seen to be working.'

Funny it didn't seem to work at Director level, but there you were. If Jacinta left, they were doomed to wind up with some femocrat toting a briefcase around the place with ruthless efficiency. The other alternative was even more horrific – some overalled feminist leftie with three earrings in one ear and one in her nose, and the hygiene! Sam put his face in his hands as the memory of a previous staff member returned in all its horror. She had told him with great pride that she always changed her underwear at the full moon. When he said he'd already guessed, she'd called him a crypto-fascist trivialiser or words to that effect.

Suddenly he had to have a cigarette. He hunted through one of his rat's-nest drawers for his secret packet, the addict's last resort. Not there. Surely one of those health freak do-gooders wouldn't have come in and taken a man's hidden cigarette supply, only to be used in direst emergencies? Impossible, they'd never find them. Straightening up, he glared round the pile of grot surging down off the desk and bookshelves and over the floor. No one who valued their health would put a toe over the threshold. The smokes had to be there. Losing his patience, he wrenched the drawer from the desk and tipped its contents onto the papers which already littered the floor. They were there, nobody had taken them.

But where to smoke the thing? It was coming up to ten o'clock now, and the timbers of the old factory were beginning to creak, suggesting at least students and possibly staff. Someone might poke a head round the door and invite him to coffee at any moment. Imagine the jeers if he were caught smoking again. He now regretted giving up so publicly after yet another row with Richard Johnston in the tea room. If that smartarse makes too many more remarks about 'as broad as he's tall' and keeps going on about how 'in a complex society, one person's selfish slackness about health affects everybody by boosting health costs', I'll rearrange his bloody face, Sam thought. If I have to stand on a chair to do it.

Palming a cigarette, he squelched softly down the corridor and into the back entrance at the top of the Rom Harre lecture theatre, a darkened haven where a desperate Klusky could soothe his nerves in peace.

Thank goodness the back door had been left open, but then Security was like that around here. He didn't put the lights on, no point in drawing attention to yourself, and anyway they mightn't be working either. Long practice enabled him to descend the inner stairs and negotiate the skeleton in front of the lectern. He lit his cigarette and began to pace slowly up and down in the gloom. As the nicotine began to restore his equilibrium, Sam began to wonder about the skeleton. What cruel fate led a person's bones to be exposed to the public gaze, the pranks of students, the screams of unprepared cleaners?

Come to that, he thought, why does a would-be hedonist like me work in a place like Barry College? Half the staff are health freaks, or religious freaks, or crazy, or just plain not nice to be with. Why do I do it? Because I need the money, he reminded himself. Life as a widower with three young children and a mortgage wasn't easy. A single mother would get help from the government, he reflected bitterly. They seem to think that middle-aged, middle-income supporting fathers have young women just falling over themselves with eagerness to take them on.

His mother had been badgering him to find another wife, a young girl who could look after the children, or a widow of independent means in need of companionship. He had tried to explain that people were less businesslike about such things here. Besides, he, himself, wasn't as European as he used to be. He liked looking after the three boys, hard though it was, and he wasn't sure how they, or he for that matter, would take to someone new. Empirical testing had shown that few women were interested after being subjected to the critical gaze of his mother and offspring over dinner. If it had been just the boys, he could have slipped some Valium into their cocoa, but somehow he didn't think Valium would work on his mother. Largactil maybe.

He paced slowly, drawing in the blessed smoke. Who wants to live so long, anyway? Gradually, a queer smell penetrated his case-hardened smoker's nostrils. Sewage, and something odd. What on earth could it be? Had his cigarette rotted or something? No, it tasted all right, despite weeks in his filthy desk drawer. Funny how tough unhealthy things seemed to be. The smell was stronger on the darker side of the auditorium, away from the lower entrance door. He wandered reluctantly towards it. The drainage system in Building 1956 was a byword for rusty inefficiency and he wondered if a drain had overflowed in the storm. He hoped it hadn't. He was meant to teach in here later on today, and raw sewage wouldn't help. Suddenly he fell over something that wasn't meant to be there.

Wet carpets, was his first thought as he picked himself up. From the flooded offices upstairs. No, wait a minute, he reminded himself, they took the last lot away a week ago and they can't have taken the next lot up yet. That smell was very nasty, now he'd got closer to it. Not even a mouldy carpet could smell like that. Familiar. His old student days as a hospital orderly, he'd done a few nasty jobs back then. In a sudden panic, he recognised it. Frantically he backed away from the thing on the floor, over to the lectern to find the bank of light switches. He flicked them. Relief that they came on changed suddenly to horror.

A heap of old clothes was lying at the end of a long smear of brown stuff.

For one appalled moment he stared at it, unsure whether to scream, throw up or just turn and run. Then the hot end of his cigarette burned his fingers, switching his mind back on. He bounded up the centre steps, back up to the top floor, and ran for help.

'Quick, someone's been hurt, quick, for God's sake!'

He galloped towards the reception area in search of a person, a phone, anything, as long as it was well away from the corpse. As he charged in, he crashed into Peter Harwell, the doctor from downstairs, coming out. Harwell, tall but slight, reeled under the impact of Klusky's bulk. Sam realised that a refugee from Medicare might be able to help.

Still gabbling, 'Quick! Quick!' he seized Peter, confident that he represented a solution to the corpse problem.

'All right! Stop doing a fucking duck imitation, I can hear you. Why are you pulling me about like that? Where are we going? Let go,' expostulated Harwell as he struggled to escape. He'd only come up from the Student Health Centre to invite Florence Lark to lunch with him.

But Sam, with all the considerable force that a solid man with a low centre of gravity could muster, hauled him back down the corridor to the now brilliantly lit lecture theatre and propelled him inside.

'There,' he said, 'do something.'

'About what?' demanded Harwell crossly. Sam pointed to the distant floor of the theatre and then realised that the thing was invisible from where they stood. The trail of dried blood across the lower level of the theatre was, however, very plain and Harwell started down the stairs. Klusky followed him, mumbling, 'You're a doctor, do something. Oh, can't you do something?'

Harwell drew breath for a sharp reply, but the whiff changed his mind. Quickly he examined the body, turning it over with practised ease.

'Well,' he said, looking at his hands with distaste, 'I may be a doctor, but raising the dead wasn't in our course and that's what he is, stiff as a board. Must have been dead quite a while. It's Richard Johnston, of course.'

Sam stared at him, speechless. He had only just managed to realise that it was a dead person; the idea of it being someone he knew was devastating.

'That's him, all right,' continued Harwell, realising Sam was beyond a reply. 'Make it easier for the police if they get a prompt identification. No great loss. I've been waiting for someone to stove that bastard's head in for years. Pity someone didn't get him sooner.'

'Stove his head in?' quavered Sam, sitting down heavily in the end seat of the first row, which banged loudly and startlingly in the silence.

'Yes. Frontal bones are completely battered in, fair bit of force used there, I should think,' answered Harwell. He looked at the remains of Richard Johnston thoughtfully. 'This is the best news I've had in years. We'd better put him back the way he was, the police get a bit annoyed if anyone but them messes around with the corpse. Come on, give us a hand to roll him back over.'

Sam sat immobile; there was no way he was touching any murder victims. Harwell glared at him but seized Johnston and rolled him back over unaided.

'Now look what you've done,' he said to Sam gloomily. 'Got me involved in a blasted police case. I'll have to be a witness, I suppose, and you know how tedious that is.'

'How can you be so callous? He was a human being and now he's dead and you don't even care,' was all Sam could find to say.

'Callous! Human being! Care! Come off it, Sam. You hated his guts, everyone knows that. Can't say I blame you. Wouldn't have been surprised if you'd stove his head in yourself.'

Sam interrupted with a horrified snort of denial.

'Well, well, you say you didn't, everyone will say that, and the fact is you found him, and you've got the strength and the motive,' Harwell continued calmly, gazing down at Sam.

'Strength? Motive?' squeaked Sam.

'Yes, yes,' snapped Harwell impatiently. 'Good god man, think. Here we have a man with a smashed head who's been dragged about twenty metres across a carpeted floor and here,' he said, glaring at Sam, 'we have a man who's used to lifting heavy weights, who has just lost his precious course to the clutches of the dear departed, to say nothing of our Loved One's nasty habit of interesting himself in your private life, and you the man who just happens to find him prematurely deceased. Adds up, doesn't it?'

'I had nothing to do with it, I only found him, I'm opposed to violence,' Sam insisted. And besides, he asked himself, how come Peter knows so much about the internal affairs of the Department? Is the rumour about him and Florence true, then?

'All right, I believe you,' replied Peter, 'but then I'm gullible; will the police believe it? Anyway, there's only one way to find out. Don't just sit there, go and call them. Call the ambulance too, but don't tell them he's dead or they won't come.'

Harwell gave a mock salute and strolled whistling away, leaving Sam sitting open-mouthed, gazing at the body.

## 2

Gaelene Trimble called the police. Gaelene was the Departmental Secretary, and widely believed to be the only person in the place who did any actual work. She had arrived to find Sam bumbling

15

around the Reception area. She couldn't quite understand what had happened at first, because all she could get out of Sam was complaints about phones not working and all the lights on the top floor being off. As she pointed out, the phones did that when they were on the night-switch system but it was a simple matter to fix it.

'What's up?' she said, once the phones were sorted out. 'The lights often go off after a storm, you know that, the water gets into the electricals, what's the big deal?'

Sam stopped muttering long enough to say clearly, 'Murder. In the Rom Harre lecture theatre. Call the police.' and so she did. She knew academics were a pretty weird lot, but if Sam said there had been a murder in the Rom Harre, then there probably had been. And if there hadn't, well, she was only following instructions. And, as Johnston had so often reminded her, she was paid to do that, not to think.

She was disappointed when Sam flatly refused to let her see the body. As a paid-up punk rocker, she loved a bit of horror, but Sam was so old-fashioned. A nice enough bloke though, probably his age; at thirty-eight you were ancient history. Gaelene hoped she died before she got old.

Sam recovered sufficiently to lock the doors of the lecture theatre, call Central Admin to explain the situation, and muster the staff in the Reception area as they wandered in to work. Just as they were trying to dispel crowds of students and write dozens of 'lecture cancelled' signs, two plain-clothes police and the Director arrived simultaneously.

'Detective-Inspector Hubel,' snapped the larger police officer, waving an identification card too quickly for anyone to read it, 'what's all this about?'

'There's been a murder,' began Sam nervously.

'Say, why don't we let the police decide that?' interrupted Nathan Goldwyn, all teeth, tailoring and perfume. The only way Nathan could keep his springy hair under control was to douse it with Eau du Portugal; a good hair oil but one with a presence.

'Who are you?' asked Detective-Inspector Hubel, sniffing suspiciously.

'I am the Director of this College, Dr Nathan Goldwyn,

madam,' Goldwyn replied. 'Pleased to make your acquaintance.'

He extended his hand and Doreen shook it dubiously.

'I don't believe I know your colleague's name,' Goldwyn began, but Doreen Hubel had had enough of pleasantries.

'We got a phone call saying there was a body in one of the lecture theatres,' she announced.

'So did I,' agreed Goldwyn.

'Well then, let's get to it.'

'You heard the lady,' said Goldwyn, peering at Sam. Who was he? Klutzy? Surely not, nobody had a name like that. Was he an academic? Some of the lecturing staff were fairly odd-looking in this country. 'Let's get to it, where's the body? Do we know who it is?'

'It's in the Rom Harre lecture theatre, er, down there. It's Richard Johnston.'

'Richard Johnston! Don't be ridiculous!' Goldwyn shouted. 'He's a very fine man, an outstanding academic. Who would want to kill him?'

Doreen noticed that nobody contradicted Goldwyn verbally.

'You knew this Johnston, then?' she asked Goldwyn.

'Yes, I know him well. We graduated from the same university in the States, not at the same time of course, he was a little younger, but a very distinguished academic, I was pleased and proud to find that he was in the College when I came here as Director...'

'Good-oh,' said Doreen. 'We need somebody to identify him, you gonna be up to it or should we get your friend here to show us? I mean you're not gonna faint on us are you?'

'Up to it? Faint?' expostulated Goldwyn. 'I served in Korea!'

To Sam's unspeakable relief, Goldwyn and Hubel disappeared into the Rom Harre, while Hubel's partner stood in the reception area eyeing them all. Sam prayed that they wouldn't need him. Apparently they didn't. About five minutes later, Goldwyn re-emerged leaning on Hubel's sturdy arm and looking very pale and sick.

'Korea must've worn off a bit,' Hubel said to Gaelene. 'You're the secretary aren't you? How about a cuppa for Mr Goldwyn?

You lot,' she added, addressing the rest of the staff collectively, 'get those students out of here, they're in the way.' She dumped Goldwyn onto a bench and strode towards the phone to call for reinforcements.

Amazing the effect of somebody taking charge. Hubel's remarks seemed to have the same effect as shouting, 'Lights! Camera! Action!' Students dispersed down the stairs in small disgruntled groups, but Sam was unpleasantly surprised when Inspector Hubel's silent friend sidled up to him and said, 'You the bloke who found the body? We want to interview you, come along this way.'

It took them about two hours, and much listening to irrelevancy and confusion, to decide that it would be a good idea for Sam to continue helping the police in more congenial surroundings. For the police, that was. The pathologist appeared and announced that rigor mortis was well advanced and that Dr Johnston had been dead some hours. He had probably died on Sunday afternoon, Mackinolty continued. The corpse had depressed, comminuted fractures of the left frontal and parietal bones of the skull caused by a heavy object wielded with great force.

Typical, Doreen thought, tell you in Greek what you can see for yourself in English.

With a rare burst of communication, Mackinolty remarked, 'Somebody's been at him already. You noticed that, didn't you? Head's three inches away from the blood.' Doreen hadn't but she wasn't going to admit to it.

'What was the cause of death?' she asked, hopefully, but knowing the answer in advance.

'Impossible to tell without a post-mortem,' replied the pathologist, running true to form.

'Could it have anything to do with being hit over the head with something heavy?' suggested Wiesel helpfully. He intercepted two glares, one from the pathologist who thought he was getting his leg pulled, and one from Hubel who wasn't about to stand there all day listening to another lecture on proximal and distal causes of death. Anyway, Wiesel had been getting above himself lately, she thought. She cut Mackinolty off before he could start on aspiration of vomit versus loss of blood. At least it wasn't going to be one of those untraceable-poison numbers, like that dreadful Bogle-Chandler case. You could never tell with these academics, they could be cooking up anything in those laboratories.'

'Thanks Doc,' she said. 'Can you tell us anything about the murderer?'

'Not the sort of thing women go in for. They're poisoners as a rule. Probably a male. Right-handed I'd think. Might be covered in blood and brains,' he said tersely. 'Not now, would have had a wash. Stained clothes. Check the men's loo, he might have cleaned himself up in there. Check with the cleaners.'

'What about the weapon?' Doreen asked a little desperately, hoping for some sort of clue.

'Like your friend said, something heavy. Try an iron bar. I'll be able to tell you more after the post-mortem.' He packed up his bag and began giving orders for the removal of the body and uttering threats against anyone entering the lecture theatre before it had been examined, measured, and dusted.

To the fascinated students outside, who watched in awe as the stretcher containing the body was humped down the stairs, Sam Klusky's arrest was the most exciting thing to have happened at Barry College since the day it all got too much for Dr Cavendish. She had been found, naked, singing, and surrounded by empty gin bottles, in the Bruno Bettelheim Lecture Theatre first thing one morning.

For Sam, things were less exhilarating. Sam was a stoical soul, not given to overt expressions of dismay. The fact that, on being told of his arrest, he had only remarked, 'Oh well, at least I won't have to give Johnston's bloody classes,' had not gone down well with the police.

'Do you want something to cover your face?' asked the policeman whom Sam now knew to be called Percival Wiesel.

'What would I want to cover my face for?' Sam demanded. 'I'm not guilty.'

'All the more reason to cover it then,' replied Wiesel reasonably. 'You wouldn't want people to get the wrong idea, would you?'

Sam found himself unable to comprehend how he had allowed himself to be talked into covering his face with a jacket and being led around his own College. The power of other people's expectations was boundless, he thought gloomily, negotiating by feel. Years of practice in power failures meant it wasn't as difficult as he had thought. Fortunately the lift worked this time.

There were police everywhere in Building 1956 by now, measuring, interviewing and photographing. Dr Lisa Thomas hung about, waiting to deny all in the interview and meanwhile looking as inconspicuous as possible. As a good social psychologist, not to mention a friend of Sam's, she felt an obligation to be close to the action. Not too close, thank you, but enough to keep an eye on things.

Sam couldn't possibly have committed a murder. Certainly he had hated Johnston, but when it came to killing, Sam just wasn't that sort of person. You only had to see him with his boys to realise that. Although, she supposed, you never could tell. Perhaps he had a brain tumour; he did get headaches from time to time. Mind you, didn't we all, having to work in a dump like this. No, of course Sam couldn't have done it. It wasn't his style. He was more into self-blame. Obese, stressed, a prime candidate for a heart attack. She wondered whether he had had time to make arrangements for the boys, but then there was always Sam's mother.

The police didn't seem to have any doubts.

'He's the one, all right,' she heard a large portly police officer say to a small one as Percival Wiesel led Sam away. Why on earth with a jacket over his head, she wondered? Was there a regulation concerning jackets, accused heads for the covering of? Lisa was thankful that no-one had said it was an open-and-shut case. She suspected that life at Barry College was imitating soap opera, and she was relieved that at least one opportunity for a cliché had been passed up. It was bad enough having large porcine policemen and small rodent-like ones going around in pairs. Perhaps they were paired up like that at training college. Did they mate for life, she wondered, like turtle doves?

'Yes, an open-and-shut case,' a strange man in a brown suit remarked down the office phone behind her.

Lisa turned around and intercepted a fierce glare from someone who wanted more privacy than he could find. She hurriedly moved out of Reception and began examining the contents of her pigeonhole. Like many academics, she usually kept three or four harmless and irrelevant documents in her pigeonhole to provide her with an excuse for hanging around the corridor.

'But,' she could just make out the man saying, 'murderers often arrange to be the ones to find the victim. What? This is an awful line, you'll have to speak up. Oh. Motive. Hell, Bruce, do we have to discuss that now? I thought we operated on the premise that all phones were tapped.'

Did we, thought Lisa, as she gazed around the open space in front of the reception area. Most of the staff favoured the informal look at the best of times. Now, unkempt, uncertain, and awaiting instructions, they looked like shipwrecked survivors. Steerage mostly.

Just to prove her wrong, one of the few exceptions to slackness of any sort materialised from Reception, where she had been doing a little eavesdropping of her own. Still beautifully coiffured despite the red-rimmed eyes and smudged mascara, Antonia Summerfield bore down remorselessly on Lisa. She could see Antonia was trying to cope with some very strong emotion, but she would still have done almost anything to escape that penetrating voice, those inexorable opinions.

'I can't believe Richard's really dead,' she said in a tight voice. Lisa was surprised to see her so upset, and gave her a sympathetic look. It bounced off.

'I don't believe it,' Antonia continued firmly. 'Sam may be a slacker, but he's no killer. Poor fellow, I must ring my friend's chambers at once and arrange proper legal counsel for him. He can't have done it, can he, Seamus?'

Seamus O'Faolain was making good use of his time, apparently unfazed by events. He looked up from the floor where he was sitting cross-legged, proofreading a handout for students.

'Seems unlikely on the face of it, knowing Sam,' he agreed, 'but there is one thing that concerns me.'

'What's that?'

'Well, if he didn't do it, who did?' Seamus rose and wandered away.

As Seamus left, the Department's only aspirant to masculine chic moved fluidly down the corridor. Wearing white drill trousers and a navy blue shirt, and with a scarlet bandana carelessly knotted round his throat, he was a vision of sartorial splendour. He lacked only a cabbage tree hat and a light coating of grime to be the Compleat Bushranger. Why can't he wear lavender everythings or tattered blue jeans and Army surplus boots, like other gays, Lisa wondered crossly. Bennett ignored her and turned to Antonia. Like most other people in the Department, he knew exactly what Antonia thought of him, but unlike the others he didn't care and he loved to tease.

'Is this wonderful news true?' he asked breathlessly. 'Is it an actual fact, or just a delightful fantasy, that Richard Johnston has breathed his last? Does this mean an end to those helpful suggestions I was forever receiving about my personal life and out-of-hours recreation?'

Antonia saw in Bennett the worst of Antipodean attitudes to sex, not to mention emotional expression. The suggestion that he was pleased by Johnston's death seemed to be the last straw. Lisa wished she could have retreated into her pigeonhole as the gust of icy dislike wafted past her.

'Yes, he's dead,' said Antonia, drawing herself up sternly, 'and I think it would do you more credit if you could show some appreciation of the gravity of the situation, not to mention respect for the dead. After all, there has been a murder committed in our department.'

'Respect? What for? That man hovered over this place like a great black cloud of bad temper, blackmail, and paranoia. You know perfectly well he blocked my promotion to Principal Lecturer out of pure homophobia. You knew that at the time but would you support my appeal? You would not. Precious Richard could do no wrong. I'm glad, and I don't care who knows it. Not even you, Miss Bossyboots.'

If looks could maim, Bennett would have been in need of all the help the combined forces of the Departments of Applied Legal Practice and Medical Engineering could muster.

'Well, if you can't show the least scrap of human decency over the death of a fellow human being, you could at least indicate some reaction to poor Sam's arrest. Poor man, what he must be going through.'

'Oh, so Sam did it, did he? Well of course, he had reason enough but I'd never have believed he had it in him,' breathed Edmund with a well-rehearsed frisson of pleasure. 'How terribly masculine of him.'

Lisa was faintly surprised that steam wasn't emanating from Antonia's ears. She wanted to escape rather urgently, but the two antagonists had trapped her in front of the pigeonholes and the only way to leave was to push either one or both of them out of the way, and this she was unwilling to do in case they noticed her and turned on her simultaneously.

'You're disgusting, that's what you are,' hissed Antonia angrily. 'Of course Sam didn't do it. The police have made a horrible mistake, and it's up to us to rally round and see what we can do to help.'

'Well, I'm certainly not doing anything to help him,' replied Bennett airily. 'I'm delighted Johnston is dead and I don't really care who did it. But I think arresting Sam was a splendid idea. Life here will be much more congenial without him. Besides, he's fat.'

Turning his back on the enraged Antonia, he plucked a single grubby note from his pigeonhole and glided away towards his office, leaving an appalled silence in his wake.

'Well!' Antonia began, but seemed lost for an ending. 'Well, I've got work to do if no-one else has,' she managed finally, turned on her heel and headed for her room. On the way down the corridor, she collided with the returning Bennett in the semi-darkness. The impact prompted him to shout, 'Lights! Mushrooms! There's been another leak! Oh, get out of my way, can't you? I'm going home.'

He sauntered away to the unguarded back stairs. Antonia, looking decidedly grim after her encounter with Bennett and the discovery that her filing cabinets were once more filled with water, began working her way through the lists of phone numbers marked 'Maintenance' and 'Cleaning Squad'. None of them answered, but as she told herself, what could you expect from a bunch of Australians? Slack.

Lisa noted with some interest that nobody except Antonia was expressing any regret for the passing of their colleague. Hardly surprising, she though with a shrug. He was a right bastard if ever there was one. Jacinta certainly won't be sorry when she hears about this, she thought, following Bennett's example and escaping from the foyer. Jacinta's office was locked, so Lisa meandered gloomily on down the corridor. She wished she had the nerve to follow Bennett even further, and go home. To her surprise, she heard the photocopier working.

'What's all the excitement about?' asked Jacinta, raising her head from a breach of the copyright laws. 'Another bomb scare?'

'Bigger than that,' Lisa replied. 'Rather nasty actually. It seems someone's self-actualised themselves all over Richard Johnston with a meataxe.'

'You're joking,' said Jacinta, hitting the photocopier to stop it from beeping.

'No, it's for real, stiff as a board. Anyway, I don't think it's funny.'

'Dead? Richard Johnston? Oh come off it, the wicked never die. I'm not going to fall for that. I'd recognise your feeble sense of humour anywhere.'

'Come on, you know I'm funnier than that. Remember the dead fish in the filing cabinet? Anyway, if you don't believe me, ask Potoch.'

Jacinta turned, and saw Reuben Potoch flumping down the corridor from the staff tea room like a mobile sack of potatoes. Reuben's aversion to all types of exercise and dietary restraint had produced a human form which made our relationship with the amoeba difficult to deny.

'Isn't it awful?' he wheezed. 'Have you heard? They've arrested Sam. I've never heard anything so outrageous. Antisemitism. It's amazing how prevalent it is in the police force.'

'They've arrested Sam?' interruped Jacinta quickly. 'That's ridiculous. He couldn't have... Hey, do you think we could have a look at where it happened?'

'How morbid!' sniffed Reuben. 'You young Australians, no sense of decency. Australian women have the worst possible taste.'

But Jacinta and Lisa were halfway down the corridor, heading for one of the more obscure entries to the Rom Harre lecture theatre.

'How could anyone have worse taste than his wife, whatshername?' asked Jacinta as they walked down the stairway.

'Judith,' mused Lisa, 'but maybe he's a great fuck.'

The two of them fell, spluttering and giggling, through the lower entry of the Rom Harre theatre, only a few feet from where Johnston had been found. There was a truly awesome amount of blood. It looked as if Johnston had been felled near the front of the lecture theatre, and dragged perhaps a dozen yards to the dark corner where they stood.

'Good grief,' said Lisa.

Her whisper alerted a young, nervous-looking policeman who had been keeping a watch on the main doors, upstairs at the back. He whirled around, looking as if he wished he were somewhere else.

'Hey!' he shouted, recovering his nerve when he saw two relatively small female people. 'Youse can't come in here. Forensic haven't finished yet.'

'Yeah?' asked Lisa. 'What are they going to do? Fingerprint a lecture theatre? Have they any idea how many people come in here every day? Anyway, my fingerprints will be all over the shop. I've been teaching in here every Tuesday for ages.'

Jacinta ignored the policeman, now moving towards them, and looked carefully at the brown stain.

'You know, Sam can't have done it,' she said quietly to Lisa. 'If Johnston was really stiff, then death must have occurred on Sunday afternoon and he was somewhere else at the time.'

'He was?' Lisa looked blank.

'Yes, you know, he was talking to the Epilepsy Association. Remember the big panic when he didn't have his slides ready?'

'Yes, yes, youse can tell the plain-clothes blokes all about it when youse are interviewed,' asserted the constable. When they continued to ignore him, he grabbed each woman by the arm and shoved them back through the doorway.

'What a cheek,' said Jacinta crossly as the door slammed on them. 'They can damn well work it out for themselves if

25

they're going to maul people about. Let's go and have a cup of coffee.'

She sprang back up the narrow fire stairs.

Lisa gazed after her for a moment with a puzzled expression on her face. Wearily she climbed the stairs and came out into the tea room just in time to encounter the Head of Department. Iain Scott hadn't been seen on the premises before one in the afternoon for some years, but circumstances altered cases. He was marching up and down, shouting, 'Extraordinary meeting. Everyone must attend. Come on, hurry up, we can't stand gassing all day.'

## 3

Iain Scott had been roused from someone else's mattress by the insistent chirruping of a phone near his head. When he finally gave up and answered it, Gaelene remarked that dealing with police officers was not in her job description. She demanded that he get his arse into gear and roll it into work. Then she slammed the phone down. Scott turned onto his back and stared at the ceiling. Had no-one any sympathy at all, he wondered, for a man abruptly awakened to the harsh glare of an Australian morning without knowing where he was, who he was with, or what on earth he had been saying? He prodded the warm lump beside him in the bedclothes, hoping that it would at least identify itself and perhaps make him a cup of coffee.

'Gronk!' it remarked crossly, wound the rest of the covers round itself and retreated until only a few strands of green hair showed.

Man's search for meaning, not to mention trousers, inspired a shivering Scott to sit up and look about him. If Gaelene had known where to find him, this green-haired creature beside him must be a regular. The room had some definitely Carltonian features. They didn't go in for seagrass matting much in St Kilda, and they didn't usually have curtains either. Seagrass matting, curtains, hand-knotted Indian lampshades – it all looked like

Carlton. Could this heavy-breathing thing be Terri, he wondered, but when could she have dyed her hair green?

Scott retrieved a singlet, skivvy, and one sock from the side of the mattress and wandered, bare-arsed and disconsolate, in search of the rest of his clothing. Where did underpants go when you wanted them? Why did you only ever lose one sock? Tipping a table over with one hand, he retrieved a pair of underpants that would probably fit and even looked like his. Funny how individual your underpants were. Why were they so recognisable? Like an old friend who's come on hard times, loyal but embarrassing.

Hopping from foot to foot, he hauled them on, wondering what the police were doing at Barry College. Not another bomb scare, surely. He found his jeans behind the tape player. Good grief, four bomb scares in five months, he thought, sucking in his paunch to negotiate the zip.

Now all he needed was another sock, some shoes and several Disprin. It certain had been a bad year for students. Scott pounced on his left shoe. Pity he'd put the sock on his right foot. All this confrontation got nobody anywhere. Negotiation, compromise, the golden mean, that was what life was all about.

Mind you, Margery Cavendish had over-reacted badly to the student complaints last year; the vision of the singing maenad in the Bruno Bettelheim returned to him in full force. He held his hand to his left eye until the stabbing pain subsided. Peering through the ill-fitting curtains, he discovered where he was. Calrton, that was Terri then. Green hair, Christ! He owed nothing to a weirdo who wouldn't even make him a cup of coffee. I have a perfect right to find my other shoe, he thought, flinging the curtains open and gazing hopelessly round the chaotic room. Terri rolled over and continued to snore.

Then they started finding mechanical contraptions all over the Department, Scott mused. A note attached to one of them had expressed an intention to 'get that pipe-smoking Pommie bastard'. Scott, a Marlboro-smoking New Zealander, had deduced that the bombs were intended for James Tate. Tate had recently set up a Centre for Creativity on the ground floor of Building 1956, and in a burst of spleen had failed several Radiocommunications students. While he admitted that one had complained vociferously, Tate refused to reveal the name on the grounds of confidentiality. After the third bomb, Scott had raised the possibility of reviewing the student's mark at a Joint Exam Standards Tribunal meeting. The memory still made him froth with annoyance. Tate had removed his pipe from his mouth and said, 'I take it that none of these remote-controlled explosive devices has actually detonated?'

'Er no,' replied Scott, 'but the point, Dr Tate, is that...'

'Well, that certainly validates my assessment of his electronic knowledge,' he had remarked crushingly, jamming the pipe back into his mouth.

Dr Dane, the elderly chairman of JEST, had taken the resulting silence as grounds for moving on to the next point on the agenda while Scott had sat, fuming and impotent. How on earth did you communicate with an anonymous maniac, he wondered? How did you communicate with your blasted colleagues, if it came to that? Aha! The other shoe, and thank God, it had the other sock rolled up inside it.

Dressed, he wondered what to do next. He had seen too many of these houses to imagine for a moment that there would be any Disprin. If there were, no-one would be able to find it in the chaos. Where on earth had he left his car? It was probably blocked in somewhere down at Bazza Tech. Still, one thing about Castlereagh Street, it was close enough to walk.

He had almost made it to Building 1956's decaying front portals before the rain started again. Dear God, don't let there be a leak as well as a bomb scare, he prayed. I couldn't stand the whining, not today. He raced past a police car and into the building. He was astonished to meet Goldwyn tottering out. Nathan rarely emerged from Building 1975 and almost never migrated north of Descartes Avenue, which cut the campus neatly in half. Nathan's reaction to the sight of a crumpled, decrepit derelict who happened to be a Head of Department was one of mingled disgust and despair.

'Pleased to see you're able to join us at last, Scott,' he said dourly. 'One of your Principal Lecturers has been murdered and the staff need someone to pull things together. You've lost your main lecture theatre – the Rom Harre – until Forensic have finished with it, but you should be able to find alternatives. The end of the semester exams, in case you've forgotten, are coming up in a couple of weeks and we can't afford to let things slip now.'

'Murdered? Who? Are you sure? Why?' asked Scott, astonished.

'Well, if he's not dead, he sure has a great act there,' replied Goldwyn. 'He just happens to be the only halfway decent academic you had – Richard Johnston. The tragedy of it is that he died just as he was on the verge of one of the greatest breakthroughs psychology has ever known. His discovery might have made psychology not only scientific but really useful to society. Instead of the pointless, self-indulgent...' Goldwyn paused, seeking an alternative to the word that rose to his mind; he prided himself on keeping a clean mouth, 'navel-gazing that you and your type indugle in, psychology could have become a vital contributor to good government and order.'

'You mean his Civilein, or whatever it was called,' hazarded Scott. With his social life, he found it hard to keep up with those of his staff who cooked things up in laboratories which cost small fortunes to set up and endless money and argument to maintain.

Goldwyn slapped his forehead. 'Yeah, I mean his Civilein or whatever it was called. Goddammit! That whatever-it-was-called would have put us on the map, let alone have made a fortune for the Barry College Consulting Services Group. You just better hope to hell that you can find his notes and reconstruct the experiments. All we've got is one hell of a mess, no Civilein, a murderer roaming around and a godawful scandal that I'll have to deal with.'

'Murdered, wait a minute. Aren't we jumping to conclusions here?' said Scott, the eternal optimist. 'If we go around saying it's murder, it's not going to do anybody any good. It could easily have been an accident. Johnston was very dedicated to his work, and the power does fail in this building from time to time. He came in at all hours, maybe he fell in the dark.'

Goldwyn gazed at Scott with something approaching respect. The man might look like a hobo, but he had just made the one useful suggestion he had heard that morning. He had tried hard, once his stomach had settled down, to convince the police to agree that it might have been a homicidal burglar, but their lack of enthusiasm had been obvious and their eagerness to interrogate Sam Klusky palpable. Goldwyn hadn't bothered to wait for the end of that because Klusky obviously wasn't the type.

'Yes, Scott my boy,' he purred. 'Yes indeed, a sudden fall, he drags himself across the floor looking for help, but he doesn't make it. Very sad, but these things can happen. An accident, yes, no damage to our reputation, no more wild accusations levelled at the staff. No nasty questions from the granting body. Yes, an accident might be just the thing to keep the lid on the whole mess.' He reached out to pat Scott on the shoulder, but changed his mind with a closer look at Scott's skivvy. He charged off, mentally reviewing which of his governmental contacts would be the most relevant to the wide acceptance of the accident theory. Would folding money be required on this one, he wondered, or would subtle hints be enough to work another cover-up?

Scott clumped gloomily up the stairs just as the lift was whirring and creaking its way down with Sam Klusky and the two police officers. Arriving at the reception area, he moaned, 'Gaelene, love, bring us a couple of Disprin, will you?', charged into his office, and started ferreting about in the piles of papers on his desk. After the standard pause to show him she didn't jump to anybody's orders, Gaelene appeared in the doorway.

'No Disprin left, Dr Scott,' she said sullenly. 'Don'tcha remember yelling yer head off about the memo last week? The one where Central Budgets said it would only buy Disprin for staff if they could prove the problems were work-related. No Kleenex either. You was goina write and tell em off.'

'Oh Christ, my headaches are work-related.'

'Yeah?'

'Yeah! I mean yes. Look, don't just stand there staring, I'm sure you must have some work to do. You could start by filing some of this stuff on my desk.'

'Needs signing, most of it, Dr Scott.' Gaelene flounced out, leaving an aura of dumb insolence behind her. Pity she knew so much, and all the wrong things, Scott thought. One of these days he'd fire her, he knew he would. Not today though, he had found the timetable at last and now he had to reallocate Johnston's teaching, to say nothing of finding rooms until the Rom Harre was back in use. This awful building, he thought suddenly, it's absolutely freezing! In an effort to build up some warmth, he risked further headache by bustling around telling all staff to assemble in room 4.24D to discuss teaching.

Sullenly, those who remained trooped in and arranged themselves as far as possible from him. Most of them were wearing ski jackets and gloves. Reuben had wound a scarf over the lower half of his face. In the present context, it gave him an unpleasantly sinister air. Scott longed to ask him to take it off, but decided an argument about personal rights with Potoch was the last thing he needed.

'Where's Sam? Not in again?' he demanded.

'He's been arrested,' snapped Antonia Summerfield.

'Oh God, not another set of classes to cover for,' groaned Scott.

He began writing initials against Johnston's and Klusky's classes, trying to avoid demanding that staff be in three places at once, but pointing out that two classes could aways be amalgamated if need be. He then read out the allocations, sternly ignoring the cries and groans around him.

'Now that you've cut all our work out for us,' Jacinta said, 'would you mind clarifying just exactly what extra work, or should I simply say work, you plan to take?'

'Yes, I most certainly would!' snapped Scott. 'It's not my habit to justify my decisions to junior members of staff.'

'That would strain anyone,' Jacinta retorted. 'But in this case a simple statement of the courses and classes would be informative if not convincing.'

The impending stand-off was averted by the exit of a sobbing sociologist.

One of the counselling group stood up, waving his hands vaguely, and said, 'It's no good Iain, I know how Florence feels. I mean a lot of us went into our areas of specialisation because we couldn't manage the numbers. I mean we obviously had positive reasons as well, um, connected with our perceived potential for personal growth and the contribution that we believed we could make to improving the quality of life...'

'Oh god, why doesn't he get to the point,' muttered Seamus O'Faolain, whose area of specialisation was disembodied voices.

Stung, Clive glared around the room, but all he could see were blandly interested faces gazing benignly back at him.

'What I mean to say is, we can't teach these classes. We haven't got the skills,' he finished firmly and marched towards the door.

'What about some sessional lecturers?' suggested Lisa, trying to avoid adding to her own workload.

Scott jumped guiltily. He really would have to do something about the departmental accounts. Something drastic at that. Now Johnston was dead, of course, it might all be possible, especially if he could get his hands on Johnston's files.

'Impossible! Ridiculous! Unnecessary! Anyway, the sessional teaching budget is exhausted.'

'At this time of year?' asked Antonia with a distinct note of suspicion in her voice.

Damn the woman, Scott thought. I suppose the Women's United Movement Party has started teaching them all accounting as well, but this was the last moment to get into a row about money. Speaking of rows, he wondered if the bookie had rung again. He pulled himself together and began reallocating the classes Clive and Florence had refused.

Jacinta, gazing over his shoulder, remarked, 'I don't see the initials IS against any of those lectures.'

'Quite right,' answered Scott brightly. 'And reading sideways too, how clever. Now you will have noticed that I am only reallocating the elementary lectures at this stage. If you had one iota of managerial flair, you would realise that there is no point in putting your top-flight staff on the basic duties...'

'But some duties might help matters don't you think,' continued Jacinta doggedly.

'Indeed they would,' said Scott, with the airy nonchalance of one who knows an opponent's weak point, 'and among my duties will be the tenure reviews for lecturers. The response you all make to this week's crisis will not go unappreciated, I assure you, or unnoticed either. Now, in my case, I have reached such an advanced level of statistics that it would be a pointless waste of time and talent to go back to this elementary descriptive stuff. I will make my contribution in other ways.'

A rude snort echoed around the room and Scott glanced up quickly, hoping, again in vain, to catch O'Faolain at it. He began handing out sheaves of scribbled-over notes.

'If we can't get sessional lecturers in,' Lisa persisted, having just taken a vertiginous glance at her new workload, 'what about getting some time off in lieu or study leave or something?' She trailed off uncertainly.

'Of course, of course,' beamed Scott. 'Just as soon as the crisis is over, we'll have a complete workload review.'

'Just a minute, Iain, before you close the meeting,' began Antonia. 'You're asking us to do a lot of work here under intolerable conditions. Is it asking too much to get the air-conditioning turned off and the heating turned on? It is, after all, mid-winter. I suppose that being a smoker, you can't detect the vile stench of decay which would tell you that there has been yet another leak into my office and Edmund Bennett's, and to cap it all off, the carpets are covered in filth of all sorts from the roof.'

'Yes,' said Reuben, weighing in determinedly. 'This building is a disgrace. If the Health Department knew about it, they'd close it down. What about the lights, anyway? They've been smashed for months. The Accident Appreciation Committee has told me to take out a Provisional Improvement Notice on the lights alone. I'm warning you, Iain, it may become necessary to invoke legal remedies.'

Scott leaned back in his chair and gave a good imitation of saintly resignation. Academics just will not co-operate, he thought crossly. Look at Richard and Jacinta. Richard had moved heaven and earth to appoint the woman and then she wouldn't collaborate with him on anything. Bloody women, they were so unreliable, and almost all academics were a pack of old women. But now was hardly the time to say so. He took a deep breath.

'I am horrified that people who have supposedly dedicated their lives to the helping professions can possibly have nothing but selfish considerations on their minds at a time like this. I am particularly surprised at you, Antonia, for all your talk of discipline and self-sacrifice, allowing yourself to get upset about a little rat shit on the carpet. At this time, when one of our most valued staff members has been carried off by a tragic accident, we should all pull together in an attempt to continue the work of our Department. I will endeavour to give my attention to these petty personal problems, if I have any time left over after I have spoken to the police and done my best to keep the Department running smoothly, but I cannot make any promises on these lines.'

He rose and swept out, leaving behind him an atmosphere unmatched for gloom and disaffection since the last days of the Weimar Republic.

'Accident? Accident?' he heard Reuben demanding behind him. 'I thought it was murder. If it was an accident, why have they arrested Sam?'

As the most numerate, untenured and consequently vulnerable members of the staff, Jacinta, Lisa and Seamus had been lumbered with the majority of Johnston's courses. Mutinously, they trailed off to the tea room to chat about how to manage with the least disruption to their lives. On their way down the gloomy, badly lit corridor, they noticed that Scott's enthusiasm for the cause of numeracy had already led to en masse departure for home among the sociology and counselling staff. The very thought of slaving over a hot statistic had caused little pieces of paper to sprout on several doors. The message on each was much the same: Dr/Mr/Ms X will not be available today due to an illness/emergency.

'Total lack of originality,' pronounced Jacinta after she had deciphered the first three in the gloom. 'Look here, Reuben's right about these lights. Does anyone know when they're going to be replaced? I mean they've been like this since the Student Orientation riots. I for one don't care to be wandering around this building in the half dark with a murderer on the loose.'

Nobody seemed to know, and they continued on to the tea room, where they sat about dispiritedly swallowing coffee. The tea room itself was not a place to inspire much cheer, at least not if your colour vision was normal. The chairs and fittings had been chosen by Gaelene, whose penchant for purple and red flowers and desire to perk the place up a bit had allowed her to ignore the fact that the carpet was a deep, decayed-looking brown and the walls a queer off-green colour.

'What annoys me,' Jacinta was saying, 'is the way some people just burst into tears, charge off, and get out of doing any teaching they don't want to do. If I did that, no-one would take the slightest notice.'

'I think they call it tenure,' said Seamus. 'If you can't get rid of people, you have to pander to them, it's easier that way.'

Lisa found herself roused to action, as so many times before, by the fact that her ability to tolerate the ghastly neo-modernist painting inflicted on them by Scott ran out at the ten-minute mark. The only vaguely discernible item in the blur of paint seemed to be a boxing glove, which might have explained his choice. There had been speculation that the decor had been deliberately designed to stop them sitting around enjoying themselves.

'Well,' said Lisa, 'Johnston is bound to have a course outline or something. If we can find those then it shouldn't be too hard.'

'Haven't the police declared his office and lab out of bounds or something?' asked O'Faolain. 'I mean they've locked the doors until further notice; how are we going to get in there?' O'Faolain himself was not averse to having a poke around in Johnston's office. There were rumours about files which O'Faolain wished to test.

'Out of bounds be buggered,' snarled Jacinta, who was still brooding over Scott and the meeting. 'I may have to teach Johnston's bloody courses, but I'm damned if I'll do any more on them than I have to. Sit there, I'll ring Maintenance.'

The maintenance men, once located, were rather reluctant to attack a door which bore a large sign to the effect that the Victoria Police had declared it out of bounds. Jacinta proved remarkably persuasive on the topic and the conversation ranged over out-of-hours perks and the facts that they could easily wear gloves and that a bit more form would hardly matter for most of them anyway. Eventually, she drew aside with the foreman for a brief chat and they returned beaming.

'You both owe me twenty dollars,' she hissed at Seamus and Lisa. The men then fiddled about with the locks for half an hour, while the academics, conscious of the onward march of time towards the hour of their lectures, stood fuming. Finally they gave up, explained that Johnston seemed to have installed his own security system and departed, twenty tax-free dollars each richer.

'No wonder nothing seems to get maintained around here,' said Lisa crossly. 'They can't even open the doors.'

O'Faolain screamed, 'Wouldn't it shit you? Even when the bastard's dead, he still gets in your bloody way!' and he hurled himself bodily against the door.

One of the few things that really did the job in Barry College were the doors. Solid oak, right through. The walls were quite another matter. It had apparently failed to occur to anyone that matching solid oak doors with plasterboard walls was something of a waste of time.

'I think I've broken my shoulder,' Seamus whimpered, rubbing it.

Jacinta was busily levering the plasterboard panels off their frame with a heavy metal ruler.

'You know your trouble, Seamus?' she said. 'You're hasty, probably all those androgens seething around in your blood. Wreck the brain, intoxicate the ascending reticular formation and send you right off, androgens do. Johnston would have told you that.'

'Get on with it,' Seamus retorted grumpily. 'I haven't got all day and reverse sexism is just as bad as anything Johnston did or didn't do.'

'Try not to wreck the panels,' Lisa interposed. 'Remember, we'll have to put them back.'

Jacinta leaned on the ruler and the panel suddenly gave way, admitting them to Johnston's office. Unlike the seething whirlpool of Klusky's cubbyhole, Johnston's office reflected a degree of organisation a fraction behind a too full life. Gloomily, the three of them mooched around the room, dominated by a giant poster of the Los Angeles track and field team of 1962 and littered with the stigmata of commitment to extreme right-wing causes. Lisa and Jacinta prodded under piles of leaflets which posed such questions as: 'Was Christ just another rabbi?'

Seamus shifted racks of test-tubes and looked in desk drawers. Nothing remotely resembling course outlines could be found. Lisa finally remarked, 'I suppose we're going to have to get those locked filing cabinets open. Stands to reason he'd have put the course outlines in there. Top drawer of the one on the left is where people usually keep them.'

'No,' interposed Jacinta. 'It's going to be awfully difficult to do it without making a mess. Anyway,' she hedged, 'I don't think it would be necessary. He will have lodged master copies of the basic outlines with the main office. That'll be enough to be going on with. Besides it's getting late and Lisa has to take the first one in about ten minutes. She has to find out where it's on too.'

Johnston's habits were well known. It was clear to Seamus that Jacinta was concerned that if they continued to search, some damaging document might come to light. He was intrigued. What did Johnston have on Jacinta? He wanted to find out. More than that, he wanted to prevent her from gathering up any other files, particularly those marked 'O'Faolain'.

Lisa stared at Jacinta, wondering what had become of her well-known commitment to Work Minimisation. Seamus could see there was no way Jacinta would allow him to have a good look at Johnston's files. He made a mental note to return alone, when things were quieter. And soon, before the police found whatever interesting things were there to be found.

They replaced the plasterboard as best they could and wandered back down the corridor towards the main office, reminiscing about Johnston – his misogyny, his Catholicism so fanatical that it embarrassed the Catholics and outraged all other denominations, his ruthless plagiarism and, above all, his dreadful research projects into abortion and insanity.

'Do you remember that awful scene when Gloria Steinem came over to give a talk on feminism in America?' asked Seamus. 'And Johnston got up and asked her if she'd ever been satisfied by a man? Embarrassed! I found myself putting my hands over my beard and trying to look feminine.'

The other two laughed at the image, but Lisa remembered how intense Johnston had been. She hadn't liked being alone with him. Only the fact that Jacinta came in on Sundays too gave her the nerve to share the building with him.

Seamus continued: 'What's the strength of all this talk about Civilein, do you reckon?'

'Well, Johnston had an article on it in *Xenobiotica*, saying it was a goer. He had a stable compound which could be inhaled. It crossed the blood/brain barrier and made the rats go slow and dozy. Probably would do something similar to people. The main problems were finding some way of purifying the stuff and producing it in commercial quantities.'

'Yes, but do you think it would have worked?' persisted Seamus.

'How was it supposed to work anyway?' Lisa asked.

'The answers are I'm not sure and it's hard to explain,' replied Jacinta. 'You know all that stuff Johnston did on abortions and insanity?'

They nodded.

'It seems he checked the blood progesterone level of women wanting abortions and found it was abnormally low compared to women who didn't. Well, other people have said that, it was supposed to be a side-effect of the stress they were under, thanks to Johnston's little friends upsetting them. Johnston's research was based on the fact that progesterone is really quite a powerful tranquilliser, knocks your ascending reticular formation for six. He thought that progesterone made you fatalistic, stopped you roaring about causing tumult and affray. But it's not enough on its own, you need a cofactor to promote the conversion of other similar steroids into progesterone and swamp the system. That way, it can affect men as well.'

Jacinta paused to negotiate a particularly boggy patch of the carpet and wait until Seamus stopped coughing.

'Anyway, his theory was that if you could over-ride the feedback loop controlling the interconversion of progesterone and other steroids in the brain, we would all accept our fate, whatever he decided for us that was going to be. Naturally there was a lot of interest in that from certain quarters. As to whether it would have worked in real life, who knows. Anyway there are only a few groups with the set-up to do that kind of research. Oh Christ, the floor's covered with rat shit!'

'I think he thought women were mad anyway, and having

abortions only proved it. You know the theory that women only exist to give birth to male geniuses? You'd have to be mad to pass up on an experience like that,' Lisa said.

Jacinta nodded. 'Pity no-one told him you have to give birth to a lot of twits before you get a genius.'

'It's my belief,' interrupted Seamus, 'that some fanatical feminists came over from America and fixed him – the Society for Castrating Men? You should know, Jacinta, you were saying the other day that they ought to send a hit squad to get the Pope.'

'Cutting Up Men,' corrected Jacinta absently. 'Look here, Seamus, don't say things like that. All we know is that Sam has been arrested and that he had plenty of motive. And I don't only mean his course. What about those photographs of the end-of-term party that were sent to his mother! Okay, so Sam wore fishnet stockings for the revue and we knew it was just a joke, but his mother didn't see it that way. We all know who sent them. Johnston never left Sam alone. And he pinched Sam's course too. I mean,' she said, conspiratorially, 'the police are all over the place and we don't want them getting the wrong idea.'

Or the right idea? thought Lisa. Jacinta had already told her she knew Sam had an alibi. What was she trying to do now?

'Honestly, Jacinta,' Seamus said. 'You were touchy about Johnston too, half of what he said about women wasn't meant to be taken seriously. Whatever you think about his research, he did get published in the *New England Journal of Medicine*, and now in *Xenobiotica*.'

Biting back a number of pithy retorts, Jacinta sighed. Seamus expressed that loyalty to the Union of Men which is the despair of feminists, she thought. Men can say and do what they like and anyone who objects to being systematically insulted is being 'sensitive', 'unreasonable' or 'touchy'. On the other hand, now was no time to annoy people. The potential for blackmail ran high at Bazza Tech at the best of times, but now, between police interviews and tenure reviews, it had never been greater. Better cut off this conversation, she thought, and replied, 'Yes, the *New England Journal of Medicine* did publish him and Reagan did quote him. Reagan was cutting off funding for poor women who needed abortions at the time, if I remember correctly. We never heard the end of that one, did we? Anyway, I'd better go and sort out these blasted lectures.'

As Jacinta was hunting through the main filing cabinets, she saw Scott bidding an effusive farewell to one of the police, who had stayed behind while his larger friends took Sam to HQ.

'Well, you've given us plenty to go on here,' he said. 'This should help us clarify a few things with whatshisname, Klusky,' He got into the malodorous lift.

Down at the police station, Sam Klusky was having an awful time. The early part of the interrogation had been comparatively peaceful. Doreen Hubel had gazed at him calmly, and pointed out that he had the motive and the means and that it would be much easier for everybody if he would just confess. Sam kept pleading with her to check his alibi, but gradually he had begun to doubt himself. Could he have given his talk on Saturday, not Sunday? He had loathed Johnston, he couldn't deny that. Could he have killed him in some sort of fugue state? Hubel seemed so certain, and in a way so soothing, even kind, that he found himself lured into wanting to agree with her and make her happy.

About halfway through the interview, Sam was saved, temporarily, by a sudden phone call. Hubel had grabbed the phone and said, 'For God's sake! I'm busy! Oh. Yes. I see. Well, put him on then.'

Her voice took on a more respectful tone.

'Yes. Yes. I quite see that. Well, I understand that an accident would be much more manageable. Yes. I know that it would be a better use of public funds to investigate the wharfie murders. Well, I think there are problems with that explanation. Um, the problem is that there was a witness before the body was moved. No, no, I don't mean him, he'd see the light all right.' She paused to gaze appraisingly at Sam, who flinched. 'When I said a witness,' she continued, 'I meant that the accused, the man who found the body, I mean, called a doctor. Yes, they have one working there. No, well it would be a bit risky, you know how touchy doctors are. He had a good look apparently and he might go a bit odd if you suggested he couldn't pick a murder. Well, Mackinolty's different, we don't know this other guy. I think so. Unless there are some other findings. I'd try Mackinolty, with respect sir, I think that's likely to be a more profitable avenue. Yes, sir, yes, I'll carry on here.'

The first fruits of Nathan's flurry of phone calls diverted, Hubel returned to putting the hard word on Sam. Just then Wiesel bounded in with the notes from their colleague's interview with Iain Scott. Hubel read them slowly but thoroughly, occasionally pausing to glance up at Sam. A most disconcerting procedure. Finally she slung them across the desk at him.

'Here you are, read this lot. I suppose you can read, being a lecturer and all.'

Sam began to read Scott's account of his relationship with Johnston and wished he had had a British upbringing to learn inscrutability. He knew his upper lip was stiff, because he kept it that way as a forlorn hope, but he was also aware of the beads of sweat on his face. It was extraordinary. Without once stooping to a downright lie, Scott had implied that the only reason Johnston had lived so long was inveterate sloth on Klusky's part. My god, there were things in here he hadn't even known Scott knew about. The course, well no-one would kill for a course, but those awful photographs from the end-of-year party! A bet was a bet, but who would have guessed Johnston would send them to his mother? So they had argued in the tea room. Well, people argue. Yes, it was all true, well, semi-true, but he hadn't done him in. Damn it, he thought, I'll go on the attack.

'Er, we seem to have been here an awfully long time,' he began. 'Isn't there something about a six-hour rule?'

He smiled weakly, only to jump a foot when Hubel suddenly barked at him.

'Look here mate, you're wasting our time. You know you killed him, your mates are just about pointing the finger and all you can do is sit their grinning! You're a big bloke with a lot of motive. You found the body and you tell us it was pure chance that you were wandering around in a lecture theatre where you had no business to be. Let's get a statement written out and signed, and then we can all go home.'

'All go home? I'd be stuck here. But I didn't kill him, I just found him. I sought medical help at once,' gabbled Klusky, his stoicism worn thin.

'Are you saying Dr Scott's statement isn't true?' demanded Hubel.

'Yes, yes, it's true, yes he pinched my course, yes he threatened me about my sex life but I didn't kill him, and I told you, I've got an alibi. Why don't you check it? And while we're at it, I want a lawyer.' Klusky asserted.

'Ah, a lawyer,' said Wiesel. 'The gentleman wants a lawyer, Inspector Hubel.'

In the ensuing silence, Klusky found himself wishing they wouldn't talk about him as if he wasn't there. It made the whole experience more like the Mad Hatter's tea party than ever. To control his rising stress levels, he gazed desperately around the room. He had never imagined a place more run-down than Barry College, but there was no doubt that the police had the same maintenance problems, an even livelier clientele, and a staff who were ninety-nine per cent smokers with some unsavoury habits in butt disposal. The desks were scuffed and worn and liberally strewn with old coffee cups with butts floating in the dregs. The paint had once been an unpleasant institutional green but had flaked off until it was now a mangy colour with pointillist mould near the windows.

Klusky was desperately trying to wrench his mind back and focus his concentration when he realised that Hubel was speaking to him again. Crossing her heavy thighs and leaning forward, she said slowly and carefully, 'As a rule, Sergeant Wiesel and I have found that the only people who want a lawyer are people who know they're guilty.'

'But I know I'm innocent,' Klusky whimpered, sweating profusely.

'You look pretty nervous for an innocent man, and it was a bit more than light-hearted chat between you two, wasn't it? I mean, it says right here, "I was afraid that they would come to blows in the last argument and tried to intervene". What have you got to say about that?'

The injustice of this rallied Klusky. Colour returned to his cheeks and he shouted, 'Intervene! Scott! That lobbas! How does he know these things? He's never in. Investigate him, then you'd find something worth knowing. All right, so I'm nervous. I'm a worrywart. I face life imprisonment and you won't make one lousy phone call.'

'I would have thought this course business, on top of everything else, would have given you quite a motive,' interjected Wiesel. 'According to Scott, he was planning to promote you on the basis of it, until you resigned your co-ordinating role to Johnston. Come on, we know you did it, get it off your chest and tell us all about it.'

Klusky sat breathing heavily through his nose and trying to think of a way to deal with the situation politely, professionally and effectively. In the silence, Inspector Hubel, supporting mother of two, found herself thinking that her taxes went to pay people like this. Her young Jarrod had expressed an interest in going to tech, and the thought that he might be exposed to this sort of person was worrying to say the least. Well, he was only young, plenty of time to talk him out of it.

Klusky, reciprocating her thoughts, said very calmly, 'Please ring the Epilepsy Foundation.'

Just at that moment, there was a commotion outside and Lisa Thomas bounded in, followed by a protesting policeman.

'I couldn't help it,' he cried. 'She just went on and on and then charged for the door before I could stop her.'

'What do you want?' cried Hubel.

'Look here,' said Lisa. 'You're interrogating an innocent man. Didn't he tell you that he was giving a lecture to the Epilepsy Foundation?'

## 4

'Look at that,' groaned Sam as they left the building. 'It's almost dark; those bastards had me there all day.'

Lisa manouevred her battered old Renault out of the Russell Street carpark, peering through a rear window almost completely covered with stickers. 'Keep Gay Whales in the Ground Now' was the general message they displayed to the world. Dodging a pedestrian, she slid the car into the traffic and headed back to Barry College.

He doesn't look exactly overjoyed at being rescued, thought Lisa, but then he never seemed to look terribly happy about anything. Still, who would, with a life like Sam's? She could guess exactly what was on his mind – his mother. Ever since his wife had died in the car accident, Sam had been tyrannised by that formidable lady who had moved in, so she claimed, to look after the children. Unfortunately, by the time Sam had realised that she thought he was one of them, it had been too late. She had sold her house and put all the money into trust for the grandchildren, and was now financially dependent on Sam. Anyway, with childcare facilities at Bazza the way they were – nonexistent – there wasn't a lot he could have done about it, even if he'd had the nerve.

Sam cleared his throat. Oh dear, thought Lisa, of course he'll be worried about whether old Ma Battleaxe has heard the news.

'Did anyone ring home and tell them where I was?' he asked anxiously.

Saved by incompetence, thought Lisa. Gaelene, the only person likely to think of doing it, was on Sam's side and spent a good deal of her time covering up for him.

'No,' she replied, to Sam's obvious relief, 'I don't think anyone got around to it; you know what they're like. Everyone's been running around in little circles trying to work out who takes what for the rest of the semester. Why don't you just tell her that you were called to an emergency meeting as a result of Johnston's death, and it went on rather longer than you had expected? After all, it's true, isn't it?'

Sam sighed, deeply relieved, and sank heavily back into the seat, only to sit back up again as if it had bitten him, and ask, 'How did you know where I was on Sunday?'

'Well, said Lisa, 'it was a funny thing...'

She had been puzzled by a number of things about the events of that day. Why, for example, had Jacinta not turned up at work as she usually did on a Sunday? Seamus had remarked on it when they had paused for a companionable cup of tea that Sunday afternoon. Unfortunately, the major responsibility for keeping Johnston's students at bay had fallen on her untenured shoulders, and she really hadn't had time to think things through carefully.

She had also had to cope with a long discussion with the police about why exactly she came in on Sundays. This had been wedged between one of Johnston's classes on statistics and one of her own on professional teamwork and communication. It had been her only free hour for the day, and she had rather been hoping for a little late lunch and a chance to think things over. But that was not to be, at least not until after the police had finished, and by then she had been feeling too upset for more concentrated thought. In fact, for any thought which was not actually required to get her successfully through the day.

She had tried to explain to the police about academic promotion, the need for publication, and the fact that this need was strongest in junior and untenured members of staff who also had the highest teaching loads and who were expected to appear on a variety of committees. Usually, she had thought but not said, as the token pleb, never listened to but always inveigled into report-writing and the like. She had tried to point out that she had no wish to be stuck at Bazza Tech for the rest of her working life – surely they could empathise with that – and that the only way she could meet her overcommitted deadlines and publish anything at all was by working every weekend. The police, however, had seemed unsympathetic. They found the concept of someone working on a Sunday when they hadn't been rostered impossible to believe. Even Lisa's explanations about the need for peace and quiet that you could develop if you lived in the Rathbone Street Co-operative had failed to convince.

Lisa had been greatly relieved, though puzzled, when the interview had ended abruptly. The mysterious man who had been using the Reception phone burst into the room and told them they were wasting their time.

'Don't bother with her,' he had said, rudely ignoring her and dropping his hideous camelhair coat on her desk. 'She's got nothing to do with it, can't you see that?'

The policeman who was taking her statement was not made of the same stuff as Doreen Hubel, by then back at police headquarters with Sam. He subsided, muttering, 'But she might have seen or heard something all the same. And I'm meant to get a statement from everybody.'

'Oh, stuff that. You won't get anything out of her,' he had said, in a tone that made it clear that he had been going to add, 'after all, she's only a woman,' and had barely restrained himself from doing so. 'Let's get down to something relevant,' he had added.

At least it had given her half an hour before the next class. Time for a cup of coffee. By then she had been so tired that poor Sam's plight had completely slipped her mind. Funny how you could adjust so quickly to just about any set of bizarre circumstances.

No sooner had she flopped into a welcoming pink and purple chair in the empty tea room and kicked a space clear of old and boring academic journals, so that she could put her feet on the coffee table, than Antonia Summerfield had come in.

'It's such a nuisance. The police finished ages ago and we still can't use the Rom Harre. I don't know where I'm going to put my Medical Engineering class.'

'Why can't we use the Harre?' asked Lisa, not because she was interested, but because any conversation was better than her own thoughts. 'Do the police still have to check it or something?'

'Not at all,' said Reuben, who had come into the room with Antonia. 'We've just been trying to sort things out with the maintenance men. Honestly, you'd think they'd be grateful, the rate of pay they get, when you consider they're only menials.'

'Yes,' said Antonia. 'Maintenance say they won't touch it because it's the Cleaning Squad's job to get rid of bloodstains. And the Cleaning Squad say they won't touch it unless they're guaranteed a Nauseous Allowance.'

'Well, is that so unreasonable?' asked Lisa. 'I mean, it's not exactly a pleasant thing to have to do.'

'Pleasant!' snorted Reuben. 'Why should their jobs be pleasant? They should be grateful they've got jobs. They think they're having a hard time. What about the Jews throughout the ages?'

Everybody ignored Reuben, but marvelled inwardly yet again

at his ability to see everything in relationship to the persecution of the Jews.

'Well, Staffing are kicking up about paying the Nauseous Allowance. They say the Cleaning Squad cleans up the dissection lab and this is no different.'

'Nonsense,' said Lisa. 'Cleaning up after a group of students have been dissecting frogs is not quite the same thing as getting human bloodstains out of the carpet in the Rom Harre. And there is an awful lot of the stuff. I don't know how they'd get it out. It'll probably be there for ever,' she continued. 'One of those stains that lasts through history, like the blood of martyred saints.' And she looked quickly at Reuben, realising too late that she had left him an opening. But he was busy slurping his tea and didn't notice.

Lisa suddenly laughed. 'Hey, that reminds me of something I read in the *New Scientist*. Apparently there was this scientist who was visiting a church in England somewhere, and he was shown a dark stain on the floor in the belfry, which they said was the blood of some martyred saint or other. And it couldn't be cleaned off. Well, it could but it always reappeared straight away. So apparently this bloke went down on his hands and knees and sniffed it, and put his finger in it and licked it, and then looked up and announced that it was bat piss. The vicar was terribly upset.'

Antonia laughed, and Reuben looked shocked. 'Oh, I suppose we shouldn't be laughing at a time like this,' said Antonia. 'But honestly, you have to let off steam somehow.'

Seamus wandered in, seeking comfort after an hour of hysterical Articled Clerks, and stopped in amazement at the sight of so much levity.

'Gaelene tells me they've got a report out of the police surgeon,' he said. Nobody knew how Gaelene got to know all these things, but experience had taught them that she generally knew what was going on well before anybody else. 'Apparently he's fixed the time of death at late Sunday afternoon.'

'Lets me out then,' said Antonia flippantly. 'I was at the Epilepsy Foundation from two until after six. Sam was there, in fact he was speaking on genetic counselling.'

There was a brief silence.

'Oh my goodness,' said Lisa, 'I forgot. Of course. Sam's down at the police station being questioned right now, and he's got an alibi. How could I forget a thing like that?'

'Why didn't you tell the police?' said Seamus to Antonia.

'They haven't got around to interviewing me yet, and I'm afraid it just didn't occur to me,' replied Antonia. 'But I said all along that Sam can't have done it, and now there's proof. What a relief. Lisa, you'd better ring the police right away.'

Why me, thought Lisa. But then again, she had been told earlier in the day about Sam's alibi, and she hadn't done anything about it, so perhaps it was fair enough. Antonia was clearly not going to act. She announced that she felt she had done quite enough for Barry College that day and she was going home at once. Lisa did feel sorry for Sam. Being interrogated by Doreen Hubel was unlikely to be much fun, and besides, being cut off from his regular top-ups of pastrami on rye, hamburgers with the lot, and Mars Bars must get to him eventually. Who knows, she thought, he might even confess out of desperation, just to get some food. Briefly she wondered whether serving a life sentence for murder would be more or less pleasant than Sam's current work and home life.

Sighing, she advanced on the tea-room phone. There had been moves afoot among the staff to have it removed; surely, they argued, they could be free from the importunity of students at least while they were having a well-earned cup of coffee. But, mysteriously, this was the only phone in the College which never seemed to be out of order.

After a struggle with the Russell Street receptionist, she succeeded in breaking through to the Homicide Squad. The sergeant who answered, however, was less than helpful, and refused to call anyone more senior to the phone. A long spiralling conversation ensued in which Lisa, to the amusement of her listening colleagues, insisted ever more desperately that yes, she knew they were busy, she knew they were being helped in their inquiries about the Boffin Murder by a staff member from Barry College, that was why she was ringing. The sergeant, for his part, insisted ever more stolidly that the very reason why she couldn't help them with their inquiries was that they were already being helped quite enough. He would, he finally and grudgingly conceded, take a message which would be attended to as soon as possible, but he was not hopeful that it would be that same afternoon.

'What do I have to do to get their attention?' she asked despairingly. 'Confess to the blasted murder myself?'

'I wonder if they know what danger they're in,' mused Seamus. 'I mean, if they keep Sam for too long without his Doggybix he'll bite one of them in the leg.'

'You'll have to go down there,' said Antonia, who hadn't moved despite her claim that she was going home. 'They won't be able to ignore you in the flesh.'

Personally Lisa doubted this. She was used to being ignored, and she had a feeling that ignoring small female people was an important part of police basic training. 'Well, all right,' she said reluctantly. 'But somebody else will have to take my class. It's on in five minutes.' And I still haven't got my cup of coffee, she added inwardly.

There was a doubtful silence.

'Well then, somebody else will have to go down to the police station,' she proposed, without hope.

Nobody moved.

'What about cancelling my class, for once?'

Reuben's shocked look was enough to squelch that one, especially with her contract review coming up. You had to be very careful what you said around here. Nearly everybody was asked to write a report on your suitability for tenure, and it was vital to appear cheerful and willing at all times.

'So what you lot want is for me to go and give my class and then go down to the police station and get Sam released?'

Taking silence for assent, she continued, 'And it doesn't bother any of you that this means Sam will be stuck there for another hour?'

The silence continued, but it did take on a slightly shifty air that suggested that, even though Lisa's assessment of the situation was reasonably accurate, at least some people there did feel a tiny bit guilty about it.

'So in the end,' Lisa concluded, as they neared the College again, 'I allowed myself to be manipulated into finishing teaching before coming down and getting you. What a pack of no-hopers! I hope they arrest the lot of them next; I wouldn't lift a finger to get them out of chokey.' It was all right to say that sort of thing to Sam; he was on her side.

'Anyway, that sergeant was a bit more easily manipulated face to face than over the phone.' Lisa did have a nice smile, after all.

She drove into the underground carpark at Barry College, past a student in a deathshead helmet who was chaining his motorbike to a sign that read 'Staff Parking Only'.

'It's all very nice, me saving you and all,' she said as the two of them climbed the stairs, Sam puffing beside her. 'But it does leave us with one little problem. If you didn't do it, and of course you didn't, then who did? I mean, Johnston was hardly Mr Popularity, but murder is a rather extreme reaction. Messy. Lacks that finesse, subtlety and wit that one might expect from the academic mind. Mind you,' she added in a rare burst of cynicism, 'that doesn't cut out very many of the staff around here.'

Wrestling the rusty fire door open, Lisa and Sam entered the tea room where the remains of the Department huddled together, preparing for the trip home.

Once the cries of joy had subsided and the others had departed homeward, Lisa continued: 'Nobody liked him, that's fair enough, but if you really had it in for somebody you'd block their promotion. Then they'd still be alive so you could watch them suffer.'

'But,' said Sam, 'what if it was someone junior, someone who didn't have a say in promotions? Or someone from outside the College? Anyway you know how hard it was to block Johnston in anything he wanted. Even Scott was scared of him. Have you forgotten the legend of when Johnston got study leave, this is way back when he was only a lecturer too, to finish the PhD that he already had? I don't know how he got away with that one.'

'Well, maybe you're right,' conceded Lisa. 'But who could have done it?'

'I don't know,' said Sam, shamelessly lighting up a cigarette. 'I was thinking about it, down at the police station. It's got to be somebody short-tempered and reasonably strong. But that doesn't get us very far. I mean, Seamus is probably strong enough, but he's just not the type. And Reuben – well, that's just ridiculous. It just doesn't make sense. Maybe it's completely motiveless, just some maniac.'

'Oh great,' said Lisa. 'Very comforting. Just what I've always wanted. A maniac on the loose; makes me feel terrific.'

Her mind was not really on the discussion with Sam. She was still trying to work out how Jacinta could have known, hours before anyone else, about the time of death. Oh well, she thought, Jacinta does have a strong biological background. I mean, she did work with Johnston at one stage, before she got her present job. And the way she was burbling on this morning about Civilein, sounded like she actually knew what she was on about. As she speculated, the subject of her thoughts appeared and advanced on the coffee urn.

'Well, that's it for the day,' said Jacinta. 'Oh, Sam,' she added. 'You're back. How much did it cost to get out?'

'Don't joke about such things,' he said gloomily. 'People have no rights in those situations. I couldn't get them check my alibi and they wouldn't let me call a lawyer if their lives had depended on it. I tell you, I really thought I was a goner until Lisa turned up.'

'It's my belief,' said Jacinta, measuring coffee into a mug, 'that Johnston probably met up with a burglar, addressed him in his usual charming style, and got exactly what he deserved.'

'What is it, I mean was it, between you and Johnston?' asked Sam. 'You used to get on with him all right. You even published something together, didn't you?'

'Well, yes, but that was before I came to this dump.'

'But didn't he make a huge effort to get you appointed?'

'If he did, it was totally unnecessary,' snapped Jacinta. 'I was the best candidate on my own merits without any interference from him.'

Which was true enough, she thought. But she would never even have applied if it hadn't been for Johnston. She'd never even have heard of the place. He'd rung her in her PhD student's office at Melbourne University, asked if she wanted a bit of casual work, and made an appointment to see her. When he arrived, he offered her five thousand dollars if she'd do the statistical sections of a paper for him. Jacinta had been young enough and poor enough to believe him when he said this was the least he could offer. He said he had a lot of money to get rid of by the end of the year so that his grant would be renewed, and he wanted the paper ready in a hurry to present at a conference somewhere.

Well, she'd done the analysis and written it up for him. He'd seemed very pleased, paid up on the dot, even put her name on the paper, and had then mentioned that she should apply for a research assistantship with him. She'd wound up getting the lectureship instead.

It had all changed, though, as soon as she was on the payroll. On her first day at work she had gone to his lab. She was looking foward to getting a look at the ultracentrifuge he'd used in the experiment she'd analysed. The lab, however, had been deserted. She'd gone in, puzzled by the absence of anything that looked even remotely like an ultracentrifuge, and had been reading his notice board when he'd come charging in, yelling abuse at her for daring to enter the lab.

She had been startled by the whole incident. Right now, she found it best to push it to the back of her mind. Anyway, there had been no collaboration, no access to research funds, no joint publications.

She turned towards the urn and seized the spigot. There was a bang and a huge spark leapt out of the electrical connection. Smoke and steam rose with a roar. From the middle of the confusion, Jacinta was thrown back, crying, 'Ah, shit!'

'Are you all right?' gasped Lisa and Sam simultaneously. Jacinta nodded. Lisa helped her to her feet.

'I think my hair's been singed,' she said.

'Shouldn't we turn it off?' asked Sam timidly, as the urn hissed and spluttered menacingly.

Carefully Jacinta advanced on it, avoiding the puddles of water on the floor, and gingerly turned it off at the mains. To make quite sure, she pulled the plug out too.

'Did you get a shock?' asked Sam, all sympathy now the danger of electrocution seemed to have passed.

'No, at least not an electrical one,' replied Jacinta, subsiding into a hideous flowery chair. 'I was just worried that all that hot water was going to spill on me.'

Moving gingerly forward through the steaming pool on the floor, Lisa emptied out the rest of the boiling water and examined the base carefully.

'Look at this,' she said, with interest, 'It's been cut.'

Jacinta and Sam peered at the flex. Sure enough, there was a deep straight cut through the plastic, down to the wires. Clearly the wires had touched the metal of the base, and the whole thing had shorted.

'It's a wonder nobody was electrocuted.'

Jacinta looked horrified. 'A booby trap!' she cried.

Lisa was appalled. 'Surely not,' she said. 'I mean, why would anybody want to do that?' She stopped. 'Unless you were right about a homicidal maniac.'

'Nonsense,' scoffed Sam. 'That's not a cut. It's Gaelene, you know how careless she is about electrical things. Every time she fills the urn she lets it stand on the wire, sooner or later it's bound to be cut through. It's just the weight of the urn and the sharp metal edge.'

Lisa was not convinced, but she was even more puzzled than before.

## 5

The sudden violent death of one of the College's most controversial staff members boosted early morning attendances the next day. Students leapt from their beds and battled Melbourne's dying public transport system with an eagerness that was otherwise completely absent from their academic lives. Excitedly they rushed into the College on Tuesday morning to watch the police, to gossip in the corridors, and to develop fantastic theories of motive and method.

Doreen Hubel, who had had to put up with a chewing-out by her immediate superior after Lisa had rescued Sam, found herself less than impressed by the students as she made her way to the administration block. Again she found herself hoping that Jarrod wouldn't show any interest in continuing his education after he left school. Fortunately Kylie had little chance of being accepted into any tertiary institution, if her progress at school was anything to go by. No time to worry about Kylie today though. Perhaps it's all true about single working mothers, she thought. Still, what would be the alternative? Single mothers at home on benefits were even more of a threat to the welfare of society in general and their children in particular. Staying home would have her bored to tears anyway, she knew that. Whatever you could say about being the only female Detective-Inspector in the Homicide Squad, you couldn't say it was boring.

She hurried past a group of students, on her way to yet another confusing interview with yet another vague staff member who, she knew in advance, would have remarkably little idea of the running of the place where he worked but would be full to the brim with stupid theories about motive and guilt which she would have to bloody listen to, just in case he confessed or something.

The students watched her go and decided, as one, that they needed a cup of coffee. At least at this hour, the floor of the cafeteria wasn't awash with discarded plates, paper cups, and stubbed fags, but the barn-like hall was cheerless enough to induce anorexia in all but the largest and hungriest of the football-playing Medical Engineering students. The atmosphere was not lightened by the ferocious old lags womanning the cash registers. Refugees from capitalism, they were determined not to oppress anyone by making a profit or indeed by serving them at all. Flatly they refused to sell the stale pink and green iced doughnuts which were their stock-in-trade to the slavering throng of students, academics, and maintenance staff, who had skipped breakfast at home in order to miss none of the day's action.

'It's no good whingeing. You don't know you're born, most of you. We can't sell you the stuff until we get the cash register made up,' rasped one of them monotonously to all requests, pleas, and arguments, 'and we never do that until the day's orders have arrived from the bakery.'

'Why not?' asked a student unwisely.

'It'll be open at nine o'clock, can'tcha wait until then?' the smock-clad gargoyle snarled ferociously. 'Wouldn't know if your bum was on fire, most of you.'

The students subsided in a muttering group. The few hungry staff members tried pathetically to look as if they were just passing and were taking a kindly interest in student life. Eventually the handsome Neos Kosmos, Medical Engineering student and Greek god look-alike, decided to exert his not inconsiderable charms. It would be a waste to squander them on the cash register women, he knew that. With a winning smile he turned to the pretty young girl who stood hopefully at his side, and murmured seductively in her ear. She blushed and looked grateful, then raced around the corner to the milk bar, where they actually sold things to make a living. Panting, she returned with a small box containing an assortment of meat pies, hamburgers, cigarettes, and apple slices to be sold at a profit to the waiting students, and for Neos himself a copy of the *Sun*.

When she returned, Neos was regaling his acolytes with a tirade about the guilt of Sam Klusky. Some were rather surprised at Neos's vehemence; what skin off his nose was it, anyway? Sam was only an academic. So, too, was Richard Johnston. Did it matter, really, if one of them killed another?

But others remembered that Sam had once had the nerve to fail Neos for his complete inability to communicate in written English. Neos had never forgotten this incident. He had pointed out that English was, after all, his second language and it was hardly fair to expect great works of art in a foreign language, was it?

Had he tried such a line on Jacinta, she would have snapped back that he was going to find himself in some difficulties when he went out to work if he had to restrict his clientele to those fluent in Greek. Sam, however, was made of softer stuff. Gently he had agreed that it was a problem; with a rare burst of self-disclosure, which Neos had interpreted as sarcasm, he had pointed out that he himself had English as his fourth language, but did seem to manage. However, if Neos would like to re-submit the assignment in Greek, Sam would be happy to mark it.

It hadn't occurred to Neos that Sam might have spoken Greek himself. Students tended not to wonder very much about the personal histories of their lecturers, and in fact were generally of the opinion that, when not actually lecturing, they were switched off and stored in a cupboard somewhere. Neos shared this view, despite the fact that he had had numerous experiences to the contrary with members of staff of the College. But it had never occurred to him that Sam might have picked up a few survival skills in the process of leaving Poland.

Of course, failing Kosmos was unthinkable in itself. His teachers had never done it at school and he had made it clear to Scott that he was not going to stand for it now. Scott had seen it his way. Most people did. Only one or two fixed ideas had penetrated that handsome head, but Neos had a remarkable capacity to repeat them indefinitely while towering over his victim. The Caff Ladies, hailing (as most of them did) from Belfast, were unimpressed by anything short of dynamite. But they were among the few failures he had had. Normally he got what he wanted in one of two ways.

The trickier strategy, one he only used if he had to, was to threaten to go to their superiors and claim they had made improper advances to him. With Neos's looks, there was every chance that such a claim would be believed; even those totally innocent in word, in thought, and in deed were reluctant to call his bluff on that one.

Neos's easy strategy was more often used. He would charm people, of either sex, into doing exactly what he wanted with the vaguely worded promise of carnal pleasures to come. Sometimes he even followed through with them, if he thought it was worth his while. Edmund Bennett, for example, had been a useful source of examination papers and inside information. Well worth keeping something going with. And Eddie was scared, really scared, about letting on, so there was scope for blackmail too. Not that it had come to that yet. But Neos knew that Edmund was re-applying for promotion to Principal Lecturer, a promotion that had been denied to him before by the poisonous homophobia of Richard Johnston. Now things had changed, of course, but Neos could see some profit for himself if Eddie really wanted to present a positive image to the promotions committee.

'Hey, Neos! Look at this!' interrupted one of his followers. Neos directed a withering look in his direction. Nobody interrupted Neos Kosmos. The student gulped, but continued bravely. 'Look, they reckon Johnston had AIDS,' he continued, waving the paper at Neos.

That grabbed Neos's attention. He turned white. Seizing the paper from his follower, he read the leading paragraph slowly. He flung it down and charged out of the caff, his face a deathly shade.

As he swung out through the cafeteria door and rushed, oblivious, down the dingy corridor, Anne Goodbody had to flatten herself against the wall to avoid being knocked over by the man who had relieved her of her virginity on the previous Saturday night. A well-heeled honey blonde, whose usual garb of pink cardigan, white blouse, tailored fawn skirt and sensible shoes made her conspicuous among her scruffier colleagues, Anne too had troubles. At the bottom of her wicker basket, full of books, notes, and sandwiches made by her mum, there lay a copy of the paper for the upcoming exam in Sociological Paradigms. This had been the return for services rendered to the now vanished Neos Kosmos.

She had taken a respectable amount of persuading, Anne told herself. After all, she was a well-brought-up young lady, not one of those slags from Medical Engineering who'd do anything for a free beer. She had always dreamed of her first time, on her wedding night, in a romantic honeymoon hideaway, with a man whose body was an athletic dream but whose face, in her fantasies, had always been blurred and indistinct. Things had turned out rather differently, she thought, remembering the quick and painful grope in the back of Neos's car, parked up a darkened alley. Quickly she repressed a sudden feeling of – surely it couldn't be – disappointment, regret even. Neos loved her, he had told her so. And sex with the man who loved you had to be the most wonderful experience a woman could have. That's what the nuns had always said, rather wistfully she had sometimes thought. And after all, she was a woman now, wasn't she? One up on Sister Patrick.

And here was the precious exam, clutched tightly to her bosom. It looked like the real thing, but where could dear Neos have got it? If it were the real thing, she mused with excruciating grammatical correctness, it was awfully sweet of him to give it to her. That just showed what a fine, honest, caring boy – Anne had difficulty thinking of her male contemporaries as men – he was.

She moved dreamily through the gathering piles of debris that surrounded the doorway to the cafeteria.

'Oh Anne, er...' said one of a group of dear Neos's friends, grinning. I really must talk to him about some of the people he associates with, thought Anne. Some of them seem quite unsuitable. Perhaps I could introduce him to some of my friends. Of course they'd like him, even if he is a bit...um... She was unable to let the phrase 'lower class' enter her conscious mind, but, guiltily, she knew it was lurking there.

'Hello John,' she replied brightly for the time being. No sense in being too confrontative, not yet anyway, although there was something distinctly unpleasant about that grin.

'Oh honeybunch, Neos told us such a lot about you,' he continued in cooing tones, while the others around him chortled and guffawed.

'Yer, he won his bet, though of course you'd have been the first to know. Yer, we bet him a hundred dollars he couldn't get into your pants, but he swore you had the hots for him. Looks like he was right! Har har har,' cut in one of the others. 'Still, I reckon it was worth a hundred dollars just to hear him describe the whole thing.'

'Yeah,' he said. 'Little bit shy she was, it seems. Had to be talked into...'

Appalled, Anne imitated Neos's speedy departure. That bastard, she seethed to herself. How could he have done it? Told his scruffy mates about them? Done it for a bet! And she thought he had really loved her. All those things he'd said, lies, all lies.

Finding a refuge in the ladies' loo, Anne sank onto a seat without even covering it with toilet paper first. For ten minutes or so she alternated between fits of weeping and desperate mutterings of, 'I can't face them, I'll never be able to look another student in the eye, I'll have to leave, oh what's to become of me, what will my parents say...'

Then, gradually, a thirst for revenge began to assert itself. She was going to get that bastard. He was going to find out that you didn't treat a lady like that, not if you were a nasty little wog from the wrong side of town. She'd fix him, and she had just the ammunition she needed. The exam. All she had to do was dob Neos in. It was a pity in a way; she'd done no work at all for Sociological Paradigms, spending all the class time chatting noisily with her friends in the Quiet Study Area of the library. But it would be worth it. She could pick someone else's brain and scrape through. Maybe she could steal some notes, just temporarily of course, photocopy and return them before their owner knew they were missing. Getting back at Neos was the important thing. She'd really drop him in it, and she'd enjoy doing it.

She looked at her watch. Half past nine. Good, things would be quiet for a bit. Carefully she repaired her natural-look makeup and practised a calm but wounded facial expression in the mirror. Still a little red-eyed, but otherwise as ravishing as artifice could make her, she headed for Antonia Summerfield's office. By now her jolly ocker tormentors had dispersed to lectures, practical classes, and the recreation room, so she could cross the campus without having to confront any more giggling, har-haring louts.

As usual, Dr Summerfield had her ear glued to the phone, and she flapped her hand vaguely at Anne and continued her conversation with the national secretary of WUMP. Interpreting this correctly, Anne sank into a yellow plastic chair and waited.

'What can I do for you, Anne; is something the matter?' asked Antonia in her usual brisk tones, as she put the receiver down.

'Oh, Dr Summerfield,' said Anne with an only partly artificial quaver in her voice. 'I can't tell you, it's just awful!' And she burst into tears again. Antonia gazed at her despairingly. Why on earth did they bother to come if that was all they were going to say? The prospect of dragging some trivial problem out of yet another weeping student held even less than its usual rather dubious appeal.

Antonia had slept very badly, and was feeling awful herself that morning. She had been fond of Johnston, but nobody asked her how she felt. Nobody suggested she might want to take today off, or even patted her shoulder and said they knew how she must be feeling. No, they were all just gloating over his death like a pack of ghouls. All right, perhaps she had been the only one to see Johnston's positive side, but there was no need for them to be quite so insensitive about the death of another human being. And yes, she was delighted that Sam had been released; but it hardly cleared things up, did it? In fact, it made things considerably worse for the rest of them, as the police had gone back to tramping around, interviewing, poking their noses in everywhere, asking personal questions.

Besides, there was that urn. If the murder had been politically motivated – and heaven knew there were enough left-wing weirdos around – mightn't she also be a target? Her politics were less extreme than Johnston's; after all, she couldn't possibly go along with the view that God had created woman, the weaker vessel, as a support and comfort for man. But even so, Antonia believed the Family was the basis of society. Being electrocuted at the age of forty-five was definitely not in her plans for her life, which were more ambitious than most people realised.

A muffled sob returned her to the present. Antonia sighed, and switched into counselling mode. 'Well now, I'm sure it can't be as awful as all that,' she began automatically. 'Everyone makes mistakes you know. The trick is not to make the same one twice, isn't it? Now tell me what it's all about and we'll see what we can do.'

Gradually Antonia's years of practice in such situations began to tell on Anne, and she unfolded the dreadful tale of how she had come to be given the exam by Neos.

'I just knew it was the wrong thing,' she said, 'and I really felt I had to tell someone.'

'Well yes, you were absolutely right of course; it does feel better to get these things off your chest, doesn't it?' smiled Antonia reassuringly, thinking furiously. Why confess? Why to her? What was this girl doing here? 'Now, perhaps you could tell me why you were so terribly upset about it. I mean, there is more to it than just the exam, isn't there?'

Anne looked startled. 'Well, I felt so guilty...'

'Oh come now,' said Antonia in the fake-motherly voice that she found so useful for getting the truth out of students, 'there's more to it than that. You'd better tell me the whole story. Are you sure you really cared for this boy? He didn't threaten you or hurt you, did he?'

Anne was briefly tempted to come out with the whole terrible scene in the cafeteria and her ghastly realisation of how she had been deceived and abused. Antonia was a very skilled interviewer, after all. But Anne pulled herself together. She knew that if she let that slip, her motive for revenge would be too obvious. She thought fast, then settled for sobbing, 'Well, I think I'm pregnant!'

Once Antonia had calmed the girl down again and discovered that intercourse had taken place only three days earlier, the smell of a rat became even stronger. But what was going on? What student, even Anne Goodbody, would report a leaked exam paper? If she just wanted to confess, why not see the chaplain, mused Antonia. Or if she's worried about pregnancy, wouldn't Peter Harwell have been more use? Perhaps she's too shy and embarrassed, Antonia speculated, but it's strange all the same. It would seem that Anne had her own very particular motives in choosing to confess in this particular way.

All the same, the leak was a serious matter and had to be followed up. There was no doubt that the dogeared paper Anne had handed over was the real thing. Antonia had proofread it herself, over the objections of some of the staff to such a nitpicking procedure.

'I think you should report this to Miss Kloof, your Head of Department.' Anne's face fell. Obviously she had been hoping that one confession would be enough. 'I will report it to our Head, and we will just have to get another version written and printed before exam week. Now don't look so miserable, Anne; you've done the right thing by telling us who gave you the exam,' she added, scrutinising the student's face intently. Sure enough, there it was, a tiny flash of malicious pleasure. So that was what she wanted, was it? To get Neos into trouble? Well, thought Antonia grimly, there's going to be trouble all right, but it won't just be Neos who cops it. 'Run along now', she said, patting Anne on the shoulder and ushering her out into the corridor.

The question we have to settle, though, she thought, gazing unseeingly at Anne's pink-cardiganed back, is where did he get it from in the first place? She had a fair idea, and she hoped that this time there would be some action. Staff members who gave out exam papers in return for sexual favours made her very angry indeed. She wasn't sure whether it was the immorality or the stupidity of the action she found more offensive, but she knew she didn't like it and she was going to see that it was stopped. It was remarkably difficult to get rid of a staff member who had been granted tenure. But there was still that rule on the books about gross moral turpitude. Gross moral turpitude indeed. She knew that this was a tricky concept to define, and that tenured staff had got away with an awful lot in the past by claiming they had the right to determine for themselves what was moral and what was not. Basically people didn't want to get involved, or were afraid that their own less-than-perfect private lives might be opened up to scrutiny if they made too much of a fuss about others.

This time, however, the consequence was going to be the rewriting of the Sociological Paradigms exam. That was going to mean an awful lot of work for an awfully large percentage of the staff. Of course, she didn't delude herself that the work would fall to the other senior and tenured members of staff who had the power to make a fuss about Bennett's behaviour. But she hoped that the junior staff members who were landed with the work would be prepared to complain loudly and bitterly enough to produce some action from Scott. If I were running this place, she thought, things would be very different.

Later, in the Head of Department's office, there was action aplenty.

Iain Scott felt like bursting into tears. No sooner had he got in that morning at the ridiculously early hour of eleven o'clock, than he was confronted with an outraged Agnes Kloof, Head of Medical Engineering. He was not at his best in confrontations, preferring if possible to stalk out with an air of wounded pride. Later, he'd come back and do things the way he had wanted in the first place. It usually worked. Other staff members were generally so stunned by his self-centred audacity that whatever he wanted would be a fait accompli before they had managed to close their mouths. Lately, he had noticed with concern that the technique was gaining other adherents, people who even had the cheek to go around behind him and reverse his decisions. He suspected that Jacinta had been putting them up to it. We'll see about that when her tenure application comes up, he thought.

But he could see that a hurt but dignified exit was not going to help this time. Miss Kloof was a large person who had single-handedly run the Medical Engineering side of a rehabilitation hospital full of punch-drunk boxers and frustrated footballers for twenty years before moving into the relative quiet of student training. She gave off an intimidating air of having sized you up and found you distinctly wanting. Anyway, they were in his office, and the chief consequence of his making a dignified exit would be to leave her in close propinquity to a number of rather embarrassing files; files he knew she would feel no compunction at all about taking down and reading. Further, he would then have to skulk in the corridor waiting for the coast to be clear again. He had learned early in his career as Head of Department that the great thing was to avoid informal meetings with members of staff. This meant no hanging around in corridors. Staff, he had found, were infinitely easier to deal with in the more formal atmosphere of a staff meeting, where he could rule them out of order when things got tricky.

Right now, however, Agnes Kloof was standing over him in a meaning way, and that was definitely a copy of the forthcoming

Sociological Paradigms exam that she was waving furiously. He recognised it, because he'd been called in to intercede between two sociologists who were near blows concerning the putative difference between a radical lesbian feminist approach to education and a radical feminist lesbian approach to education.

He'd solved this problem in his usual dymanic way by pointing out that it would be tantamount to academic censorship for him to side with either in the struggle, and suggested they get another sociologist to propose an entirely different essay question. The fact that the third sociologist did not teach in the Sociological Paradigms course, and produced a question which was completely irrelevant to anything covered in classes, wasn't important. It was all the same, he argued; students only ever prepared one essay topic, and wrote on that regardless of the actual question. The undeniable truth of this declaration worked. The sociologists had been too stunned to reply, and when they did they fell to bickering among themselves. Another problem resolved satisfactorily, Scott had thought.

He was jerked sharply back to the present by the sound of Miss Kloof's strident voice raised in fury. 'You're not getting away with it this time, Scott!' she shouted, leaning menacingly forward and exposing an ill-fitting set of false teeth to his fascinated gaze. 'I want a full inquiry. I want to know where this exam came from and what exactly is going on. This sort of thing is completely intolerable.'

'Well, perhaps you could start by leaning on this Kosmos chap,' suggested Scott, desperately trying the old ball's-in-your-court trick. 'After all, it was him this student got the paper from. There's always the possibility of legal proceedings against him. I mean, it is burglary.'

'Burglary my foot,' expostulated Agnes, waving that portion of her anatomy in a worrying way. 'He was given that paper.'

'Oh, he says that, does he?' replied Scott nastily. 'Is he aware of the provisions of the laws of libel?'

'Now hang on a minute,' said Miss Kloof, nonplussed at finding herself on the back foot quite so early in the conversation. After all, she did have right on her side, didn't she? 'I haven't spoken to him yet.'

'Haven't spoken to him?' repeated Scott, trying to hide his immense relief and pleasure. 'So this is all baseless accusation, then? Just trying to stir up trouble on the off-chance? Why haven't you spoken to him?'

'I would, if I could find the bastard,' admitted Kloof. 'But nobody's seen him since he rushed out of the cafeteria yesterday.'

'Must've eaten something,' surmised Scott. 'Poor chap. Have you noticed how reminiscent the cafeteria is of a morgue?'

'Stick to the point!' shouted Miss Kloof. 'And stay off the subject of morgues, will you? I mean, with one of your own staff not yet buried, it's hardly decent.'

'So, I should concern myself with some little tart from your department and this cock-and-bull story she's come up with to stop herself feeling guilty about getting carried away last Saturday night with some other lowlife, again, I note, a student in your department?'

'No, you should not,' foamed Kloof, wondering how on earth anyone could work closely with this man. The answer to that, of course, was that nobody could and that was why he had managed to get away with so much over the years. 'The point is not what Miss Goodbody did or whether she should have. The point is Kosmos. Where did he get the exam from? That's what I want to know, and I want to know it soon, or I'm going to the Director. You're not getting away with another cover-up, my man.'

'Look,' hedged Scott desperately, 'if your students get in here and steal copies of our exams, that's hardly my fault. I think the investigation belongs squarely in your department. What do you teach them over there? Burglary 1A? Assault and battery as an advanced option? You have the nerve to come over here and threaten me, because one of your students has been stealing exam papers. I think that if any investigation is called for, it's called for in Medical Engineering, not here.'

'Stealing my arse!' screamed Kloof, with a rather infelicitous turn of phrase. 'It's that old poove Bennett, up to his tricks again. Your department is a human cesspit. The only member of this outfit with any morals at all was Richard Johnston. He at least had the courage of his convictions. He managed to block Bennett's promotion last year, and a good thing too. And look what happened to him!'

A horrible thought crossed her mind. Had Edmund Bennett finally flipped? He'd been absolutely livid about missing that promotion, and everyone knew how unstable poofters were. Surely not? An even more horrible thought: she had been on that promotions committee too, in fact she'd supported Johnston strongly over Bennett's unsuitability. Was her own safety at risk?

Scott, oblivious to Agnes's fears, groaned inwardly. If she pushed the moral angle, there'd be trouble. There had been a number of unfortunate incidents, all happily hushed up, concerning Dr Edmund Bennett and some of the more attractive and dim-witted of the students. The male ones, that is. It was embarrassing, to say the least. Now good old heterosexual liaisons with students – well, that was something else entirely, completely understandable when you considered the number of attractive young ladies among the students, and the undeniable savoir faire of the male staff...

He was torn away from some rather pleasant reminiscences, involving a number of attractive female students he had unnoticingly scarred for life, by the ringing of the phone. Hoping for a reprieve, he reached for it eagerly. It was Gaelene.

'Oh, Dr Scott,' she said in that tone of hers which was exactly halfway between respectful and sarcastic. Nothing you could actually put your finger on, but Scott always felt that Gaelene was laughing at some private joke of her own. 'The police are on the line. I told them you'd be happy to speak to them.'

She's done it again, he thought. Amazing how powerless one is against such simple strategies. I can't exactly ask her to tell them I've gone out, can I? He wondered again if he should try exerting his charms on Gaelene. She was a worthy opponent; imagine what an ally she would be. Between the two of them they could have the entire College sewn up. But he had a nasty feeling that she would probably just laugh if he tried anything with her. Sighing, he pressed the transfer button on the phone.

'This is Detective-Inspector Hubel from the Homicide Squad,' he heard with a sinking heart. 'I thought, in the light of the forensic evidence, that you might have a few interesting things to tell me.'

'Forensic evidence? My dear, what do you mean? It was all just an unfortunate accident, I thought that was already established.' He glanced warily at Agnes Kloof, who was drinking it all in.

Doreen Hubel sighed. She hated being called 'my dear', especially by people who made it obvious that they feared and despised her. Doreen had no illusions about the reactions she could expect from the public, and most particularly from the insecure male members of it, who she could be reasonably sure were guilty as hell, if not of murder then of something far more nasty. 'Don't you read the papers?' she inquired.

'Well, no,' confessed Scott. 'I never seem to pass a milk bar.'

'Are you trying to pretend you haven't heard about the results of the blood test?'

'No, of course I haven't. I've got a busy and responsible job to carry out, you know. I've been flat-out keeping this place going in spite of you lot crawling all over it with magnifying glasses and lists of personal questions. What could there be in a blood test to interest the newspapers anyway?'

'AIDS.'

'AIDS? You're joking,' spluttered an astonished Scott without thinking. Miss Kloof gasped and looked grim. Oh well, thought Scott, it's in the paper, I've hardly let out a secret. Obviously she hasn't seen today's paper either. He gathered his wits to reply. 'AIDS? That's ridiculous. How could Johnston possibly have AIDS?'

'That's what we'd like to know,' replied Doreen. 'I'm getting the feeling that there's a lot of things you're not telling us, Scott. And I want to know what those things are and why you're being – shall we say – less than forthcoming in helping the police with their inquiries. I wouldn't like to have to charge you with obstruction,' she added in a tone of voice which implied that there was little she would have preferred to doing just that.

Scott was once again overwhelmed with a desire to burst into tears. As a strategy for making things go away, it hadn't actually worked since he was three years old, but as a psychologist, Scott was well aware that people tended to revert to earlier patterns of behaviour under conditions of stress. And conditions of stress were exactly what he was under.

Johnston with AIDS? He knew that didn't necessarily mean that Johnston was – had been – gay, but it was the first, impossible, picture to rise before him. Johnston, of all people! The pompous, judgemental, sanctimonious old fart! Picking up boys in public lavatories or cruising in St Kilda – the images which rose before him – seemed too risky for the likes of Johnston. Carrying on a clandestine relationship, then. Perhaps with one of the students? Oh no, this exam business couldn't be connected with Johnston, could it? Neos Kosmos was well known as someone who'd fuck anything if there was an advantage in it. Scott liked his problems separate and straightforward, and the implications of possible links between an AIDS-infected Johnston and some corrupt, exam-stealing student were more than he could handle. And what about Bennett? Everyone knew about him; he at least didn't make any secret of it. If anything, a bit too up-front for Scott's liking. Still, we were all liberated now. Did Bennett have AIDS too? Worse, the disease was contagious, wasn't it? Could you catch it from using a dirty coffee cup? And what about the men's toilets? He'd have to make some discreet inquiries.

Inspector Hubel was still quacking down the receiver. With an enormous effort, Scott managed a reply.

'Look, this comes as a complete shock to me. There couldn't be some mistake, could there?'

'Don't come the innocent with me, Scott,' replied Hubel angrily. She was having a tough time dealing with all these so-called intellectuals. They appeared to believe that the rules of ordinary society just didn't apply to them, except of course when it suited them. She was firmly of the opinion that Scott was the worst of the lot. Guilty as hell, she could tell that. Probably not of the murder, but of all manner of other sordid, tacky crimes, that much seemed certain. 'I'll be over there in an hour, and I want you to tell me a few things,' she said firmly.

The phone line went dead. Scott sighed deeply, and looked up to see Miss Kloof regarding him with a baleful expression.

'Johnston too, is it?' she said grimly. 'You and your department of perverts, preying on innocent students.' Richard Johnston, she thought. How can it be possible? So had there been something more complicated behind Richard's distaste for Bennett? Her mind shied away from the possible entanglements. 'I'll see something is done about this, you just wait,' she continued angrily. 'How would you like a nice new job at the Yularu TAFE College? Cleaning the cafeteria? I'll give you a week to get this whole messy business tidied up, and then I'm taking it all to the Director.'

'Him? What makes you think he'd be interested? He's as bent as a hoop snake on heat, everybody knows that. He'll laugh at you, you know.'

Kloof glared. Goldwyn was a dark horse, she knew that. After all, why had he left America? All sorts of funny things in his past, no doubt. Still, that was true of most of us. But were he and Scott actually in league over something? Hard to say. Each loathed the other, but that had never stopped people working together, had it? Especially their sort. She just wasn't sure. 'Well, if I don't get any action from him, it'll be the newspapers. You think they'd turn down a story about homosexual love tangles at Bazza Tech?'

Scott could see that she just might do it, and that of course had to be avoided at all costs, if any of them wanted to be around to collect their less-than-generous superannuation allowance. The Yularu TAFE College sounded positively inviting by contrast.

He was not in a good position; even the sunniest of optimists would have agreed to that. But even so, he wasn't having a fat sow like Kloof ordering him around. He rose to his feet in an effort to tower over her threatingly, but ruined the effect by falling over a mouldering heap of unmarked essays.

The pain in his elbow made him more petulant than ever, and climbing to his feet he shouted, 'How dare you barge into my office, listen to my private and confidential telephone conversations, and then have the nerve – the sheer, unmitigated gall –' he knew it was a cliché, but it did sound good, and it was long enough to give him a chance to work out what to say next '– to threaten me? The Johnston case has nothing to do with you, and there's nothing to suggest it's in any way connected with this exam-paper nonsense. It's highly likely that this little Goodbody tart is just out to make trouble – I mean, we've only got her word for it that the Kosmos lad gave her the paper. It's probably just one of those spiteful lovers' quarrels. And besides, that's highly unlikely to be a real exam at all. It looks to me like a practice exam. My staff prepare them regularly as revision for the students; a custom, I might add, which reflects positively on their dedication to helping your less than brilliant students to cope with the conceptual complexities of our subjects. Now get out of my office; I've got enough to do without you coming in here wasting my time with groundless accusations.'

He stopped, panting and rubbing his poor elbow. Kloof glared at him. If looks could kill, there would have been a second murder investigation underway.

'You lying hound!' she said, with grudging admiration. 'I'm going straight to the Director.'

And she swept out of the office.

Wearily, Scott pulled towards him the draft agenda for Thursday's staff meeting and began to make alterations.


## 7

Even the solidly built Agnes Kloof was momentarily stopped by the Barry College wind as she left Building 1956. Years of practice enabled her to progress slowly down the narrow alley-way between Building 1956 on one side and Building 1934 on the other. Shouldering her way through gaggles of students, Agnes emerged at the brow of the Barry College hill. The old emplacement which had once allowed surveillance of the activities of all below was still there.

Agnes began the descent of the steep bluestone steps alongside the towering walls of Building 1872 and it occurred to her that Barry College, during its various metamorphoses, had always been a repository for the socially inconvenient. Initially, parts of it had been a Victorian model prison. Its buildings had been converted first into unsuccessful little factories and now into a re-education camp for those too middle-class to be on the dole, but not rich enough to work in Daddy's business. Barry College was a shabby, gritty, city campus with little to commend it to the eye and less to the nose when the nearby tannery had its weekly vat-cleaning. There was a rumour that the old paint in one of the basement rooms in Building 1872 still gave a positive benzidine test for the blood spilt in floggings. Quite a reasonable place for a murder, really, thought Miss Kloof. Several, she added, compiling a mental list with 'I. Scott' at the top.

At the bottom of the stairs, she froze the leader of Disabled Individual Student Activities Behind Longer Education with a look. Miss Kloof was a strong supporter of euthanasia, compulsory where necessary. The country had problems enough without supporting people who were incapable of a hard day's work. She turned sharp right into the maze of renovated nineteenth-century cottages fronting Descartes Avenue and pressed on in her quest for Building 1975, known as the Power Tower.

Thy brother's blood cries unto me from the ground, she thought, now where did that come from? Really, she decided, all this business must be driving me silly. She crossed Descartes Avenue, daring a student on a motorbike to run her down. Deaths-head helmet or no deaths-head helmet, he braked and swerved, and allowed Miss Kloof to cross unhonked. Immediately deducing that he had to be enrolled in Medical Engineering, she made a mental note to track him down and tick him off for roaring around campus at an unsafe speed and menacing the staff.

A few more twists and turns and she came on the only purpose-built area on the campus – the Administration block, Building 1975, Nathan Goldwyn's pride and joy. He had even managed to persuade the architects to leave room for Barry College's only trees – all three of them. The scene suddenly reminded Agnes of her South African girlhood. The whites got trees, the blacks got concrete. The professional staff must occupy some sort of Cape Coloured position in the administrative mind, she decided. Her Department's roof didn't leak, not like the Department of Psychological and Sociological Enquiry, but the accommodation was nothing to shout about and the few windows gave onto views of rusted pipes and blank walls.

Arriving at the low, rounded building, she swept through the electronic doors, flinching yet again at the once-modish pink and apricot decor. Stolidly, she ignored all offers of help on her progress to the Administrative core, where the seldom-seen Director reportedly lurked. In the course of her journey, the appurtenances rose steadily in their numbers and luxuriousness until ankle-deep carpet pile muffled even Agnes's thunderous tread as she advanced on the Director's doors. Cries of: 'No! Stop! You can't go in there, he's got his red light on,' resounded from various acolytes, but Agnes ignored them. Reaching the Director's door, she barrelled through its oaken portals like Matt Dillon shouldering into the Last Chance Saloon. The sybaritic furniture within was matched by the activities. These ended with a thud as Goldwyn leapt to his feet, spilling a hapless clerical assistant to the floor. For a moment the trio gazed at one another.

'Well!' fumed Miss Kloof, recovering first. 'Now we know why they all get RSI working for you! Special duties indeed, I would say so! Yes, Lurline, you might well go!' she stormed at the retreating assistant before turning to Goldwyn. Used to life's alarms, he had made good use of the time to readjust his clothing, sit down and assume his usual air of bland affability and charm. Years of experience dealing with battleaxes had taught him that charm was their weak point.

'How very nice to see you, Miss Kloof, even if it is a little unexpected,' Nathan began. 'I do pride myself on being accessible to the staff...'

'I can see that!' roared Miss Kloof.

'...but I prefer people to make appointments, you know, so that I can plan my day,' Nathan continued imperturbably. 'But as you're here, what can I do for you?' he asked with a winning smile.

He waved his arm at Agnes, to suggest that she might sink into one of the black leather Ultimolux Reklinas scattered about his vast office.

'Plan! You plan this sort of thing?' stormed Agnes. The cold wind, the confrontation with Scott, and the sudden discovery of a man using one of the more ancient methods of combatting nervous stress had done little for her temper. With an effort she pulled herself together. What she had come about was far more important than in-house fornication. Set-faced, she advanced on the seated Goldwyn, who blanched and revved his Reklina a foot backwards.

'Listen, Goldwyn,' she gritted, 'this college is in trouble...'

'You mean the tragic loss of Dr Johnston? Well, these things are terribly unfortunate, but accidents do happen you know. I've complained for years about the low level of funding for basic maintenance for the fabric of this college, but the Australian government just doesn't have the same level of commitment to tertiary education that you get in the States, and the Alumni Association spends most of its time getting pie-eyed in reunions instead of organising a bit of the old razzamatazz and fund-raising. Mind you, the college didn't even have an Alumni Association until I got it off the ground, I can't understand how this kind of basic oversight can occur in this country.'

'Accident? Tragic loss?' said Agnes. 'It was murder. You and Iain Scott are hand-in-glove. I know a cover-up when I see one.'

'Not at all,' Goldwyn replied. 'I have just been discussing this with the police at the highest level and it appears that poor Johnston died as the result of a fall down the staircase in the dark. The main problem now is the whole question of the Civilein production contracts which were signed just before Johnston's death between the Justice Barry Research, Consulting and Professional Services Unit and Lexington Biosearch Corporation. I have not yet been able to raise Lexington by phone, but surely they will realise that the loss of the principal researcher will make those dates a little hard to meet. That stuff he was working on would have been worth a fortune to this college, so his death was indeed a tragic one. In every way.' he added.

'Typical!' snorted Agnes. 'All you can think about is research contracts! The college does have some kind of responsibility to the students and to the community. I'm talking about academic standards and professional responsibility. Forgotten concepts here I know, but the parents and the taxpayers still believe in them and even the politicians still pay homage to them when they do the triennial funding. You've got one scandal here, accident my foot, and you're going to have another.'

She paused and was rewarded by the sight of a man imitating a terrified bullfrog. The phrase 'triennial funding' had got him where he lived, she thought venomously, and she pulled the Sociological Paradigms Semester I Examination out of her voluminous handbag.

'As you know,' she began 'the Joint Exam Standards Tribunal has had several reports concerning failures of examination confidentiality. I believe at least two of them have been forwarded to you?'

She gazed threatingly down at Goldwyn's sallow features.

'But, but,' he persevered, 'I had those allegations thoroughly investigated and nothing whatever came of them.'

'Well, what do you call this?' Agnes demanded. 'I've told you over and over again, Goldwyn, there is a ring of staff members providing exams, in return for favours of all sorts. But those psychologists are giving the exams out like sweeties now. It's Scott's fault, you should know that. Well! You would know that if you had any time to spare between getting all over the secretaries like a rash and roaring round the country on junkets.'

'The job of Director requires a certain amount of public relations work,' protested Goldwyn.

'The job of Director! If you did the job of Director, you would have got rid of that odious man back in 1982, when...'

Goldwyn sensed another scandal coming round for a rerun. He had two current ones and enough was enough.

'Now look,' he said, 'that's all in the past and anyway Scott explained to me that he was making a film on counselling the disabled, and he'd got that girl, the student, to act the part. The special effects got a little out of hand, that's all. We have to take some risks to stay in the forefront of the field and there was no lasting harm done. The cameras were soon mended, no college property was damaged, not even the wheelchair, and they had no trouble resuscitating that poor girl, what was her name now? Seriously Agnes, the way you return to this incident makes me wonder whether it has more than a merely professional significance for you.'

'Miss Kloof turned a deep outraged purple. She had had a very difficult interview with an outraged Cypriot father over that incident. It was not, it had emerged, that the darkly beautiful Irene had nearly broken her neck as she ricocheted down the stairs in a wheelchair which had annoyed Mr Kalokerinos. It was the fact that she had been unchaperoned with a male who was not a relative. Word had spread about the careless approach taken at Barry College toward a maiden's honour. As a result, the Department of Medical Engineering had never again qualified for an attractive government subsidy designed to assist students of migrant backgrounds.

'His films on counselling, as he calls them, are nothing less than a sordid excuse to exploit innocent students and ruin the good name of the college in pursuit of his own advancement,' she shrieked. 'For God's sake, Goldwyn! The man has no control over his staff, and the whole process of assessment over there is a mockery. You've got away with calling it "allegations" up until now. Well, here's the proof. One of my students has handed this exam in, now will you investigate where it came from, because he won't.' She flung the dogeared exam across Goldwyn's marble-topped desk. He lunged and caught it before it hit the ground.

Goldwyn really had no desire to meddle in the internal affairs of his departments, he had worries enough being Director. She did not seem to realise that there was little hope of proving that a staff member had given an exam to a student unless one or the other confessed. This was something that neither party had ever shown any inclination to do in his extensive experience of these perennial allegations. It was utterly hopeless but there was no way he could admit it. The whole blasted business of exam scandals was a worry if any hint of it reached outside funding bodies. It began to look as if his relief that the ink had dried on the Lexington contract had been premature. Had Johnston been killed by someone in the exam ring, he wondered. But having started the accident theory, there was no hope of letting it go. Playing for time, he began reading the exam aloud while he thought furiously.

'Compare and contrast the approaches taken by Marx and Hegel to the ethical problems of human in vitro fertilisation,' he read.

Suddenly hearing what he was saying, he stared at the paper to check that he hadn't made it up. 'Common First Year Sociology and this is what they ask?' he demanded. 'Are you sure this isn't some kind of joke?'

'Pah!' retorted Miss Kloof.

A conviction that he was missing some vital connection forced Goldwyn to persist. 'Look,' he said. 'Aside from the fact that Marx and Hegel died long before in vitro fertilisation was ever even thought of, why on God's green earth are they teaching this sort of thing to first-year students? I mean, just how relevant are Marx and Hegel to Electronic Engineering students, not to mention Graphic Arts? I suppose it would help the Articled Clerks a bit, though,' he concluded lamely.

Agnes sighed wearily and waved a pudgy hand. 'We wondered that,' she said. 'James Tate told me he was going to raise the whole question of the relevance of in vitro fertilisation to Radiocommunications Engineering at last month's JEST meeting. It would have been okay if Psycho had sent the usual representative, you know, Dr Lark. We could have soon resolved the matter after a collegial discussion, but she was sick and Johnston came instead. These socially aware people are often sick, have you noticed that?'

Nathan nodded, spellbound. He had. 'So, so, what happened? Did he ask?' he demanded.

'Yes and no,' replied Agnes. 'No sooner had Tate taken his pipe out of his mouth and started "when I was at Reading..." than Johnston was on him like a tiger.'

Serve him right, thought Goldwyn. Honestly, it's a wonder I'm not a screaming wacko myself, sitting listening to all those tedious reminiscences about Reading. Reading! Why not Blueing? But all those English places had extraordinary names. Much Nether in the Wallop. Thank God that didn't have a university or he'd have to sit listening to boring stories about England's answer to Podunk, Ohio.

'Are you all right?' Agnes demanded, peering at him through her glasses.

'Well, things have been getting a bit much lately,' Goldwyn admitted. 'But go on. You were telling me Johnston's explanation for all of this.'

'Johnston just turned to him and said, "When you were at

Reading, baby" – you know the way he talked – "the place blew sky-high with Commies and agitators. Now you guys told us that you wanted the bean-brained dyslexics that you select into your damnfool courses to be turned into Renaissance Men, sensitive, aware, and tuned-in to social issues. Well, you got it. So don't moan to me about how we do it. The end justifies the goddamned means, Tate." Then he glared at the chairman and said he had research to do if no-one else did, so how about hitting that agenda and getting the hell on out there. It was the shortest JEST meeting on record.'

Goldwyn had to admit that Johnston's gall, arrogance, and rudeness was, rather had been, on such a grand scale that it had always aroused a certain sneaking admiration in him. How he had yearned to tell Dr Dane to hit that agenda or words to that effect, but would it work if he did it? Could he pull it off or would they just think he had gone over the top like poor old Bayliss before him? Probably. He sighed and turned back to the exam.

'Well, well,' he began, with the beaming, gold-tinged smile for which he was justly famed. 'There may seem on the face of it to be some security problem, but it would never do to jump to conclusions without a thorough, searching and bipartisan investigation first, now would it? Of course, I don't have to impress on an academic of your standing and years of experience the need for confidentiality. Yes, indeed, absolute discretion must be the keynote of our approach to this complex and demanding issue.'

It sure must, he thought, thinking gloomily of that litigious lot of loonies over in Psycho. At least in the old days of writs and counterwrits, the place hadn't been lousy with corpses, not to mention the boys and girls from Homicide. All the same, it had been a worry for a peace-loving Director. Thinking of previous times of gloom and doom reminded him, he hadn't had the statutory visit from George Irwell, Union Rep and pain in the ass. He usually managed to drop by just when he was least needed to put Goldwyn straight on the Academic and Professional staff's point of view, as if he needed to be told. If there were people more capable of making their wishes known, he hadn't met them yet. His voice was rolling on and he hurriedly switched himself back into control of it.

'I'll certainly ring Scott and discuss the matter with him and see what action he has taken. If this is in fact a practice exam, as I suspect, no action may be necessary. But if not, I'm sure you'll find that he's right on top of things...'

'Quite!' snorted Agnes, but Goldwyn, by now in full flood, continued as if he hadn't heard, while rising to his feet and conducting her out.

'The security of examination papers is a very serious problem and we may have to discuss allocating funds to tighten the existing security arrangements, when we have our next Barry College Council Meeting. Naturally, this will involve certain costs as well as benefits and funds may have to be removed from some areas to meet felt needs in others. Nevertheless we cannot afford to spare any efforts in upholding our good name and the academic integrity of Barry College of Technology, one of the oldest and most prestigious tertiary colleges in the Southern Hemisphere. Founded in 1850 to serve the needs of an expanding, thrusting colony, think of that, Miss Kloof, well over a century ago, men had this vision of a liberated, educated technological sector ready to lift the Australian community into the next century and beyond by applying the theories discovered in musty philosophers' studies and making them relevant to the call of life itself. In those days, of course, people had a simpler view of a settled, hierarchical society where everyone, brainworker or craftsman, knew his place, and teachers and learning were more respected. Students nowadays are so much more assertive than they used to be and they make demands which not all our staff members are equally well equipped to handle. They have become accustomed to practice exams of course, and so the line between practice and reality has become a little blurred for some of them, and then there is still the element of youthful high spirits to deal with, but I'm sure we all remember those days of youthful gaiety and light-heartedness from our own youth, when activities, perhaps thoughtless, but not vicious, were entered into which we wouldn't consider today...'

Goldwyn remembered, momentarily, the shy, tongue-tied student he had been and wondered where, on the road to middle age, he had acquired this ability to ramble on meaninglessly for so long. Miss Kloof, holder of the Botha University Gold medal for Physiology (1957) wondered, not for the first time, how Goldwyn managed to breathe during these diatribes. Some hidden spiracle perhaps? While she was wondering, she found herself outside the inner sanctum and realised that the old survivor had done it again. Partly mollified, she began the long trek back to Medical Engineering to brood in her office.

Wasting no time once he had eased Agnes out, Goldwyn leaped across his office, grabbed the phone, and shouted, 'Get me Scott!'

While waiting for things to happen, he relieved some of his complicated tensions by storming around his office kicking things. To hell with exams, to hell with corpses, he had to meet those research contracts. Did nobody understand that Barry College was in the red, that the Lexington money was not only committed, it had been spent? Who could replace Johnston? Dammit, he'd arranged for an understudy himself. 'Just in case' he'd said, talking Goldwyn into lifting the staff ceiling to get that woman a job. What was her name? Mac something? Matilda MacQuide? No, Jacinta? His thoughts were shattered when the phone rang and he shouted, 'Scott!' into the receiver.

'Sorree, Dr Goldwyn,' came Gaelene's resigned voice. 'But Dr Scott is tied up at the moment.'

'Get him untied and onto this phone!' roared Goldwyn.

'Don't think I can, Dr Goldwyn, he's got the police with him,' replied Gaelene. She was used to people demanding Scott with a note of homicidal fury in their voices.

'Unh.' said Goldwyn, momentarily stymied. 'Right, okay, well tell him I want to speak to him right away, not tomorrow, not the day after or when he darn well just happens to feel like it but the moment the police leave I want him. I want two things. I want an explanation for that exam. He'll know what I mean. What's more, I want those blasted accounts. He's way over the deadline and this time I want action and I don't want excuses. Have you got all that?'

'Yes, Dr Goldwyn, I'll be sure to tell him,' said Gaelene.

She picked up her knitting, after all she had to do something to pass the time, and went back to eavesdropping. Behind Scott's door could be heard the rise and fall of furious, placatory, and even pleading voices as the police tried desperately to extract something consistent and comprehensible – they had given up on accurate – from Scott.

The interview had begun badly with a heated discussion about who had levered the panels off the wall in Johnston's office and turned his papers over. Wiesel had asked Scott what he had to hide. Scott had pointed out simultaneously that his life was an open book and that he knew enough about the law to have Wiesel dismissed from the Force for character assassination. The culprits were, Scott insisted, fun-loving students looking for souvenirs. He had got most annoyed when Doreen Hubel had remarked that those fun-loving students had a lot of uses. After enduring a lecture on the proper relationship of academics to eager hot-headed youth, she had signalled Wiesel to take over a renewed investigation of the murky relationships between the academics.

'Now the last time we talked to you, Iain...' Wiesel began chummily.

'Dr Scott,' corrected Iain.

'Dr Scott, you told us that this Klusky bloke was a dead cert to have done Johnston in, and now you're telling us that Johnston was well liked by all and had no enemies?'

'Well I understand now that there is no question of murder but rather that the unfortunate Johnston died accidentally by falling down the stairs in the dark,' Scott replied blandly.

'How often do we have to tell you, Scott,' asked Doreen wearily, 'that Johnston's injuries are simply not consistent with falling down a set of carpeted stairs, and in any case, however he died, he was then dragged by a person or persons unknown. Our aim in this interview,' she continued heavily, 'is to find out who on earth they were and we would appreciate some help.'

'Perhaps a burglar?' suggested Scott.

'We have had the entire place checked and double-checked by the Break and Enter Squad and there is no sign whatsoever of forcible entry,' repeated Wiesel flatly.

'A cunning burglar,' suggested Scott, lighting another cigarette, 'bright enough to duplicate the keys or hide in the building overnight.'

The police looked at each other sadly and decided by mutual consent to change the subject.

'Your staff tell us that you and Johnston didn't get on too well and that you had quite a few rows,' insinuated Wiesel. He paused and consulted his scribbles. 'There was the time he threatened you with legal action and there are rumours that he was blackmailing you.'

'Blackmail? Me? Whatever could he blackmail me about?'

Quite a few things, I bet, Doreen thought, but Scott was burbling on.

'As for the legal issue, well that was all a misunderstanding and soon resolved. If you're going to go around collecting gossip from my staff, you will have to realise that this place is alive with rumour and every small interpersonal difficulty is magnified out of all proportion. Certain staff members, Edmund Bennett for example, and I might also name Margery Cavendish, had their own problems which impeded their developing a smooth transactional relationship with colleagues, Johnston in particular. When one person is successful and others are not, well I'm sure you understand. Now Johnston was a very dynamic researcher and an inspiring lecturer, but as a colleague he was prone to overuse the defences of projection, reaction formation, and denial, and I would say that he had a mild case of religiomania, but that doesn't mean that he wasn't a valued member of staff.'

The police looked at each other again. They simply couldn't be sure whether Scott talked like this all the time or whether he was putting them down by forcing them to ask for explanations. Doreen inclined to the latter theory.

'Scott,' she said sternly. 'I don't think you're trying to help us.'

'Me?' cried Scott. 'I am a strong supporter of the police and I think our boys in blue, um, look I mean you do a wonderful, socially essential job.'

'Well in that case, give us a bit of help for god's sake!' snapped Hubel. 'Who was Johnston on with?'

'Nobody. Believe me. The man was a bloody ascetic! I mean, everyone has the right to make their own choices in the area of sexuality, and œlibacy is a viable lifestyle, but perhaps his views were a little extreme in an academic setting.'

'Look,' said Hubel, patiently. 'Johnston had Stage III HTLV in his bloodstream.'

'Good heavens,' murmured Scott. 'This jargon is all too much for me. Could you explain what that means?'

'It means he was on with somebody, now who was it?' shouted Hubel, her patience suddenly giving way. Why on earth did I ever agree to interview this man in his office instead of mine, she wondered. A quick trip down the stairs would clear his head in more ways than one.

'For heaven's sake, Miss Huber,' protested Scott. 'I don't know what you think I do all day long, but I can assure you that watching over the morals of my staff is not a part of it. I really do not know who he could have had a relationship with. My impression was that he was totally bound up in his work and had no close relationships with people.'

'What about a student?' asked Wiesel, before Doreen could correct Scott about her name and title.

'What are you suggesting?' Scott said huffily. 'That would be quite unethical and whatever they may do at universities, I can assure you that we don't do that here. Besides, there are at least fifteen thousand students, plus God knows who else milling around on this campus every day. If Johnston was murdered, and I am by no means convinced that he was, then any one of them could have done it.'

Was this the time, Doreen thought, to explain to this man yet again that whoever killed Johnston had to have access to keys? He was supposed to be intelligent, after all. Or perhaps he was intelligent. That Goldwyn had been very keen on a mad burglar before he settled on the accident theory. She had noticed Scott's affection for the accident point of view. There certainly were a few cover-up vibes on this one. She stood up and moved to the door.

'Murder isn't too ethical either, but one of your staff members doesn't seem to object,' she said as a parting shot. 'Meanwhile, you could at least try to think of something that would help us.'

Hubel stormed out, followed by Wiesel.

'Oh, Dr Scott,' called Gaelene. 'Urgent message from the Director.'

'I just can't stand it,' said Scott. 'Tell them I've gone home sick.'

## 8

The following morning, Lisa was enjoying the unwonted opportunity to prepare for a lecture. Through the one pane of clear glass in her window, she could see the little tent of blue that academics call the sky. It was difficult to concentrate on the derivations from Central Limit Theorem with the hideous memories of recent conversations going round in her head.

She sighed, wondering where Sam was. He seemed to have vanished lately. Presumably he was regathering his wits at home after the shock of being arrested. She began to prepare projections of normal distributions and gradually drifted away from the troubles of the present. Nothing disturbed her but the glad cries of the construction workers four storeys below. Conflict resolution in the building industry was rather different from the processes followed in academia. Probably, she mused, a reflection of the limited access that the average male has to solutions such as bursting into tears, dropping his pneumatic drill, and storming off.

There was a rapping on the door, which she firmly ignored. Seamus O'Faolain, whose claims to ESP proved to be not entirely unfounded, came bounding in.

'Quick!' he said. 'What's a grand multipara?'

'A woman who has had four or more children,' Lisa replied from some distant textbook, 'increased risk of rupture of the uterus, um, why?'

'Oh, I've got to give a lecture on it this morning,' said O'Faolain, scribbling furiously.

'If you don't know anything about it, why are you lecturing on it?'

'You know how it is,' Seamus said airily. 'Curriculum Committee writes, and having writ, moves on, to clobber some other poor twit. Besides, I know more about it than they do, so I'll be fine. That wasn't all I wanted to talk about, anyway.'

O'Faolain carefully closed the door. Oh no, thought Lisa. Barry College fairly rustled with conversations behind closed doors. The habit had increased of late, as people all over the campus followed in the footsteps of Lombroso, muttering to each other that so-and-so certainly looked the type to commit a brutal murder. She had found herself fighting down the impulse to ask how many brutal murderers the speakers had actually seen.

'Look,' O'Faolain began. 'You know the staff meeting that's coming up?' Lisa nodded. 'Well, something's just got to be done about Scott. There are the endless rumours about the man's private life. We've all got used to those, but Antonia's very worried about the financial situation. You know she's on the Finance and Budgets Interdepartmental Committee? Well, apparently Scott hasn't handed the department's accounts in yet, and we're months overdue.'

'Like a grand multipara really,' murmured Lisa.

'What?' said O'Faolain, but rushed on. 'And then there's this exam business, which Iain just hasn't done anything about. Whenever it comes up, he just changes the subject, that's when you can get hold of him to talk to him. I tell you, we're looking very bad with the rest of the college. I understand Goldwyn's finally on the warpath.'

'What exam business?' asked Lisa.

'You mean no-one's told you?' asked O'Faolain, amazed. He himself kept his ear to the ground so consistently that he was rapidly becoming scoliotic.

'They wouldn't have had much chance lately, would they? I mean all I do is work. If I'm not lecturing or tutoring, I'm sitting in here trying desperately to prepare for the next onslaught of lectures or tutorials. In the few moments I can spare from that, I'm learning how to communicate with the police in such a way that I don't get arrested for murder, libel, or hindering the police in their inquiries.' Lisa paused long enough to check whether O'Faolain was going to take the hint and leave, but as he obviously wasn't, she quickly went on before he could get a paragraph in edgewise. 'Can't we get some sessionals in? This is ridiculous. Isn't that on the agenda for the next meeting?'

'No it isn't,' replied O'Faolain. 'That's one of the problems. Scott just keeps saying that there's no money left in the sessional fund, but it's only June, and as Antonia pointed out, we haven't had any sessionals, so where has it gone? But getting back to the exams; apparently Bennett has been giving them out to his chosen ones.'

'Now look, hang on,' said Lisa wearily. 'Not those old stories again. I may not have worked in academia long, but even I have managed to notice that these rumours are endemic. They gain in strength annually, like mushrooms in the Spring, just when the tenure reviews roll around. If it isn't the exam-for-a-fuck routine, then it's the old oral in absentia or perhaps the mysterious list of ninety-seven students' marks when only ninety-six actually sat the exam. There are many versions of this but what they all have in common is that you can't prove them.'

'This time,' said O'Faolain, 'you're wrong. This time we've got the bastard.'

'Well,' said Lisa warningly, 'I hope you remember what happened when Johnston was accused of being in the National Front. Writs flying all over the place. All this sounds frightfully defamatory to me. Are we sure Bennett actually handed the exam out?'

O'Faolain sighed. 'I only wish someone had told me that you had to have an iron grip on the law of defamation to function as an academic. I could have done an extra unit in Law. But yes, you're right of course. It seems that one of the students handed in the paper and alleged that a fellow student had given it to her, having got it from Bennett.'

'So, what does Bennett's alleged friend have to say on the topic?'

'The story seems to get a bit blurry there. Antonia is hardly the kind of person who can be cross-examined about the sexual habits of Medical Engineers. She seems to be quite convinced though, from what she told me. There has to be some sort of investigation. So far Scott's confined himself to yelling at Jacinta and then going home.'

'How did that go down?' inquired Lisa.

'Not too well, really. I mean you can imagine. He was on the way out of the building, and he met Jacinta on the stairs and told her off about it. She reminded him about his memo about the importance of collegial criticism, and then she gave him some.' O'Faolain grinned. 'Therapeutic really, they both enjoy a good slanging match. She's been storming about vowing vengeance ever since. But that brings me to this meeting. Apparently Antonia's found a provision for deposing heads of departments and putting in an election system.'

'What, you mean like crews getting rid of the ship's captain when he goes stark, staring mad in mid-ocean?'

'Er, well, something like that.' Seamus was surprised by this note of fantasy from the level-headed Lisa. The strain must be getting to her. 'But the point is, if it comes to a vote, which it might, we need your support. Have we got it?'

'Who's we?' asked Lisa suspiciously.

'Well, myself obviously, Antonia, and certain other senior members of the staff who want to see changes in the way this Department is run.'

He gazed at Lisa eagerly but she looked decidedly noncommittal.

'Um, well. I mean, I know Scott's got a number of glaring faults, but at least he keeps out of your way most of the time, and I don't have a total commitment to Antonia either. She's completely untried and she flies off the handle under stress. The other thing is, if I definitely say who I'm going to vote for, and that person doesn't get in, I'm going to be in trouble next time I want conference money, aren't I?'

'Right, right,' said O'Faolain cheerily, 'just trying to whip up some support, find out how the land lies, all that sort of thing. Look, how about a cuppa? It's nearly twelve o'clock and work makes you go blind.'

'Oh, all right,' said Lisa, turning aside to get her coffee, a moment which O'Faolain used to write a 'Y' surreptitiously next to her name on his list. He knew an academic's 'yes' when he heard one. They didn't call him 'Toecutter O'Faolain' for nothing.

Lisa reflected that O'Faolain resembled the famous semiotician who had joined the Mafia. He was always making you offers you couldn't understand. George Irwell was President of the Union, but somehow it was O'Faolain who managed to organise such things as the Union Wine-Bottling. He had sold most of it too, before its true nature revealed itself to the trusting socialists who had bought it. She wouldn't be at all surprised, she thought, if O'Faolain had done the reading about elected headships and put Antonia up to it. She could knock Scott over, copping all the flak and the writs, and Seamus could succeed smoothly to power at the next round of elections. Nevertheless he remained likeable. Probably due to his firmly held belief that you couldn't cheat someone unless he had larceny in his heart. As a result, his victims usually accepted that they had been at least partly to blame. There was also the fact that, almost alone of the academic staff, Seamus had retained a belief that life was within his control, that things could be done. It seemed to work for him and gave him an aura of optimism.

As they neared the tea room, it became clear that the possibility of herding together was exerting a strong attraction for those unable to think of an excuse to stay away altogether. Lisa brewed up her usual cup of double-strength Jamaican and gazed at her colleagues. The drama of Johnston's death had struck them in different ways, but the common factor was hysteria. Jacinta and Peter Harwell were happily engaged in a technical discussion of temperature, rigor mortis, and the curious modus operandi of killing people and then dragging them about. Harwell had made a neat pencilled list of Psycho staff members and begun writing pros and cons by each name. Peter, of course, had no right to be in the Psycho staff room, and should have been downstairs writing referrals and Pill prescriptions for the students. But he was moonstruck over Florence, and spent a good deal of time hanging around in the hope of bumping into her by accident.

'The murder must have happened on Sunday,' said Jacinta. 'That, in itself, rules a lot of people out. We're looking for a big, bad-tempered, eager beaver who comes to work on Sundays and loathed Johnston enough to do him in. Does anyone know where Scott was on Sunday?'

'Scott's by no means an eager beaver, and anyway he would have been at the Moonee Ponds racetrack. Loathing Johnston doesn't cut too many people out though,' replied Harwell thoughtfully. 'Couldn't stand the man myself. He seemed to think he had a God-given right to use my laboratory as well as his own. I wouldn't have minded doing a bit of research myself, but no hope while he was around. Anyway, there's one thing we do know.' Peter paused, as was his maddening habit, in mid-sentence to tap his pencil reflectively on his teeth.

'The dingo is innocent?' suggested Jacinta, to hurry him up.

'Whoever did it was fit, strong enough to fracture skull bones, and capable of lugging eighty-five kilos across a carpeted floor,' continued Peter as if he hadn't heard. 'And Equal Opportunity or no Equal Opportunity that puts a lot of people out of the running.'

That, thought Lisa, was the key to their reactions. Anyone with the kind of physique remotely capable of hauling a corpse about was loudly assuring all who would listen that a lot of the insults they had hurled were purely in jest. When they weren't doing that, they were telling the police about everyone else's involvement in weightlifting, boxing, karate, and just about every other manly sport known. Edmund Bennett, who had surprisingly turned out to be an expert in martial arts and was registered with the police, had pointed out huffily that there were others with similar backgrounds; the shape of Scott's nose testified to an enthusiasm for boxing which apparently had exceeded his skill level on more than one occasion. Besides, there was no reason to suppose that Johnston had been murdered by a psychologist, Johnston had enemies everywhere.

Those slight of frame reacted differently. They had taken to jumping nervously when people came up behind them, and clamoured for more lights and better security.

To everyone's surprise, Scott seemed to think it might have been an accident. But when Clyde passed on this theory, he had been howled down by Harwell. Peter pointed out that he himself had examined the body and there was no question of an accident.

'He was dragged there by his feet. You can tell by the position relative to the bloodstain,' he had pointed out.

There seemed to be some unspoken support for Jacinta's homicidal burglar theory. She had elaborated on this by pointing out to successive groups of scoffing coffee-drinkers that there had been a series of murders in New South Wales by someone who seemed to have a fetish about killing people and then dragging them about. He might have moved, she had said, and be prowling around the campus at this very moment waiting to strike again.

'But why,' Reuben had asked, 'would anyone have a fetish about killing academics?'

'You seem to think,' Jacinta had replied, 'that there has to be some rational reason for these things. Read your Colin Wilson. Anyway, there might be. Johnston's equipment was worth quite a bit. He might have surprised our murderous friend in the process of carting it away. Maybe the murderer decided to enrol in Electronic Engineering, you know, build a better bomb and all that, and then suddenly discovered he had to do one of Johnston's courses in Psychoneuronics in the name of being well-rounded. That would give any reasonable person a motive.'

The thought of a student-murderer had led to mass hysterics that Tuesday, and allegations that no-one could possibly care enough about a course to eliminate the perpetrator. All the same, there had been those bomb scares by someone who wasn't at all happy with Barry College's viewpoint on his academic standing. Could it have been the same person? Nobody could be sure.

Lisa gathered up her cup and wandered over to the huddle of chairs in the centre of the room. Seating herself, she picked up *Lyrebird*, the student newspaper, in the faint hope of avoiding getting involved in the energetic game of 'Guess the Murderer'. The Student President, an unsavoury-looking man called Frank Hodges, described the vigilante groups that he planned to form with the aid of students enrolled in Chemical Engineering, Metal Science, and similar courses better endowed with brawn than brain. He planned, he said, to have every late-night class escorted around campus. Pick-up points and times were listed. Lisa found herself wondering, for the second time that morning, which was the worse of the two choices offered. Meeting a rapid end from some homicidal maniac or being slowly bored silly by some student heavy.

She flicked over the pages. Seamus was denying that he had felt any animosity about Johnston torpedoing his grant application two years before. She didn't want to get involved. She hunched over the pages of *Lyrebird* and began to read an article headlined: TELL IT NOT IN GATH. One thing about the Student Christian Movement, she thought, it has led to more literate headlines. Under a large picture of a grinning Nathan, the article explained the wonders of the new Revelations Programme which was, according to him, making great strides in integrating knowledge which had hitherto been fragmented into bite-sized chunks called faculties. Lisa had been puzzled by Goldwyn's enthusiasm for this programme, and even more by the choice of people to staff it. Didn't the man realise that the students simply did not want to learn? They just wanted to get their little pieces of paper, and go out and make money in what they touchingly called the 'real' world. Dear, naive little things! She had found them in general to be quite good-humoured about the process, but the Revelations Programme seemed to have rather a large percentage of staff members known for their ability to drive students wild. She dreaded to think what would happen when they actually got round to teaching them some of this new, wonderful, holistic and integrated knowledge.

Giving up on the idea that reading *Lyrebird* could distract her attention from her colleagues, Lisa reluctantly surfaced to gaze around at her companions. Undeniably, a miasma of anxiety hung over them. The chatter was noisier than usual, with a strained, tight edge to it.

Klusky, apparently trying to create a diversion in the unremitting discussion of post-mortems, had foolishly tried telling Peter a joke.

Harwell looked him up and down with distaste.

'I see you're still putting on weight, Klusky,' he said. 'Really you should try to get some more exercise...'

'I know, I know,' snapped Klusky. 'Twenty laps around the pond will make me tall and slim and blond.'

'Well, I was thinking of preventive medicine, not miracles...' hedged Peter.

Klusky's fragile bonhomie vanished.

'For heaven's sake!' he shouted. 'I was arrested yesterday. I have twice the workload I used to have. This morning I ran over the cat in the driveway and my little boy hucked me all the way to creche with "Fix it Daddy, why don't you fix the cat?" and now I can't sit in here and breathe without someone telling me off!'

He broke off at the now familiar sight of Doreen Hubel standing in the doorway.

'We've come to have a look at this tea urn which was supposed to be sabotaged,' she announced. 'Christ, you're not still using it, are you?'

'Gaelene put in a requisition this morning, or at least she says she did. These things can take months, but meanwhile...' answered Harwell, guardian of health and safety.

Doreen ignored him. 'Weren't you the one who was supposed to be electrocuted?' she asked Jacinta.

'Eh? Oh yes, very frightening,' agreed Jacinta.

'And you have some reason to suspect that it may have been deliberately done?' asked Wiesel.

'Only in the sense that whoever killed Johnston might be prowling around, waiting to...' began Jacinta, but Doreen cut her off.

'Very rare, you know, that sort of thing. Gets into all the books, but most murders are committed by relatives or friends of the deceased. You've all got to face up to the fact that it's someone Johnston knew. If it wasn't a relative, then it was one of you. Once you all understand that, we might get the help that we need.'

She glared intimidatingly at the silent group, and left.

Lot of fuss about nothing, Lisa thought. Of course it had been an accident. They had told Gaelene a hundred times not to leave an urn full of boiling water pressing on its own flex. She had taken to saying that if they wanted things done differently, they could do it themselves and while they were at it, they could wash up as well. It wasn't in her job description, was it. This riposte had quelled criticism most effectively.

It's just Jacinta overdramatising things again, thought Lisa. The police will never find out who did it if they have to go on following up all these dead ends. The group, she noticed, didn't seem to be too bothered. They had returned to jokes and banter; even Peter joined in.

They were telling some of the oldest and silliest of undergraduate jokes she had ever heard, she thought sourly.

All the noise, however, died down again suddenly as Antonia Summerfield came in. She looked tired and upset as she wordlessly threw the day's *Sun* on the table.

AIDS BLOOD LINK IN BOFFIN MURDER SHOCK screamed the headline which had caught her eye and prompted her to buy a paper she usually never read.

'What?' said Seamus. 'Don't tell me Johnston had AIDS. I don't believe it.'

'Forensic experts today confirmed earlier reports that the murdered academic, Dr Richard Johnston, had antibodies to the AIDS virus in his blood. The Director of Barry College has refused to comment on whether this might have had any connection with the brutal murder,' read Peter Harwell, who had annoyingly taken charge of the paper.

'Oh go on!' said Clyde. 'You're not going to get me to believe that Johnston was gay. He was always going on and on about marriage being a sacrament and homosexuality being an abomination. Poor old Edmund used to cop it all the time. No wonder he never comes into the tea room, he could hardly show his face without Johnston trying to reform him.'

'You're over-reacting to this gay business,' interrupted Sam, who had recovered from his sulks. 'Eddie's all right. You know as well as I do,' he continued, looking at Clyde, 'that Eddie made far more enemies doing research into whether counselling really helped people than he ever did by being gay. This AIDS business is a red herring. Someone murdered Johnston for the Civilein. It's obvious.'

'Nonsense,' said Jacinta loudly. 'Nobody would get that worked up about an untested, unproven compound.'

'Having AIDS doesn't prove you're gay,' said Antonia.

'Yeah?' asked Peter. 'What are you suggesting? Transplacental infection? Holidays in Haiti? He sure as hell wasn't a haemophiliac; I can tell you that.'

'Look,' said Antonia and then stopped, and swallowed hard. Everyone turned to stare at her. 'Look, speculation and idle, hurtful gossip isn't going to bring him back. I think we should maintain our dignity in this situation. The important thing now is to find out about this leaked exam paper; who gave it out and what's to be done about it.'

'That's a rather odd set of priorities, isn't it?' asked Jacinta. 'I mean when you're so caught up in your job that you're more concerned about an exam paper than a human life, it's time to get a bit of perspective. Anyway, we all know who gave it out, it was that bloody Bennett, sucking up to some student again. And the murder's the most interesting thing to have happened around here in years.'

Antonia turned very red. 'You watch your tongue, young lady,' she said. 'How dare you go around making baseless accusations like that? You're the co-ordinator of the subject. If you did a halfway decent job this would never have happened. Any of it!' and she stormed out.

'Dear me!' said Jacinta. Everyone looked thoughtful, suddenly realising that, whatever their own feelings about Johnston's death, perhaps Antonia was genuinely upset about it.

'Don't let her worry you,' said Seamus to Jacinta, his mind on voting patterns. 'She's upset, that's all. We know you're probably right about the exam, of course it's got nothing to do with your co-ordinating, nothing at all.'

'All the same, why pick on Eddie?' persisted Sam. 'His big mistake in life is not coming to the tea room. That's why everyone picks on him.'

'And I'm getting bloody sick of this "Have a hack at Jacinta" routine,' Jacinta continued. 'This bloody coordinating is all responsibility and no power. She's the second person to blame me for the exam leak, and both of them were the ones who were so keen on this stupid collegial criticism lark. Scott started it and Antonia backed him up. Who gets the blame when things go wrong? Not them, not bloody likely. I told Scott right at the start that circulating the exam to the whole staff was the way to security problems, but would he listen? No way. I mean you've got

Cavendish for starters. She never knows whether it's Mucking Out or Shrove Tuesday. She could have left the bloody thing anywhere. On a tram. In the cafeteria. In the bloody library return chute. Then there's the vicious element, but I don't want to go into that right now. If Scott and Antonia want to circulate exams to all that lot, they can take the blame when the shit hits the fan.'

'But,' said Lisa, 'why would Edmund have given the exam to Anne Goodbody? He isn't into girls.'

'Well, no,' agreed Jacinta reluctantly. 'Look, it's all academic anyway. He's got a cast-iron defence if he just says they found the blasted thing in the corridor or broke into his room. But we know better, don't we?'

Sam sighed and shook his head. There was no point in trying to reason with any of these people.

'Unless,' said Lisa, and stopped.

'What?' asked Seamus eagerly.

'Well, you know how Edmund picks on the fairly stupid type who don't seem to work out what he's after for a while? If he did give it to someone like that, it seems pretty likely that he'd have a girlfriend.'

'Maybe,' said Jacinta. 'But is it likely that he'd rush off to her and say, "Look what I got for fucking Dr Bennett"?'

'I dunno. Some of these students aren't too strong on the social graces. And if the Good Body was his girlfriend and he did say that to her, she might have got seriously pissed off and decided to make some trouble,' answered Lisa. 'I mean, you'd be a bit pissed off if you were a young, innocent student whose boyfriend suddenly announced he'd been having a homosexual affair with a staff member.'

'Sounds convincing,' said Jacinta in an unconvinced tone. 'So what's the strategy for tomorrow? I mean, it's bound to come up in the staff meeting. Florence Lark told me she'd raise it in Any Other Business if it wasn't on the agenda. We can't exactly ask Bennett directly whether he gave the paper out to his latest young man. He'd sue us.'

'I don't understand you lot at all,' broke in Seamus. 'Johnston is dead for heaven's sake, and if it isn't the exams it's moaning about workloads. The exam is trivial. All we have to do is circulate the stolen paper to all the students, tell them it's a practice exam, and give them an altered version in the actual exam. It's not important. The important thing to face is that someone in this department, or with access to it, killed Johnston. Who was it? It could be one of us sitting here and quacking about this bloody exam!'

'Yes,' said Lisa thoughtfully. 'All the same I keep having this funny feeling that the murder and the exam are somehow connected. But I don't see how. I can't really imagine that someone killed Johnston to get the paper.'

'Impossible,' Jacinta agreed. 'He doesn't teach the subject, I mean didn't. He wouldn't even have seen the paper. Unless someone bloody well circulated it to him for some collegial criticism.'

'I think it's the AIDS that's the connection,' asserted Seamus. 'I mean, if we do assume that this Kosmos boy got the exam from Bennett.'

'So what are the implications of Johnston having AIDS?' Lisa said quietly as if she were thinking aloud. 'It means he might have been gay, more than that, he probably was. Where does that get us? Did he give the paper to Kosmos? No, unless he stole it or found it, which seems unlikely. Was he carrying on with Bennett? No, that means he might have got AIDS from Bennett, which in turn... No, I can't work it out at all.'

Seamus looked at his watch. 'My God, is that the time? I've got a class at twelve thirty.'

As he raced down the dim corridor towards his office, Seamus almost crashed into Edmund Bennett, who was deep in conversation with a dark, heavily built young man.

## 9

'For heaven's sake be quiet, Neos!' Edmund was hissing anxiously. 'Stop that awful blubbering this minute. Please.'

He looked worriedly round at the sound of thundering feet,

and saw O'Faolain's chunky Celtic form bearing down on them at speed. He mustn't make people any more suspicious than they already seemed to be.

'Quick, into my office,' he whispered. Opening the door with one hand, he jerked Kosmos through the door behind him with the other and backheeled it shut in one fluid move. O'Faolain, who just had time to notice the figures looming up in the semi-darkness, reeled, recovered, and hurried on towards the Feyerabend Communication Space, where his lecture was scheduled to begin. Thank god he had once played centre forward for Moonee Ponds, he thought, surprising the skills which came in handy in academic life. Bennett had doubtless heard a few of those rumours about the exam paper and had plenty of reason to be jumpy.

Harder to explain his hauling that student into his room like that. Even the most promiscuous of the staff generally displayed a little more cool. Although the boy didn't seem to mind. In fact, thought Seamus, he had some dim recollection of having seen him hanging about the Department of Psychological and Sociological Inquiry a fair bit. If I didn't have a lecture to go to, he thought, pattering furiously downward, I'd damn well listen outside that door to find out just what Bennett is going to concoct with that boy.

Unfortunately, there was no hope of employing this stratagem this particular Wednesday. He had five classes to give. This one, on cross-cultural aspects of childbirth, was a late addition to his already overloaded schedule. It was not one of Johnston's, but had until recently been the job of Ms Redperson (Redman that was), who had suddenly been seconded to the Education Department's Office for the Removal of Gratuitously Anachronistic Sexist Material (Secondary School Curriculum Division). Rumour had it that her sudden removal to ORGASM, where she sat in air-conditioned, designer-coordinated judgement on the writings of great thinkers down the ages, had something to do with her blossoming friendship with the head of that unit. Seamus had met this career femocrat only once, when he had attended the compulsory lecture on Affirmative Action, and had decided then that her hubris was exceeded only by the size of her bum.

So far, Griselda Redperson (Fudge to her friends) had succeeded in banning Henry Handel Richardson and Miles Franklin from the Australian Studies curriculum, on the grounds that they constituted an over-representation of male writers. As she had now moved on to English Literature of the Early Modern Period (A), Seamus supposed George Eliot would be next cab off the rank. Fudge was probably sharpening her pencil at this very moment. Thank god the Brontës had decided to come clean.

Emerging from the litter-infested stairwell, Seamus began his long march across the grey, dirty campus, brooding on the injustices of this life, especially as far as being male was concerned. Whatever had happened to good old merit, eh?

A furious blast from a horn returned him to his present surroundings and he leaped out of the way of a roaring motorbike. He swore futilely at the diminishing cloud of dust and smoke. Deaths-head indeed! Bloody deadhead would be nearer the mark. What was he meant to be lecturing on? Oh yes, cross-cultural aspects of childbirth. Hardly a subject that interested him.

He gazed over the neo-Brutalist concrete of Building 1957 to the Byzantine towers of the Law Courts behind and sighed deeply. For perhaps the seventeenth time that day, he wondered what you had to do to get out of this place. Without fucking gay public servants, that is. He had been applying for jobs, but he knew that the Barry College letterhead on his applications hardly helped. Should he apply for study leave? Should he go off on compo? Wasn't there some new government scheme now to reduce the unemployment figures, where you could get RSI and vanish semi-permanently? He really ought to investigate that last one. Equal Opportunity for RSI and men, he thought, marching determinedly into the Feyerabend Communication Space.

Back in the Department of Psychological and Sociological Inquiry, Edmund Bennett had regained some of his composure. The office was still a mess, with carpets pulled back and sodden books and papers balanced on the arms of chairs. The smell of decay was increasing hourly. He sat down gracefully and gazed in wonderment as Kosmos blundered about his office. Looks and brains just did not seem to come in the same package. What could the creature want, he thought. Finally he gave up and asked, 'Now that you've made a public display of yourself, and of me, you blithering idiot, would you be so good as to let me know what it was you wanted? No! Don't pound that print of "David" with your fist! Culture is precious to some of us!'

For an awful moment, as Kosmos whirled around in a Rambo-style pose, Bennett wondered if his passions were about to be expressed on Bennett's own unprotected body. The time was long gone when he had enjoyed that sort of thing. As he had explained at tedious length on Tuesday to that lumpy policewoman – what was her name again? Huber? Tuber? – it was true he had learned karate in his youth, but his whole experience of unarmed combat had biased him in favour of guns and knives. Encroaching middle age had slowed his reflexes and turned his tastes towards a quieter style of pleasure. But the gorgeous hulk subsided, sobbing, into Bennett's spare armchair.

'Listen, you gotta help me, you just gotta!'

'Perhaps if you explained what all this passion was about?' inquired Bennett airily, inspecting his nails now that the danger appeared to have passed.

'Listen, that Dickie Johnston... I mean Dr Johnston... Listen I, listen I... well... I fucked him.' Kosmos blurted and began to sob again. 'Well, the papers say he had AIDS.'

Bennett found himself able to understand each word separately, but he was having considerable problems extracting the meaning of the whole. Johnston and homosexual liaisons? It was just unbelievable. He had never encountered such poisonous homophobia in his life. It had pretty well put paid to any hope of promotion, as well as making Barry College a very lonely place for him. It hadn't been all bad of course, because it meant that he had avoided the nonsensical chatter in the tea room, but it had been dreadfully wearing. What on earth was going on?

'Kosmos,' he said in a kindly tone, 'now think carefully, Are you quite sure that you and Johnston had homosexual intercourse?'

'Yeah, well, it was the same as we done it,' came the belligerent reply.

It's no good, thought Edmund, after trying to put Johnston's face to some of his seamier mental images. I just don't believe it.

What could Johnston have wanted from this lump? Whatever it was, mused Edmund, every instinct told him it was more than the simple lusts of the flesh.

'Okay, I give up,' he said. 'Tell me. How did it all start?'

'Well,' said Kosmos slowly, lifting a bleary face, 'you gotta earn money these days, to go to college, keep the car goin' and get the girls. It's hard to get part-time jobs and the pay's rotten so I used to deal a bit, you know.'

Edmund nodded. Actual work simply wasn't Neos's style.

'Well I had this really great supplier, but then he got hit by a bus and said he'd found Christ and given up his evil ways. Well there I was, I mean I was really stuck on how to get the stuff, but Johnston gave all those lectures on drugs and the brain and I sort of thought, you know, he might have connections. So I went round to his lab, you know, and I asked him a few questions about the lectures and I was goina kind of lead up to whether he had tried the stuff, but he just glared at me and said he was busy and why didn't I come round to his house to talk about these things.'

He glanced up warily at Edmund, who was trying to cope with the alien concept of Johnston actually having a home to go to.

'Yeah well, he lived real close, in Castlereagh Street, round the corner, so I went round there an we had a natter an he told me that he could get me Angel Dust and LSD but nuthin else. Well that was okay, so I said yeah why not.'

'Yes, yes,' said Edmund, 'so where does that leave us with the fucking?'

'Ah, well, that was all in the price, like I got a discount for letting him fuck me and got to keep more cash. Well I figure I done it with you anyway, so so what?'

Suddenly the horrible suspicion which had been forming in Bennett's mind had to be answered. And soon. Suppose this pest had been having an affair with both of them simultaneously? He knew, or at least he thought he could be pretty sure, that he couldn't have given Johnston AIDS via Kosmos. Bennett tried hard to stick to virgins or else safe sex – preventive medicine, broadly defined. But suppose it had been the other way around? Cold fear washed over him.

Rising to his feet, Bennett opened a neatly arranged filing cabinet and extracted a file indexed under 'Notes, semiliterate'.

'I think we'd better discuss your little billet doux...'

Kosmos looked blank.

'I meant to say note... in detail at this point. Now what have we here, ah yes: "Its all off. Im Goina have a good tiem with Jonstin. Neos." Really, Neos, didn't anyone ever teach you to spell? But I must admit that you convey your meaning fairly clearly. Were you having intercourse with both of us simultaneously?'

Confused, Kosmos stared at Bennett, who tried again.

'Neos, were you on with both of us at once?'

Kosmos looked startled.

'Well, of course not,' he said to Bennett's immeasurable, but premature, relief. 'Come on, surely you would've remembered if it'd been all three of us at once. Wuntcha?'

Bennett made an elegant gesture of despair.

'Not both at the same time, you dingbat,' he sighed wearily. 'I meant during the same time period.'

'Oh' said Kosmos, light dawning. 'Well. I did, well it was all so quick, you know, these things happen. I wasn't too sure, and then I changed my mind about you...'

Neos stopped, impressed by the colour change in Bennett's face.

'You mean to tell me that you came to me after you had had sex with that – that – ' he stuttered, momentarily lost for invective – 'that foul, diseased, creature who wrecked my career?' he screamed.

Kosmos went back to looking blank.

'Do you realise what this means?' screeched Bennett.

'Yes,' moaned Kosmos, recognising a straight question when he heard one. 'It means I might have AIDS, and how am I going to tell me mum?'

His mum, a small fierce woman who had suffered endlessly from Anglo-Saxon attitudes, had always said that her favourite boy would show them. Quite what he was to show whom Kosmos had never been entirely clear, but he was quite sure that AIDS did not figure in his mum's plans for him.

'I don't suppose that it has occurred to you that my mum might not care to hear this news either,' enquired Bennett. His mum had died years ago, but he wasn't going to let that stand in his way. Long practice in tertiary teaching had taught him that form was more important than content.

'Eh? But your mum doesn't even know me,' said Kosmos, puzzled. Bennett sighed. This was definitely one of those slow conversations.

'If you have AIDS, you great lump, then so might I,' he said with grim clarity. Kosmos stared at him.

'Oh, don't bother expressing your concern at this late stage; you've already impressed me quite enough with your grace, charm and sensitivity, you useless heap of parrot droppings.'

The possible implications of what he had learnt were beginning to sink in. Edmund had read *Time* magazine on AIDS and found some of the nastier photographs crowding into his field of thought. Feeling something close to panic, he demanded angrily, 'What on earth did you come here for anyway? To gloat? To give me the bad news in person? Or couldn't you manage another of your charming little notes? Can't you spell incurable?'

Kosmos was puzzled by the turn the conversation had taken. It had not occurred to him that Bennett would take things as personally as he had. Kosmos firmly believed that lecturers hung themselves in cupboards when not lecturing and had no life of their own whatever. Bennett's interpretation of events came as a bolt out of the blue to him. He had anticipated that Edmund might come across with a few kind words at least, and perhaps even some good advice. And who else could he possibly talk to? Not his mum, that was for sure. And the thought of how his cronies would react to the knowledge that he was a poofter – worse, that he had fucked members of staff – sent shivers down his spine. That thought spurred him to action.

'Who are you calling parrot droppings?' he asked belligerently. 'What are you on about?'

'What I'm on about, as you so elegantly put it, is that you first scrawl me a note telling me you've given up on me in favour of some foul philistine...' he stopped, momentarily lost for words '...and then you come crawling around here to tell me that you were two-timing all along and that you've probably given me a ghastly and incurable disease. To top it all off you want my bloody sympathy! Sympathy! Get out!'

Coming from the medium-sized Bennett, the order seemed ludicrous, and only added to Kosmos's rising fear and rage.

'But what am I going to DO?' he bellowed. 'Where am I going to GO?'

''Do? Go? Do what you like. Go to a doctor. Go to Fairfield, go anywhere, but get out of my sight,' said Bennett.

This was the last straw. No-one spoke to Neos Kosmos like that, especially not a middle-aged, scrawny pervert. Rising to his feet, he towered over Edmund and announced, 'You done it, dincha? You killed Johnston cos you was jealous of him and me. You think you're so smart, Mr Lecturer, but you won't get away with this. I'm gonna tell the police about you, I am. And if they don't do nothing then me and my cousins are goina beat up on ya.' He paused for breath. 'Maybe we'll do it anyway. Yeah. If you're on the loose we can find ya. It aint gonna be fun. For you, that is.'

In search of police, cousins, and vengeance, Kosmos slammed out of the room and thundered off down the corridor. His departure was punctuated by furious punches to the wall, much to the amazement of Sam Klusky and a class of Computing Applications students on the other side of the fragile asbestos-packed partitions. Sam lumbered out of the lecture theatre shouting, 'Stop that!' after Kosmos's retreating back, only to encounter Edmund Bennett glaring in the same direction. Edmund had had previous altercations with students, but Sam had never seen him look as upset about it before. Poor Eddie, he thought, he really doesn't seem to be coping all that well. It must be tricky to know how to react when someone you've always loathed is brutally murdered.

'Sorry, Eddie,' he said. 'I didn't see you there. But that oaf was making such a noise. It's hard enough taking all these extra classes about things I've never heard of, without students practising martial arts in the corridors...'

He trailed off because Bennett had wordlessly turned his back on him and gone back into his office, slamming the door shut again. In fact, he had not even registered Sam's presence. He had far too much on his mind. He could probably discount Kosmos's threats to inform the police; Kosmos, he knew, would have to admit all sorts of things in order to be believed. Anyway there was the drug-dealing aspect; he wouldn't talk to the police, he was sure. Still, the odd anonymous note or phone call was always on the cards. Okay, they couldn't make the murder stick, or he hoped not, but they could do some very embarrassing investigation into his private life once they got started. Infamous conduct, he thought, Nauru School of Mines here I come. Where on earth could he get another job if he lost this one? Could he manage on the dole? No, that was ridiculous, but then again, if he was doomed what did it matter?

One way or the other, there seemed to be early graves looming up all around him. There was the AIDS for one thing. Would they be able to give him any answers at this, presumably early, stage? Not if he knew doctors, he thought gloomily. Then again, it would be foolish to take the threat of Kosmos's cousins lightly. There had been a nasty incident of some sort at Kosmos's high school, he now remembered having heard. The details were a bit vague. Who had told him? Klusky? He'd have to ask him. He had an idea it had involved at least one teacher being retired on sick pay and three others resigning to take up country posts.

Desperately, he tried to pull himself together. First things first, he thought, dialling the number of AIDS Counselling and Diagnosis to make an appointment. But what on earth was going to happen, thought Bennett, with something close to terror, with Johnston's beastly infections reaching out from beyond the grave?

## 10

Wiesel sighed, scratched his nose, and looked thoughtfully at his superior sitting beside him in the squad car.

'Can't make it out at all,' he said. 'I mean, it seems that it's usually perfectly obvious who the murderer was. Just look for someone who seems awfully pleased with himself and there you are. But this lot! Bunch of loonies if you ask me. None of them seems in the slightest bit upset about Johnston's death, which would be suspicious, only none of them seems terribly pleased either. All more concerned about this ruddy exam, it seems to me.'

Doreen Hubel took a thoughtful bite of her meat pie. It was Wednesday already, and she had the feeling that, rather than getting closer to discovering the murderer, her investigation was getting more and more confused. It was important to her that it came out well. It would help her in her most recent application for promotion. Fat chance that she had of getting promotion, she thought. Equal Opportunities or no Equal Opportunities, women just didn't have the same chances for promotion as men in the force.

At least, that's what seemed to be the story. Although just lately she'd been wondering. Perhaps it was her. Perhaps she wasn't as good a police officer as the others who had gone up in the last round of promotions. Pure coincidence that they had all been men?

'Perhaps we're barking up the wrong tree,' she said indistinctly through pie and nagging doubts.

'A lunatic, you mean?' said her assistant hopefully. 'That'd explain why we can't work out the motive. You remember that series of murders in Sydney last year? All hacked to death with a butcher's hook and then dragged up the nearest flight of stairs? They never did catch that bloke, did they? Maybe he's moved.'

Doreen looked at him in disbelief. 'Lord, why me?' she asked religiously. 'Haven't I enough to worry about without having this idiot as an assistant?' She paused, and took an emotional chew of her pie. This twerp, she reminded herself, is highly likely to wind up a lot further up the ladder than I'll ever get, and a lot sooner too. It's amazing what going to the right school and picking your gender carefully can do to compensate for a total lack of common sense.

'Listen, Wiesel,' she said in a strained voice. 'You're young, you've got a lot to learn. Now let me just explain about those Sydney murders, all right? Listen carefully, you just might learn something. Then we'll get back to the case in hand.'

The younger officer nodded enthusiastically.

'First off, it wasn't a lunatic. It very rarely is in lunatic cases. This time it was Slasher Harris. Remember his wife? Used to run a knocking-shop in Oxford Street.'

'Yes, but wasn't she one of the victims?'

'Exactly. They had a bit of an argument and he did her in. Then, to stop it looking too suspicious, he went around and knocked off another half-dozen the same way, and spread that line about his wife having been followed home by a man with a walleye and a limp.'

'But...' said Wiesel, clearly finding this all a bit much.

'Yes, I know,' explained Doreen patiently. Really, it was just like reading a bedtime story to Jarrod. 'But he's a useful man, Slasher Harris, and he's got a number of friends, if you get my drift. So they let him off with a caution, understand?'

'Um,' said Wiesel thoughtfully. 'They do things differently up there, don't they?'

Inspector Doreen Hubel sighed. This Wiesel creature clearly still had a lot to learn. Didn't she have troubles enough of her own, without being lumbered with a useless assistant who probably still believed in the tooth fairy? Her mind slipped away to Kylie's worrisome progress, or lack thereof, at school. At the last parent-teacher night her class teacher had recommended that Doreen supervise her homework more carefully. How in hell can I supervise Kylie's homework when there's Jarrod to bath and put to bed, not to mention the fact that once I've done my overtime and got to the shops and got home it's usually high time the pair of them were asleep?

And all this media stuff about latch-key children and callous greedy working mothers doesn't exactly help. What they expect a girl to do when her husband shoots through with a barmaid I do not know. He'd lied about his income so the Family Court would set the maintenance payments low. Which they had. Hard to see why he'd bother to perjure himself; he'd never had any intention of making the payments. And going to the Family Court again had been no help at all. They'd seemed to find it funny that a policewoman couldn't make her ex-husband keep up the payments. Funny! Mind you, it wasn't just the money that she was working for; Doreen did enjoy her job. Mostly, she was proud of policing. Sometimes, though, you couldn't help but wonder... She wrenched her mind back.

'Let's talk about the case in hand,' she said. 'What's the first thing to consider?'

'Motive?'

'Well, it'll do. So who's got a motive and what is it?'

'Well, the man's got no family, few friends, few interests outside his work. That means we should probably be looking at his colleagues.'

'Right,' agreed Hubel. 'There's more possible motives there than you can count. I started going through some of the folders in his filing cabinet. And that reminds me, we've got to put the hard word on that Scott bloke because some of them were obviously missing. But anyway, he seemed to have a lot of dirt on a lot of people.'

'Well. There's Klusky, who found the body. He's got an alibi so it can't be him, unless the time of death has been faked somehow.'

'Oh come off it,' groaned Hubel. 'That stuff about faking time of death just doesn't happen, not in real life. It's too technical. The best anyone can do is to confuse us by freezing the body or something, like that guy did in Adelaide.'

'Oh yes,' said Wiesel, remembering. 'He was a poofter too, wasn't he? Basically unstable, I reckon they are. So you reckon Klusky's in the clear?'

'Yes, yes, yes,' hissed Hubel. How could anyone be so slow and still be able to wander around Melbourne without being hit by a tram?

Doreen had been secretly glad that Klusky had had an alibi. Of course, it was always a nuisance when you pulled in the wrong person; it wasted valuable time and damaged friendly community relations. But at the same time, and despite her rather abrupt manner in the interrogation, she had quite liked Sam Klusky. When you considered the other people that worked in the place, Sam's straightforward manner had been a delightful contrast. He had a way of listening to your question and thinking about the answer that suggested he recognised you as a fellow human being. A fairly basic skill that seemed to be lacking in most academics she had encountered. They seemed to be quite friendly among themselves, some of them at least, but most were endowed with an arrogant contempt for the rest of the human race, people who worked for their money instead of hanging about pontificating to students. Sam, she thought again, had been different.

'Who else is there?' she prompted. 'Who's next?'

'Well, that Scott is a fairly nasty piece of work, I reckon,' said Wiesel. 'Though he did seem pretty surprised about the AIDS, which would suggest that he wasn't having an affair with Johnston.'

'No, I think we can safely say that Johnston wasn't Scott's type. Rather aggressively hetero, our man Scott.'

'So it can't have been him,' argued Wiesel.

'Oh come on,' sighed Hubel. 'There are possible motives other than sex, after all. I keep getting the feeling that it might be all connected with this course-stealing business that Scott was on about. You know, Johnston stealing Klusky's intellectual property, or whatever. Or that business about Johnston blocking Bennett's promotion. Maybe Johnston knew something that could ruin Scott's career too. It's funny that there don't seem to be any nasty little files on Scott. And some of the files are clearly missing. Probably he was trying to blackmail him.'

'I'm confused,' admitted Wiesel.

Doreen sighed deeply. 'Let me just tell you a few things the uniformed boys have come up with. It might help you, knowing a bit more about that side of things.'

Wiesel nodded eagerly. 'That sounds great. The last guy I worked for never told me anything. He just used to give me little jobs to do – watching a house, checking files, that sort of thing. That's not what I joined the Force for.'

Doreen could sympathise with Wiesel's previous superior. But as a single mother she knew the importance of making do with the materials to hand, and she had a vague hope that, with encouragement, Wiesel might one day become a competent assistant.

'Well,' she said. 'The Uniformed Branch went round to Johnston's house. He lived in Castlereagh Street, just round the corner from the college really.'

'Yeah, funny that,' mused Wiesel. 'I mean, if I worked in a dump like that and earned as much as he did, I would have found somewhere really nice to live. Somewhere away from it all, you know. Kew, or Hawthorn, or somewhere with trees and things.'

'Yes, Perce,' said Doreen. 'But then again, you're normal – more or less anyway. This Johnston guy was definitely a bit queer. I mean peculiar. Didn't seem to have much of a life outside the college. Hardly any friends, used to work late, never went out . . .'

'Have they talked to the neighbours?' asked Wiesel, hoping to impress.

'Yes,' sighed Doreen. 'They've talked to the neighbours. They've read the procedures book too.'

'So what did they find?'

'Well, there's a warehouse on one side, nobody's there after five, so that was no help. But there's an art student lives on the other side. And you know something interesting? She said she knew Johnston worked at the college, not because she'd ever spoken to him, but because her boyfriend works there too, and he'd recognised him one day.'

'Ooh,' said Wiesel. 'That sounds suspicious.'

'Yes, and you know what's even more suspicious? Her boyfriend is Iain Scott.'

Wiesel's mouth opened and closed silently. He couldn't work out quite how to respond to this bit of information.

'What does Scott say?'

'Oh, I haven't asked him specifically. But it does raise a few possibilities, doesn't it? The idea of blackmail is one we can't rule out yet.'

'But you can't blackmail a guy just because he's going out with your next-door neighbour, can you? I mean, Scott's not married or anything, is he? Surely he can go out with this art student if he wants?'

'Mm. Scott's got an ex-wife somewhere. Who knows? Maybe she's making trouble. Maybe she was on with Johnston. I'm not sure, maybe there's kids and some sort of custody battle.' Though why anybody would fight for the offspring of somebody like Scott was beyond Doreen, fond of children though she was.

'Motives,' she reminded Wiesel, returning to an earlier phase of the conversation when they had both known what was going on. 'Sex and money. Maybe power, occasionally revenge. And then there's the blackmail angle.'

'Sex?' said Wiesel. 'Johnston must have got AIDS from somewhere.'

'Yes, you twerp. Didn't you read the coroner's report? Clear evidence of recent homosexual contact. So that's a possibility for investigation. Who did he get AIDS from? And more to the point, who did he give it to? We'll have to sift through all those blasted anonymous letters we've got, just to see if any of them has any truth in it.'

'Hey, I've just remembered something,' said Wiesel. 'Just before I left I overheard that Bennett character making a phone call... purely by chance you understand...'

Hubel smiled approvingly. 'Of course. But what about it?'

'Well, he was making an appointment to see a doctor!'

'And?'

'And so he's caught AIDS from Johnston and the murder was to get back at him.'

'Hmm. Maybe. These academics all call each other doctor. He might have just been phoning a colleague or something.'

'Oh yes, I hadn't thought of that,' replied Wiesel, crestfallen.

'It was a good suggestion, though,' said Hubel encouragingly. 'Worth following up. There's always the possibility they were on together, though it seems pretty unlikely from the way Bennett's reacted. But maybe there was some sort of lovers' triangle. With a student, maybe. Which brings us to the stolen exam, perhaps.'

'Getting back to motive for a minute though,' said Wiesel, 'we do need to follow this sex thing up. I wonder if we could get all the staff to have blood tests?'

Hubel regarded him sadly. 'Don't you know anything about the rights of murder suspects? I'm willing to bet this lot do, and that's not the sort of thing I'd even whisper around that place. That Jacinta for one. She'd be on our backs in a second. Remarkably well informed on police procedure, she is.'

'Do you think that's suspicious?' asked Wiesel eagerly.

'No, just nosey,' replied Hubel. 'I don't think she's a habitual criminal, not quite the type, and anyway I don't think this is a habitual crime. Crime of passion, I reckon, one way or another.'

'Yes, exactly. That's why blood tests would be so useful.'

Inspector Hubel again called on the Lord for guidance. 'Don't be so silly,' she continued, transferring her attention to Wiesel. 'In the first place there's more kinds of passion than sex, you know.' Wiesel looked somewhat startled because, in fact, he hadn't known. 'And in the second place this guy's sexual activities seem to have been a secret, so it's highly likely he was into gay bars or pickups or whatever. He could have caught AIDS from a perfect stranger. And besides, even if he's been fucking half the school he mightn't have given any of them AIDS. Still,' she continued thoughtfully, 'they all know about the AIDS now, don't they. I wonder if we can follow up on your idea, and find out who's been making hurried visits to doctors lately?'

She fished in her handbag. 'Then there's this,' she said, passing him a large brown envelope. Wiesel hesitated. 'No, it's all right, I've had it fingerprinted, you can have a look at it.'

Wiesel opened the envelope and drew out a glossy photograph. He gasped. 'Whew. I haven't seen anything like that since I did my stint with the Porno boys. Where did you get it? And who the hell is it? What's he got to do with the case?'

'I'm not sure,' said Doreen. 'But I would be willing to bet that those ... er ... private parts he's ... um ... doing things to ... belong to Johnston.'

'You think this is one of Johnston's boyfriends?'

'I'd put money on it.'

'But who is he? And where does he fit in?' puzzled Wiesel. It was an unfortunate choice of words, considering the activity shown in the photograph.

'I don't know,' said Doreen. 'Not yet, anyway. And it's going to be a bit difficult to find out. I mean, I can hardly wander around the college flashing this photo and asking if anyone recognises him, can I?'

'Pity, isn't it,' agreed Wiesel. 'It's nice and clear.' Clear it certainly was, nice, perhaps less so. But there was little question that anyone at the college, once they had overcome their shock enough to look carefully, would have recognised the fine features of Neos Kosmos. 'But how did you come by it?'

'It was on the floor of Johnston's office when I went in this morning,' replied Doreen, giving him a meaning look.

'What!' replied Wiesel, completely misinterpreting the look. 'But I went over that office on Monday. You're not suggesting I would have missed something like that, are you?'

'No,' replied Doreen. 'Not even you could have missed a pornographic eight-by-ten glossy lying face up on the floor.'

Wiesel sighed with relief. These women superiors were generally tougher than the men, or so he'd heard. Generally had more to prove, or something.

'So how did it get there?'

'God, you're thick!' cried Doreen in exasperation. 'It got there because somebody put it there.'

'Somebody put it there?' Repeating the statement helped Wiesel to make some kind of sense of it. 'But why? And who?'

'That's what I'd like to know. But I'd bet that Scott thoughtfully took it from one of those files he's got and put it there for us. He's tried the accident theory, tried the mad burglar theory, and now he's trying to pin the whole thing on this guy, whoever he is. But was Scott blackmailing Johnston, or this other guy? Or was Johnston blackmailing this other guy? And who is he? Is he a friend of Bennett's? That could lead us back to the exam again. I think we could have a very interesting chat with him, if only we could track him down.'

Wiesel sighed. It all seemed terribly difficult. Someone had done Johnston in, they knew that. But otherwise, they didn't seem to be getting terribly far. Here it was, Wednesday already, and the whole thing seemed to be getting more confusing by the minute.

'We'll have to see if we can find him. Maybe he's a student.'

'Maybe. He's more likely to be one of those St Kilda boys.'

'Well, let's try another tack,' suggested Wiesel. 'What about that Lisa character?'

'What? You want me to show her this photo? She'd probably faint.'

'No, I meant as a separate approach.'

'You think she was having an affair with Johnston? You must be joking; she loathed the guy. It was quite clear. She even said something about how uncomfortable he made her feel. He must have been a creep.'

'That's not what I meant,' replied Wiesel. 'And anyway, that could all be a front, couldn't it?'

'Oh, no,' groaned Hubel in reply. 'You're not going to say she did it. She couldn't be more than half the guy's size. You're not seriously suggesting she attacked him with an iron bar and then dragged his body right across the room? Think about it.'

'That's not what I mean either. Would you listen for a sec?' said Wiesel, huffily. 'What I mean is this. She admits she was in the place on the day Johnston died.'

'So?'

'So maybe she can tell us something.'

'And you think I haven't asked her? What sort of an idiot do you think I am?'

'Well,' he said defensively, 'maybe she saw something without realising the implications. Or maybe she didn't see something that usually was there, or . . .' His voice trailed off. It didn't sound very convincing, he thought.

Hubel sighed again, and began fishing for her seat belt. 'For heaven's sake, Wiesel,' she said, more in sorrow than in anger, 'if you'd only stop wasting your time with Agatha Christies, you might turn into a halfway good policeman one day. Now let's get on with interviewing, much good though it is likely to do.'

## 11

It was damp and gloomy the next morning in Sam's office, where he was trying to organise a dishevelled folder of notes into a stimulating and memorable lecture. A bit hard, he felt, when the topic was 'psychological aspects of repetitive strain injury' and the audience Articled Clerks. Repetitive brain injury was more like it with that lot, as Jacinta had once remarked. Half of them would attack him for saying RSI was all in the mind, and the other half would attack him for saying it wasn't. They seemed unable to comprehend that sometimes there was no simple answer.

With a sigh, he rose to his feet. Too far into the day to dare have a cigarette; by this time the anti-smokers would be out in force. Besides, the last time he had sneaked a cigarette in this place the consequences had not been pleasant. A cup of coffee might soothe his troubled mind, he thought. He trudged down the dark corridor to where the tea-room windows let in the grey light that passed in Melbourne for bright day. He hoped Harwell wouldn't be there this time when he needed a hot coffee and a soothing chat, and was pleased to discover Jacinta, standing alone by the window.

'Hi, Sam,' she said, 'Come and have a look at this lot. You know, I'll never understand it.'

'Understand what?' replied Sam, clutching his warm mug in frozen fingers. Outside was a soaked group of crippled demonstrators. Pinned to their wheelchairs and crutches were posters reading, WHEELCHAIR ACCESS, EDUCATION FOR ALL.

'Well,' replied Jacinta. 'They've got this far into the complex, which proves they can manage. So why don't they just club together and buy themselves a flying fox?'

'A what?' asked Sam, thinking the rain must have got into his ears.

'A flying fox,' repeated Jacinta impatiently. 'You know, one of those boy-scout things. Didn't they have them in the Young Pioneers? They could swing from building to building through the windows and not have to bother about the stairs. They could stop all this demonstrating and just get on with it.'

Sam considered the sight of a group of wheelchair bound students letting themselves down into a lecture theatre on ropes. Like a scene out of 'Brazil', he mused.

'Perhaps they think there's a principle involved,' he ventured cautiously. You had to be careful, expressing any opinion in front of Jacinta. She didn't like people disagreeing with her.

'Principle!' snorted Jacinta, true to form. 'That's what's wrong with this country, you know; that's why the economy hasn't got any money in it. It's because people hang around moaning about principles when they could be helping themselves.'

Christ, thought Sam, scratch a feminist and you find a neo-Fascist self-help merchant. Still, he wasn't going to give up. He was sick of people telling him what to think.

'Perhaps they believe that the college expresses certain exclusionary and unfair principles in its architecture, which takes no account of the fact that not everybody gets around on two feet.'

'You think they should get Amnesty into it?'

'Amnesty?' asked Sam, trying desperately to work out what smart remark she was leading up to.

'Good grief, Sam, what's the matter with you?' laughed Jacinta. 'Remember, every prisoner is a political prisoner. The only reason this college has millions of stairs and no reliable lifts is the inequitable distribution of resources between the physically handicapped and the rest of them, whose handicaps are less obvious. Now if that isn't political, you tell me what is.'

Sam sipped his coffee and stared at her. She certainly was twitchy lately. Did it have anything to do with Richard Johnston's death? Certainly she had always made a fuss about how much she had disliked him. But then, there was that story that he had had a lot to do with her getting the job in the first place. Not that he'd let her get involved in his research, so it was hard to see why.

His thoughts were interrupted by a rapid thudding of feet on the metal internal staircase. The steel fire door at the far end of the tea room swung open and Lisa bounded in, looking annoyed.

'Don't let Reuben catch you doing that,' warned Jacinta. 'He hasn't been the same since they made him Chairman of the Safety Committee. He claims that using the fire escapes as short cuts sets a bad example.'

'Nonsense,' said Lisa, out of breath. 'It's a community service. I'm checking the condition of the stairwells. Besides, you do it all the time. And I'm much less likely to run into any students this way. The bloody computer has gone down again. I tried to log in and it just beeped at me.'

'Did you report it to the Duty Programmer?' asked Jacinta.

'Well, I tried,' said Lisa. 'It was Harry Holderness on duty, though. It took me a good ten minutes to drag him away from the 'Beat the Bookies Betting System'. That bloody programme seems to engage his interest rather more than actually providing a service to users. Hardly surprising, really, when you consider who most of the users are.'

These dreadful women, thought Sam, where did they get their energy from? If they weren't arguing politics, they were charging about programming things and shouting. It had turned out to be a tough week, and there was this staff meeting to go to later on this afternoon. Now what had that article in the *New Scientist* said? Something about the average level of testosterone in the blood of Western men falling by half, or something frightening, in the last decade? That was it, of course, men were losing their oomph, and women were sort of expanding to fill the gap. It could only be a matter of time really before...He came out of his reverie abruptly to find that Lisa and Jacinta were both staring fixedly at him.

'What?' he asked, shifting uncomfortably.

'I said,' repeated Jacinta, 'that I think it would be a good idea for us to get a strategy together for the extraordinary staff meeting this afternoon.'

Sam looked at her in silence, cautiously reserving his remarks until he found out how the land lay. Seamus had had a chat with Sam too, and, like Lisa, Sam had instantly worked out that the winning side was the one to be on. On the one hand he wanted to be rid of Scott. He had a feeling the whole ghastly murder business would never have happened if Scott hadn't been chairman. But did he really want to throw in his lot behind Antonia Summerfield? He suspected it would mean work. He also perceived that if he wasn't at least seen to be supporting whoever finally won, his chances of promotion would be less than none. Still, it gave him something definite to think about, other than confusing and apparently insoluble murders.

'This isn't the extraordinary one. That was on Monday. This is just a regular one, but I suppose all staff meetings around here are fairly extraordinary,' said Lisa.

Jacinta glared at her. 'It's all right,' she said. 'I know exactly what's going through your tiny mind. It's just this sort of weak-kneed pusillanimity that's allowed Scott to stay on.'

'It's not, you know,' returned Lisa stoutly. 'It's the lack of an alternative. I mean, have you looked at our senior staff lately?'

'There is that,' admitted Jacinta. 'Most of them are total deadheads. But what about Antonia? She'd be okay.'

'Well,' said Sam, trying to get a word in, 'if she really thinks that way about Australia, why doesn't she go somewhere else? She could try Poland or Libya perhaps.' He flopped back into the groaning chair.

'Besides,' added Lisa, 'how come you've turned into an Antonia supporter all of a sudden? You've always been so rude about her, calling her Plutonia and mocking her accent and so on.'

'She's got to be an improvement on Scott,' insisted Jacinta. 'This department is a chaotic mess, nothing ever gets done, exams are given out to students and he won't investigate it, there's something very suspicious happening with the accounts, and to top it all, somebody has been murdered and he hasn't even got around to advertising the position yet.'

'I don't know that advertising someone's position would be my first reaction,' Lisa was beginning, when the door to the corridor opened to admit Antonia Summerfield herself, looking crisp and efficient in blue and white stripes.

'I've just come around to organise who's going to Johnston's funeral,' Antonia said. 'It was to have been tomorrow, but they've put it off till Saturday so that people will be able to go without missing classes.'

None of them, of course, wished to go, but Antonia was not an easy person to deny. Besides, staying away from a murdered colleague's funeral might not look good to the police. All murmured assent and Antonia wrote down their names.

'I suppose you know this department has an elected head,' she began, 'and I believe the time for an election is about due.' She gazed at three smoothly polite faces, which gazed back at her.

'Well, I hope to raise this matter during the staff meeting,' she continued.

'I don't recall seeing it on the agenda,' said Lisa, as neutrally as she could.

'Well, not as such,' replied Antonia cautiously. Years of working with Antonia had taught them that 'not as such' was Home Counties English for 'no'. 'I intend to raise it under Any Other Business,' she continued.

'I thought we had a one-hour limit on these meetings,' said Sam. 'I mean, there already seems to be an item to do with exam security and another about Johnston's death.'

'The sooner the better,' said Antonia firmly, and swept out. She knew it was hopeless asking them for any indication of their opinions, much less believing their answers. Few of her colleagues could lie straight in bed at night.

'I tell you,' said Jacinta, as soon as the door had shut, 'we ought to have a strategy.'

'A strategy for what?' asked Lisa irritably. She wasn't putting herself on the line to save Jacinta.

'A strategy for keeping us, the peasants, out of the firing line.'

'What about a secret ballot?' interjected Sam.

'Good old Klusky,' said Jacinta.' 'I always knew you'd come in handy for something. You must have at least two neurons in there, and they're even talking to each other!'

'Yes,' said Lisa. 'That's a good idea. Even the unions have them these days, so it's surely not too much to ask. You can play your cards very close and miss out on a lot of mudslinging with a secret ballot.'

Satisfied, they wended their various ways around the campus – Lisa to the Feyerabend Communication Space to teach assertiveness to the Kindergarten Trainees; Jacinta to hammer the rudiments of qualitative research methods into the heads of the Medical Engineers; and Sam right across the campus, buffeted by the wet wind, jostled by students, and jeered at by the disabled protestors to teach elementary psychology of work to the Articled Clerks.

By mid-afternoon, the staff of the Department of Psychological and Sociological Inquiry – or possibly Enquiry; the matter had never been fully resolved, despite numerous heated debates – began to foregather in the James Frazer Room. This was on the first floor of Building 1956, along with the student health service and the audiovisual store. Its walls were lined with cupboards crammed with nameless junk from previous eras, which the audiovisual officer refused to part with.

'Oh my God, those students are thick, thick, thick,' moaned Jacinta, subsiding into a chair. 'And why are they all so huge?' she demanded. 'They tower over me.'

Some of the more sensitive of the dispirited and non-quorate huddle flinched.

'I tell you I've met more intelligent pussy cats,' Jacinta continued, unwrapping a hamburger with the lot. Then she noticed that Scott was wearily lighting up another cigarette.

'Oh no, not again! Don't tell me you're going to fill this tiny little unventilated room with smoke for the entire meeting. What about that motion which was passed nem con at that meeting last year? The one banning smoking?'

'Nem con it might have been, dear lady,' replied Scott, using Jacinta's least favourite form of address with a nasty smile, 'but the meeting itself was non-quorate.' And he leaned back in his chair and blew a smoke ring.

'No it wasn't,' said Reuben. 'I remember.'

'I wrote the minutes,' replied Scott, 'and I say it was.'

'Never mind, Reuben,' interrupted Jacinta. 'Just remember our glorious leader's motto – he who writes the minutes rules the day. Honestly, Iain, your lungs must be two black, hideous, filthy bags of corruption.'

Scott glared at her as she tried to find a safe spot out of range of the thick blue smoke. Fresh from Encounters of the Third Kind with Agnes Kloof and Doreen Hubel, he had no intention of allowing any other women to gain the upper hand, however momentarily. He wondered for a moment whether it had been Jacinta who had suggested that he had had a motive, several in fact, for the murder of Johnston. It had taken some fast talking on Wednesday to persuade Nathan Goldwyn that the Department did not require the attentions of the Fraud Squad and that the accounts were almost finished. They were too, and a work of art they had turned out to be. I wouldn't put much past Jacinta, he thought, she could well have dropped a hint or two to that blasted policewoman about the finances. He decided to reassert his authority. Some nasty gibe about monstrous regiments of women floated into his mind, but he couldn't quite remember it. He knew Jacinta better than to think he could get away with a misquotation, so he fell back on the safer ground of personal attack.

'My dear girl,' he purred. 'Nobody who consumes your diet can possibly have much insight into medical matters. But if you would read more widely into the history of medicine, you would discover that tobacco has a healthy curative effect. It soothes and preserves, as long as it isn't that nasty French muck. That's the stuff that gives you cancer.'

Jacinta snorted in utter and unconcealed contempt, and there was some suppressed giggling among the staff. Scott decided to give it up as a bad job. He had far too much on his mind and no time or inclination to bandy words with people who should have been beneath his notice.

He gazed gloomily around the room at the small group. He had a horrible suspicion that one of them had murdered Richard and was going to get away with it. It seemed clear how things were shaping up. The police were not going to go away until they got their murderer, and he, the unpopular authority figure, was going to be the scapegoat. They could do it quite easily, a few words to the police at the right time . . . God knew he had motivation enough.

Jacinta munched her hamburger and glared at him. How unfair that anyone so fierce and intelligent should look so relatively normal, Scott thought. It would be so much easier if feminism had some outward and visible mark, like a crewcut, or at least a big bum. Perhaps that was only lesbians, but anyway what was the difference, really? Of course, he and Jacinta had been through all this in the course of that nasty sexual harassment charge she had brought against him shortly after starting work. Thank god for the probationary period, he thought. That had been what had got her off his throat, the veiled threat of getting the old heave-ho in twelve months' time.

Jacinta looked up, and gave him a glare so fierce that he decided it might be a good idea to rest his gaze elsewhere while they waited for the last few staff members to trickle in. Punctuality is the thief of time, Lisa used to say whenever she was kept waiting by latecomers at these meetings.

Scott's gaze came to rest on the departmental politician. Seamus O'Faolain had, as usual, dragged a green beanbag into the room and subsided into it. All that could be seen of him now was a grubby foot encased in a sandal – funny how some people's feet seemed immune from the cold – and a head munching its way through a huge, crumbling, all-natural sandwich. No wonder the place was overrun with all-natural rats, thought Scott. And I wish people wouldn't eat their blasted lunches during staff meetings. He had raised the question once, but had been howled down by the others, who had declared that they didn't get enough breaks from teaching, and had to take their sustenance when they could. They had pointed out that they couldn't exactly eat while lecturing. He'd had to give way on that one, but he hadn't liked it.

Antonia Summerfield, bolt upright in a chair near Seamus, was crunching an apple. Scott noticed that she was wearing blue and white stripes again. Didn't the woman own anything else? Further around, poor old Dr Cavendish nibbled her lettuce leaf. She'd never been the same since that awful day in the Rom Harre. Did she really know where she was now, Scott wondered, observing her cease munching and stare vaguely into space. Surely they ought to do a subtle mental status examination on her, it shouldn't be too hard. Jacinta had suggested creeping up on her in a corridor and asking, 'What do you think of Menzies' performance these days?' But she did seem to keep her classes going, and most of the students passed and nobody complained, so really what more could one want?

Lisa and Reuben were whispering together at the back in a way that struck Scott as vaguely sinister. He was drawing in breath to quell them when Bennett strolled in and languidly remarked, 'Well, you're sitting there as if you have the weight of the world on your shoulders, darling, when you could be sharing it with us.'

Bennett loved teasing Scott even more than he enjoyed teasing Antonia.

Scott glared at him. As if sharing my difficulties with you would help, he thought, you seem to be the main problem.

'Well, I can't start the meeting until it's quorate,' he began.

'I don't see why not,' objected Reuben. 'After all, you seem to decide whether meetings are quorate or not at some later point.'

'Now look here, Reuben,' Scott snarled in what he hoped would be misinterpreted as a jocular manner. 'I'm not having those sorts of defamatory statements; I mean, the minutes are always circulated for confirmation. And besides...'

Besides what was never discovered, because at that moment Alan Hoxha bounded between the two protagonists, beaming on each with the detachment and tolerance that only prolonged and frequent absences could confer.

'Hello everyone,' he said. 'Now what's this meeting all about?'

'Oh hello whatsyername, Alan, a long time since we've met but so glad you could spare the time to drop in,' snarled Scott, 'but now we're quorate I suppose we can start. It's patently obvious that none of you read your agendas or you'd know what this meeting was about, damn it. This meeting has two main issues. The first is, who the hell gave the exam out? Don't bother with that crap about it being a practice exam either. It might work sometimes, but it's not going to work on me.'

He stopped for breath, satisfied that he now had the attention of the entire group. That's stopped them whispering, he thought.

'I intend to find out who is responsible for this exam business, and that person will be fired.'

'Fired?' inquired Alan Hoxha innocently. 'But what if they're tenured?'

'Tenure! Tenure! Haven't you heard of Infamous Conduct?' Scott shouted. 'If you came to work a bit more often, you'd know a bit more about academic life, Hoxha. And giving out exams, probably to secure the sexual favours of randy Medical Engineers, is the most infamous conduct there is.'

'What about murder?' Lisa asked. She had resolved to keep very quiet in this meeting, but the words were out before she realised. Oh well, I've started, she thought, so I might as well go on. This meeting is going to be so thick with drama that nobody will remember, let alone care. 'I mean, why are we so obsessed with this exam when there's an unsolved murder right in front of us? Doesn't that concern anybody but me?'

'Murder?' said Alan Hoxha. 'Murder? What murder? Is this another of your silly jokes?'

A collective moan arose from the others. How could he possibly not have heard? Didn't he read the papers? Didn't he ever watch the telly? Didn't he come to work? The meeting was in uproar.

Eventually Scott regained control. 'Alan,' he said. 'I'll see you in my office afterwards. Now let's get on with the business at hand. To start with, poor Johnston's death was just an unfortunate accident.'

'That's not what you told the police when you were dobbing poor Sam in,' retorted Reuben. 'Just what exactly do you believe?'

Scott ignored Reuben with the ease of long practice.

'First things first,' he said. 'This business of exams for sex and drugs.'

And he glared at Jacinta.

'Are you glaring at me?' she squeaked. 'You're not seriously suggesting it was me? Sex and drugs? What do you mean?'

'Ah,' replied Scott. 'A guilty mind reveals itself.' He knew it wasn't true, but he wasn't going to pass up a chance to anger Jacinta. 'Now what made you think I was looking at you, my dear, when I was addressing the meeting in general?'

'I am not your dear and if you continue to behave in this obnoxious manner I certainly never will be,' Jacinta snapped. 'I thought you were looking at me because you were looking at me. So for heaven's sake stop this ridiculous FBI stuff.'

Klusky suddenly spoke up from behind Reuben's ample form. 'Hadn't you better tell us how you are going to investigate this matter?' he asked mildly. 'I mean, most of the staff are suspects because it was the exam for the introductory course, the one that's in the Common First Year. We're all suspects,' he went on a little frantically, 'of one thing or another.'

'Tell you how I'm going to investigate this matter?' asked Scott, rolling his eyes to heaven. 'I mean, really, Klusky, you are so simple. If I tell you all, the guilty person may be able to forestall my efforts. But make no mistake, it is being investigated. We are narrowing our investigation and one person is a very clear suspect.'

'Honestly, Scott,' said Bennett. 'I do think all that time you've been spending with the police is beginning to rub off. But you must have picked up on one fundamental little fact – even suspects have certain rights...'

'Order,' shouted Scott.

'What do you mean, shouting "Order"? Bennett retorted. 'You haven't been running this gathering along the rules of meetings; as far as I can see it's just a discussion and people are free to contribute.'

'The best thing you could contribute is a confession,' replied Scott. Bennett blanched.

'Aha!' cried Scott, triumphantly. 'Another one turning pale. Yes indeed, a confession is the only thing that just might, and I emphasise might, persuade me to write the culprit a passable reference.'

There was a subdued snarling from the rest of the staff, who were not quite sure which side would be less dangerous to be seen to be on. Confusion was uppermost until Antonia Summerfield's clear voice was heard, piercing the hubbub like a high-quality industrial diamond.

'If all you had in mind in calling this meeting was to waste our time by throwing baseless accusations at one staff member after another,' she intoned icily, 'then I for one think it's disgraceful. Poor Edmund there has grounds for legal action already. Don't you realise that you could impair his capacity to make a living?'

'I definitely do,' began Scott, who was losing his cool spectacularly, but Antonia simply changed her voice up a gear and rolled inexorably on.

'Even the order of this agenda is disgraceful. First the exams and then poor Richard's death. What sort of perspective is that? Whatever you may have thought about Richard Johnston, he suffered a ghastly death at the hands of some maniac. You have to look at the facts,' she continued remorselessly. Her hearers sat rivetted. They knew nothing would stop Antonia once she got started. Edmund Bennett leaned forward in his chair, his hands pressed to his forehead. His unfortunately close, albeit inadvertent, links with Johnston had come flooding back to him. Close behind them were anxieties about his own possible fate if he fell into the hands of Neos's relatives. Behind them, yet another anxiety, what of his professional future? The spectre of public exposure and dismissal hovered on the edge of his awareness.

'Richard Johnston was bludgeoned by a madman and then dragged, possibly still conscious and in dreadful agony, right across the lecture theatre. I, for one, believe that the exam leak and the murder are connected. Whoever gave that exam out knows a lot more about Johnston's death than he should, but the whole thing is a matter for the police, not some internal...'

A soft thud momentarily diverted even Antonia, and all eyes turned to see Bennett sprawled on the floor.

The meeting broke up instantly, with one group clustering around Bennett and the other furiously continuing the battle for leadership of the department. Antonia had gone to Bennett's assistance, so O'Faolain was left to fight his battle for himself, and eagerly waded in with a couple of inflammatory insults. Scott responded in kind.

On the other side of the room, Antonia knelt beside Edmund. 'Perhaps he's had a heart attack,' she said. Frantically she began administering mouth-to-mouth resuscitation. Klusky scrambled forward and pulled her off.

'Not like that,' he said. He turned Edmund onto his side. Still breathing, thank goodness. He didn't fancy mouth-to-mouth with Eddie, whatever the books said about saliva.

The others' attention flickered, like spectators at a three-ring circus, between the heap on the floor, now moaning softly, and the battle between O'Faolain and Scott.

'I move a vote of No Confidence,' shouted O'Faolain, leaping up from his beanbag. 'He's wasted our time, terrorised everybody, and now he's planning to abrogate our basic human rights.' He waved a furious finger at his fascinated colleagues. 'Come on, you spineless bastards, vote him out. You've put up with him for years too long, like a pack of useless bloody masochists. Now stop whingeing and do something.'

'Don't bother with your stupid vote. I resign as Head, run it yourselves, you bunch of gormless no-hopers, I'm going out.' Scott slammed the door behind him and silence descended. Bennett rose on one elbow to receive sympathy, but the crowd's attention had moved on.

Antonia was the first to rally. 'I nominate myself as head,' she said firmly.

'Seconded,' shouted O'Faolain, still on his feet.

Confusion, as so often in Barry College's history, passed for consent, and Antonia closed the meeting. The first thing to do, she thought, is to find Goldwyn and convince him to go along with this stunt. She strode purposefully off down the corridor, while the rest of the staff scrambled down the fire escape and repaired to the Alaska Hotel to discuss the events of the day. Sam alone remained behind with Edmund, now sitting up but still looking horribly pale.

'Can I drive you home?' he offered sympathetically.

Edmund looked at him as if he'd never seen him before.

'Just leave me alone,' he whimpered. 'Just fucking well leave me alone, can't you? You've caused enough trouble, now just piss off.'

Stung by the injustice of this remark, Sam caught up with the staff of Psychological and Sociological Inquiry crossing Martin Street. They swarmed into the front bar of the Alaska. A quick whip round and some cooperative effort soon covered a table with jugs of beer and Smoky Bacon potato crisps. The manufacturer of these had recently announced that these contained absolutely no meat product, so they were acceptable to all, regardless of creed. After a couple of rounds and a general post-mortem of the putsch, talk turned to The Murder.

Margery Cavendish had eschewed the beer, preferring her own order of very dry martinis. She drank quickly and efficiently, and had soon reached the blood alcohol content at which she functioned best.

'But my dears,' she said huskily. 'It's all so obvious.'

'What?' asked Seamus, who was always intrigued by the way Margery reverted to her showbusiness past when somewhat pickled. A car accident in her twenties had forced her to re-train as a psychologist. She said it was all the same really, one form of showbiz was much like another. These days, of course, it was hard to believe she had once been Norma the Nude Contortionist. Fattening, all that gin. Seamus gazed at her inquiringly.

'Why, who did it, of course,' replied Margery, holding out her glass to him imperiously. 'Get me another of those, will you dear boy? And tell them that when I say dry, I mean dry.'

'Well,' said Seamus, returning from the counter in record time and handing over her drink, 'don't leave us in suspense. Tell all.'

'As you know,' began Margery, taking a delicate sip. Amazing how steady her hand was once she got a few of those inside her, mused Seamus. 'It would be fair to say that Iain and I don't really get on. As a matter of fact, I loathe him.' She paused to gaze at Seamus. 'Scott did it. You know Johnston was fond of blackmail – does anyone know what happened to his personal files, by the way?'

'I think someone from Admin got them,' said Jacinta quickly. 'But why would Scott kill Johnston?'

'Because of the gambling,' said Margery, draining her glass. 'Surely you knew about Scott's obsession with the neddies? He was always in and out of the computer building, taking Harry Holderness out to lunch, that sort of thing. Research he called it. Hah! He was right in on the "Beat The Bookies" special. Must have been a few bugs in the system though. He was in debt up to his neck. Well, Johnston wanted something. I don't know, money, power, first crack at the research budget. Maybe just liked seeing Scott squirm. I know I did,' she added, with a nasty smile.

'Anyway,' she continued, 'Scott paid him, whatever it was, to keep quiet. But when the sessional money ran out and Goldwyn started to carry on about external auditors, well that was when Scott found it too much, and dotted him off.'

There was a short silence. Nobody really believed Iain could have murdered Johnston. Certainly it would be a convenient solution, but it was just too unlikely. But the sessional money, now there could be something in that.

'Are you saying Scott was paying Johnston the sessional money?' asked Sam.

'No, no,' replied Margery. 'Weren't you listening? Where's my glass? Empty already?'

Sam took the hint, and returned quickly with another martini.

'So, what about the sessional money?' he prompted her.

'Oh, yes, dear. That was what Scott was using to fund his gambling. Not considered quite the thing, really. Revolver-in-the-library stuff, really.'

'But,' objected Lisa, who had been thinking furiously but so far had only succeeded in becoming even more confused. 'I was in the building on Sunday and I didn't see Scott.'

'Then again, you didn't see Johnston, did you?' pointed out Jacinta through a mouthful of crisps.

'It is a big building,' Lisa admitted, but she was puzzled. Her suspicions tended in a different direction. Besides, didn't Iain have an alibi? She didn't see how Margery's story could possibly be a motive for the murder.

'It's a downright creepy building,' observed Reuben.

Lisa ignored him. There was a great deal she still wanted to think about.

Jacinta's absence from work on Sunday had been so unusual that Lisa had asked her what she had been up to. Jacinta's reply that she had been working at home in the company of her cat came as a surprise; Lisa knew that Jacinta worked only at work, and Sunday absences were usually explained by something more sociable. Perhaps she had been out with some of those funny anarchist friends of hers, and didn't want them to get mixed up with the police. Still, it was odd. And then there was her sudden interest in Johnston's research work. She'd refused to have anything to do with him ever since she'd come to Barry. At least, that's what some versions of the story said. Others said that it had been he who'd thrown her out of his lab. But apparently he'd tried to get her interested again, shortly before he'd died, and Jacinta had refused. Peculiar.

And then, what about Seamus? He was a very large, solidly-built person. When exactly had he got into work on that Sunday? He had seemed calm, cheerful, and blood-free when chatting in the tea room, but then he always did. It was all very odd.

## 12

When Antonia finally tracked Goldwyn down the following morning, he was less than enthralled by the series of events she unfolded to him.

'You're a bunch of wackos!' he opined. 'Can't you do anything right?'

Antonia held her ground and gazed at him coolly. 'To be honest, Dr Goldwyn, that wasn't quite the reaction I was expecting from you.'

Antonia's freezing English accent had little effect on the American Goldwyn, although he had observed its demoralising influence on others. Now he leaned back in his seat, foolishly ran his fingers through his hair, and said wearily, 'Now, let's take this again slowly. On the basis of an unwritten offer of resignation informally accepted by the meeting, you moved that you be made Head of Department and nobody complained. Scott hasn't been seen since, and you want my blessing to take over. Is that right?'

'You could describe it that way if you chose,' replied Antonia. 'But it hardly detracts from the fact that I do have the support of a significant majority of the staff, and that an election was three years overdue.'

Goldwyn reached for a cigar, lit it, and contemplated Antonia. She looked very crisp and neat. She reminded him of a nursing Major he had known in Korea. He felt she could be a more redoubtable adversary than Scott had ever been, and he wondered if he could possibly get her on his side. Unlikely. The blasted woman was some kind of femocrat agitator. Difficult to understand, really, the left-wing attitudes of so many of these people. Surely they could see the benefits of a society which allowed a place for everyone, a role for women which allowed the cream to rise, as it should, to the top? Pulling his mind away from the inexplicable politics of this country – a socialist Prime Minister again, for heaven's sake, don't these people learn from their mistakes? – he rose to his feet and paced to the window. Before his unseeing eye lay the derelict Victorian cottages which were labelled 'General Purpose Space' but were really the exclusive preserve of that hateful organisation, the Student Union, led by the rabid Frank Hodges.

Well, he thought, if this bitch can keep that lot in order for five minutes or so, she'll be doing better than Scott, and I'll have a chance to get on with running the rest of the place.

'Okay,' he said, returning to his chair. 'You have my support. With,' he added, leaning forward for emphasis, 'certain provisos. One, there has to be an investigation into this leaked exam business, somebody's head has got to roll and I don't much care whose it is; two, I want those Departmental accounts and I want them fast; and three, I want someone to continue Johnston's Civilein project. That Jacinta McBride. Send her over to see me.'

'Of course,' said Antonia.

'Fine. If Scott makes trouble tell him to come to me about it. I'll shift him sideways. He can work on the new Revelations Programme. Can't do much harm there.'

Noticing a startled look on Antonia's face, he stopped abruptly and changed tack. Odd how even the toughest of academic women could be surprisingly naive when it came to money and power. Briefly he wondered whether it had been entirely Antonia's idea to challenge Scott.

'We have to compensate the man somehow,' he pointed out. 'As it is, you've just given yourself his job because some of the other staff were persuaded into thinking it might be an improvement. I mean, it's hardly standard procedure, is it?'

'Well, if it's standard procedure we're on about, I think there's a number of matters of procedure which the Government Academic Review Panel might find interesting,' retorted Antonia, with a sweeping gesture that took in the antique desk, luxurious shag-pile carpet, and original Pro Hart on the wall. For good measure, she cast a meaning glance through the glass panel in the direction of Goldwyn's personal assistant, the beautiful but illiterate seventeen-year-old whose presence in his lap had startled Agnes so much earlier that week. She appeared to be buffing her nails while Goldwyn's business secretaries worked their butts off in the outer regions.

'It's like that, then, is it?' said Goldwyn sternly.

'Yes,' replied Antonia. Goldwyn sighed with relief. They were back in his area of expertise – blackmail.

'Well, it's up to you, I suppose, but I'd rather wrestle live alligators than be directly responsible for that bunch of loonies over in Psycho.'

Stubbing out his cigar, he pressed the tips of his fingers together, leaned his chin on them, and gazed intently at Antonia. It was a position he had practised at home in front of a mirror, and he fancied that it gave him a wise and world-weary air. However, during practice sessions, he had made sure his hair was lying flat.

'You'd be surprised just how much filters its way upwards to the Director's office,' he began, musingly.

Antonia wasn't entirely sure that things could filter upwards. Downwards and sideways, perhaps, but not directly against the laws of gravity. However, this was clearly not a time to be correcting Goldwyn's English expression, so she put on her best bright, alert expression and beamed silently back at him.

'There are quite a few unanswered questions hovering over that Department,' he went on. 'It certainly isn't a good time to be going in as Head.'

So what else is new, thought Antonia, smiling brightly. There never has been a good time to go in as head of any department anywhere. What's he getting at?

'For a start,' said Goldwyn, 'there are those accounts. I suppose you knew about Scott's gambling habits?'

So that was why there was no sessional money. But Antonia knew better than to shake her head. Heads of departments had to appear to know everything that went on, even if they made a fair bit of it up on the spot.

'One hears all sorts of rumours,' she said cautiously. Could this be some sort of trap? 'But there was never any proof...' Don't want to give him the impression I'd slander my staff.

'There is a theory,' continued Goldwyn, escalating the battle in the hope of getting some reaction, 'that Johnston knew a bit more than Scott would have liked about Scott's gambling habits.'

That's got her, he thought with satisfaction.

'What are you suggesting?' she said, her mind whirring.

'Oh, nothing, nothing,' soothed Goldwyn, all kindness and understanding now he had her on the run. 'But in any case, the fact remains that I haven't had any statements out of your Department in eighteen months. And what I'm suggesting is that you straighten things out as quickly as you can. And make sure nobody gets in the way of the police. We don't want them to take it into their heads to investigate that place any more closely than is absolutely essential, so tell your staff to cooperate and then lie low.'

Antonia could see his point. 'Are you sure somebody in Psychological Inquiry murdered Johnston?' she demanded. Perhaps they could just point the police away from the place.

'Who the hell else?' replied Goldwyn. 'People generally get murdered by their nearest and dearest, you know that as well as I do. The man had no family and no friends and I can tell you that he made a habit of menacing his co-workers. Now I never liked Johnston. He was a pompous, arrogant ass. Wasn't he?'

Antonia sat like a stone, smile fixed in place, inwardly crying out at her betrayal of Johnston. She alone, she thought, had been able to see his good side. And now he's dead.

'Johnston was a bastard,' continued Goldwyn. 'Always going on about Christianity and making offensively anti-Semitic remarks. But I don't particularly care for having murderers on the payroll. If they do catch whoever did it, I won't lift a finger to help him. However you look at the man, however hard he was to get on with, he was a very effective academic. He brought in a lot of grant money, he did a lot of research, and he put this little backwater on the international map. Most of the people in this college are too timid to go on an exchange to Sydney. Johnston gave guest lectures all over the world. He was a big shot in the Australian-American Education Foundation too. And this Civilein project was going to be very big for the College. There's a lot of unreasonable unrest in the world these days.'

Antonia left Goldwyn's office reasonably happy. After all, he had confirmed her headship, and he could have made a lot more demands. All that money unaccounted for, that was a worry. It had never occurred to her that Scott might have been gambling it all away. Perhaps they could make up some of the leeway with salary savings. Nothing like a murder to make a few salary savings, she thought, and felt shocked at her own cynicism. She was developing an Australian outlook, with these slack attitudes to human life and moral values. Not good enough, she said to herself, in exactly the way her old headmistress had said it, in morning assembly following yet another disgusting episode with a used sanitary napkin.

Better get on with it, she told herself sternly. There's a need to bring a better approach, especially to work, to the Department of Psychological and Sociological Enquiry. Inquiry. Some definitive decision on how to spell the blasted place might help.

But who could have given that exam out? It must have been Bennett. Who else? But, as several staff members had pointed out, the man had an iron-clad defence if he simply said that this Kosmos chap had found it lying about in the corridor. There was, after all, a precedent. Some people were awfully careless.

She paused to look critically at Building 1872. Festoons of brilliant orange computer cables detracted not at all from its gloomy majesty. It displayed them like the banners of an army which has yet to discover it has been defeated, its last path of retreat cut off. Setting up a computer system at the College had proved unexpectedly difficult. Twentieth-century masonry drills and technology had buckled in the face of nineteenth-century granite and craftsmanship. The computer cables had had to be let in at the few and narrow windows. At least it gave the students something to hang their horrifying slogans from during Rag Week.

Now why couldn't they have had a murder in there, she wondered. Much more suitable. In fact, there probably had been any number of murders there already for all anyone knew. Barry College was very dark about its past. Look on the bright side, she thought, struggling on, all these stairs do make you fit.

She hurried on. As Head of Department there were important decisions to be made. Who to ring to discuss a replacement for Johnston. What to do about the sessional money. Whether the portrait of the Queen would go better over the cocktail bar in Scott's – her – office or on the bookshelf. Rounding the corner at last, she bumped into Lisa Thomas, on her way from one class to another. Lisa looked at her oddly as she apologised and walked straight into the building, giving no sign of recognition.

Lisa sighed, retrieved the folder Antonia had knocked from her hands, and followed her into Building 1956. No matter what manner of upheavals and disasters were occurring in the department, it seemed there could never be any suggestion of cancelling a class or two. For heaven's sake, she thought, surely one class more or less isn't going to make all that much difference to their professional competence. Everyone moaned about the number of classes, but if you even suggested cancelling a few, you got all that rot about people coming down from the country specially for that very class. Academics could be very odd.

There was, of course, no replacement for Johnston yet; Fudge hadn't yet been replaced, and they were still haggling about the wording of the advertisement, so that was going to be a long slow business; Scott had disappeared; and Bennett was still feeling too frail to front up. So the load was heavier than usual on those who were still on deck.

She had found yesterday's staff meeting a little puzzling; Bennett's reaction to the description of Johnston's body had been a little extreme, or had he been reacting to something else? Scott too had been under a lot of strain. Doesn't mean either of them is guilty, whatever Margery said. It's not exactly pleasant having this sort of thing going on around you. Jacinta seemed to be taking things in her stride though.

There were still several things she wanted to think through, but lack of time made it impossible. And now she had one of Scott's classes to take. She'd had only fifteen minutes to prepare for it, but had found to her relief that it was a practical class on relaxation strategies. Gaelene had found her a relaxation tape and tape-player in Scott's room. We could all do with a bit of relaxation, she had thought as she hunted through the confusing list of class bookings. Allegations had been made that the Computer Centre used a random number generator in the programme that produced them, and by the end of the first semester they were a thicket of alternatives and crossings-out.

The students assembled in the James Frazer Room were a bunch of Medical Engineers, dressed in their uniform of sloppy joes, faded jeans, and runners. Lisa knew a few of them from previous classes. Neos Kosmos, for example, well known as a trouble-maker and persistent applicant, first for exemptions and later for special consideration. Some of the others looked vaguely familiar, but they were hard to tell apart. Who was it who had suggested to her that each year's crop of students was not actually new? Seamus of course. He had explained to Lisa about the vast student recycling factory at Broadmeadows. That's why we have such a long vacation, he had said. It takes them that long to wipe their memory circuits, re-buff their teeth, and hammer out the dents in their self-satisfied world-view.

She began the class. The students seemed quite enthusiastic about the idea of actually trying out a technique instead of just sitting around talking about it. Cheerily they took off their shoes, pushed their chairs against the cupboard-lined wall of the James Frazer Room, and deposited themselves on the floor.

'I'll just put the lights out to stop us getting distracted,' said Lisa.

'Oh!' gasped one of the larger students.

'Problem?' asked Lisa, somewhat surprised.

'Well,' stammered the student, who appeared on close inspection to be female. Lisa had a feeling she'd had her in a class last year. Dona Ferentes, she thought the girl's name was. 'Yes, Dona?'

'Well, it's just that...I mean...Well, I don't feel comfortable with the light off. Really.' The girl blushed.

'Oh Dona,' said another student sympathetically, 'you poor thing. She doesn't have to do it, does she, Dr Thomas. Not if she's got a compulsion.'

'Phobia,' corrected Lisa absent-mindedly. Funny how even Medical Engineering students could show vaguely human characteristics from time to time, she thought. 'You really feel bad, do you, Dona?' she asked as sympathetically as she could. Were the students trying to get a rise out of her? No, Dona did look genuinely upset, thought Lisa, and if she can fake a blush like that she doesn't need to get any more in touch with her body anyway.

Dona nodded. 'It sort of comes and goes,' she said. 'I'm okay in places I know well, but sometimes in strange places I just feel like... well... like...'

'Well,' said Lisa, 'why don't you try it, and if it does get too much for you, just get up and leave quietly, all right? But it would be good if you could stay, because the relaxation technique might help you to deal with the feelings anyway.' And she put on her best encouraging smile.

'All right, I'll try,' said Dona reasonably happily, and the class settled down on the floor.

'Make yourselves comfortable,' said Lisa, turning off the light, 'and just listen to the tape.'

She would have liked to lie down on the floor and join them, heaven knew she could do with some relaxation, but there didn't seem to be any room left, so she squeezed herself into a corner and sat listening to the gentle breathing.

The tape was a good one, and the students were giving out an air of total bliss. The room was quiet and awfully peaceful, and Lisa began to relax herself. Suddenly the quiet atmosphere was disrupted by a crash, as one of the vacated chairs was tipped over. There was a scuffling sound, and Lisa saw the door open and close quickly, as a figure passed out through it. That must be Dona, she thought. Pity she couldn't manage to stay a bit longer. She considered going outside to see that the girl was all right, but the thought of treading on or tripping over the other students stopped her. She'd chase her up later and see if she'd like to get some help with the problem.

The tape continued; the other students seemed barely aware that anything had happened. Lisa heard a student giggling; someone else was snoring softly. Not quite the idea, she thought; still, it doesn't do them any real harm to drop off for a minute or two.

The tape finished; Lisa switched the light on. Some of the students sighed slowly and dreamily, others lay still. There was a pause.

'Take your time,' said Lisa, since it was obvious that people were, 'and sit up when you feel ready.'

A student sat up. To Lisa's surprise, it was Dona Ferentes.

'Dona!' she said. 'Then...'

She looked around. All the students seemed to be there, but something appeared to be not quite right. The chair she had heard fall lay on one side, and a cupboard door seemed to have swung open. Nearby, another large student lay oddly still.

'Timeo,' said Lisa, hoping that was the student's name, 'are you all right?'

If she had been trying to maintain a calm atmosphere, she couldn't have done worse. All the students, with the alarming exception of Timeo, sat up suddenly. Timeo lay without moving. Lisa moved towards him, as the student beside him let out a scream.

'Oh no, he's dead!' cried the student, recoiling in horror.

There was a sudden silence. Got to take charge, thought Lisa. She stepped up to the motionless form; the student was right, that much seemed obvious. The boy's eyes were slightly open, and glittered from beneath still lids. His face was grey. He looked dead to Lisa, but she steeled herself and knelt down beside him, turning him onto his side and searching at the throat and wrists for a sign of a pulse. An odd thought came to her: if you're not meant to touch a body that's been murdered, how are you meant to see if they need first aid? Lisa had no medical training, but she could see Timeo was beyond first aid.

'Who's not here?' demanded Lisa, sitting back on her heels. 'Somebody got up and left while the light was off. Who was it?'

The students looked at each other in confusion. Nobody could quite remember who had been there in the first place, but they were all under the impression that nobody was missing. Lisa counted them. There were eleven – no, twelve, counting Timeo. Nobody had gone. She addressed one of the largest students, who had been right next to the door and well away from the body.

'You,' she said, wondering desperately if she was doing the right thing. 'Go straight down the corridor to Student Health. Tell them to send Dr Harwell. Page him if he's not there. Tell them there's been an accident.' Much good he'll be able to do, she thought. 'And tell them to call the police as well.'

The sound of student voices outside signalled the end of one class period and the beginning of another, but Lisa felt a bit uncertain about letting her students go. Some were looking very pale; two sat down on the floor, the rest crowded near the door, as far away from the body as possible. To stall for time, Lisa found a piece of paper and got each student to give his or her name and address.

'Look,' said Lisa, 'I'm not sure, but I think we should all stay here until the police arrive.'

'Oh, Dr Thomas,' said Neos Kosmos, 'I'll have to go soon, I've got a train to catch.'

'For heaven's sake, Neos,' snapped Lisa. 'You can't just walk away from a dead body because you have to catch a train.' Neos looked decidedly mutinous. 'The police won't be impressed if you do,' she warned, and was relieved to see his expression change.

'Well, my mum will worry,' he said with an air of aggrieved innocence, sinking into a chair.

God only knows what about, thought Lisa, it would take a front-end loader or a Leopard tank to make much impression on Mrs Kosmos's little boy. Fortunately she was spared the strain of trying to work out a polite reply by Peter Harwell's sudden entry. He strode over to the body and quickly confirmed Lisa's judgement.

'Dead all right,' he said with an air of gloomy satisfaction. 'Strangulation, I would think. See the bruise on the neck? Are the police coming?'

At that moment, the student messenger reappeared. 'The police will be here right away,' he panted. 'Student Health rang the Director too, and Mr Goldwyn said everyone stays here until the police arrive.'

Neos kicked his rucksack with an air of sulky dissatisfaction, but Lisa felt a great wave of relief. Not only had she done the right thing in keeping the students there, but somebody had told her so and that made her feel a lot better. Nobody tells you what to do if a student is murdered in your tute, she mused. You'd think there'd be something in the Terms and Procedures Manual. The headings would be interesting. Something like:

Section 13.1. Murder
    13.1.1 Of a fellow staff member
    13.1.2 Of a student
    13.1.3 Of a member of the College while not on the premises

and so forth. It should go nicely in front of superannuation, because she dimly remembered that your rellies got fifty thousand smackers if you snuffed it in the glorious service of the College. A horrible thought struck her. Whoever had killed Timeo Danaos had done it in the dark. Could they have been aiming for her? Was there really a maniac roaming the College? Surely nobody could have had a motive for killing Timeo. He was totally harmless, although Lisa gathered from the way Dona was carrying on and being comforted that he had meant something special to her.

'... don't you think, Dr Thomas?' said a voice at her elbow.

Lisa jumped. 'Sorry. What?' she said, turning to face the student who had spoken.

'Well, you were sitting up, you might have seen something. Don't you think there must have been someone in the cupboard? Because we're all still here, except – er – well, we are still all here, and somebody did go out, I heard the door.'

It sounded quite feasible. Obvious really, when you thought about it. But it wasn't exactly a nice thing to think about. Somebody lying in wait, hiding in that cupboard, waiting for the class to start ... it was horrible. Lisa pushed it firmly from her mind. 'I think we should leave speculation to the police,' she said firmly. 'It's their job, not ours.'

Then, fortunately, Dona Ferentes fainted and Lisa was distracted from her own thoughts.

## 13

Fortunately the police arrived quickly; sitting in a tutorial room with eleven students and a corpse was not Lisa's idea of a good time. After announcing death, Peter Harwell had pissed off. Dona Ferentes had done her best to create a diversion once she came round, but even the strongest nerves quickly wearied of hysterical sobbing. Her colleagues had begun a spirited discussion of the relative merits of cold water or a slap in stopping the awful noise.

Lisa knew that they all thought she should do something, but it was all she could do to keep herself together, let alone work out how to slap someone six inches taller than she was. To Lisa's disgust, Doreen Hubel's entrance had stopped the sobs instantaneously.

'Anybody touched anything?' barked Doreen at Lisa.

'No, that is not after I couldn't find a pulse. They've all put their names and addresses down. Here's the list.'

'Good, good. Right, let's get everyone out of here so the pathologist can do his job. I want the students in that tea room of yours, until we can interview them. Use your office, can we? Good-oh.'

'Er, just a minute, I think the Head of Department should be told, I mean you can't just have murders happening without telling her,' Lisa said, trying to keep some semblance of authority.

'Told the Director, haven't you?' said Doreen. 'All right, all right, I'd like to get him here anyway. Too many things going on in this place.'

'Her,' said Lisa.

'Eh? The Head of Department, you said. Paunchy chap. Scott. Look, come on, I've got a lot on at the moment,' snapped Doreen.

'There's been a change. Of Head. We had a vote. Sort of. It's Antonia Summerfield. I think you've met her.' Lisa noticed that she seemed to be having trouble putting words together and wondered if it was one of the side-effects of shock.

Doreen paused on her way to get a closer look at the corpse.

'Summerfield? Blonde? Pom? Blue-and-white clothes? Oh yes. She was a bit more organised than Scott. Yeah, get her down here. No, wait a minute, I don't want you wandering around on your own. WIESEL! GET IN HERE!' she bellowed.

Wiesel leaped through the door from where he had been ushering whimpering students down the corridor.

'Wiesel, get hold of the new Head of Department. Ring up the old one's extension, don't leave the students alone. Tell her to come down here and collect one of her staff. She can keep an eye on her while we talk to that lot.'

Her assistant rocked back and forth, processing all these conflicting commands, but eventually he sorted it out and went after the students to phone Antonia. Left without guidance, they had bunched in the corridor and the faint sheep-dog-like cries of, 'Come on now, let's move on up to the tea room, yes of course it'll be all right to go in there,' echoed back to them. Lisa, carefully keeping her eyes of the remains of Timeo, stood near the door. At last the welcome clicking of Antonia's sensible middy heels could be heard. Doreen left Timeo, opened the door and propelled Lisa through it.

'Right, so you're the Head now, are you?' she demanded. Antonia nodded. 'Okay, well there's been another unexplained death as you probably know, and you can help us in our inquiries by keeping an eye on your colleague here until we can get around to talking to her.'

'How about a cup of tea?' asked Antonia dubiously, looking at Lisa's pallid face. She hadn't known, but she wasn't going to let on.

'Yeah, anything you like, just don't let her talk to anybody until we see her first,' Doreen had answered, marching back into the room.

The two went upstairs in silence. Lisa collected her cup and followed Antonia along the gloomy corridors into the Head of Department's office that was now hers. On the first floor, Mackinolty the police pathologist shambled past them, clutching a huge black bag. The corridor outside the Head of Department's office was piled high with assorted heaps of Scott's rubbish. Inside, the mingled smells of Lysol and Pine-O-Kleen fought desperately with the odour of sweaty socks and stale Marlboro.

'Take that chair,' said Antonia kindly, putting the kettle on. 'It's the only one I've had a chance to scrub yet.'

'You've certainly made a difference already,' said Lisa.

'Well it wasn't easy,' answered Antonia, gratified. 'I was here until nine o'clock last night just cleaning things out. You would be amazed, the things that man kept in his drawers! I got in here at half past seven this morning and started scrubbing it out. I simply couldn't bear living in all that awful smell. Gaelene was a great help to me, of course, with the lifting and carrying.'

Gaelene? Lisa was astonished. Lifting and carrying? Gaelene was always helpful to people she liked, but somehow Lisa hadn't thought of Antonia coming into that category. Perhaps the woman did have unsuspected leadership qualities.

'I'm afraid you'll have to excuse me now. I was talking to Goldwyn this morning about the Departmental accounts. Scott promised him they were nearly finished, but I can't seem to make the subtotals add up to the total.'

Antonia returned to her desk.

Lisa sat drinking the hot and unpleasantly sweet tea prescribed by Antonia. Her brain showed a disconcerting tendency to replay the awful moment when she had discovered that Timeo was not just play-acting on the floor. In order to get control of it, she tried to reconsider the facts of the case. She was not entirely convinced that the murderer had been after Timeo. That was Scott's class. Was the killer after Scott? Why? Heaven knew there were plenty of reasons for wanting to knock him off, but which one? What was the pattern behind murdering Johnston first, and then Scott? Did it have something to do with this stuff about gambling? She remembered O'Faolain offering her a bet that the empty files in Johnston's cabinet had been swept up by Scott. She had thought it had been Jacinta, but perhaps Seamus was right. Perhaps Scott had read them and knew too much about somebody. But the idea that Scott was the intended victim was unconvincing. Surely the killer would have noticed that Scott wasn't there. He could simply have waited until the class was over and left again, or sneaked out without harming anyone.

The disinfectant smells seemed to be getting ever more overpowering and Lisa was uncomfortably hot. I must be getting feverish, she thought, and put down her cup preparatory to unwinding the outermost of the many layers of clothing she wore to prevent occupational hypothermia.

'Too hot?' asked Antonia, glancing up.

'Yes, I wonder if I'm getting the flu or something,' answered Lisa.

'No, it's just that I turned the heating on,' replied Antonia with pardonable pride.

'Really? What was wrong with it?' asked Lisa, surprised. They had gone without heating for so long that she had ceased to expect it.

'Nothing at all, except that the attendant is Vietnamese or Chinese or something and he couldn't read the instructions. Once I got in there, it was a simple matter to press the button marked 'on' and move the setting to the place marked 'warm'. Extraordinary that nobody did it years ago. Typical Australian slackness and she'll be right. Anyway, I have to get on with these accounts. Really, the more I look at them, the more problems I seem to find.'

Well, stop looking at them, then, thought Lisa mutinously. Antonia's voice reminded her of fingers scraping on blackboards. James Tate is English anyway, she added, mentally, and all he ever did about the cold was tell you it was a lot colder at Reading. 'Think of all the power we're saving, Miss Thomas,' he had added occasionally. Why was it, she wondered, that women could never, never be addressed as doctor? She dragged her mind back to the murder. It was a relief, after all, from the tangled relationships of everyday life.

Scott had been planning to use relaxation tapes, she thought, but who else would have known that it would involve plunging the class into complete darkness? Surely that had been part of the killer's plan. That aspect alone tended to rule out bookies' runners. It did suggest somebody with a reasonable knowledge of the curriculum. Perhaps another student then? Maybe this murder had nothing to do with Johnston. Surely, though, you couldn't have murderers suddenly running riot in the place.

She tried a new tack. Perhaps the murderer had been after Timeo Danaos after all. Perhaps he had enemies. It sounded awfully melodramatic, but then she knew hardly anything about him. Could it possibly be related to this exam business? Surely Johnston's death didn't have anything to do with the exam. Did it? Would a student have gone as far as murder to get hold of an exam? A student might murder to cover up his or her tracks once the exam leak had been found out, especially if Johnston was making trouble. Of course, students didn't think of lecturers as human beings, so perhaps they wouldn't regard the killing of a lecturer as murder. More like disposing of vermin? It was a horrid thought, chilling for being all too easily believable.

And if they thought that way about Johnston, they could think that about me, she argued to herself. Suddenly she didn't feel very safe. With an effort, she pulled herself together. I'm getting hysterical, she thought, getting things out of all proportion. It's got nothing to do with me. The police are here now, they'll sort it all out.

Inspector Hubel's reactions, had she known of them, would not have been very comforting to Lisa. She had been grimly pleased to be informed of the second death.

'Well, things are starting to happen now,' she had said to Wiesel in the police car on the familiar route to Barry College. 'It's very likely we could get both deaths tidied up this afternoon.'

The rapidly mounting pile of ill-spelt anonymous letters on Doreen's desk pointed to a widespread system of exchanging exams for other commodities. Certain names recurred in their accounts of academic life. The Department of Medical Engineering had been mentioned more than once, and now, it seemed, it had proved fatal to one of their students. She had a short list of students in that Department she wished to interview.

Her feeling of satisfaction had increased when she reached the tutorial room and found that Lisa was there. Doreen didn't think she liked Lisa. She had tried to pin down the feeling and decided that Lisa reminded her of Kylie's class teacher. She knew it was silly but she couldn't help it. Now, as she sat in Lisa's office, she was determined that she would get something concrete, and preferably damaging, from her.

The appearance of the name Kosmos on Lisa's list, too, was fascinating. That name came up in many of the anonymous letters. It had taken only a moment to recognise the profile from the pornographic photograph when she entered the tutorial room, and Doreen had been absolutely sure, even before she had checked, that the face and the name went together.

She got little from the interviews, however. Whatever Lisa's faults in Doreen's opinion, the students had liked her. When Lisa suggested that they all relax, they all had. So much so that none of them had noticed much except for the door opening and closing. Even so, they had thought it was that dreadful Dona girl going out. Doreen had had to give up on her. The mere idea of telling two police officers what happened had turned her hysterical. Doreen had sent Wiesel out to arrange for her to be sent home in a taxi, while she compared the students' statements. About Kosmos, they had been carefully vague, denying any knowledge of his extracurricular activities at Bazza. Doreen wondered whether Kosmos had caught Timeo writing a letter. Kosmos himself, predictably, had denied ever having seen an exam, met Anne Goodbody, or talked to staff members at any time.

'I dunno where she got the exam, I dunno nuthin about it,' he had repeated until even the hardened Hubel could have screamed.

'She coulda found it,' he had finally said, under extreme pressure. 'Some kids did once yuh know, yeah, they found an exam, just lyin in the hall.'

Hubel contented herself with promising to interview him again later, making a mental note to bring the pornographic photograph with her to confront him, and he slouched out.

'So what do you think?' asked Wiesel anxiously.

Doreen had hoped there would be more than this, enough evidence to arrest Lisa on suspicion at least. But since the debacle with Sam Klusky, she had had to take it easy. She'd seen Sam a few times since, but he had always been rather distant. Hardly surprising, really, but she had rather liked him. She brought her mind sharply back to Dr Lisa Thomas. Doctor of what? she wondered irrelevantly. She wasn't sure yet of Lisa's involvement in the first murder. Lisa had admitted to being in the building almost all day, but insisted that she had noticed nothing. Was she hiding something, protecting someone perhaps? Kosmos was, she knew, but then she knew who he was protecting – himself.

'Looks like she's in the clear in this one, anyway. Five of the students noticed somebody leaving the room.'

'Couldn't that have been faked?' asked Wiesel eagerly. 'She could have opened the door and stood there, and then closed it again.'

Hubel had thought of that too. 'No, I'm afraid that can't be it. Three of them said they remember somebody stepping over them in the dark...'

'So, that must be her!'

'I'm afraid not. They all said that whoever it was had trousers and heavy flat shoes on, and she was wearing a skirt, and boots with heels. It just isn't on. Anyway, I could see this Timeo guy had a neck on him like a bull, there's no way she could have done it.'

'Then she must be innocent.'

'Well, I'm not so sure about innocent. It's a bit fishy that whenever you get a murder in this place, sooner or later up pops Dr Lisa Thomas. What is she doing? Setting them up? Keeping cocky?'

'Maybe she gave whoever it was a hand to drag Johnston about,' suggested Wiesel. 'But I've never understood why he was dragged anyway.'

'Well, when we catch up with the murderer, you can ask him yourself,' said Doreen. 'Anyway, go and collect Dr Thomas and let's have a little chat with her.'

The interview with Lisa was no help. Doreen began by cross-examining her about her relationship with Timeo.

'Don't be silly,' she had annoyed them both by saying, 'He was just another student. There's a lot of them about, you know.'

'Don't try to get smart,' said Doreen. 'You knew his name, didn't you?'

'Well, yes, he came top in Psychology last year.'

'Oh, so you were coaching him then? Spent a bit of time together, did you?'

'No; and I don't appreciate your insinuations.'

'Oh come on, sweetie,' persisted Hubel. 'We know what's been going on here. We've had a stack of anonymous letters a foot high about the exams. A women's libber like yourself would want to get in on the action, eh? Equal opportunities and all that. After all, the men have been doing it for years, why not you?'

'I don't know what you mean,' tried Lisa, as a stalling strategy to hide her confusion and outrage. How could she have thought these two were here to protect her interests?

'Stop acting dim,' replied Hubel.

Lisa stared stolidly at her, thinking that a minute ago she was being told off for acting smart. Was there no way to win? This interrogation stuff was a bit unsubtle but there was no doubt it was designed to try to put her off balance. She braced herself for the next shock, and sure enough, Wiesel hoed in.

'Did you give out exam papers in return for drugs?' he asked brightly.

'I most certainly did not,' snapped Lisa. Watch it, she thought, watch it, this is all set up to make you get angry and start saying things you might regret. Should she ask for a lawyer, she wondered, or would that only make them more suspicious?

'But you knew there were drugs on campus?' he persisted.

'I suppose so,' answered Lisa cautiously.

'You supposed so? Why didn't you report it to the police?' demanded Wiesel.

'Because all I had to go on was the annual article in that awful student rag about how to inject yourself one-handed and I thought it was probably a lot of hot air,' Lisa replied stiffly. She had, of course, seen The Old Dope Pedlar on his daily visit to the former prison gate. She had decided he was probably spreading a little joy and minded her own business, but now did not seem the moment to discuss it.

'What my colleague is talking about,' weighed in Hubel, 'is the drug problem among the staff. Our informants tell us that it's quite extensive and that it's gone beyond the salaries of a few of them. That's why they give the exams out, to get a supply for the next few months. Well, what do you know about it?'

'Nothing whatever,' said Lisa shortly.

'What about the A-For-A-Lay business, then?' demanded Doreen, hoping in her heart that such things were not true. Her Jarrod and Kylie might go to Tech one day, and she couldn't bear the thought of either of them exchanging sexual favours for marks. Mind you, the way Kylie was going at school, it might be the only way. God, her mind was wandering off again. The strain of the job plus the responsibilities of parenthood were starting to get her down.

'What utter nonsense!' said Lisa. 'That sort of thing is just not on; and besides, undergraduate students are hardly my style.'

'Oh, come on,' persisted Doreen. She was enjoying the pleasant sensation of having someone on the defensive. 'There's a lot of good-looking young men around here. Just the thing for a busy professional like you. Or are you gay, like your friend Edmund Bennett?'

'He's not my friend,' answered Lisa, confused, 'And I'm not gay, and anyway I don't see that it's any business of yours or even what it's got to do with the murder. That poor boy's dead, and I'm sure he was killed by mistake for someone else. Now please stop asking irrelevant questions and get on with finding out who killed him and why, and stop them from doing it again. Just leave me alone while you're doing it.'

Doreen knew that this was the time to keep pushing. The drive that had got her this far rose to the surface. She was convinced Lisa was hiding something. It was just too good to be true the way she was always there and never saw anything. Besides, there were a lot of funny undercurrents in this place, as the anonymous letter writers had made clear. One hundred and forty-two letters since Monday, Christ! There had been some wild allegations about bodies in the concrete pour when Building 1975 had gone up, but Doreen had enough problems as it was.

'Killed by mistake, you say? People are never strangled by mistake, sweetie. They're killed by someone who wants them dead. That student who had the exam; he was in the class. I'm sure somebody's not very happy with him at the moment. Is he next on the list?'

Lisa had been so involved in trying to work out whether it was her or Scott, or even Timeo himself, that had been the target, that she hadn't considered the other students. Neos Kosmos would certainly have to be a possibility; a nasty piece of work like that would be bound to have enemies, lots of them. Now she thought about it, she had seen him meeting the Old Dope Pedlar. To say nothing of whoever had given him the exam. The exam... well, everybody had a fair idea of where the handsome hulk had got that, but that seemed to imply that Edmund Bennett... Surely not.

She realised that the two police were watching her intently.

'Another student?' she asked, trying to keep them busy. 'You mean the murderer wanted to kill a student, not an academic? I hadn't thought of that. But it doesn't sound very likely, does it? I mean why would anyone want to murder one of the students?'

Neos Kosmos had certainly thought of a reason. At that very moment, he burst into Lisa's office.

'Thank Christ you're still here!' he gasped to the two police. 'I just gotta talk to you. It's about the murder. Youse have got to protect me. Please, I bin thinking about it. I know he was after me. Next time he's gonna get it right, I know he will. He's sure to get me, the same as he got Johnston!'

'Calm down,' said Hubel, a great feeling of satisfaction welling up inside her. Now they were getting somewhere. She had visions of a confession, of the whole thing tied up in no time, that elusive promotion finally hers.

Lisa was fascinated, then greatly annoyed, as she was thrown out of her own office so that they could interview the student in private. Wiesel told her he'd get a formal statement from her later, so that meant she couldn't go home. What could it mean, she mused as she headed for the tea room. Wasn't Neos the one who was supposed to have given the exam to that silly girl, Goodpasture or whatever her name was? That all pointed to Bennett being the murderer. But it didn't seem quite right to her. There were odd things that didn't fit in. And, for once, she definitely didn't want to discuss her thoughts with Jacinta.

## 14

The atmosphere in the tea room was fraught and gloomy. Although the last of the students had by now escaped, they had eaten all the biscuits, drunk the last of the milk, and left fag-ends and dirty coffee cups everywhere.

'It's the total lack of consideration that gets me down,' Reuben was grumbling. 'I mean, why put the students in here in the first place? If they had to put them somewhere, why not a tutorial room? In any case, students should know better than to help themselves to the staff's biscuits and milk.'

'Well, you know how it is when people are stressed,' Sam said soothingly. 'Their blood sugar falls, so naturally they need to replenish it.' This was his excuse, and he saw no reason why the students shouldn't benefit from it too. Potoch gave a derisive snort.

Staring into his milkless tea, O'Faolain reflected that murder seemed to have become a way of life. Last Friday it would have been unthinkable. Now it was one of those minor inconveniences that led to people nicking your milk and bikkies.

'There doesn't seem to be anybody else here,' continued Sam, trying to divert Reuben. 'Where's Iain? I haven't seen him since the staff meeting. Have you seen him, Seamus?'

'No, but I think he's still sulking,' replied Seamus. He knew perfectly well what had happened. Scott's first reaction after he had spoken to Goldwyn had been to lay a complaint with the Union. A worried George Irwell had consulted his faithful secretary, Seamus, about what he should do and Seamus had advised masterly inactivity. This was simply Seamus-speak for waiting until the dust had died down sufficiently for the winning side to appear through the haze. He wondered whether George was sharp enough to realise this. Probably not, he decided.

Goldwyn was shrewd, though, Seamus thought. He had put the fear of god into Scott concerning the irregularities in the accounts and Scott's known gambling activities. He had pointed out that if Scott hadn't blown the whole of the sessional teaching budget, there wouldn't be all the problems of sharing out Johnston's workload amongst an already overworked staff. And, he had added, if the staff had been treated a bit more like adults and less like indentured labourers they mightn't have been so quick to give him the old heave-ho when they got the chance. Besides, Goldwyn had concluded, he should by rights have instituted an election for the Headship three years ago and didn't have a leg to stand on. Summerfield was the Head of Department, and if he couldn't put up with that, he could always go elsewhere.

Scott knew the chances of his getting a job, any job, elsewhere. He also knew where elsewhere was, and had no ambition to live in Alice Springs, Australia's answer to Siberia. In any case, even the Yularu College of TAFE wanted references, didn't it? Scott had gone to the racecourse to forget his troubles.

Others had sensibly gone to ground. Office doors bristled with notes reading, 'Working at home today'. Margery Cavendish, like a shy woodland creature, had become a presence more sensed than seen, though the occasional sea-shanty warbling from her office in a breathy contralto suggested that she, at least, was happy.

'I can hear a noise like somebody singing,' remarked Sam in a puzzled tone, and the others turned to listen. Faintly, against the background of big-city traffic, tramping feet, and power drills came a human voice.

'Well, well,' remarked Seamus, as he identified the familiar sounds of "Swansea Town Once More" echoing down the mouldy corridors. 'I suppose there's nothing like seeing your enemy's downfall and having an excuse to get on the outside of a large dollop of Mother's Ruin to cheer a person up. It's a real triumph for her in a way; she's always hated Scott.'

'Not surprising, really,' agreed Sam. 'I mean, everyone knows about his blocking her promotion on the grounds that her PhD hadn't come through yet.'

'Yes,' agreed Seamus. 'And when she finally complained to the university, they told her that they were waiting on an examiner's report from Scott himself.'

'All things considered, it's a wonder she didn't take to murder herself instead of drink,' broke in Florence airily. 'Oh hello, Antonia. Where's Lisa?'

'In with the police. They wanted me to sit with her until they'd interrogated all the students first for some reason, so I'm having a late lunch. What's that singing I can hear?'

'It's Margery,' replied Seamus. 'I never knew her knowledge of ballads was so extensive. Listen, she's starting on "My Darling Maggie Mae" now.'

Antonia allowed herself a moment's dark reflection on tenure and the less suitable academic. Was there, she wondered, some system whereby tenure always went to the less suitable, or did they just go that way once they got it?

'There don't seem to be many people about,' she commented. 'Where is everybody?'

'Oh, people are around,' answered Florence hurriedly. 'I know I saw Edmund this morning, Jacinta's gone to the library she said, Margery's, er, in her office, the others are working at home I think. No, wait a minute, Clyde's gone to a Spontaneity Training Workshop.'

'Spontaneity Training?' echoed Antonia blankly.

'Yes,' said Florence brightly. 'It's supposed to get you in touch with your inner life so that you respond appropriately to the environment.'

Visions of a class practising tantrums by numbers or grimacing to order flashed through Antonia's mind. Sighing, she turned towards the blackened urn, repaired now but not, of course, cleaned, and started to fill her cup.

'Don't touch that!' shouted Reuben agitatedly.

'Why not?' asked Antonia, leaping back. 'Has it bitten somebody again?'

'What? Oh, that? No, but haven't you realised?'

'Realised what?'

'That somebody's after the staff? That poor boy, Timeo Danaos, was murdered by mistake for one of us. The murderer could well have put poison in the urn. I've brought some boiling water from home in a Thermos; come over here and have some. We can always refill it from the Caff later.'

Antonia stared at him incredulously. Reuben's pale, moustachioed face gazed calmly back, like an amiable walrus in a fleecy-lined skivvy. Could the man be serious? Another horrid thought crossed her mind. Could he be crazy? After all, quite a few of the staff in this building had gone right over the top after a few years. It had something of a name for it in the College. Rumour had it that it was old Bayliss's peculiar sense of humour which had led to him ordering the transfer of Psycho to Building 1956. Shortly after that, of course, he had started gibbering himself in a meeting. Now Reuben was showing distinct signs of paranoia. Well, in this case you would have to say 'more distinct'. Paranoids, she recalled, had a deservedly bad name in psychiatric circles. Perhaps there was poison, not in the urn, but in Reuben's thermos.

Antonia shook herself. Don't be an idiot, she thought. Reuben isn't a murderer. He's just a second-rate academic. He wouldn't get inside the door of even a redbrick university in England. Besides, he wouldn't offer me poisoned thermos water in front of witnesses. Or would he? Could this be some complicated double bluff? She was aware that, after the first moment of hesitation, her body and face were going through the required motions of gracious acceptance, crossing the room and taking the proffered flask. No matter what you thought, you really couldn't refuse. An advertisement for rat poison came into her mind unbidden. Its chief selling point, she remembered, taking the cup back across the room to add sugar to whatever else might be in it, was that the poisoned rats didn't die at once. They crawled away and died somewhere more convenient to the householder. Could this be what Reuben had put in there?

The strain must be getting to me, she thought, joining the small, gloomy group around the table. Probably comes from spending too much time trying to persuade Scott's figures to follow the conventional rules of arithmetic. Gaelene had eventually suggested that Central Admin would be so surprised to get a budget statement from Psycho that they would be most unlikely to check it too closely. If they did, well, she said, 'Goldwyn oughta know by now, he can't expect too much right away.'

Could she be right? Antonia certainly hoped so. She had done her best, but there were certain subsections which wouldn't bear the light of day. Still, she had sent it off. Why on earth had she wanted to be Head of Department in the first place? She let her mind stray fleetingly to the job advertisement she'd seen in the paper last week. Would the Cape York College of Rural Arts and Sciences be an improvement on stagnating here? But it was so dreadfully hot in Queensland, she thought. Worse than Melbourne. The summers gave her prickly heat down here as it was.

Seamus had been listening to Reuben's suspicions, but he shook his head vigorously. All the same, he had accepted Reuben's hot water too, if only to shut him up. He felt a bit dubious about the idea of a murderer with an obsessive hatred of the staff at Barry College of Technology.

Johnston certainly had been different, he mused. Why on earth had he stayed here, wondered Seamus, with his publication record and connections in high places? He had been very big in the Australian-American Education Foundation. It wouldn't have been hard for him to find a cosy nest in a university somewhere more congenial than Melbourne. Perhaps he had wanted to be a big fish in a small pond, perhaps he had signed up, like Beau Geste, in order to forget? Unlikely, Seamus thought. If there was one thing which had distinguished Johnston, it was a capacity for remembering, particularly in the grudge and pay-off departments. He probably stayed on purely for the pleasure of tormenting us, and I suppose for the special access to research grants. But hadn't that been negotiated with the government shortly after he arrived? Of course, that was when he had arranged for Jacinta to start. She had gone from strength to strength since then. But why had she never collaborated with Johnston? She had hated him since Seamus could remember. What had gone wrong? Realising that Reuben was demanding something of the group at large, Seamus pulled himself together in case a rapid dissemble was required.

'What is going to happen to Scott, now that he isn't Head?' he was asking.

Antonia gazed modestly into her lunch and replied, 'I believe that he and Goldwyn have discussed some career strategies this morning, but I don't know the outcome. If I did, I really wouldn't see it as a suitable topic for tea-room gossip. I believe that staff are entitled to expect that their affairs will be dealt with in a confidential manner.'

The others stared at her, nonplussed. What were they going to do in the tea room if not gossip? Sam finally decided that he must have missed Antonia's message and ventured, 'I think he'll wind up in the Revelations Programme, won't he, Seamus?'

'Yup,' he replied, with his mouth full of chocolate doughnut. 'Seems to be where old academics go to die these days.'

It was Antonia's turn to be nonplussed. How on earth did they do it, she wondered. Goldwyn had only mentioned it to her as a possibility that very morning on the other side of the campus, and now here they were discussing it in the Building 1956 tea room. One might just as well live in a fishbowl. She really must try to take control of this sort of idle, pointless chatter. It would have a bad effect on morale if people went about saying the Revelations

Programme was a sort of academics' graveyard, instead of a new and vital initiative to make tertiary education relevant to the needs of Australia in the twenty-first century.

'I'm not sure that Dr Scott will want to enter the Programme, nor that his talents will be entirely suited to it,' she began.

If she had hoped to intimidate Seamus, she had misjudged him. He stared back at her and replied shortly, 'I don't think you'll find it's a question of wanting or talent. Scott can't be fired, he has to go somewhere and there's nowhere else for him to go.'

'What do you mean, he can't be fired?' demanded Reuben. 'What about the infamous conduct provision?'

'First,' replied Seamus patiently, 'you've got to prove it, and in the process a great deal of very nasty muck would be publicly raked. No. You'll find the Revelations Programme is the cheap and painless option for everyone.'

Antonia decided it was time to change the subject.

'If the police don't let poor Lisa go soon,' she interjected, 'I think we'll have to give up this pretence of normality and cancel a few classes.'

The rest of the staff looked at her in surprise and admiration. When Scott had been Head there had never been any suggestion of cancelling classes; in fact, one of his really infuriating habits had been nominating junior and untenured staff members to take his classes at short notice. He claimed this was to develop flexibility and confidence, but in fact it meant he had a hot tip for the races and wanted to be there in person.

Antonia dispatched her second boiled egg, and started on the cheese. Her arteries must be a wonder, thought Seamus, but he knew better than to comment on others' dietary habits. The arguments that had raged over coffee, Caro, and Decaf had left their scars. The wall over the sink was still decorated with articles clipped from the newspapers describing the death-dealing properties of each. The prohibition on gossip revived the atmosphere of pensive gloom which Antonia's arrival had briefly dissipated. In the silence, the distant singer could be heard distinctly. She, too, seemed to sense the atmosphere, because she made a determined onslaught on 'Amazing Grace', although her contralto clearly didn't stand a chance of reaching the top notes.

'BE QUIET!' roared Reuben, and the singing subsided.

Reuben's main contribution to teaching and learning at Barry College was a series of counselling classes on Death, Loss, and Bereavement. Now he decided it was time to apply some of the skills he so arduously imparted.

'We should learn to accept death and realise that it's not something to be glossed over or ignored,' he began sanctimoniously.

'That's all very well,' snapped Antonia, 'but I haven't finished with my life yet and I don't want people stopping it for me... Oh Lisa! They've let you go; how wonderful.'

'Yes, have some coffee,' said Reuben, reaching hospitably for his Thermos. 'There isn't any milk though, those little beasts of students drank the lot, that's if the police didn't pinch it themselves.'

'I'm so glad you're all right,' continued Antonia warmly, ignoring Reuben. 'I was beginning to get worried that we'd have to cancel that introductory statistics class that you so kindly took over after poor Johnston's death.'

To everyone's surprise, the usually phlegmatic Lisa sank back into a chair and burst into tears. A confused uproar began over her head, with Antonia being roundly told off for her heartlessness but stoutly defending herself on the grounds of practicality.

'Honestly,' Sam protested to Antonia. 'This is not a department for teaching statistics. That should be clearly understood in the first place. And secondly, to say that to Lisa now is a bit heartless. For heaven's sake, she's just missed being murdered, then the police questioned her, which I can tell you is no fun, and all you can think about is whether she can teach statistics.'

'It's all right, really, it's all right,' sobbed Lisa, 'it's just that I can't stop crying.'

'If you can't stop crying, then it can't be all right,' said Sam. 'Here, have a hankie; oh, mine's all grubby. Have you got one, Seamus?'

Seamus scrabbled about in his jeans, his vast baggy poncho and his collarless shirt, but no hankie was forthcoming.

'My father always said that you could tell if a man was a gentleman or not by whether he had a clean, white handkerchief,' snapped Antonia, on the principle that attack is the best method of defence.

Lisa sprang to her feet in order to escape before the next round of shouting began.

'I just want to go away somewhere on my own for a bit,' she muttered, setting off down the fire stairs to that unfailing refuge in times of trouble, the ladies' toilet. She ignored the 'Out-of-order' sign on the door. That was only a desperate attempt on the part of the staff to gain a little privacy from the students. There were times, after all, when you frankly did not want to overhear the sorts of things that students talked about, or did, in ladies' toilets.

Sitting on the lid of a toilet, Lisa succumbed to a fresh burst of tears. Two police interrogations and two murders, all in one week, were beginning to take their toll. She sobbed for a while, giving herself up gratefully to the sheer awfulness of it all.

After a while, she began to feel better. She looked around for some toilet paper to wipe her swollen, tear-stained face, but was not surprised to find that there was none. She left the cubicle and gazed at herself in the mirror. Yes, she thought, I look terrible. Can't face the students like this.

Surely there would be some tissues in Johnston's laboratory, which was a little further down the corridor and well away from the haunts of all but the most persistent of students. Rounding a corner, she heard a voice above her head announce, 'I want to go back to Liverpool town, Liverpool town where I was born.'

It died away into a fruity gurgle. Lisa jumped uncontrollably. Disembodied voices were just a bit too much. She ran down the gloomy corridor towards the laboratory. The door was open, sending a blaze of welcoming light into the gloom. Rushing in, she startled Jacinta who was sitting at the main laboratory bench going through a large untidy collection of notes.

'There's somebody singing in the corridor. She sounds unhinged!' shouted Lisa.

'Quite right,' said Jacinta, recovering her composure, putting her notepad into the folder and shutting it quickly. 'It's only Margery Cavendish, you know she's been unhinged for years. Harmless. I was just thinking though, her voice is quite nice really and she sings all the right words as... wait a minute; you look awful. What's the matter? You can't have been arrested or you wouldn't be here. Did you escape? Or are you on bail?'

'I've had an awful time and nobody seems to care and I really would like a few tissues to clean up my face,' replied Lisa, taking a few deep breaths in an effort not to start crying again at this indication of concern. Honestly, she thought, with all this practice at interrogations I've had lately, I shouldn't crack up the first time someone says a kind word to me.

'Right. Yes. Definitely. Here.' Jacinta briskly hauled a box of them out from under the bench. Lisa was upset, but not too upset to notice that Jacinta had known where the tissues were without even having to look. What was she doing in here, anyway? She'd hated Johnston like poison. Was she looking for personal files as well?

Jacinta hurried on. 'Florence told me you were being held in Antonia's office so the police could interrogate you. How did it go? Is that what upset you? I mean, you seem really broken up; you shouldn't speak to them without a lawyer, you know.'

'Did you have a lawyer when they interrogated you?' asked Lisa.

'No, but then what was the point? I wasn't in on Sunday, and anyway they were looking for a man. I've got an iron-clad alibi for this latest one, not that they've asked me yet. I've been making myself scarce in here, it's the only way to get any work done with all this murder and mayhem going on around us. Have they got any suspects for this one, apart from you that is?'

How could this be happening, Lisa wondered, sitting calmly in a laboratory used by one murdered man and discussing the murder of another. She blew her nose and replied, 'I don't know really, they turfed me out of my office just as a student with a lot on his mind turned up.'

'A student suspect, do you think?' Jacinta began tidying up the notes. 'God, that's a worry. I hope they don't start blowing poisoned darts at us in the lectures, paper planes are bad enough.'

On a brighter note, Dr Cavendish's voice suddenly announced, 'When I was a young man in my prime, I'd fuck them young girls two at a time.'

Jacinta grinned at Lisa, who raised a puzzled face from her tissue.

'It's the air conditioning,' she explained.

'Well, I knew it could affect you,' replied Lisa, feeling a little better, 'but I didn't know it went straight to your head.' She was now fighting back the urge to laugh uncontrollably.

'No, you berk, that's the gin. The reason we can hear her so clearly from down here is that she's bellowing down the air-conditioning vent. God knows why, it's hardly the sort of thing you can ask someone. Honestly, I begin to feel almost sorry for Johnston. She must have driven him bonkers.'

'What did Johnston do to you?' asked Lisa bravely. 'He seems to have upset everyone else.'

'Way, hey, Santy Anno!' interposed the voice, giving a quite credible imitation of sweating lascars raising the anchor.

Jacinta, picking up a large pair of scissors, climbed onto the bench top, reached up and banged loudly on the main duct with the scissor handles. The singing stopped abruptly.

'That should fix her for a while,' said Jacinta briskly. 'You can see by the marks in the paint that Johnston must have done that a fair bit. I bet the banging would really echo in her office, if we can hear her singing so clearly in here.'

'But this is the first time I've ever heard her singing,' objected Lisa. 'And you can hear her in the corridor upstairs and in the tea room too; it's not just in here.'

'Well, maybe he just liked upsetting her. You know her office is the only one upstairs on this side of the lift shaft; it must be directly above. I bet this air conditioning duct doesn't go near any of the other staff offices, so he'd have a free rein to torment her.' She looked thoughtfully at the duct. 'He'd probably just wait for her to settle down to some work and then have a go. No wonder she hardly ever came in. I mean, can you imagine her complaining to Scott about hearing strange noises? She wouldn't have dared; he'd have had her in the funny farm before you could say involuntary committal.'

Lisa made an agreeing noise. The marks in the paint definitely looked as if somebody had been banging away on the duct with something fairly heavy. You could see dents in the metal.

'Johnston would have had a free hand and there wouldn't have been a thing she could have done about it. Motive for murder, don't you think?' finished Jacinta flippantly. She was now rearranging notes into large, red folders as she spoke, but Lisa couldn't really raise enough energy to ask her what they were or what she was doing with them.

Jacinta helpfully remarked, 'I'm arranging these so I can go and see Goldwyn next week about taking over Johnston's research programme.'

The last thing Lisa wanted was to talk about neurochemistry. She blew her nose again, and chose her words carefully.

'But those marks look as if they were made by something much heavier than the scissors,' she said, gazing around. There was nothing that looked quite right for the job in the laboratory.

'Did the police upset you?' Jacinta asked again, interrupting her train of thought.

'Well, they made all sorts of unpleasant insinuations about my relationships with students. But what really upset me was coming into the tea room, only to be told that they were glad to see me because they didn't want to cancel a class.'

Jacinta nodded sympathetically and stacked the folders up on top of each other. 'No chance of getting Scott to take on a few extras now he's not Administrative Head, I suppose?'

'Well, that seems to be one of the problems. No-one's seen Scott since he had a free and frank exchange with Goldwyn. It seems that he's sulking in a way permitted only to senior staff. Anyway, remember what he said to you when you suggested it? That his statistics were too advanced for him to go back to the introductory level.'

'He certainly has a great line in excuses, no contest, except Johnston of course. I mean, being dead is fairly hard to argue with. Well, tell me all about it, have the police got a suspect yet?'

Lisa sighed. It certainly had not been fun, although Wiesel's comments had been a revelation about the possibilities of academic life. She had got the distinct impression that the police thought she was covering up for someone.

When she related all this, Jacinta, now putting folders away while she listened, said, 'Well, it's a technique you know. They reason that while you're all upset about poor whatshisface, or more to the point about being narrowly missed yourself, that you'll be less careful and start saying things about the other murder that you'd otherwise regret. And perhaps you did hear a noise or see something unusual, perhaps you even saw who did it and decided not to say.'

She glanced at Lisa, who was too wrapped up in reliving the interrogation to discuss possible murderers' identities.

'Well, I can't understand why they can't just come out and say that, instead of doing the mock sinister bit. They're as bad as Scott, trying to influence other people's reactions. I wonder, you know, exactly who it was that that person lurking in the cupboard was really after.'

'You don't think they were aiming at you, surely?' replied Jacinta quickly. 'I mean, what set of motives could anyone possibly have that would include both you and Johnston? It just doesn't make sense.'

'You said yourself that murderers don't always have sensible motives,' returned Lisa. 'The police said that it might be a cover-up for the original murder.' She decided she definitely wanted to leave the subject of the interview before Jacinta could ask too many questions.

'But I don't care what the motives are, I just don't want to be one of the victims. Come on, let's get out of this place, it's spooky with all Johnston's things lying around in it,' she concluded.

'Yes, it is a bit, you almost expect him to come roaring in demanding to know who's been at his precious equipment,' replied Jacinta, evidently feeling a need to justify her presence there. 'He never would let anyone else in here. We all contributed to this marvellous set-up because he hogged all the research funds, as well as the external grants. I wonder how Goldwyn let him get away with it, he is on the Research and Grants Committee you know. But Johnston never let anybody so much as look at the equipment. I think Goldwyn might want me to take over the programme, and the first step is to familiarise myself with what's here. The police turned this place over and that plain-clothes bloke left the notes in a frightful mess. Goodness knows what he thought he was looking for. Come on, you'd better get on with things if you're giving an extra class at five.'

Jacinta firmly ushered Lisa out and locked the door behind her. Lisa noticed that she had got the spare key out of Gaelene and wondered how long it would be before she had one of her own cut. Jacinta took her by the arm and started off up the dim stairwell and through the tea room towards her office. Suddenly a figure leapt out of a doorway and grabbed her.

'It's Johnston!' shrieked a trembling Margery Cavendish. 'He's back! I heard him banging again. He's back to haunt us!'

## 15

The day of Johnston's funeral was brilliantly clear but cold. The weather was no comfort to Goldwyn as he searched for somewhere to park near the Cathedral. Where were all these people going, he fumed to himself. If they had any sense they would be where he wanted to be – in bed. At last he spotted an empty space and accelerated into it a split second before another contender.

'Yes, buddy, yes,' he nodded, lip-reading. 'I know, yes, my father said the same thing.'

Goldwyn made a last-minute check before leaving the car, shoes polished, fly zipped up, shirt tucked in, hat on head. Where in hell was his hat? No, hang on, he didn't need a hat for this one. Why do they do it, he wondered, I mean they take a perfectly good religion, road-tested for millennia, guaranteed for many more thousands of years and then they mess it about. They don't think up a new one, oh no, they get hold of somebody else's ideas and change them round and cause confusion. Did they do it to annoy, he wondered, or was it a subtle send-up?

This is not the right attitude, Nathan, he admonished himself. Here you are, going to the funeral of a good man, who was an ardent practitioner of this faith, so think positive. He got out, checked all the car doors twice, and set off. He wished fervently that Leah had come, but she had pleaded official business, an excuse which he suspected deeply, since he used it himself. Well, it certainly wasn't all fun being married to the Mayor of Cheltenham.

The crowds of people surprised him. He had not realised that Johnston was this popular. Was this where he had lavished the social skills he had so conspicuously lacked at work, Nathan wondered. Good god, the times he had had to smooth things over, and he had good reason to believe he had only heard about half of what went on. While he was musing, the crowd swept him into the main body of the Cathedral, where he spotted a pew empty except for Antonia Summerfield. So it was the right funeral. But who were all these people? On his way down the aisle towards Antonia, he sensed he was being watched. Glancing about, he saw Doreen Hubel, sitting lumpily at the end of a pew. How on earth could women let their figures go like that, he wondered. And come to that, didn't she ever take any time off? Couldn't a man go to a colleague's funeral without being stared at? In a haze of righteous indignation he strode on up the aisle.

Presuming Antonia would have located the Barry College pew, he sat down next to her. Now what on earth did one do, he wondered. He settled for looking as inconspicuous as possible, and trying to get comfortable. Whoever had built the pews had understood very little about the mechanics of the average human body, he thought, wriggling slightly to try to find the best average fit for knees, spine, shoulder blades, and head. On the other hand, a lot of these Christians were into suffering, weren't they? Perhaps it was deliberate, a foretaste of Purgatory, or possibly it served to keep the congregation awake.

From where he sat, he could see the coffin, standing on its bier, heaped with wreaths. How odd to think that Johnston's body actually lay in that. But did it? Somehow at all the funerals he had ever been to, he could never escape the feeling that the coffin was really empty and the Loved Ones were somewhere else. Who on earth had killed Johnston, he wondered, and why? He had reluctantly been forced to give up on the accident theory, once the impossibility of implementing it had been explained to him tactfully by a highly placed source. The fall-back option of homicidal burglars seemed to arouse nothing but scorn from that dreadful fat woman. It seemed so extraordinary that Johnston had actually been murdered. Goldwyn discounted the blackmail theories. He had never seen any evidence of it, as he had told the police. Moral indifference had reached such a pitch that it was hard to imagine a blackmail attempt succeeding. Nobody cared what other people thought of them. Why should they?

Still, the police had been fairly easy to deal with, compared with the other guy and the odd series of questions he had asked. He had been introduced as 'a colleague from the Commonwealth side of things', and the police had left. Warming to a fellow American, Goldwyn had tried to break the ice by asking whether his interlocutor was from Boston, but he had got the answer, 'Somewhere like that.'

Chilly, Goldwyn thought. The man had opened his notebook and stared into it for a considerable time before asking his first question. Long enough for Goldwyn to register that it was deliberate. As long as it stayed at this childish sort of level, he didn't really mind, but he wondered where it was going to end. He also wondered how many Americans the Commonwealth Police had working for them. Didn't you have to be a citizen, or something?

'You saw Johnston at a board meeting approximately two days before his death, is that right?' the man had asked, gazing intently at Nathan through horn-rimmed glasses.

'Those present are listed in the minutes,' Goldwyn had replied. On closer inspection, his spectacles seemed to be made of plain glass. Why was he wearing them, Goldwyn had wondered. To change his appearance? To make himself look older?

'Did you see him again at any time subsequent to that meeting?'
'No.'

'During the meeting, did anything odd strike you?' the man had asked.

Most things about academic life in Australia, and Barry College in particular, struck Goldwyn as being extremely odd. But he had decided it was probably not the moment to go into broader questions and had asked, 'Odd about what?'

He had anticipated the man's long, offensive stare and braced himself to sit through it. I know what you're up to, it had said, you're trying to put me off my stroke.

Eventually, though, Goldwyn's will had proved stronger and the man had been forced to say, with contemptuous distinctness, 'About Johnston's state of mind.'

'No,' Goldwyn had replied flatly. He was enjoying himself; years of childish games in academic meetings were finally paying off.

'Would Johnston have come to you, if he had been worried about anything?' the man had asked with some asperity.

Goldwyn had paused to give the appearance of considering this deeply. Finally he had said, 'That would depend on what it was.'

'Did Richard Johnston ever say to you that he was in fear of his life?' had been the next, rather melodramatic, demand. Reasonable in retrospect, Goldwyn mused. Yes, reasonable in retrospect, the man had, after all, been killed. It was in prospect that the whole thing was so extraordinary. Nothing that Goldwyn had ever seen appeared to produce any emotion in Richard Johnston. Would such a man have been in fear of his life?

'No, he didn't. Say, who are you anyway? Why are you asking me all these questions? I've talked to the police already. Isn't this a police job?'

He had regretted it as soon as he'd said it, because he realised he had given his advantage away. The man took it.

'No,' he had answered, and left.

Leah had immediately suggested a CIA connection. It was, she had said, perfectly obvious. Goldwyn had rejected this one and he remained unconvinced. From what he knew of the CIA, they were fully occupied in places like Libya and El Salvador, and he doubted whether a bona fide CIA operative had ever been near a one-horse town like Melbourne. Oh god, his backside was going to sleep already, how on earth would he last out the service. He writhed desperately round to a different position.

Antonia glanced up at him and smiled. She was quite pretty when she smiled, so he whispered, 'There seem to be a lot of people here.'

'It's a custom they have,' she whispered back. 'If there's a funeral for a member of the congregation, everyone makes a special effort to come.'

So that was the explanation. He gazed round the Cathedral. Why didn't they allow smoking in these things? Suddenly the priest appeared in the pulpit and the congregation rose to its feet. It was certainly a relief to get the weight off his backside and Nathan had a sudden insight into the reasons why Catholic congregations seemed to be in perpetual motion: standing, kneeling, sitting.

An unctuous voice intoned, 'We are gathered here today to remember our friend Richard who has gone to God.'

To his great annoyance, Nathan realised that this was going to be a modern service in English. If he had to listen to nonsense, he preferred it unintelligible. He had regretted the passing of the Latin Mass, if no one else had. Still, he thought, the next funeral – for that poor student – was almost certain to be in Greek, which was one comfort about the whole thing. Had the Greek Orthodox church gone trendy and translated its services into English? He devoutly hoped not, but it seemed he would shortly find out. That had been the end, when the Drug Squad had come to see him about Neos Kosmos's approach to working his way through college. On the whole, Nathan thought it very likely that someone was trying to terminate Kosmos. Probably an academic; it seemed some of the staff still had standards.

'Some of Richard's friends,' continued the voice, 'are here with us today, to celebrate their love for him in song.'

Nathan hoped that the worst was not going to happen, but it was. Three drably dressed women trudged up the aisle to take up their position behind the altar rails, carrying guitars. Do-it-yourself hymns, oh no, he thought, what next? Why on earth didn't they just pay someone who could sing?

In the stomach-churning pause while their twanging efforts to tune the guitars echoed around the vast Cathedral, Goldwyn tried to work out just exactly what it was about their clothes that was so, well, wrong. He fancied himself as a connoisseur of women's clothing, although Leah swore he drove her mad on shopping expeditions. Even at this distance he could see that there was nothing objectionable about any individual item. It was rather something about the way they were put together, the way they were worn, they didn't hang properly. He accepted that they might have reasons for dressing right up to the neck, but did there have to be quite so much navy blue and bottle green? It was a funeral, true, but he suspected that they dressed so as to be in permanent readiness to attend one. When they finally started strumming away at some crime against music, he realised that tolerance of other people's religious foibles could only go so far. He simply had to divert his mind from that cracked singing, so he leant down and whispered to Antonia, 'Are we the only two from Barry College?'

'Yes,' she whispered back. 'I don't understand it.'

Goldwyn looked down at the top of Antonia's neat blonde curls. Another one who wore her blouses buttoned right up to the neck. But this one at least had the taste to buy a rather charming little white lace number. Could she have nice tits under it? It was hard to be sure. The challenge of finding out diverted his mind for some time. What did one do, he wondered. How on earth did one get started with this sort of woman? He thought wistfully of his maternal grandfather, a disgraceful old reprobate who had seduced his way across Russia in pursuit of the fur trade. A light traveller, he usually got his clean underwear from the wardrobes of the men he had cuckolded. Now there was a man who would have been able to set about a seduction at a funeral with confidence. Goldwyn sighed. Being brought up as an American gentleman was very inhibiting.

Just as he was about to give up on the whole idea, the ghastly singing ground to a halt. The priest then made the unexpectedly useful suggestion that the congregation should each turn to a neighbour, take their hands, and say, 'God be with you.'

This caused a certain amount of confusion in the more crowded pews with people turning the wrong way and getting left out, but it was one Christian custom Goldwyn was happy to try. Seizing Antonia's hand, he gave it an affectionate squeeze, gazed into her startled blue eyes, and whispered, 'How ya doin there, chuck?'

With a muffled squeak, she snatched her hand back. Goddammit, he thought, I've blown it. The congregation sat down to listen to the eulogy. Most of it went past Antonia. In Johnston's few friendly moments, he had addressed her as 'chuck'. She sat, feeling terribly alone, thinking about the nicer side of the man who had been generally loathed. Why hadn't anyone else come? They might have done that out of politeness, at least. But politeness was definitely not one of their strong points.

Antonia had allowed herself certain hopes over Johnston, although her more realistic side had warned her they they stood very little chance of being realised. Still, when he wasn't thinking about work, politics, and money, he could be very charming. There certainly had been a fanatical side to him which she had found disturbing, but in these days of the Great Man Shortage a woman had to be prepared to overlook certain things. Let's face it, if she wanted to put into practice what she preached from the platforms of WUMP about the joys of family life, she'd have to get a move on. She was, after all, forty-five. Still reasonably attractive, but there were so few opportunities.

Now that he had gone, what was there left to dream about? What would give her days any sort of interest or colour? There was always work, but was work enough? She was beginning to wonder, even as Head of Department. That was another thing; she enjoyed being strong and competent, but at times even the strongest yearned to be looked after by someone stronger. Johnston, she had rather hoped, might have supplied something of the sort, but now there seemed to be no-one remotely likely to notice or care that she was a woman who wanted to be cherished.

Lost in her gloomy reverie, Antonia was luckier than Goldwyn, who found himself unable to distract his mind from the awful drivel which now filled the cathedral.

'While Richard had a powerful intellect, he also had his faults,' it began.

This, thought Goldwyn, is a eulogy? What if they actively disliked you? By a logical process that eluded Nathan, the speaker had now reached the point of reminding the congregation that Christ had died to redeem Johnston, and indeed all present. Really, he thought, is that all they can offer? At least a rabbi would have tried to draw some sort of conclusion about the man's life, what he had offered to the community, even, in extreme cases, what sort of things were better avoided. And why had he been so dumb with Antonia? He should have known you had to take it slower with those cool English types. Staring straight in front of him, with an expression of earnest concentration fixed on his features, he suddenly heard a repressed sobbing on his left. Good god, she was actually upset. Thinking moodily that the eulogy was enough to upset anybody, he produced a clean, white handkerchief and offered it to her. Rejected or not, a gentleman was a gentleman. To his great surprise she took it, and started sobbing into it with renewed vigour.

Comforting damsels in distress, he thought, was a move that could hardly go wrong, so he quietly wrapped his arm around her shaking shoulders. There didn't seem to be any perceptible objection to this manoeuvre, which was encouraging. Brotherly physical contact was at least a beginning, though he frankly doubted whether it would get any further. Still, you never could tell and his natural optimism began to flourish once more. Remembering that he was in a place of worship, he blended a touch of soulful concern with the concentration already on his face and kept gazing at the eulogiser. He appeared to be used to these sorts of goings-on in the pews because he stared straight through them and rambled mindlessly on, 'Among Richard's faults was the sin of pride, the sin of pride in intellect. At times he was impatient with his slower brethren.'

Whatever happened, he didn't believe he could take much more of this. Seizing his opportunity, he leaned down to Antonia and whispered in her ear, 'Are you all right?'

She nodded, her face covered with his handkerchief. Damn it, he thought, and tried again, more firmly.

'I really think you'd better go, come on, I'll go with you, I'm sure they won't mind.'

Suiting the action to the word, he raised her gently to her feet, nodded meaningly at the priest, and swept Antonia down the aisle. The priest nodded back and continued without a pause.

'But Christ, who died for all our sins, will extend his matchless compassion to Richard, knocking on the gates of Paradise and . . .'

Passing Doreen, Goldwyn remembered to give her a perfunctory nod, although he had an uneasy feeling that she had guessed what his plans were.

They were out in some kind of entrance hall. The outer door was open, letting in the fresh, cold air. What a relief. Goldwyn felt like throwing up his arms and bounding away down the steps whooping with joy. He was, however, diverted by Antonia throwing her arms around him and sobbing into his shirt. Conflicting thoughts rushed through his mind, many of them concerned with whether or not Antonia's make-up would leave tell-tale marks. Various people, mostly elderly ladies, wandered past the pair of them without sparing a glance. Apparently people sobbing their hearts out on other people's chests was accepted as standard practice in this neck of the woods. The sobbing slowed down a bit, and he gently peeled Antonia away. Yes, as he had thought, make-up everywhere.

'Listen,' he said kindly, 'I think I should take you home.'

'No, no, it's all right, my car's just near here and I don't live far away. I can manage.'

'I don't think you're in any state to cope with driving,' persisted Goldwyn. 'In any case, you shouldn't be alone in this state. Let me drive you home.'

He took her by the arm and they started down the steps with Antonia still protesting, 'But how will you get home?'

'Look, I can manage, don't worry about me. You and I were real friends of Johnston's. We've got to stick together. There weren't too many people smart enough to see the real man, you know. Which way is your car?'

'This way,' muttered Antonia, in imminent danger of a fresh burst of sobbing. It was such a relief to be taken care of, especially by someone large, personable and American, that she quite forgot that only on Thursday he had referred to Johnston as a bastard. She never quite understood how she found Goldwyn at the wheel of her car driving her home to her flat. So like Johnston in so many ways, she thought, these Americans seemed to have a certain natural courtesy that Australian men couldn't even come near. Once there, it was only manners to invite him in for a sherry and only manners for him to accept.

Once she was away from the enforced gloom of the service, Antonia's mood rebounded and she found herself sitting drinking coffee and sherry simultaneously and actually giggling with Goldwyn about the more extraordinary bits of the service. Once she noticed that his shirt was smeared with her make-up, she had insisted on making amends by cleaning it. He had helpfully offered to remove it. Things progressed smoothly from there. Not quite so smoothly that Antonia didn't have time to wonder how this would affect their working relationship. It might be quite useful, in its own way, she thought as she wrapped herself around him.

## *16*

One of the many problems of being poor, Lisa thought as she sat gloomily in the rain-sodden Monday traffic, was a plethora of soul-mates. The very rich, she had noticed in her avid reading of biographies (Lisa hankered to have her own biography written one day, but so far there was remarkably little to be put in it), the very rich were always moaning on about the lack of companionship in their lives. The poor, she mused, had to fight their way through their companions to get to the fridge. Who was it who had said the poor were always with us? Some Jewish philosopher, wasn't it? Well, he was right, especially when you were one of the poor yourself and were trying to get a bit of peace and quiet.

She briefly returned her attention to the traffic, which was remarkably slow, even for this particular section of Sydney Road at half past seven on a Monday morning. Another old lady hit by a tram, she supposed, and sure enough, there ahead of her was an ambulance. A very young-looking policeman was directing traffic. It's all true about the policemen, then, she thought gloomily.

Mind you, she thought, settling down to wait another eight minutes before inching forward again, the last house meeting had been different. The main topic of conversation had, of course, been The Murder. Nige, of the frizzy hair and luminous pink socks, had been totally unimpressed by the fact that an All Points Bulletin had gone out for Bennett. Shifting a large portion of mung bean sandwich to his other cheek, he had mumbled, 'Rot! S'usual plot 'gainst gays.' Swallowing the piece of sandwich with evident difficulty, he continued enthusiastically. 'Can't you see? He's just the obvious victim. That Johnston was up to his neck with the CIA, I just don't understand what a sensible person like you is doing with your brain.' At least Nige thinks I'm sensible, Lisa thought. I doubt that Doreen Hubel would agree.

'Can't you see it?' Nige had continued, waving his sandwich to and fro. 'That Australian-American whatnot thing he was in is a well-known front for spies. If you ask me, there's been a bit of an argument back at the ranch and Johnston was for the chop. Terminated with extreme prejudice. But something went wrong and they were rumbled. Somebody probably interrupted them, might even've been you. No, more probably that Timeo character. That would explain why he was done in as well. Anyway, you can't leave bodies lying around a nice tidy place like Melbourne without an explanation' (here he waved away an interruption from Kathleen to the effect that there were already large numbers of dead bodies secreted in odd spots around Melbourne) 'and poor old Bennett is the explanation. Bloody New Right, they've always had it in for gays.'

Lisa concentrated on her ideologically unsound Black Forest cake, purchased with her own money because the rest wouldn't have a bar of it coming out of the kitty, and reflected that not for nothing was Nige known locally as Marvin the Paranoid Android. Kathleen NiHoulihan was the first of the others to reach intelligibility.

'Jeeze Nige,' she said. 'If I didn't object to male-oriented psychiatry, I'd suggest you go and have a bloody lobotomy, all you men are the bloody same, I mean you've got spies on the bloody brain. Of course it wasn't Bennett, he's far too obvious, but it wasn't the bloody CIA either. All we need to do is forget about this spy stuff, get a pencil and a piece of paper, and work out who could have been there, who's got the motive, and we'll know who it was.'

Kathleen, despite the overalls which made her look like a rather lumpy apprentice plumber, was a student of computer programming and had the tidiness of mind that went with it. As she said, she couldn't in all conscience urge other women to enrol for Electronic Engineering because it was so bloody boring, but she seemed to be making a go of it. She had got her pencils, needle sharp as always, and written down all the names. The trouble had been, of course, that there were so many people for whom the assembled multitudes could think of motives, and so few for whom they could think of alibis. At least, that was so for Johnston. Precisely the opposite appeared to be the case with Timeo Danaos, so they had decided to leave him out of the problem.

'We do it all the time with engineering problems,' Kathleen assured the others. 'The answers come out so much neater that way.'

There was Jacinta, who had hated Johnston's guts. Lisa recalled that Jacinta had not set foot in Johnston's laboratory since shortly after she had taken the job at Barry, when he had apparently thrown her out and threatened her with violence if she ever went near his equipment again. Or was it that she had refused to work with him? Lisa wasn't sure; it had all happened before she had got her job there anyway. Odd that Jacinta was so keen to pick up his research now that he was dead, or was it some sort of revenge? She said she had been home at the time of the murder, but her only witness had been Muscles T Malone, her cat, and he apparently refused to confirm or deny her story. There was Bennett, now presumably on the run, whose live-in lover also refused to confirm or deny his alibi, and who had proven to have registered his body with the police as a dangerous weapon. An entirely understandable interest in self-defence, given some of his late-night activities, Nige had maintained. Klusky and Summerfield had confirmed each other's alibis – they had both been at the Epilepsy Foundation meeting. Lisa had no idea where Margery Cavendish or Reuben had been on that Sunday; Florence Lark, she presumed, would have been out doing something ineffably tedious and improving, possibly in the company of Peter Harwell. Seamus was on the scene, as usual, and denied having seen anything.

Lisa manoeuvred her car out of one traffic jam and into the tail end of another. Where were all these people going, she thought crossly. Why didn't they all stay home in bed for once? Didn't they know this was Australia, land of the long weekend? Her mind drifted back to the untidy, overcrowded kitchen, full of munching, arguing people, with Kathleen proceeding inexorably through her list.

'What about this Iain Scott guy?' she had asked. 'Christ, why is it that all men have names like Fart or Burp, or else they spell them in some bizarre way to stand out from the crowd?'

That had let to yet another diversion, with Nige roaring about sexism and even the quiet Colin raising his head from Rolling Stone long enough to say crossly that his name wasn't anything like Fart or Burp. But when order was restored Lisa had to assure them that Scott's presence in his usual spot at Moonee Ponds had been attested to by a large contingent of menacing-looking bookies with no reasons for doing him any favours.

'Time for a spot of dope,' suggested Colin, thowing down his magazine. This had been greeted with general acclaim and had had the effect of distracting them rather from the subject at hand, so they had never got around to extending their list to include Johnston's many other sworn enemies. His habit of keeping files on everyone he ran across had not endeared him to many, and there was a rumour that he had been the anonymous source of one or two particularly juicy, and apparently accurate, bits on the love lives of Admin staff which had appeared in *Lyrebird*.

Lisa and Nige had, however, got back to the subject of files at some stage during the evening. Odd, Lisa had said, how interested everybody seemed to be in those files.

'You ought to go in some time when it's quiet and have a quick look,' Nige had suggested, invading her personal space in a manner clearly proscribed by the Rules of the Collective.

'Oh give up, Nige,' Lisa had replied crossly, pushing him away and stomping off to her own room, but the idea had made sense. If Jacinta found those files so interesting, then there might just be something there to help Lisa shake off the awful suspicion she had been forming over the past few days. Surely, Jacinta couldn't have bumped off Johnston. It was ridiculous to think that there could be motive for murder in that lab. But someone had murdered Johnston, and the lab was the place to find out who, and why. It was silly. Jacinta wasn't a murderer, she was her friend. Anyway, there was the second murder. No way would Jacinta have been involved with exams and drugs. It would be best to find out, and clear her mind of this ridiculous suspicion.

So here she was, with the distant white towers of Barry College looming into view through the grey morning drizzle. What were those towers for? Nobody seemed to know. Nige was a silly bugger. Funny how fond men were of putting everything down to a CIA plot. Not to mention jumping on every woman they ever shared a commune with. Lisa had met a fair number of those young men from the Australian-American Education Association. At least, it had seemed that she had been introduced to several of them, but they were all so alike it was hard to be sure. They all came equipped with heavy glasses, firm but dry handshakes, and that curious walk that American men seemed to have. Johnston, Lisa remembered, had been distinctly unamused when Jacinta had suggested that he tell the laundry to put less starch in his knickers. Surely they couldn't be spies, nobody would be stupid enough to entrust anything important to them. But then again, perhaps they were being particularly cunning and trying to throw her off the scent.

Sighing, she concentrated on the daily miracle of parking the car round an S-bend between two enormous pillars in the basement.

Perhaps coming in so early wasn't a really good idea, she thought as she entered the darkened stairwell and groped for the light switch. The rest of the Rathbone Street Cooperative were no doubt still tucked up in bed, and here she was, facing heaven knew what. The old building creaked. Reminding herself that she was, after all, a logical positivist, she pressed the light switch again and ran upstairs, reaching the fire door into the tea room just as there was a majestic click and the stairwell was plunged again into darkness.

'Blasted time-switches,' she muttered, pushing the door open and gratefully letting it slam behind her. The tea room was not the nicest of places, but it was one up on the steel fire stairs. Lisa hurried down the corridor to the secretary's office. A quick and expert shove at the door, and she was in. Evading departmental security with a rapidity born of long experience, she quickly found Key 66. She covered up the signs of her visit, closed the door, and hurried back to the tea room. No danger of being discovered by a member of the academic staff, not at this hour, but it was always possible that Gaelene could be coming in early to finish some urgent typing.

She braced herself for another onslaught on the fire stairs – funny how different they were with the day switch on and no danger of being plunged into darkness halfway from one step to the next – and suddenly found herself outside Johnston's laboratory.

Quickly she let herself in, and stood with her back pressed against the metal of the door, heart pounding and mouth dry. There was, she reminded herself uncertainly, nothing to be afraid of. In fact, less now than there had been before Johnston's death. A notoriously early starter, he would have torn a strip or two off any staff member found in his precious laboratory. If he had had such an effect on Jacinta, he must have been ferocious.

Now to settle exactly what Jacinta had been so interested in last week, to try to answer the nagging questions that kept floating unasked into Lisa's consciousness whenever she thought of Jacinta in relationship to Johnston's murder. Jacinta couldn't be a murderer. And what was her motive? This Timeo business didn't seem to fit. Doubtless there was some perfectly ordinary explanation for Jacinta's behaviour, she thought with more hope than conviction. Perhaps, she thought with even less certitude, if she could find the file she could work out exactly what that innocent explanation was.

The filing cabinet was, of course, locked, but this didn't deter Lisa. A quick look in the top right-hand desk drawer, the place all academics put their valuables, and the keys were in her hand. Lisa's mind was racing, turning over possibilities. Could Jacinta possibly have overcome the vigorous Johnston? He had been a regular early-morning jogger around the campus; he said he usually aimed to get in an hour's work and a two-mile run before nine o'clock. And what could have driven her to murder? Anyway,

Lisa had been in that Sunday and she hadn't seen Jacinta. They usually made sure they had tea together on weekends as a protection of sorts against Johnston's dissertations on the essential irrationality of women and their need to find fulfilment with husband and babies.

Opening the filing cabinets one by one, she found herself confronted by row upon row of bulging files. This was not the usual academic's filing cabinet, in which lecture notes mixed with reprints out of journals and the occasional ancient sandwich. The files were all neatly indexed, and labelled with titles like 'cortical imbalance' and 'gonadal hypertrophy and sex hormone binding globulin'. If only she hadn't been so upset on Friday, she thought, she could have demanded that Jacinta show her what she was doing. Jacinta had been looking through red folders, and all of these were green. Where were the red ones? Hurriedly she opened and closed the drawers. They rattled and clanged as she pushed them in and out, but there was really nothing to worry about. It was still only eight o'clock, hours before anyone would come in.

No red folders. Distractedly she began searching through the cupboards, marvelling at the enormous array of expensive laboratory equipment neatly tucked away in them. No wonder there was never any money for her communication-skills workshops. At last, she swung open a small cupboard and was confronted with a squat, old-fashioned safe with a combination tumbler lock. Nige's CIA plot floated back into her mind. Perhaps it was full of sensitive information. Microdots, whatever they were.

Nonsense, she told herself. Probably hazardous chemicals or something. But where else could the red folders be? Unless Jacinta had taken them. She considered the option of just going away, quietly, and getting on with preparing yet another unexpected lecture. But she knew Nige would want to know what she had found. Bloody Nige. Who cared what he thought? How to open the safe, though, that was a problem. If only there was a stethoscope, she had vague memories of people in films listening to the tumblers drop through a stethoscope.

There must be a stethoscope in this place somewhere. She went back through the cupboards. Johnston probably had half a dozen sphygmos in the lab, but they all seemed to be that modern automatic kind that puffed themselves up and down while you just sat by. No use. Anyway, she had no idea what to listen for, and she had more than a suspicion that if she started listening to safe doors at this hour she could well go screaming mad before the day was out.

From some long-lost memory of cheap student film nights, Peter Lorre whispered, 'You can open half the safes in Germany with the date of the Nazi accession to power. The other half are easier, they just open to Hitler's birthday.'

Well, thought Lisa, it'd be worth a go, if only I knew the dates. Hang on a minute, she did know Hitler's birthday. It had featured in an introductory psychology lecture on the context of knowledge, or something equally peculiar. It was, she recalled, the simplest question you could ask in Nazi Germany, and if you didn't know it you were likely to wind up getting involved with the Gestapo. Well here goes, 20 to the right, 4 to the left, and 89 to the right.

Nothing happened.

Lisa stared at the safe. A minute ago she had wanted to run away, but now she was determined. What set of numbers had Johnston used? How on earth could she work that out?

Another voice rose up from the past. This time her old German teacher, explaining how Germans wrote the date. Month first, she remembered, then the day, then the year. Johnston was just enough of a pedant, she thought, it might just work. Anyway, didn't Americans sometimes write the date like that too? This is silly, she thought, but again she fiddled the knob – 4 to the right, 20 to the left, 89 to the right.

The safe swung open.

She stretched her right arm in, face averted. No way was she going to put her head inside that safe. It might just bite her. She pulled at the contents, and a heap of red folders fell onto the gleaming laboratory floor.

If she had wanted to know what interested Jacinta, well, here it was. She must have hidden them somewhere else while the police searched the lab. Or, more likely, just put them in the filing cabinets and put them back here later for security. Inside the first red folder was a neat lined writing tablet, covered in Jacinta's formal, upright handwriting. She left the red folders where they had fallen, and sat on one of the high stools to read Jacinta's notes. It had been quite a time since her struggles with physiology, but she recognised the familiar shape of the serotonin group of transmitters. Her memory was certainly getting a workout this morning. Jacinta had helpfully drawn a few circles and added exclamation marks on her diagrams, so Lisa began gradually to work out that these were artificially produced nervous system transmitters. As all psychologists knew, impulses were transferred from nerve to nerve through the brain and nervous system through the action of chemical transmitters. Different chemicals had different effects, and the body produced various sorts for various processes. Many psychotropic drugs worked by imitating these chemicals; they were similar enough to the real thing to be able to take their place, but different enough to produce some rather interesting effects. There were a few differences in these chemicals, Lisa was sure. All that talk about artificial psychoses, and that Civilein stuff, that made people docile and quiet. Could it have been true?

She began flipping through the pad quickly, but the notes were beyond her. In the middle of a maze of notes and diagrams was the notation, 'Christ, it might even work'. But what? thought Lisa crossly. If only I'd taken more physiology and less social psychology.

An almighty crash returned her to her surroundings. She dropped the pad and leapt up off the stool, narrowly avoiding spraining her ankle. Johnston's ghost, Jacinta with an iron bar, the police... There was silence. Nobody came in. She strained her ears. Nobody. Silence. No, not quite.

In the distance, she could hear an odd gurgling sound.

She tiptoed to the door and looked out. Nobody. Nothing. The old building creaked and groaned, and the odd gurgling sound continued.

Must have been outside, thought Lisa, a truck unloading or something. She glanced at her watch. Nine o'clock. Better tidy up in here and get back upstairs, she thought. Quickly she replaced the red folders, Jacinta's notebook among them, in the safe and twirled the tumblers. Better get upstairs and put this key back, she though, Gaelene must be here by now. But first, a quick visit to the ladies' loo.

As she walked down the corridor, the gurgling sound re-established itself. Peculiar, she thought, it sounds like water running, no, that's not quite it, something more sludgy. The sound continued, and as she put out her hand to open the swing door into the ladies' loo it became clear that it was coming from inside. Something must have broken, she thought, given way under its own weight and age. Better have a quick look, then call up Maintenance. Fat lot of good that will do, mind you, she thought, swinging open the inner door that led from a small row of basins and mirrors to the toilet cubicles themselves.

The sight that met her eyes was bad enough; the smell that assailed her nostrils had her falling back in revulsion against the swing door. A fat pipe in the ceiling over one of the cubicles had broken, and a disgusting brown sludge was glopping out of it in fat, overripe lumps. Beside it, a smaller pipe had cracked, and spat water, or what Lisa hoped was water, in a thin spray all over the ceiling and upper walls. Beneath it, something even more horrifying protruded from under the cubicle door. A wicker basket, and a foot clad in a sensible fawn shoe. Lisa rushed forward. The door swung in, and then stopped as it struck something soft but solid.

On the floor lay the unconscious form of Anne Goodbody. Tied tightly around her neck was one end of a pair of pantihose; the other end had a loop tied in it, and must have slipped off the pipe when it broke. Anne's face was a nasty purple colour and her breath was coming in uneven gasps. One of her legs was bent up beneath her in a very unnatural-looking position. Brown globs of goo slopped slowly from her face and body onto the floor.

Lisa held her breath and reached in, trying to get to the knot. Anne had fallen in an awkward position, with her head down behind the lavatory, but with an enormous effort Lisa got her fingers to the stocking. It was wet, and Lisa restrained herself from wondering what with. Frantically she tore at the stocking, but the knot had pulled tight in the fall. Her ideologically sound fingernails were hardly the right tool, but they were all she had. Finally the knot loosened, and the gasps took on a less frightening sound.

Anne showed no signs, however, of coming round. Lisa struggled to her feet and backed out into the corridor. Peter Harwell's office and surgery were on the next floor down. Peter, surely, would be here by now. He usually had a fairly full appointment diary in the mornings, or so she'd heard him say. She ran frantically down the fire stairs, now fully lit.

Bursting into the Medical Centre, she cried, 'Where's Peter? There's been an accident.'

Funny, she thought irrelevantly, how it seemed so natural to call it an accident, when it was almost certainly a suicide attempt. Even when you were trying to galvanise people into action, you didn't say anything too shocking.

Harwell's secretary looked up, and gave that world-weary smile that doctors' secretaries are so well trained in. The one that said, 'Well, dear, you do seem to be in a tizz. Now the doctor and I know that it can't possibly be anything important, because it's not happening to us, is it? But I'll humour you because I'm such a well-brought-up person.' Tricky to get that all in one smile, but she managed. 'Doctor Harwell is giving a lecture, dear,' she said slowly, as one would to a crying child. 'Would you like to wait?'

'Oh bugger,' said Lisa, 'Where?'

That threw the secretary.

'Upstairs in the Rom Harre,' she replied before she could think.

Lisa sprinted back up the stairs. At the far end, Peter was giving his annual talk on safety-in-the-workplace to the Articled Clerks.

'As you can see,' she heard him say, as he gesticulated towards an overhead projection, 'paper cuts were the most common cause of injury in this survey. These do not generally require anything beyond a bandaid and a cup of tea. Teabags should be available in the first aid box as a matter of urgency. Second on the list, assault by clients and their relatives...'

She dashed in. 'Peter,' she cried, 'Peter, come at once, there's been an accident.'

The Articled Clerks were not born yesterday. They knew what it portended when a psychologist rushed into a lecture screaming about disaster. Some took careful notes, others scanned the walls for the hidden cameras, still others took their own pulses.

Peter stared at Lisa. He could see that something really was wrong, but he had given this lecture so often that his brain was in neutral, protecting itself from the stultifying boredom. Gradually he regained full awareness.

'Not again,' he said in a peeved manner. 'Oh well, lecture cancelled – no, postponed,' He remembered the College's official view on cancelled lectures just in time. 'What is it this time?' he added, following Lisa out of the room. 'Not another stiff I hope. We doctors can't treat that, you know, and I'll be very peeved if you've disrupted my lecture for somebody who's already carked it.'

Lisa found that Peter was yet more peeved when he found that the patient was still alive but dripping with raw sewage. Trying hard not to retch, he checked her over carefully.

'Well, at least she doesn't need mouth-to-mouth,' he announced, momentarily becoming slightly less gloomy. 'She's bashed her head though, as well as that leg. Give us a hand to get her out.'

Together they held their breaths and manipulated the still form out of its awkward resting place.

'Wait with her here, will you,' said Peter. 'I'll organise an ambulance.' And he raced off.

Lisa sighed. This day wasn't turning out to be a good one at all, and it was still only half past nine. Wearily she settled down on the toilet floor to mount guard over the malodorous and bedraggled form. This wasn't in the job description, she mused. Her mind strayed away to the files she had read. It was only half an hour ago, but already it seemed like days. What did they mean? Was Johnston really onto something big? And what was Jacinta's interest? The research money, of course, but surely Jacinta wouldn't have murdered Johnston for the sake of research funds. There must have been more to it than that. She and Jacinta were fairly open about most things, but when it came to Richard Johnston she seemed to clam up. But murder was a bit extreme, wasn't it? Trying to hang yourself with a pair of pantihose in the ladies' loo, though, now that was downright peculiar.

Peter came back in. 'You can go now if you like,' he said. 'My secretary will send the ambulance men up, and there's not a lot more you can do.'

Lisa was delighted to be relieved. Coffee was the first thought to enter her mind as she left the loo, and she went straight back up the fire stairs to the tea room.

Antonia was there. 'You're late this morning,' she said. 'I'm getting a bit concerned about some people's attitudes to their jobs. And don't forget you're taking one of Johnston's lectures at ten.'

## 17

'Well, how was I expected to know she'd been standing guard over an unconscious student in the downstairs loos?' inquired Antonia aggrievedly, in reply to an accusing look from Sam. By this stage, Lisa was ensconced in Gaelene's office down at the front of the building. Her tears had been cleared up, she had been found an aspirin from Gaelene's bag, and Florence was making her a cup of herb tea. She had also managed to slip the laboratory key back into the key cupboard while Gaelene had been distracted in the search for aspirins.

Sam made no reply, which made Antonia feel even more uncomfortable. 'I've got a lot on my mind at the moment,' she explained lamely. The main thing, of course, was the new development in her working relationship with Goldwyn and the effect this was likely to have on the necessity of getting the departmental accounts to reflect life rather than art. She did hope that Goldwyn wasn't the sort to kiss and tell; it would be a bit hard to hold their secret over him if he'd already told half of administration. Unlikely, though. Goldwyn played his cards pretty close to his chest. This suicide attempt, too, she was a bit worried about that. Why had the girl chosen this building? Antonia felt oddly responsible. After all, it was to her she had come for help. She thought she'd done what she could. Did it have anything to do with Johnston, though? She sincerely hoped not. There were suicide attempts every year.

Antonia's thoughts were interrupted by the ringing of the tea room phone. Wearily she reached for it. It was Gaelene.

'That policewoman on the blower for ya,' said Gaelene in her inimitable secretarial style.

Antonia sighed, and walked slowly up the corridor to take the call. Lisa had been on the point of announcing that she was quite recovered and had better go and see about the lecture she was meant to be taking, but the thought of being in close proximity to one end of a potentially interesting phone conversation caused her to come over all woozy again and have to slump down in a spare chair.

'What?' she heard Antonia say with disbelief. 'All of them? For heaven's sake, why? What on earth do you mean, standard procedure? We're trying to run an educational establishment here, you realise.'

There was an angry quacking from the other end of the phone, and Antonia sighed again. Heavy sighs had always been a feature of academic departments, mused Lisa, and things were definitely getting worse. 'Oh very well,' capitulated Antonia. 'They've a lecture scheduled for ten o'clock; I'll cancel it and your men can see them then. Will that be soon enough for you?' And she rang off.

'Well, Lisa,' she said, turning around. 'You can stop pretending to be overcome; you've had a reprieve. Inspector Hubel has insisted that her people interview all the Medical Engineering students, right now. What the rush is all about I cannot begin to imagine. They seem to have no concept of how a tertiary institution operates, no concept at all. But I have made a concession in the interests of good public relations, and they will be taking over your lecture time to deal with the students.'

That was the best news Lisa had had all day. Not, of course, that there had been much competition. But she cheered up sufficiently to go off in search of a cup of coffee and a nice soothing chat with Sam Klusky. The other things on her mind could wait.

Even the disillusioned Doreen Hubel would have preferred a chat with Sam just then. In fact, the more she got to know about Barry College the more she came to feel that she had misjudged

Sam Klusky. Anybody who worked in an environment like that and still maintained some recognisably human characteristics was doing well, she felt.

Doreen was quite pleased with how the case was progressing, but there were still a lot of ends to be tied up. Interviewing the students was one of those things. She dispatched Wiesel with a group of six new recruits to take statements. The only things of interest that were likely to come out of that would go to the Drug Squad, which had already developed an interest in Neos Kosmos. Somebody would have to check up on this dratted suicide business too, although she was reasonably sure that had nothing to do with the case. At least, she hoped not. Like Kathleen NiHoulihan, Doreen was of the opinion that things were quite complicated enough already.

Not a lot for her to do now, until Bennett was found. She had intended to get the whole thing wrapped up on Friday night. After Neos Kosmos's shocking disclosures she had decided to arrest Bennett at once. A slight hitch in her plans had arisen when Gaelene had obligingly rung all four of Bennett's numbers, late on Friday afternoon, and had drawn a complete blank.

'Happens all the time,' she said. 'We can't find them, they can't find themselves. Sorry, you'll just have to wait till he comes in.'

'Oh,' said Doreen, 'I don't suppose you'd have a list of when his classes are on?' She had little hope that such a thing would exist or, if it did, that it would bear any relationship to reality. But she was following procedure. Gaelene confirmed her suspicions.

'Works of fiction, those lists are,' she replied cheerily. 'Anyway, Eddie hardly ever came to his classes, even before he was wanted on a murder rap. No chance of seeing him in here this side of payday.' And she turned away and went on typing flat out.

Doreen had accompanied Wiesel to the College, but she left him in charge of organising the interviewing. She had already heard a few stories from the more forthcoming of the students, and she decided, unwisely, that it might be a good idea to see if she could confirm them with Miss Kloof.

Miss Kloof assured Doreen at the top of her excellent lungs that she was, after all, a professional and deserved to be treated with respect.

'But hang on a minute,' said Doreen. She had had an old superintendent who had yelled at her like that, and she wasn't going to let it faze her. Come to think of it, Miss Kloof did remind her rather of that old guy, except of course for the moustache. Miss Kloof's was noticeably thicker. 'Just hang on there. Those people over in the Department of Psycho Whatever, they'd be professionals too, wouldn't they?'

Agnes let out a full chestful of air in a deep heartfelt sigh as she searched through a number of potential replies for the nastiest.

'Look, Constable,' she began.

'Detective-Inspector,' replied Doreen, huffily.

'Whatever,' proceeded Agnes. 'You got that story from a student, and I must say, Neos was not one of our better selection decisions.'

Doreen looked at her.

'I mean, he's very thick. We'd love to get rid of him.'

'Well, why don't you just fail him, then?' asked Doreen.

Agnes sighed. This was not the time to launch into an explanation of students' rights and their reactions to being failed. She continued: 'Look, we have an arrangement with the Department of Psychological and Sociological Inquiry. They agree not to believe what the students tell them about us, and in return we agree not to believe what the students tell us about them. It's called reciprocity.'

'It's called protectionism, more like,' retorted Doreen. 'This is exactly the sort of approach that permits these sorts of abuses to occur, where young people can be blackmailed into these disgusting liaisons. It's the only way they can see of getting out of this dump, and you can't blame them for taking it, but you can and should blame the people that are organising the system.'

Agnes gaped like a stranded fish, but drew a deep breath and waded in.

'Oh, very pretty,' she replied. 'But you can't get away with casting Neos as an innocent abroad, you know. That young man is warped and vicious, and has been since the age of six. Edmund Bennett did not teach him anything he didn't already know. Now stop wasting my time with this ridiculous hearts-and-flowers nonsense about the corruption of pure virtuous youth, and get out and arrest that man.'

Doreen left. There seemed little point in staying. The interviews with the students were now well under way, and there was still no sign of Bennett. It was a bit early for lunch, but Doreen was hungry. She walked out of the college gates towards the Victoria Market. The walk would do her good, and she could get something to eat and look for some bargains for the kids while she was there.

Lisa, meanwhile, was concluding another interview, just as unsatisfactory in its own way. She had padded down the corridor to get her coffee mug, planning to go and have a friendly chat with Sam. Lisa did worry from time to time about how much coffee she seemed to be putting away lately, but she decided that now was not the best time to try to cut down. Maybe at the end of term. Unfortunately, after locating her mug, she had paused in her office to look at her fern. Lately it had seemed to find the atmosphere far too damp and chilly, and developed an alarming list to starboard.

Too late, she discovered Iain Scott breathing down her neck. Scott's masculinity was of the aggressive, exuberant variety and he always stood far too close when he talked to you. Lisa glared at him and picked up her coffee cup in a marked manner, but non-verbal subtlety was lost on Scott. Opinions were divided as to whether this was because he was particularly thick, even for a psychologist, when it came to the practical aspects of interpersonal communication, or had simply learned that if you ignored people's wishes it was much easier to get what you wanted.

'I've come to wish you a personal goodbye,' he said with a self-satisfied smirk. He sat down and gazed at her expectantly, forcing her to ask, 'Goodbye? Why? Where are you going?'

'Well,' Scott began, 'confidentially of course, the Director has personally invited me to contribute to the new Revelations project. They need a sound thinker like me in at the ground floor, to get them off on the right track. So I'll be resigning as Head of Department and letting Antonia take over in my absence. It'll be good experience for her, after all. I'll still be on hand, of course, to offer her advice when she needs it. But of course, Nathan knows a good man when he sees one, and he certainly has made it worth my while. Much as I have enjoyed my contacts with the students,

I think it's a sign of psychological health to know when to move on, and Nathan has made some very satisfactory arrangements.'

I'll bet he has, thought Lisa. Iain Scott knows far too much about what's been going on around here to let him get pissed off with the place. Scott continued to burble on about the Revelations Programme, the oneness of all knowledge and the Yoga of Physics until the jolly lads on the site of Building 1988, already three years behind schedule, started up a piece of noisy equipment. This provided Lisa with the chance to make non-verbal signs indicating that she was terribly sorry to be rendered unable to continue this fascinating conversation, and Scott moved off.

Miserably, Lisa set off to find consolation with Sam. Scott had told him and sworn him to secrecy, not five minutes before battening on to Lisa.

'But maybe he will do some good there,' argued Sam. 'For many of our students, it would be a revelation to know where to find the library.'

'Oh, Sam,' said Lisa. 'That man is a useless fraud and for all we know an embezzler as well. He should get the boot, but does he? No. Bloody Goldwyn kicks him sideways into a cushy job and pays him a huge bonus. What's the bloody point of trying to be a halfway decent academic if it's only the crooks who get any rewards for it?'

'But,' Sam replied soothingly, 'look at it from Goldwyn's point of view. He can't sack Scott, or any of the others, or they'd sue. The College's solicitors say we couldn't stand the legal costs, even if we won. And he can't leave them roaming around causing havoc. So what's the cheapest and tidiest thing to do? Set up a silly new programme, give it a fancy name, and tuck them all away there where they can't do any damage.'

Lisa swallowed, and Sam looked at her anxiously. He perceived that she had never quite looked at the Revelations Programme in that light before. Sam sighed. It was not the first time in his dealings with Lisa that he had picked up the distant crystalline tinkle of another ideal shattering. What cruel fate had selected him, peaceful Sam Klusky, to be a shatterer of ideals, a squasher of pussycats... Oh hell, he interrupted himself. The bloody cat.

It had completely slipped his mind, what with all the work. Coming in through the ground-floor door just as a suicidal student, smelling rather too much of mortality, was being carried down on a stretcher (the lift having apparently gone the way of all lifts) hadn't helped him maintain a clear grip on things either.

Four-year-old Joshua had refused, amid screams and tears, to accept the finality of death. He had insisted that if Daddy couldn't mend the cat, he could at least go out and buy it again. It had been obvious, at the dinner table last night, that Joshua firmly believed that if only the adults around him really tried seriously they could get Captain Moggie back. He had supported the strength of this belief by going off his dinner. This hitherto unheard-of symptom in the Klusky family had panicked old Mrs Klusky. She had screamed, 'The child wants a cat, so buy him a cat! Joshua, for grandma! Eat your dinner, eat!'

Foolishly Sam had promised that yes, he would go up to the market and see if he could find a cat. Now he said dubiously, 'Do you know if they sell cats in the Victoria Market?'

'Cats? I don't know if that's actually on in Australia. I mean, I'm sure a lot of migrants eat all sorts of things, but as far as actually selling them...'

'No, I mean live ones, you know, pets.'

'Oh! Well, yes, I think they have kittens. Why? Are you all right? You look a bit pale.'

'Yes,' said Sam. 'Let's go on down to the market and look at the cats, I mean kittens.'

There was an awful lot to do, despite the fact that Lisa's lectures had now all been cancelled for the day. Automatically she stood on tiptoe to inspect the little tent of grey that lecturers call the sky, in the hope that it would produce an excuse. But no. Melbourne had moved abruptly from winter to summer. Suddenly the idea of wandering around the Victoria Market, munching hot dogs and looking at animals in the pet shops, was irresistible. It was very very different from standing guard over smelly, unconscious students, anyway.

The thought of getting out of the mephitic atmosphere of Building 1956 swayed her. She could go out and mingle with people who had never even heard of a sociological approach to sex and death, and wouldn't give a bugger if they did.

'Oh all right,' she said. 'Why not?'

On the way, Sam confided the ghastly truth about Captain Moggie, and still more his fear that if they did settle for a small and vulnerable kitten, Joshua might love it to death in very short order.

'The good thing about Captain Moggie,' he said as they headed for the northern gate, 'was that he was very big and very tough. It was just unfortunate that he was dim enough to sit in the way of the car.'

'Oh, I wouldn't worry,' said Lisa. 'Kittens are remarkably robust. And I doubt that Joshua will even notice that Captain Moggie has lost a lot of weight and got a bit more lively.'

The north gate was definitely a hangover from the prison era. People used the shelter of its massive bluestone blocks to sell all sorts of interesting things these days, and you had to be a bit careful about who you stared at. Today, though, there was a vendor positively demanding public attention. He was a scrawny middle-aged youth, clearly a leftover from the great days of student politics and protest marches. The leather jacket bore the marks of many scuffles with police, and the denim cap still bore its red star as a tattered reminder of the glories that had passed. This was Frank Hodges, perpetual student and self-styled revolutionary. He was marching up and down and shouting, 'Read all about it! Corruption in high places! Director exposed! CIA involvement!'

Lisa's attention was caught by the headlines, which screamed in cheery red, MURDERED LECTURER CIA OPERATIVE... STUDENTS EXPOSED TO RECRUITMENT ACTIVITIES... DIRECTOR COVERS UP ON RESEARCH MONIES...

They interrupted the expedition temporarily to buy one. Leaning on a pillar, they read about the small fortune that had been poured into Johnston's experiments by someone, Lexington Biosearch ostensibly, but (said the leader writer) definitely someone who had a deep interest in artificially induced passivity and resignation. Johnston was described as a senior CIA recruiting officer. No mention was made of homosexuality; in the worldview of Frank Hodges, the CIA was clearly on the side of the baddies, while any member of an oppressed group (which homosexuals equally clearly were) was automatically a goodie. Rather than attempt to deal with this ideological conflict, Hodges had chosen to ignore the homosexual angle entirely.

'I thought we already had TV to keep us resigned and passive,' ventured Sam, reading over Lisa's shoulder. 'And tertiary education for anybody who escapes. Anyway, now we know what Jacinta's after with all her rootling around in the lab. Half a million smackers, it says here. It's a good thing for her all round, this murder, isn't it?'

'But how could she have known that?' objected Lisa. 'We didn't know, did we?'

'Well, you did ask why she was such a fervent supporter of Antonia Summerfield yourself,' Sam pointed out. 'She's on all the committees, I bet you anything that Antonia set things up with Jacinta – you know, you organise the votes and I'll give you an inside run to take over this grant.'

'But,' objected Lisa, 'it was Seamus who rigged the votes. Even I noticed that.'

'Mm,' replied Sam thoughtfully, 'that probably just shows how clever Jacinta is. Catch her doing her own dirty work.'

'Look what he says about Goldwyn,' Sam continued. '*The police have described Goldwyn's attitude to them as "unhelpful"*. . . He'll love that.'

'They must have made that up,' objected Lisa. 'The police wouldn't say something like that to a student.'

'Yes,' said Sam, 'but I bet it's true all the same. Goldwyn is going to do a cover-up on this one. Nothing will happen. He'll find some other issue to distract Hodges with, and none of the other students will notice. I mean, nobody actually reads *Lyrebird* these days. It just sits around in the cafeteria.'

'Mm,' said Lisa. 'So you don't thing this "usually reliable source" that he mentions is anybody important?'

'No, of course not. What I think you might be worrying about, though, is who's that man in the peculiar suit reading a copy? I'd be worried about it if I wasn't allergic to worry.'

Suddenly he remembered the cat.

'Look,' he said hastily. 'I really must get down to the market. Are you coming?'

But Lisa was taken by the man in the camelhair coat, and was even more interested by the sight of Goldwyn leafing through a copy. It was always interesting to see something happen that you had only ever read about, and on this occasion Lisa was entranced by the sight of a man actually gnashing his teeth. Only momentarily though, because Goldwyn crumpled his copy and strode off.

'Oh,' said Lisa vaguely, 'no, look I really think I ought to be getting back.' She have been overcome with anxiety at being seen leaving the College during working hours; when you were applying for tenure it was surprising the small but important details that could be remembered against you. Besides the day was no longer as pleasant as it had been ten minutes ago. The grey clouds had regrouped and the bitter south-easterly wind struck icily from the Antarctic. 'I'd better get back to work.'

So Sam meandered on to the market on his own. Hovering vaguely at the pet shop, trying to decide between a tabby and a black-and-white job, he was rescued by Doreen. She was surprised to find that she was really quite pleased to have bumped into him, and the two of them completed the purchase of the kitten and adjourned to a nearby cafe. Over cappuccino and several hot jam doughnuts they compared notes on the difficulties of single parenthood, and apologised to each other more times than was strictly necessary for the unpleasantnesses that had attended their previous encounter.

While understanding, or possibly even friendship, was blossoming shyly near the Victoria Market, an entirely different sort of interpersonal experience was under way in the Director's office. Goldwyn crashed through the doors into his inner sanctum, shouting, 'Get Quinn in here!'

The lovely seventeen-year-old goggled at him. She had been assured that the position of personal assistant would not actually involve anything work-related. Purely personal, Goldwyn had explained to her. There was a need for a busy man to relax, to be assisted in winding down from time to time.

'Oh, for heaven's sake!' bellowed Goldwyn. 'Get Quinn, can't you?'

The seventeen-year-old began to whimper. With a deep sigh, Goldwyn's public secretary came to her aid.

'I don't know why I bother to do this sort of thing for you, when you've chosen to hire that totally incompetent little slut instead of paying me a decent wage. But anyway it can't be done. He's in a meeting.' she said sharply.

'Well, get him out of it!' he roared, glaring at the inoffensive seventeen-year-old with such ferocity that she retreated into the executive washrooms to sob. Goldwyn was further outraged by the discovery that the ink from the article had got all over his hands and was now leaving smudges all over everything he touched.

Quinn drifted unobtrusively into the scene of Goldwyn striving to de-ink himself while maintaining a high level of rage. A frail-looking, elderly man, Quinn was much tougher than most people thought, and had the added advantage of not really giving a stuff. However, it was wearing at times to be buffeted by Goldwyn's rages and enthusiasms, and he often wishes that someone more phlegmatic and English, or even calm and Indian, or, come to that, anyone but a yelling American, had got the job.

'Where the hell have you been?' yelled Goldwyn. 'Have you read this awful crap? He's gone too goddamned far this time. I'm gonna sue his arse off, I'm gonna kick him out of the College, I'm gonna burn him in effigy, no I'm gonna burn him for real, and then I'm gonna think of something really awful to do to him. Well, don't just stand there, read the bloody thing!' and he slung the battered *Lyrebird* over the desk at Quinn, while continuing to fume, mutter, and rub his palms.

Quinn peered over his glasses and slowly read the article. He had of course read it earlier; one of the important aspects of being a good Registrar was keeping an eye on what the student malcontents were up to. But he knew that taking his time would further increase Goldwyn's rage, and he wanted to see how he would react. In his spare time Quinn dreamed of writing a novel about a tertiary institution in Melbourne, and he was always keen to collect information that would increase its verisimilitude.

'Well?' demanded Goldwyn eventually. 'What are we going to do about Hodges this time?'

'Hodges?' asked Quinn blandly. 'But this article is clearly signed "Anne Tenney". Isn't she an actress or something? It can't be her.'

Goldwyn emitted a snort of rage that anyone so slow of wit could ever have become Registrar of a large metropolitan tertiary institution. The possibility that Quinn might be sending him up never occurred to him; he was, after all, an American.

'Well,' reflected Quinn. 'There's no point in suing him. He hasn't got any money. And anyway we'd have difficulty proving he wrote it.'

Goldwyn breathed deeply through his nose and calmed down to the point where his tightly wound black curls stopped quivering. He smiled grimly and said, 'Well, that guy has been a thorn in my side ever since I came to this place, and I've been doing a little bit of research of my own. Oh yes, indeed, I've been going through the regulations. Interesting things regulations, Paddy my boy, ever read any?'

Suspecting some sort of trap but having no idea what was coming next, Quinn compromised by nodding dumbly. Goldwyn retrieved a gold-tooled, leather-bound volume from his shelves and opened it to page 1313.

'It says right here, that this College has been opened for the purpose of providing a technical education for the sons of Presbyterian gentlemen. Furthermore, it goes on to say that any student may, at any time, be asked to furnish proof that he is the son of a Presbyterian gentleman. Hodges's father was a well-known commie atheist. And a goddamned pacifist. Now, Paddy, whaddya say to that?'

Quinn thought for a while, trying to choose the most diplomatic of the answers which rose to his mind.

'Well,' he said finally. 'Let's leave aside for the moment the problems of the legality of that sort of thing in these days of EEO. Let's just consider the fact that neither of us is the son of a Presbyterian gentleman.'

Much to his surprise, Goldwyn beamed at him.

'Well, Paddy, you're right there and that's the beauty of it! I've been right through this whole book and there is not one thing that even suggests that either the Director or the Registrar has to be the son of a Presbyterian gentleman.'

'Now that you mention that aspect of things,' said Quinn, 'there is a slight problem there.'

'Problem, whaddya mean, problem?' shouted Goldwyn.

'It's like this,' Quinn began. 'Barry has always had a Chancellor and it's always had a Registrar because, well, I mean, you always have them. But, um, well I think it was in Deakin's time, that he found the strain of being Chancellor and simultaneously trying to con the great Australian public into becoming a Commonwealth, well, just too much of a strain. Anyway Deakin got a Director in, just a six-month appointment at first, some struck-off lawyer he owed a favour or something, and it's sort of gone on that way ever since.'

Goldwyn was taking this big. Quinn had his horrified and undivided attention.

'So what I'm trying to tell you, Nathan, is that there isn't really any provision in the regulations for there being a Director at all. But um, well, the job's just sort of grown, and the Director started signing the qualifications around about the 1920s. Just the trade certificates at first, then the diplomas, and now the degrees. The Chancellor, of course, doesn't do anything any more, except the odd bout of shaking hands at graduation.'

Goldwyn was staring, white-faced.

'But, but,' he said. 'Don't the trustees notice? We're federally funded now. Don't they care? Why haven't they done anything to regularise the position?

'Ah yes,' replied Quinn, a happy smile lingering about his lips. 'Well I remember back in fifty-two. We had a secret commission into that, but it was all too hard. Nobody's actually noticed since. I mean, they're pretty boring things, regulations. Nobody reads them if they don't have to.'

Goldwyn put his head in his hands. 'Do you think Hodges knows about all this?'

'Believe me,' said Quinn. 'If he knew, the world would know. But the point is that if you start scrabbling through the regulations, he'll do the same, and somebody will be bound to notice that you don't exist.'

'But how can I get rid of him?'

'Well, I don't know if we can,' said Quinn thoughtfully. 'But we've got to get him off the murder and the funding quick smart. I think distraction is the best thing.' He thought for a moment. 'Of course! This attempted suicide, over in Building 1956. Ghastly place. Let's feed him a whole lot of stuff about insensitive staff and amazing workloads, and get him all worked up about that instead. The human angle, these bleeding-heart commies can never resist the human angle.'

Goldwyn sighed. Why had he ever come to this bloody country?

## 18

The police finally caught up with Edmund Bennett in the South Melbourne flat he shared with Denys. He had dropped in that Monday afternoon to exchange his luminous white jeans for the drill trousers with which he graced Barry College of Technology. Several days of patronising the St Kilda and South Melbourne conveniences had also rendered him in need of a bath and a freshen up, but he could see the minute he walked through the door that there was going to be little chance of that. At least not in his own scented bathroom with all his favourite body oils and creams.

'I suppose I've been expecting you,' he sighed when he unlocked the door to find two large constables ensconced side by side on the sofa.

'Where have you been for the past few days?' asked the policeman on the left.

'Oh dear,' replied Bennett with a faint smile. 'You sound just like my mother.' And he glared venomously at Denys's beautifully tailored back as it retreated into the deeper regions of the flat. 'Anyway, you know how it is. Nobody loves you when you're old and gay.'

'No,' said the policeman on the left, 'we don't know.'

When formally arrested and charged with the murders of Dr Richard Baines Johnston and Mr Timeo Socrates Danaos, he looked extremely surprised.

'Who?' he asked in bewilderment.

They drove him to Russell Street, where Detective-Inspector Hubel had just returned. She had enjoyed her meeting with Sam in the market, and was feeling refreshed and more positive about her job. The news that Bennett was waiting to see her confirmed this sudden and unfamiliar feeling.

However, the feeling didn't last very long. Bennett was a difficult person to interview. He was quite cheerful and open about Richard Johnston, although he vehemently denied having murdered him.

'Creepy old toad,' he said. 'I wouldn't want to get close enough to that bastard to do him in. Never know what might happen.'

But there was something odd in the way he flatly denied any involvement in the second murder. His attitude to the whole thing was not one she was used to.

'I don't know anybody called Timeo Socrates Danaos,' he averred. 'Who is he? Not that tall dark...'

'Timeo Danaos was a student of yours,' interrupted Doreen.

'Oh! A student!' He stopped and thought. 'Timeo...Timeo... No, I'm sure I would have remembered one called anything as silly as that. I mean, many of our students do have ridiculous names, but one does tend to remember them.'

Hubel sighed deeply. Another bloody drongo, she thought, don't any of this lot read the papers? If I'd done someone in I'd certainly be keeping an eye on the news.

'Don't you read the papers?' she asked.

'I like to use the weekends to catch up on my social life,' explained Bennett. 'And, frankly, the lighting in the South Melbourne toilet blocks is a disgrace, you couldn't read a paper in there if you wanted to. Not that most people go there to catch up on world events, it's more of a relaxation for most of us. But I digress. Could you please explain who this mysterious stranger is? Don't keep me on tenterhooks another moment.'

Doreen picked up her copy of Neos's statement, cleared her throat, and went on doing it by the book.

'I have here a copy of a statement from a student named Neos Kosmos.'

Bennett twitched noticeably, and tried hard to look nonchalant.

'Yes,' said Doreen. 'He's still alive. You got the wrong boy in the dark. Which was very unfortunate. Unfortunate for the student, unfortunate for his friends and family, and very very unfortunate for you.'

She paused. Bennett was looking very sick indeed.

'Yes, you did have an effect on Neos, even if it wasn't exactly the one you'd intended. You frightened him into coming to me. According to this sworn statement, Neos states that you were at the centre of a network of corrupt academic staff who have a practice of exchanging exam papers for sexual favours. He came to an arrangement with you along these lines, but things turned bad for you when he became involved with Johnston as well. How are we góing so far?'

She smiled at him. She knew that he was in a corner and that things were going well. Making an effort to retain his cool, Bennett replied, 'I am afraid that both you and Mr Kosmos mistake the nature of my feeling for him. A man who farts during sex is hardly likely to retain my affections for very long.'

'So you don't deny that you exchanged exam papers for sexual favours?' asked Doreen incredulously. She had always cherished a faint hope that this was not true. Her own educational experiences had been limited to St Jude's Convent and the police training school. Of course there had never been anything of that sort at the convent, although there had been a rumour about Sister Michael and the advanced chemistry exam. But nobody believed that, and besides, the girl who was supposed to have been involved had later gone governessing and got herself into all sorts of trouble, so you couldn't really believe anything she might have said. By the time Doreen had arrived at police training school, her thighs were already developing their resemblance to Dean Lukin's, and the attentions of the few lecherous members of staff were directed elsewhere.

'Oh, my dear,' replied Bennett airily. 'The whole education system is a joke, everyone knows that. We pretend to teach them things, they pretend to listen, later they pretend to have read up on the subject and thought about things. I'm just injecting a bit of fun into the system.'

Doreen stared at him in amazement.

'Oh, for heaven's sake, I'm not the only one, not by a long shot. You should follow up a few of those respectable old pussies in the Kindergarten Training course.'

'But...' began Doreen, and hesitated. She tried again. 'Don't you have any sense of pride in your work? Or responsibility? I mean, you're an educated man in a good position, you're meant to be educating these people, fitting them to take responsible places in society, and you just give out exam papers like lollies to any student who takes your fancy? Then you murder a student because he drops you for someone else?' Doreen was finding it all a bit hard to take in. Her interrogation of Sam Klusky, difficult as she had found it at the time, was fading to a quite pleasant memory in contrast with this one.

'I did not murder Neos. For heaven's sake, the vindictive little toad is still walking the streets. How can I have murdered him?'

'But you did murder Timeo,' insisted Doreen.

Bennett gazed silently at her, trying to remember what his rights were.

There was a short pause, which Doreen broke with a desparing sigh. Bennett recognised it instantly as springing from disillusionment with higher education and its proponents.

'My dear,' he began in a soothing tone, 'we are discussing Barry College of Technology. I find it difficult at times to maintain my faith in higher education in that place. As for murdering Johnston because he had won the affections of a stupid boy... well, if I had fifty cents for every time a large handsome creature had dropped me for someone with more money, I would be set up for life in Madras, where the most beautiful men in the world may be had for one rupee each. Nevertheless, and despite the fact that I most emphatically did not do Johnston in, I did wonder what the source of the attraction was. On Johnston's side, that is. I wouldn't have thought he was the type to go for Neos's somewhat empty charms.'

'Well,' said Doreen. 'That's really got nothing to do with it, has it? But I understand that Johnston was interested in the boy's potential. There's something in Kosmos's statement about the possibility of a job some time in the future.'

'A what?' asked Bennett. 'But that's ridiculous, I mean Neos is really dim. And the only people that Johnston ever employed were oppressed little research assistants. And he underpaid...' Edmund stopped as comprehension dawned.

Doreen had seen that look on people's faces before. It usually heralded something interesting.

'Yes? Well? What were you going to say?' she persisted, trying not to sound to eager.

'He was recruiting them,' said Bennett firmly.

'Recruiting who? For what?' asked Doreen.

'It's quite all right, I won't blow his cover,' replied Bennett. 'Of course, you'd have known all about it right from the start, wouldn't you? I know the police like to work closely with the security forces.'

'Eh?' said Doreen. It was hopeless. No matter how far ahead you started with this bunch, you always seemed to lose control of the conversation at about the same point. Here was a man who had been charged with two murders, and who knew that a student had made a statement heavily implicating him in both, and he seemed totally in control of the interview.

'That man with the execrable taste in tailoring,' inquired Bennett. 'I suppose he's the one, is he? Just sent down to see fair play?'

'He's talking about George Agnew,' Wiesel interjected. 'The man from the American Embassy.'

Bennett laughed. 'From the Embassy! That's not very subtle, is it?'

Doreen decided that the time had come for her to take charge. She had been very pleased with the way things were progressing so far. If she managed to get Bennett on two murders after only a week's investigation, her promotion should, surely, be in the bag. The way he was carrying on at the moment, though, he would be guilty but insane. Doreen knew that the Commissioner, a rabid believer in capital punishment, strongly disapproved of that sort of verdict and she wasn't going to let any frailty of Bennett's mind stand in the way of her advancement.

'Right,' she said firmly. 'So far you've admitted to murdering Timeo Danaos.'

'Have I?' asked Bennett incredulously.

'Certainly you have,' replied Doreen. 'Now you seem to have plenty of motive for murdering Johnston as well, so why don't you just admit to that too, and I'm sure it will go easier for you when it comes to sentencing.'

Now it was Bennett's turn to be astonished at Doreen Hubel's effrontery. He too had watched the old Crawford productions, but he had never actually believed that the police were crass enough to say those sorts of things. It was a day of disillusionment all round. On the other hand, though, it did seem that the evidence against him for the death of Timeo Danaos was pretty convincing, damn the boy.

'Look here,' he said. 'I don't know anybody called Danaos or Timeo or even which is his surname. I didn't set out to kill anybody.'

Doreen gazed back at him with the stolid stare that experience had taught her caused unwary suspects to start babbling.

'All right. I accept you've got a body that looks like Neos, but that doesn't prove it was me who killed him, does it?' demanded Bennett.

This was beyond dispute, so Doreen didn't bother to answer. Bennett glared at her. She realised that he knew perfectly well what she was doing and had decided to try and sit it out. From what she had learned of academics, she thought he probably wouldn't have had much practice at keeping his mouth shut, so she decided to wait a while and see if anything came of it. Let him think about what evidence Neos might have given the police. Her hunch proved right and Edmund began again after a brief pause.

'Okay, okay,' he said. 'It was me in the room and I was planning to give Neos a scare. Scaring is a very different thing from killing people, and it certainly isn't murder. You have to mean to kill people before it's murder.'

'Just how did you plan to scare him and why?' asked Doreen.

'A little pressure, for a brief time, on certain parts of the neck,' replied Edmund. 'Enough to terrify him, nothing more than that. It's a horrible experience, you know.'

I bet it is, thought Doreen. She continued her silent treatment, since it seemed to be working so well. Edmund had a nasty feeling that even if she believed his rather unlikely story there was still something called 'reckless indifference to human life' that they could get him on. He searched desperately for another tack.

'You must know by now that Neos threatened my life and attempted to blackmail me,' he said, thinking furiously. 'Perhaps you could charge him for that?' A hopeful note came into his voice, then died out again. 'I didn't want to lose my job. I'd never be able to get another senior one, not even at the Yularu College of Simple Life Skills. But,' he said emphatically, 'I did not murder this whats-his-name, nor did I murder Johnston. I never went near Johnston, I could not bear the man. Sweaty, for one thing. If I had murdered Johnston, I'd never have done anything quite so vulgar as hitting him over the head with an iron bar. I mean, can't you see that it's just uncharacteristically butch?'

Doreen shook her head. She had seen Timeo's body and she knew that Edmund could be quite nasty if he put his mind to it. Besides, she was beginning to recognise bullshit when she heard it from academics.

'How did you happen to know it was an iron bar?' she inquired.

'Oh come now,' said Bennett. 'Aren't we getting a little heavy-handed? Everyone knew Johnston had a big solid iron bar in his laboratory. We have had a lot of burglaries, as the local lot should have told you, and Johnston was convinced they were after something magic out of his precious lab, so he wanted to be prepared. He was always going on about it. Come the murder, he's found to have been hit with something heavy and the iron bar's gone. Your mob wander about the College asking whether anyone happens to have borrowed an iron bar from the lab. What does that suggest to you, Inspector Hubel?'

'You're pretty cool for a man who's already confessed to one murder, aren't you?' asked Doreen, in an effort to stop herself from thumping him for being so patronising.

201

'I keep telling you I did not murder that student and I don't believe I even touched him. It's just as likely that I pressed Neos's neck and he turned on Danaos himself in the dark. In any case, Inspector, what would you recommend? A little tearing of the hair? A spot of garment-rending perhaps? Or would you like to see a grown man cry?'

'A little more recognition of the fact that you have murdered two people might be appropriate,' Hubel replied. 'Have you no respect for human life? Don't you feel any remorse? Aren't you sorry for what you've done? Or anything?'

'I have not murdered two people,' shot back Bennett. 'You're not getting that past me in a welter of melodramatic nonsense. Anyway, as for respect for human life, you seem to be totally unmoved at the idea of Johnston's activities and what they undoubtedly meant in the lives of the young men he seduced and blackmailed into betraying themselves and their ideals.' He stopped, breathing heavily. 'At least they got exams and a good time from me.'

'Look, I have no idea what crackpot theory you have about Johnston or what the hell you are going on about. Let's get him charged and get on with things, Wiesel.'


At Barry College the following morning, there was a certain amount of relief in the air. Bennett's arrest had been announced on the early morning news programmes, and there had been a very bad, fuzzy, photograph of him in the *Age* that morning.

'Well, I'm certainly glad they've arrested the killer,' announced Reuben. He had now gone back to using water from the urn for his tea, risking death from electrocution quite calmly.

'Just a minute,' said Sam. 'We don't know he's guilty yet, he hasn't been tried.'

'What I don't understand,' broke in Seamus thoughtfully, 'is the motivation. Why would Bennett kill both Johnston and a perfectly harmless young student? I mean, he didn't have a thing going with this Danaos person, did he?'

'I think it's perfectly obvious,' sniffed Reuben. 'You know how unstable these poofters are. He's just cracked up under the strain. It could have been any one of us. Pure luck that he picked on those two. It's frightening, isn't it?' He turned a wild eye on a frankly disbelieving audience. 'All these years we've shared our lives with him, drunk tea together, gone to meetings, discussed students... It could have happened at any time!'

'Good heavens, Reuben,' retorted Seamus. 'I don't understand how a man can be a trained psychologist and still hold to all these ridiculous notions about gays. They're no more unstable than anyone else. Anyway, if he had been off his head, why come in on the weekend, kill Johnston, then wait a week, hide in a tute room cupboard, wait for the room to go dark, and kill someone else? Why not just leap on the nearest person? Why stop at two? He could have killed a dozen people and made a proper job of it while he was about it. There's nothing crazy about Bennett.'

Reuben was stung by the suggestion that his training in psychology might not have taken, as it were.

'I'm well aware that it is now fashionable to assert, on the basis of very little evidence and a lot of wishful thinking, that we all have a latent homosexual component. We all have a latent capacity for epilepsy too, but no-one suggests we all go and have foam-ins at the City Square. As for the rationality and reasonableness of killing people, which you seem to have been asserting, well all I can say is that there were a lot of people like you in Hitler's Germany.'

Seamus sighed.

'No,' he began patiently, 'I don't think killing people is a good idea at all.' Although like most people, he thought flippantly, I do have a list. And the way you're going, you could well be near the top. What was that quote about it being the little niggling faults in other people that really got to us? Something about halitosis being harder to forgive than adultery, he thought. 'I just think it wasn't completely random. He had a reason for killing each of those people.'

'But,' Sam put in unhelpfully, 'mad people have their reasons too, it's just that they're mad ones. Like they attack people who remind them of their mothers, things like that.'

'You're not suggesting that Johnston reminded Edmund of his mother, are you?' asked Seamus. 'Or that student, for that matter?'

'No, no,' explained Sam, oblivious to being sent up. 'That was just an example. I mean...'

Seamus interrupted. 'Well, if Johnston was the dead spit of Edmund's mother, it could well explain one or two things about poor old Eddie.'

The rush of laughter that this provoked broke off nervously as Antonia Summerfield strode into the tea room.

'Have you heard the latest?' she cried, a little inelegantly for one who prided herself on the retention of her accent. But then she was deeply disturbed by recent events. She had met Goldwyn crossing the campus only half an hour earlier, and he had stared straight through her as if she were a total stranger.

'What?' asked Sam.

'Well, it seems that poor Timeo got it by mistake. It seems Edmund said he killed Timeo by accident.'

'Whatever do you mean, by accident?' demanded Lisa. 'How can you find out that a tute is going to be held in the dark, go early and hide in a cupboard, come out and put a killer hold on someone's neck, and then tiptoe away, by accident?'

'No, no,' said Antonia. 'That's not what I meant. I meant he intended to kill Neos Kosmos, and got Timeo Danaos by mistake in the dark.'

'That's horrible!' said Lisa. It could have been me, she thought.

'Well, no matter who gets it in the neck, it's just as horrible for the victim,' objected Seamus with his usual maddening reasonableness. 'But that still doesn't answer our puzzle, does it? Why would Bennett want to kill Neos Kosmos? Although it does make more sense than killing this Danaos chap, who to all appearances was a harmless young lad.'

'He was studying Medical Engineering,' reminded Sam.

'Well, yes, harmless for a Medical Engineer,' amended Seamus. 'I mean, I presume that Eddie and this Kosmos character had some unsavoury thing going – they're the two most unsavoury things around this place so it makes some sort of sense – but whatever could have possessed Eddie to try and do away with him?'

'That's quite enough, Seamus,' interrupted Antonia, at her frostiest. 'It's not our job to deal with the motivations in this case, and I will not have idle speculation of this disgustingly ghoulish nature taking place in my department during office hours. The police force are perfectly well equipped to discover the details of the case, and if you're really interested then no doubt you can read all about them in the evening press, together with a lot of damaging speculation about the College.'

The assembled staff avoided each other's eyes. How was it that Antonia could make them feel like naughty schoolchildren, when they all knew perfectly well that her ghoulish fascination with the case was higher than anyone's?

She certainly was in a foul mood this morning, mused Lisa. Was it because nobody but she had bothered to go to the funeral? Or had she been upset by the service? Or something else that had happened?

'Well, it's all over now,' said Antonia briskly, aware that she had gone too far. She didn't want any of the staff to imagine she might be upset about something. 'The ad. for Johnston's position is all set to appear in Saturday's *Australian*, and we can start thinking about a replacement for Bennett fairly soon.'

And that's it then, is it? thought Lisa. All close ranks and carry on as if nothing had happened. Stiff upper lip chaps, and thumbs-up for the cameras. It wasn't right. Apart from the human angle of the danger to life and limb from quietly studying relaxation techniques, there were the other, frankly disconcerting, glimpses of the darker side of life at Barry College. Sexual harassment, CIA involvement, drug rings, exam stealing... was it all just to be swept under the carpet again, now that they had a sacrificial victim to carry all the sins? Well, yes, he had committed a fair few of them, that seemed fairly clear. But all the same, was the College really just going to carry on as normal? It certainly seemed that way.

Sam echoed her thoughts. He felt rather sorry for poor Edmund. The police could make your life rather uncomfortable if they wanted. Sam himself had managed; after all, he was used to that sort of thing. But Edmund didn't have an elderly mother living with him, and might not have had as much practice.

'But has Edmund really confessed to murdering Richard Johnston?' he asked.

Antonia paused. 'No, funny that. He denies having anything to do with that. Perhaps he thinks he'll get off lightly or something.'

'Well, it seems a bit odd to me,' said Seamus thoughtfully.

'How should I know?' said Antonia with a touch of asperity. There was nothing she would have enjoyed more than a good gossip session about all the thrilling but awful aspects of the previous week. But the responsibilities of leadership and the need to maintain decorum were uppermost in her mind. There were, after all, standards to be maintained. Blast that Nathan Goldwyn, men were all the same really, when you came down to it. 'Listen,' she continued icily. 'You all spend far too much time doing things that aren't in your duty statements and not nearly enough time doing the things that are.'

In the frozen silence that descended she wondered if she had finally gone too far. But it was true. Too much time fooling around. Discussing murders and playing Dungeons and Dragons on the computer were both high on her list of Things To Be Stopped. Discipline, that was what was needed. 'Perhaps,' she continued, trying to lighten the atmosphere, 'he really is crazy. Perhaps he can't remember murdering Johnston. I don't know how his mind works, or whether it's still working after whatever came over him to make him kill Johnston in the first place.'

'It is odd, though,' said Lisa, in an effort to maintain the lighter tone. 'I mean, nobody ever saw Edmund in here on the weekend. He was hard enough to find during office hours. It seems strange.'

'Well, there's nothing strange about that bit,' objected Seamus. 'Of course he came in specially. He knew Johnston would be in here and that the place would be pretty deserted. I mean when would you choose to murder someone? Ten o'clock Tuesday morning?'

Antonia was relieved to see that her remark seemed to have been forgiven. Or possibly accepted as the truth. She made another effort to restore some dignity to the proceedings. 'Well, I don't like this idle speculation,' she said in her best brisk voice. 'It's time to get things back to normal. I'd like a volunteer to clean the stuff out of Johnston's lab and sort through it.'

'I'll do that,' said Jacinta eagerly. It was the first time she had spoken, which struck Lisa as odd in itself. Definitely out of character. Volunteering to clean up somebody else's mess, particularly a man's, particularly Johnston's, was hardly in character either.

Nobody else seemed to find it odd. Lisa wondered if she needed to get a better grip on herself.

'Thank you Jacinta,' said Antonia. 'Now, we've got the duplicate exams to make up for Sociological Paradigms. I'll need a few people to work on that with me.'

Eagerly people volunteered. A concrete, straightforward job, one they could do successfully and finish with, that was what they needed.

## 19

After arguing about the Sociological Paradigms exam for a steady three hours, Lisa realised that she had learned something important. She had discovered what a mistake she had made in volunteering to stay around and help with it. She knew never to do that again, and that was, after all, a useful thing to have learned. Even Sam hadn't made that mistake. He had flatly refused.

'I've got an important appointment,' he had explained earnestly to Antonia.

He had not, however, been able to resist whispering to Lisa that it was to have lunch with Doreen Hubel. Partly celebration, partly to make up for the discomfort he had suffered last week. He had looked ridiculously happy.

A confused but earnest psychobabble dulled Lisa's senses like a slow-action nerve gas, and combined with the memory of too many narrow escapes to blunt her usual wariness, and somehow prompted her to ask the most foolish question of the morning. Imagine asking them how they knew which social institutions were important. Stress certainly did reduce the efficiency of high level cognitive performance. Of course they knew which social institutions were important, they had bellowed, and her role was to be a scribe for their inspirations on this topic. Still, she thought, she had allowed them to experience at least a moment of unity.

It was while she was sitting, Pentel in hand, waiting to scribe their thoughts, that she let her mind wander to what Jacinta might be doing. Of course, in typical smart-aleck style, she'd managed to avoid this little task. Tidying Johnston's papers instead. Odd, that. What meanings might the verb 'to tidy' encompass in Jacinta's mind, Lisa wondered, but just then Reuben poked her in the ribs and shouted, 'Anyone home? Florence has been dictating a question to you on the relative importance of family, work and the media in inculcating attitudes to drug addiction.'

Lisa began scribbling furiously. The convoluted result of the committee's democratic decisions was fascinating though mysterious. She wondered if anyone would remind the author that many of Barry College's students had begun their education in Turkey, Greece, or Vietnam and finished it abruptly on arrival in Footscray. Short, simple questions were really all they could comprehend in English. Glancing across, she saw that Seamus was wearing his best calm, professional expression. So that was all right, then, the final form of the exam would bear little resemblance to this, and some of the students might even understand it. Many a slip between meeting and word processor, these days. Well, if that was the plan, Seamus could put up with the screaming when the double-cross was revealed, multiplied by one thousand four hundred and twenty-three in the form of the final exam papers.

'Excuse me,' she said, rising to her feet. 'I've got an appointment.'

As she walked to the door, rejoicing in her temporary freedom, Florence and Reuben began fighting it out over whether Marx would or would not have approved of artificial insemination. Cries of, 'But it's the ultimate alienation from the means of production!' mingled with, 'Rubbish; you're mixing people up with tractors!'

Seamus's voice could be heard faintly across the din, suggesting to somebody that it would be a good idea to write the exam now and decide on the marking system later. Once they had a marking system, they could then resolve the issue of whether to deduct points for wrong answers.

'You know what happens,' he was reminding Clyde wearily as Lisa escaped down the corridor, 'when we try to get the gnomes over at printing to rev up the means of production. Total chaos. Remember the time when they collated some of the pages of the confidential report on sexual harassment with the Director's welcoming address to the freshers? We don't want another episode like that one, with half the students refusing to go near that bloke from Medical Engineering, and the other half queuing up to get into Mrs Golightly's self-expression class. Let's get the new exam into the printers as soon as possible, and sort out the details later.'

He hasn't got a hope of getting that lot to listen to reason, thought Lisa, as Reuben began to defend the oppressed printshop workers and Clyde wanted to know what was the good of an exam without a marking system. Still, reminding one and all of the printing section's well-known creativity should lay the foundations of a good excuse later. That'll teach him to go around saying that exams are trivial compared to murders; they hadn't expended nearly as much emotional energy on the murders as they werre doing at the moment.

They can get on with it, too, Lisa thought; I've done my bit, and at last there's a chance to get hold of Jacinta and see what exactly she's up to with Johnston's stuff. As a social psychologist, Lisa had always maintained a considerable scepticism about biological determinism. This scepticism had been made a lot easier by simply not reading much about human biology. Lately though, her easy complacency had been tested. The last time she had seen Johnston, he had been smirking in the tea room about the imminence of producing a tranquillising compound that could be inhaled.

'Half of you guys are on Valium as it is,' he had scornfully remarked. 'You accept oral tranquillisers because they've been around for ages, so what's the big deal about administering the stuff by a different route?'

They had tried to convince him that there might be some other ramifications to his research, but Lisa suspected that he had been perfectly well aware of that. The news about the sources of his funding had confirmed her fears. Now, of course, Johnston was dead. Had he been bumped off by someone who didn't want the air filled with calm? Or by someone who thought that the hand on the air-conditioning control marked 'Soothe' should be a different sex, colour, or creed than Johnston's?

What was it Jacinta had written on the notes? Yes, it was 'Christ, it might even work.' Might it? Could she make it work? That was a worrying one. Jacinta had some very firm ideas about false consciousness and Lisa thought she might have even fewer scruples about re-jigging other people's thought patterns than Johnston would have had. Then of course, there was the money, the fame, the lot, but could Jacinta get it going?

Lisa suspected she would have a darned good try. Johnston's notes were meticulous and he would have left precise directions as to how to manufacture it. But it seemed that nobody had found the recipe. Or if they had, they had kept it quiet. Of course, they might not have recognised it for what it was. The man who'd been wandering about the department had impressed her as someone who would not have recognised pure science if it had bitten him on the leg. Goldwyn would, though. What had he majored in? Biochemistry, wasn't it? From what she had seen of Goldwyn, the chance of the CIA getting out of their side of the funding contract was nil. Hell had no fury like a director on the trail of a research budget. He might well have whizzed in early one morning while all was in disarray and removed some of Johnston's notes.

Heading down the corridor towards the laboratory, she was astonished to find signs of maintenance in the gloom. You could say that for Antonia Summerfield, thought Lisa admiringly, she certainly gets things done. Those lights had been smashed for months, ever since the Student Orientation Riots. Scott had tried, or so he had claimed, to get hold of Maintenance, but without success. It looked as if a brisk memo, hand-delivered by the redoubtable Antonia, had finally worn down the resistance of the Chief Maintenance Engineer, who doubled as shop steward in times of industrial unrest.

Lisa was, however, wrong about the Maintenance men's motives for being there. They were not replacing lights, but were tramping about inside Johnston's laboratory. The various planks, ladders and tarpaulins lying about the darkened corridor were apparently intended to raise hope and divert suspicion. Negotiating the obstacles skilfully, Lisa reached the door of the laboratory in time to hear Jacinta saying, 'Well, that's about the last load. Thank you so much for your help.' In the background, Lisa heard the sound of folding money changing hands. She entered the laboratory, to find all the cupboards and the safe standing open and bare. Two large men in overalls were grunting under the remaining cardboard boxes. Catching sight of Lisa, Jacinta waved a cheery hello and sent the men off in the direction of her car.

'Oy,' said Lisa. 'Antonia won't be too happy when she finds out about this. She's spent her life's blood persuading them to leave their warm little cubbyholes and come over here, and now you've gone and hijacked their labour power. Incidentally, since when did "tidy up" mean "take all the papers home"? I assume you are taking them home.'

'Now, now,' replied Jacinta with maddening calm. 'I know you've spent hours having your head bitten off in the name of the New Order, but don't go all grumpy on me. After all, you did volunteer, you know.'

'Yes, but...' replied Lisa. 'The lights...'

'Oh come on, I wasn't going to hump all those boxes down to the car on my own. Anyway I'd probably have hurt my back if I tried, and I'm sure Antonia doesn't want any more industrial accidents this week. Have you seen the latest *Lyrebird*? Something about FEMALE HEAD LACKS HEART – FEAR AND LOATHING IN THE DEPARTMENT OF PSYCHOLOGICAL INQUIRY. You've got to hand it to Hodges, he's right up with the latest; he's got a special edition out on Anne Goodbody already. Anyway, you know Antonia doesn't really believe in the Maintenance men, she things they're in the same class as piskies or something, and who can blame her? Don't worry, she'll never know.'

'Hmm. So when you get these boxes home, leaving aside whether you have any right to take them, how are you going to get them out of the car again? I don't suppose you're planning to take all those men home with you and continue exploiting them, are you?'

From the shifty expression on Jacinta's face, Lisa deduced that this was indeed what she had in mind.

'It's definitely lunchtime, you know,' Jacinta said. 'I've got enough meat for a barbecue. Look, honestly, they're happy to do it. They'll have a good time, get out into the open air, eat sausages, drink wine, relax a bit, and do a trivial amount of work. These guys have muscles on their muscles, humping boxes is nothing to them. Now if you call that exploitation...'

'How do you do it?' broke in Lisa crossly.

'Get them to do things, you mean?' asked Jacinta, looking thoughtful. 'Well, it's hard to describe exactly, but I find if you fix them with a hypnotic stare and just keep repeating a simple command clearly and firmly, the average man will...'

'No, no. I mean how do you justify it to yourself?' Lisa snapped.

'Ooh, you are in a bad mood, aren't you?' Jacinta picked up her shoulder bag and started switching off laboratory lights, preparatory to following Nicko, Fred, and Nguyen from Maintenance.

'Look,' replied Lisa, standing firmly in the doorway and trying to keep her temper. 'If you take those men off to do things for you, they won't mend the lights and the rest of us will go on stumbling around in the dark. Poor old Margery just about has a fit whenever she meets anyone in this corridor. Be fair, she sees two of everybody most of the time, anyway. I mean, it's hardly correct-line socialism, is it?'

'Lisa, for heaven's sake,' said Jacinta crossly. 'Anyone would think you'd majored in naivety. How do you think Scott got his pergola erected? What about Goldwyn's swimming pool? Why all this morality anyway? If we're going to get into correct lines, you should realise that morality is no more than one of the many traps of our socialisation. It encourages us to put up with crap from men on the ground that they're less moral than us and they can't help it, poor dears. It means we don't make perfectly sensible use of the means to hand and we don't get things done. Anyway, those boxes weigh about a ton, and I can't shift them on my own.'

She moved impatiently towards Lisa, who stayed where she was.

'No problem,' said Lisa. 'I'll help you. And I'll help eat the barbecue too. I'm just hanging out for some nice unhealthy charred flesh. You can get awfully sick of ideologically sound food, you know.'

'Ah,' said Jacinta, stopped in her tracks, hoping it wasn't too obvious that she was stuck for a reply. 'Umm...look, really, that won't be necessary. Nicko and the boys will be happy to give me a hand. And besides, you're a weed like me, and what about your lecture?'

'If it's that much of a problem, which I doubt, why can't we pinch a trolley? And the lecture's been cancelled to celebrate Bennett's departure. Besides,' she added, taking a bit of a risk, 'you said yourself that you were getting into a bit of experimental work and that I should do the same if I ever expected to get a promotion. I might take up one of the aspects of Johnston's work.' A look of alert suspicion flashed across Jacinta's face, and Lisa suddenly wondered whether she knew someone else had been reading Johnston's notes. 'That wouldn't worry you, would it?' she added, in order to confirm her suspicions.

'No, no, not at all,' Jacinta said, recovering not quite quickly enough. 'There seems to be a lot of work to do from my reading of the notes, and science could do with a little more sisterhood. Anyway, if you want to come home with me, fine, but the Maintenance blokes are coming too. I can hear them clumping up the stairs now.'

Nicko bounded into the laboratory.

'Look, sorry love,' he said in a furtive whisper. 'We got all that stuff in your car for you all right, but one of them Printing peanuts trapped us into promising to deliver some boxes of urgent stuff to Accounts. Like he was a bit dark on us, you know? He thought they'd gone months ago, but then he found the place where Franco puts things he doesn't want to deliver. Dunno how he did it, but there you are. Looks like our little trip will have to be called off. Sorry, but that's how it is round here. Got to toe the line sometimes.'

'Oh,' said Jacinta. 'Well, that's all right. I'll get Lisa here to give me a hand. Thanks for all your help.'

Nicko looked at Lisa, stuck out his lower lip, and said, 'Geez, love, I dunno how you two girls are going to do it. Them boxes feel like they got lead in them.'

Lisa waited, fascinated, for Jacinta to remind Nicko that they were both women. But she merely gazed fondly at Nicko and asked, 'Well, do you reckon we could have the trolley, what do you call it? That moonwalker thing that goes up and down steps. Then we could just drag the really heavy ones onto that.'

'Sure love, I'll tell Fred to put it on top of the rest of the boxes. But I reckon you'd be better off waiting till termorrer and we could come and give youse a hand. Still, gotta rush. That peanut was gunna dob us in if we didn't get that stuff over there today.'

He charged off down the corridor and Jacinta flicked off the laboratory lights. As they negotiated the obstacle course in the corridor, she muttered, 'All that fuss about the blasted lights and you can see they never had any intention of fixing them. They've only left the stuff here to keep Antonia quiet.'

'Tell me just one thing,' Lisa replied.

'Anything, possum, just run it past me,' returned Jacinta, wrenching at the fire door.

'Why don't you give Nicko and his mates a course on sexist language?'

'What? Oh, that. Well, you've got to give them the idea that they're actually useful and necessary if you want them to do things,' answered Jacinta airily.

The two went down the back stairs in silence.

Getting out of Barry College, however, had a cheering effect on both of them.

'I've always admired the way you do it,' said Lisa. 'You really should come and give a talk at the next Behaviour Mod Conference. I can see it now: "How to train large men to be helpful". It really would go down a treat.'

Jacinta smiled and revved the station wagon through an orange light, narrowly missing a motorcyclist in a deaths-head helmet who was turning right across her bows, and said meditatively, 'Well, I think you might as well make use of them. After all, men are there, aren't they? I see them as a vast, untapped natural resource, like...'

'Heroin and radiation?' suggested Lisa.

'Nature put them all there for a purpose,' said Jacinta firmly. She turned right at the 'No Right Turn' sign blocking off Deeming Street. 'But I look forward to a time when relations between the sexes aren't quite as fraught as they are now, and try to think of the large men I meet as serving an apprenticeship against a happier time. There you are, number forty-two, we're home.'

'Do you always drive like that?' asked Lisa, thankful to be in one piece.

'Well of course I do, I'd never get home otherwise, would I? How about a spot of lunch? It'd give us the strength to cope with all this lot, and I could give you a brief history of how the Carlton City Council brought enlightment and blocked streets to the inhabitants, whether they wanted them or not.'

Lisa shook her head.

'No,' she said firmly. 'I think we'd better make a start at least. I mean you know how it is, you sit down, have a glass of red, and before you know it it's half past eight and there's nothing for it but to send out for pizzas.'

'Right,' replied Jacinta. 'We'll have to get changed, can't hump boxes about in our good go-to-work jeans. I've got quite a few old pairs, I'm sure one set would fit you.'

Transformed into a worker, complete with hair tucked up under a Mao cap, Lisa looked worriedly at the narrow corridor. Jacinta's house was full of bits and pieces, and a hatstand and tall cupboard made the corridor even narrower.

'I'm not sure all of these boxes will fit through here,' she called.

Jacinta came back from opening the back door and wedging the shed open. 'Mm, we might have to shift the cupboard, what a bore. But let's see if we can manage to hoik things around it, or maybe even over it. We could even put the boxes in the corridor and unpack from there if we have to.'

Jacinta would go to an enormous amount of effort to avoid work, thought Lisa absently as she went back out to the car for the first box. The boxes were fairly small really, and she decided that the Maintenance men had greatly exaggerated their weight as a way of getting a cash bonus out of Jacinta.

The idea of exaggeration wore off after the first two or three staggers down the corridor. The boxes were an awkward shape which meant that the two of them had to take an end each and shuffle carefully, one forward, one backward, along the cramped corridor. The trolley proved unable to cope with the right-angled bends beloved of nineteenth-century builders. There was silence except for grunts and heavy breathing as the two struggled with their load, and deep, relieved sighs as they dropped the boxes in the shed. At about the fifth box, Lisa began hoping rather urgently that Jacinta might go back to the idea of lunch. But Jacinta seemed to be thriving on the work. With her long blonde hair in a ponytail and dust smeared down one side of her face, she bounded indefatigably about. As they walked back for the sixth box, she confided that she had done some judo in her youth.

'It's all in the technique, you see,' she explained. 'You don't have to be particularly strong if you know what you're doing.'

Lisa was a little surprised.

'You've never mentioned all this judo stuff before,' she said. 'I wouldn't have thought it was quite your thing.'

'Well, I saw what happened to poor old Eddie when people found out he was registered as a Work of Art or whatever it was. Anyway, I discovered at quite an early age that yelling is so much kinder to your hands.'

She hauled a box out of the back of the station wagon and balanced it on the tailgate, gazing meaningfully at Lisa, who decided to play for time. She needed a breather anyway.

'But Eddie wasn't just arrested because his body was registered as a dangerous weapon,' she objected. 'It was what he did with his body, and uncomfortably close to me, might I add, that was the problem.'

'Oh yes, yes,' replied Jacinta impatiently, 'but you remember after the first murder, how everyone was rushing about casting suspicions on everybody else, when the news got out that Eddie had a black belt in karate, that really brought the amateur sleuths out of the woodwork. Now I think that isolated Eddie, so that when whatever it was happened between him and that student, he couldn't discuss it with anyone in the Department. So he went right off his rocker and took an extreme solution like trying to scare him and then knocking him off.'

Lisa stared at her. Could this ponytailed moral theoretician really be the same person who had sat for hours in the tea room discussing the finer points of rigor mortis with anyone who would listen?

'What about Johnston, then? How did the isolation make him murder Johnston?'

'Well, he denies that. I don't know. Look, this box is getting awfully heavy. How about giving me a hand to get it inside, eh?'

Silence took over, as they struggled to lift the box and manoeuvre it down the narrow passage. This was a particularly heavy one. Probably full of Johnston's lead-lined underwear, thought Lisa. The box slipped in her hands, her foot caught in the carpet and she staggered sideways against the hall cupboard, dragging Jacinta and the box with her. The cupboard rocked solemnly on its base, and for an awful moment Lisa thought it would fall on her, but it settled back again. Then the door swung slowly open and a long, heavy piece of metal fell with a solid thud onto the box. It was a very clean piece of metal, and it didn't have any suspicious brown stains on it, but Lisa knew at once what it was. She could see how ideally suited it was for bashing on air-conditioning ducts, not to mention...

She looked up. Jacinta was still holding the other end of the box, breathing heavily. Her face was about three feet away. Lisa regarded her carefully. There was a short pause.

'Lunch?' said Jacinta.

## 20

A wave of relief swept over Lisa. Clearly Jacinta wasn't planning on bumping her off right now. On the other hand, the suggestion of lunch was a brilliant way of getting people into kitchens, with all that kitchens implied in the way of anti-flesh devices. She stood rooted to the spot until she realised that Jacinta was talking to her.

'Put it down,' she was saying. 'Can't you hear me? Put the box down, my arms are coming out of their sockets. I can't stand here all day and I can't put it down unless you let me.'

They put it down and Jacinta strode off towards the kitchen, while Lisa leant against the wall feeling dizzy and wondering whether she should just go while the going was good and the front door was open. Gradually curiosity reasserted itself. If Jacinta had left the front door open, she clearly wasn't planning to knock her off, and she obviously didn't expect her to race off and tell the police. These all seemed to be good signs for a person who desperately wanted to know the inside story of Johnston's murder. If, as seemed unlikely, Jacinta hadn't done it, then her possession of the weapon showed that she knew a great deal about who had.

Besides, the smells and noises from the kitchen seemed distinctly lunch-like. Odours of burning sausage and steak, the plop of a cork being withdrawn, the shuffling of notes being pushed to one side, the crash of books being shoved off chairs, and cried of 'Get out of it, you stupid cat!' lent a reassuringly normal air to a house which had begun to seem like the set of 'Amityville Horror'.

Lisa ventured down the corridor and into the kitchen.

'Oh, there you are,' said Jacinta. 'I was just about to send out an expedition for you. Find the loo all right?'

'Eh? Oh. Yes, no problem, I found it.'

'Good-oh, well we're about ready here. It's interesting that whenever other people come round, it sort of motivates you to do something about the tidemark of books and notes and things and rediscover some of the furniture underneath it all. Mind you, some of the things you rediscover in the fridge don't bear too much thinking about, but then nobody could work at Barry College unless their blood was stiff with circulating antibodies, so I don't imagine it'll worry you.'

While she was talking, Jacinta was whirling around retrieving knives, forks, plates and so on and assembling them on the dining bench in her kitchen into a reasonable facsimile of lunch for two. Lisa climbed onto one of the stools and decided that this was no time to open a discussion on the role of Natural Killer Factor in the human immune response.

'All right, is it?' asked Jacinta, plonking the mustard onto the dining island and leaping onto the opposite stool. 'It can't be too bad, poor old Muscles was quite interested. I had to discourage him from carrying it off.'

Lisa nodded, and made enthusiastic noises through a mouthful of steak. It certainly was a change from mung beans, you could say that for it at least. Jacinta, she knew, subscribed to the serious school of eating, meaning that she tended to go at it like a Tasmanian wielding a chainsaw on a redgum. She dipped a charred sausage into the Moutard a l'ancienne and wondered how to open the conversation. She could see that the swiftly chomping Jacinta was rapidly thinking of a thousand and one innocent domestic uses for a heavy metal bar of the exact dimensions to fit Johnston's head wound, and she really wanted to hear the truth. More than that, she wanted to establish quite firmly that Jacinta wasn't going to decide to bump her off next.

'Well,' she said finally. 'Why did you do it? I mean, I know you hated him, we all did. But murder is – well – a bit extreme, isn't it?'

Jacinta grinned and reached for the bottle of red.

'Some would say extreme, I suppose,' she replied. 'Others might say messy, nerve-wracking, or downright inconvenient. Refresh your glass? Good. Anyway, why do you think I killed him?'

'It was nearly getting brained with the murder weapon, or a very good facsimile of same, which set off my nasty suspicious mind,' said Lisa, carefully removing bits of cork from her glass. 'So come on, tell me why you did it, I'm . . .'

'Dying to know?' asked Jacinta. 'Surprising how these turns of phrase come back at awkward moments, isn't it? Is that wine badly corked? I keep meaning to buy a better bottle-opener, you know, one of those jazzy Swedish numbers which just blows air into the cork or something and it all happens by magic.'

'The murder,' said Lisa, gazing at her implacably.

'Ah, the murder. Good grief Lisa, what a gundog you are. Well, I suppose anything could be discussed hypothetically, couldn't it?' asked Jacinta, evidently deciding that at the worst it would be Lisa's word against her own. 'If I had killed Johnston, which I didn't, I might have had a lot of reasons. But specifically it was the job.'

Lisa listened in silence.

'You know how I was going to spread my talents for teaching large men to be useful? At the SEC? How I was just about dead set to get that Senior Research Officer job? Now that would really be something. Completely open slather to investigate the effects of working near high voltages on the human nervous system. And a million-dollar research budget to do it with.' Jacinta sighed and spread more mustard on her steak.

'Yeah,' said Lisa. 'I was that jealous too. I mean, getting out of Barry College. I can't think of anything I'd rather do. So what did Johnston have to do with it all? Was he going to make trouble? What's it to him where you work? I mean, he'd never liked you. I would have thought he'd have been pleased to see the back of you.'

'Well of course, his first line of attack was that he wasn't going to have a red like me wandering around the SEC disrupting all that vital power for communications and satellites and god knows what else. I couldn't believe he was serious at first. I explained to him that the La Trobe Valley was thick with Trots, Maoists, Marxists, you name it. They'd all be far more left-wing than me, not to mention being far more into the practical side of revolution. You know, blowing things up. Have some salad.'

Jacinta dolloped Greek salad onto Lisa's plate and returned to devouring her lunch.

Lisa pondered this unlikely story. She had the distinct impression that Jacinta's socialism was more theoretical than practical, and tended to lapse when it came to things that concerned herself. It sounded too far-fetched. How could a political disagreement over an appointment get as far as murder?

'That's crazy, though,' she protested. 'What the hell did it have to do with him? And how do we get to the bit where you bashed his brains in? It just doesn't make sense. Why should he care so passionately about the La Trobe Valley?'

Jacinta sighed. 'Let's keep the party polite, shall we? Remember, what we are discussing here is his reactions to my leaving Barry, nothing to do with people getting their brains bashed in. I must say I got a bit hot under the collar when I heard that he had gone out to lunch with two SEC blokes and lectured them on my many personal failings. Silly thing to do. I had a call from my inside contact at ten past two asking what on earth it was all about. So I wandered on down to the lab to have a word or three. That was when he explained that he didn't give a damn about the La Trobe Valley, he was worried about the Company.'

'The Company?'

'Lisa, where the hell have you been? Sitting on a toadstool at the bottom of somebody's garden? Johnston worked for the CIA. They funded all that work on neuronal transmitters, and let's face it, they still are. You won't see Goldwyn stopping the programme. But Johnston was having trouble coming up with the goods. If those experiments were going to work, he needed help fast. I was the obvious choice.'

Lisa was stunned. She had read *Lyrebird*, and heard the rumours. But somehow it hadn't sunk in that her colleagues were – had been – spies. That was what the CIA meant to her. She sat there, opening and closing her mouth, but nothing came out. Jacinta swallowed some more claret and continued.

'Basically, he told me that his need was greater than the SEC's.'

'But hang on, he couldn't just tell you not to resign because he needed a research assistant. And why didn't he get you in on the project when you first arrived and were all keen?'

'Have some more bread,' replied Jacinta.

'I don't think I'm hearing the whole story,' persisted Lisa.

'Well, few people have,' was the reply.

Lisa ate a piece of fetta and tried another tack. She didn't know how things would turn out, but it couldn't be any more dangerous to find out the full story.

'Why was he so keen to take you on in the first place if he didn't want you at the time?' she asked.

'Ah, the old "get women in on the soft research money, exploit their brains and give them the boot" trick,' said Jacinta, gazing thoughtfully out of the window.

'But you published an article with him, didn't you?' persevered Lisa. 'That was just after you got to Barry, wasn't it?'

'It most certainly was not,' snapped Jacinta. 'It was just before I got there, that's the whole point.'

Lisa was frankly puzzled. The whole point of what? If Jacinta and Johnston had been happily co-authoring scientific papers even before she had joined Barry College, why had Johnston refused to work with her when she got there? Until last week, that was. She ate in silence.

Jacinta sighed and remarked, 'I suppose Seamus has told you some garbled version of it all. Does that man have nothing else to do but gossip? Well. Very few people know about this, but when I was a postgraduate student I was very short of cash. So I used to analyse people's data on the university computer for a small fee. That's how I met Johnston. Charming? You wouldn't read about it. Doubled my hourly rates and said he didn't want to see me being exploited – hah – and there was more in the kitty. I bet there was. He used to bring the data over to me and he'd chat away for hours. Of course my PhD was in that area and I thought I might learn a bit from listening to him. Well, I certainly did, but not quite what I'd expected. But how was I to know back then? I ran the programmes, made a few suggestions about the statistics, and then, next thing I know, there's Johnston beaming at me, reprint in hand with both our names on it, saying will I be his research assistant?'

'You mean you didn't even know he was going to put your name on it?'

'No, really all I did was give a little bit of advice and run the analysis he wanted, purely mechanical, it was on a fee-for-service basis, not as collaborators.'

The conversation was suddenly interrupted by a large ginger cat leaping across the bench and snatching up a rejected piece of meat as it flew past.

'Muscles! Get out! You know you're not supposed to do that!' bellowed Jacinta, setting off in pursuit of the cat which had retreated, snarling, under the sofa. Jacinta reappeared, muttering, and sat down on the stool again.

'Now where was I?' she asked.

'Johnston was kindly offering you a position as a research assistant,' answered Lisa helpfully, relieved that Jacinta was now talking again and the risk of imminent death seemed past. 'But that's unusual, isn't it? Not to mention out of character. I mean, putting your name on the article like that?'

'Well, no, it's not done, not with hired help,' said Jacinta, 'and it really should have put me on my guard. But it all seemed so wonderful, going straight from study into a job in the area I wanted to work in.' She sighed. 'One of the problems with psychoneurotransmitters is that the chemical compounds are so tricky that you need really big equipment to tackle it. You know, ultracentrifuges, mass spectrometers. Well, the first morning of the new job, I was that keen, I bounded into the lab at five past eight. Everything was open but Johnston wasn't there, so I wandered about, waiting. Gradually it penetrated that, for the measurements I'd put through the computer, the lab was, well, sparse. So when Johnston came in, the first thing I asked him was where the measurements had been done. I mean, you can't hide a mass spectrometer, and there wasn't one in that lab. Well, did I get a shock. He hit the roof and told me my job was to run the statistical side of things, not nosy around in laboratories.'

A horrible suspicion dawned on Lisa.

Jacinta nodded. 'Yes, he made them up. I checked and there was nowhere he could have got them done in the time. They take ages to do.'

'But I always thought you started at Barry as a lecturer, not a research assistant.'

'Well, the minute that happened I knew I had to get out. I couldn't prove it but I didn't want to be in it. The lectureship was being advertised. I hadn't applied because my friend Johnston had told me I wasn't sufficiently experienced to get a lectureship, but after that I went straight out and put my application in.'

'But he always said he'd got that job for you.'

'Bullshit,' said Jacinta. 'In fact, he tried to stop them appointing me. But they said I was perfectly well qualified for the job, and if he had had no qualms in taking me on as a research assistant he had no right to object to my being offered a lectureship. So yes, I was his research assistant, but only for six weeks, and of course I didn't actually work for him in that time.'

'So you just stayed home for six weeks?'

'No, I was too keen and conscientious back then. I'd do it without batting an eyelid now of course. But when he wouldn't let me get my sticky fingers onto a test tube I used the time to do some of the background reading I should have done before. And that got me even more concerned. As far as I could see, the brain just doesn't work as simply as that. Well, he got very cross and tried to convince me that it does. He was certainly convinced, I could see that, but at the time I just couldn't accept that a compound with a simple chemical structure could be inhaled, cross the blood-brain barrier, and exert those effects on humans. Whatever it did in animals, it doesn't mean it would work that way on people. Well, he gave me a very meaning look and said, "What makes you think I haven't done the preliminary tests?" Not at Barry College, I thought, because the amount of screaming and plotting that went on was incompatible with there being anything soothing in the air conditioning.'

'So he made some Civilein?' asked Lisa.

'Oh yes. He just couldn't be bothered going through all the safety tests with animals and so on, so he made that stuff up and hoed right in on people.'

'So who had he used? Not the students, surely,' interjected Lisa.

'Well, if he had it doesn't work. No, I'm not too sure, but he did give me the impression that someone, somewhere fairly close, had been given a sniff of the magic stuff and had lain about looking beatific. Anyway, I got out of being his research assistant back then, and when he started up again I had no intention of getting back in. I told him I was going to the SEC and he'd have to take his chances on developing Civilein without me. After all, he'd done all right on his own up till then.'

'What happened then? I mean why, hypothetically, did you get to the point of bashing his brains in?'

'That's where it got really, really nasty. He gave me one of those sharklike sort of grins and said that I was the last person he would have seen as opposing research on ethical grounds. I asked him what he meant and he explained that if he'd re-run the tests on that old article and discovered that I'd made up the analyses it would be his duty to expose me, wouldn't it? Of course he'd got a lot more equipment by then and anyway it would have been his word against mine.'

'So what did you do?' asked Lisa.

'Well, I decided to play for time, so I agreed to do at least some of it so that I could get out of there and think. I said I'd have to do some reading first because I'd been doing all that stuff on electromagnetic radiation for the past few years and the human memory can only hold so much.'

Lisa finally noticed that her bum had almost died and she was getting cramps in her calves from sitting on the preposterously high stools Jacinta favoured in the kitchen.

'Look, if this is going to be a long story, do you think we could go and sit on the sofa?' she suggested, wondering if the cat would be sufficiently satiated not to be interested in the human ankle.

'Right ho,' said Jacinta, gathering up various bits and pieces in order to re-establish the party. In the living room, Lisa was horrified to see the iron bar leaning casually against the gas heater. Bloodstains, she reassured herself, she'd never kill me here, they'd prove it through the bloodstains on the carpet.

'Well,' continued Jacinta, 'after this famous moment when Johnston revealed he had the goods on me, or so he thought, our whole relationship took on a new character. He turned positively charming, like he had been at the beginning. But this was different, he was so sinister behind it. Or maybe I was just noticing better this time around. He used to do things like wait for me to come in to work and then appear from his lab and start innocent conversations with me, offer to make me cups of coffee, open the door for me – all that sort of thing. But all the time he was smiling away to himself to indicate that he had me in his power. At the time it was downright unnerving. Have a Macadamia nut?'

There was a pause. Then Jacinta continued, 'You see, I got onto my mates in the SEC right away and told them Johnston was circulating ridiculous rumours and I thought he was going off his head. They couldn't really care less, they thought all academics were a bit weird. I had the ear of a few senior people and they had the Equal Opportunity people breathing down their necks anyway, not nearly enough senior women and I would have redressed that a bit. But that wouldn't have stopped Johnston from trying, not a bit of it. The other side of it was, suppose I didn't get the job? You know how it is, it's all promises, promises, but nothing is certain until you get the letter with the Chairman's signature on the bottom. If I got stuck in Barry College, I could see I was going to get some invitations I couldn't refuse.'

'But couldn't you have sabotaged the results?' asked Lisa. 'Why would he have trusted you?'

'I think he'd thought of that, and he realised that he could check a proportion of the work, which would still leave him ahead, and then the shit would really hit the fan if the results didn't add up on what he'd checked. Of course, I would be a useful scapegoat too, insurance if he couldn't get it to work. All my fault. Anyway, my plan of life didn't include staying at the SEC for ever. I was planning to go there, get administrative experience, publish some stuff on applied psychology and then come back into academia at a rather more senior level. The life of a senior academic,' remarked Jacinta thoughtfully, 'strikes me as idyllic.'

'True,' murmured Lisa. She wasn't entirely convinced that Jacinta was being strictly truthful about the nature of the damaging story Johnston had had on her. But Lisa was hardly in a position to question Jacinta's accuracy, and the way things were going, she wasn't sure she could cope with the whole truth. Another retreat from principles, she thought with an inward sigh.

'And now, with Johnston out of the way, I can get on with the Civilein project when I finish at the SEC,' continued Jacinta. 'But as long as Johnston had the old research notes in my handwriting, there was no way I was going to get another academic job. I mean the Port Hedland College of TAFE is not the biggest institution in Australia, and I suspect they have quite a waiting list as it is. So it all added up to the fact that I had to get hold of the bloody things.'

She shifted her weight back on the sofa and there was a distant snarling from under the cushions.

'Oh shut up, cat! I don't know why I put up with it, it's like coming home to a small furry terrorist,' she muttered crossly.

Lisa thought privately that it was a case of like attracting like, but she thought that now was not the time to communicate that insight. Instead she asked, 'But how did you know where he kept them?'

'Well, I decided that he wouldn't be silly enough to leave them in the filing cabinet, because he would have realised that the odds of me coming to look for them were pretty high. But I'd been in his lab a few times, because we both taught that Psychoneuronics course, and I'd had to check a few things with him. I'd noticed that safe hidden in the cupboard, so I thought that might be a likely spot.'

Lisa emptied the last of the red into their glasses, sensing that the moment of truth was coming up.

'So how were you going to get in there when he wasn't around?' she asked.

'Well, I knew that he took an extra long jog on Sundays, and there was early Mass as well, and everything added up to him being out of the way until eight o'clock at the earliest. I'd done a bit of reconnoitring about spare keys, not too easy with Gaelene watching everything like a hawk, I can tell you, but I knew which one and where it all was, so I could get into the lab.'

'But how were you going to break into the safe?' asked Lisa.

'Well, I hadn't really thought that far ahead. You have to realise that I wasn't thinking too clearly at the time. I thought I could maybe fiddle with the tumblers, or if he came in, I was even going to have a shot at persuading him to give the stuff back. What a joke! Besides, it wasn't only the blackmail problem I was worried about, though that was pretty high on my list. Some of the things he'd said in that tea-room row about Civilein had worried me quite a bit. I mean, he'd explained the organic chemistry of the thing to me so, unlike Reuben, I knew perfectly well it wasn't just the "fatuous fantasy of a Fascist". Anyway, when I got there, surprise, surprise, the lab door was open but he wasn't there. Must have ducked out to the loo or something. Well, that was the end of the fiddling with the tumblers idea. I could hardly start fingering his safe if he was going to come back at any moment. So I went in to wait for him, and started reading some of the papers on the bench. Now those papers are very interesting. They were notes on the purification and large-scale manufacture of the accursed muck and I haven't seen them since. They disappeared at about the time that man in the brown suit appeared on the scene. And Johnston definitely had CIA backing for that work on abortion and psychosis, and it was that which led on to the whole idea of social control by inhalation of chemicals.'

She paused to drink some more wine and look up at Lisa. Her audience, while hanging on her every word, was also wondering why Jacinta hadn't removed the papers herself.

'Just as I was taking that in, he grabbed me from behind and started yelling and shaking me. He was really angry and I didn't know what he was going to do. I was so frightened, being grabbed without warning in that spooky old building, and angry too, that I just lashed out behind with my elbow. Got him in the stomach. He must have slipped on the lino, remember how clean and slippery everything always was, and he fell over and hit his head on the bench.'

'Oh come on now,' said Lisa, forgetting about being tactful. 'That's an old one. Nobody believes that one any more. Anyway, I read the reports and the man's head had been completely stove in with an iron bar. You aren't going to tell me a dingo did it, are you?'

'No, no, give me a chance.'

List felt distinctly pale and wondered whether Jacinta was going to give her a demonstration, but she could see that her friend was off in her own world, reliving the thing.

'It's a funny thing, you know,' Jacinta continued thoughtfully. 'The number of times I mentally rehearsed killing that man, I would have thought that all I would have felt when I stood over his body was a pure sense of triumph. No way. Standing over one's fallen enemies is most alarming, but especially when you notice that they're still breathing. I realised that the minute he came round, he'd accuse me of having attacked him. But worse, he'd know that I'd seen the full documentation on how to manufacture the staff and that there was no way I'd keep quiet about it. It's reasonably easy to leak things to the Press, even if you have to do it overseas. Sooner or later, the news would even filter back to Australia and possibly cause a few inconvenient things like public debate on what was being manufactured in our Colleges of

Technology. That would give him a lot of good reasons to have a go at me in any way he could, and all I'd managed to do was add a perfectly good charge of assault to the dirt he already had on me. I mean I'd already had quite a bit of being given the idea that I was in the man's power and I didn't want any more of it. I guess maybe if I'd been a bit calmer I might have been able to think of an alternative, but I decided that there was no way I could let him come round. I dragged him out of the lab, across the corridor, and into the lecture theatre.'

'Whatever for?'

'Well, I figured the CIA would be sending somebody along to have a look at things. If I left him lying dead with all that documentation out on the desk they might get a little too nosy.'

'But why would it have come back to you? There were lots of people with plenty of motive to kill him. Look at Scott for instance, not to mention poor old Margery.'

'Well, I was thinking about it from the point of view of someone who knew perfectly well who had done it. Um, well hypothetically, you realise.'

'Oh yes, definitely purely hypothetically,' agreed Lisa hurriedly.

'Christ, it's freezing in here,' said Jacinta, getting up and lighting the gas fire. 'How about a little music to lighten the tone? I've got a really good new record called Songs of Mediaeval Women.'

Plangent dulcimers had the same effect on Lisa that fingernails scraping on blackboards had on students. She shook her head and continued, 'It still doesn't make sense. Couldn't you have stolen the papers? Or burnt them, or something?'

'If you meant the Civilein research papers, there was no stealing them. Johnston kept his notes in a numbered series. Didn't you notice?'

'Pardon?' said Lisa. 'Notice what?' Her heart was thundering and she swallowed the last of the wine in an effort to hide her confusion. Listening to other people's confessions was all very well, but she wondered what Jacinta's reaction would be if she knew for certain she had been spied on.

'In a purely hypothetical way,' began Jacinta with a wicked grin, 'I might mention that I know darn well that someone other than me and our friends in blue went through that lab. It would have to be you, because you're the only one in the department with the wit to break the safe code.'

'Well, in that case,' said Lisa, putting down her glass and hoping that her hands weren't trembling too visibly, 'how did you open the safe? You did open the safe, didn't you?'

'Simple, I found the combination taped to the underside of the drawer next to the sink. Incidentally, would you mind not looking so worried? I'm not going to knock you off. Why should I? The way things have worked out at the moment everyone's happy except Eddie, poor chap, but a third murder would cause all sorts of confusion. Relax, relax, the only creature likely to harm a hair of your head, or ankle, in this house is Muscles.'

'Um, I see, well in that case you were telling me why it was so important that Johnston not be found in the laboratory.'

'Yes, so I was, so I was to be sure. You seem to have forgotten that in the matter of documentation there were two problems. One was the specifications for the Civilein and the other was the so-called evidence against my character and integrity. Frankly I was more worried about the latter, because at the time when Johnston was lying on the laboratory floor, I hadn't even found those old notes and so I would be right in the gun on motive when the police found documents in my handwriting in his safe. And if they worked that out, someone might just wonder whether I'd been poking around the lab, which would lead to the possibility that I might be suspected of knowing too much.'

'Knowing too much! In Australia? You've been reading too many spy stories!' snorted Lisa.

'Well, I must have reassured you, you're back to your usual cocky contradictory self. A little more Dutch courage?' Jacinta opened the second bottle, refilled the glasses, took a swallow, and continued.

'Yes, knowing too much in Australia. You may have noticed the high death rate among Australians who become involved in Royal Commissions, talk to the police, take strolls in the wrong parts of the country, and generally engage in things other people don't care for. Heart attacks are a prime candidate or heroin overdose failing that, and then there's always suicide. Good old suicide, where would the country be without it? Anyway, I had no particular wish to end up starring in a coroner's report. So that left me with convincing whoever was planning to come around and investigate Johnston's sudden departure that he hadn't even been in the lab at the time he was offed. What I hoped was that they'd assume he'd heard a noise, gone to investigate, met a burglar, and been attacked. Maybe it was a bit silly, but I was rather stressed at the time. Remember, I had to think all this up in thirty seconds or less. So, I dragged him by the feet, out of the lab and into the lecture theatre. I raced back and grabbed that metal bar. When I got back he was sitting up and moaning. All I could think of was Rasputin. The first thing he said was, "I'll see you never work again for this." Well, Sydney or the Bush, I thought, and I hit him three times. He was down on the floor, I was standing over him, so it wasn't all that difficult.'

'But why drag him around the lecture theatre?' protested Lisa. 'You'd already dragged him from the lab, and anyway weren't there drag marks in the corridor?'

'Have you taken a close look at the carpet in the corridor lately? No? Well, I certainly did, and there is just no nap left to show marks. Anyway I scuffed it up a bit later, just in case. Once he was actually dead and not a direct threat, I felt a lot calmer and started thinking a bit more collectedly about how to convince the police it couldn't have been me. I thought it would be best to try to give them the impression that it must have been a man. I mean, they tend to assume it's a man anyway, and I thought a few more helpful hints would throw them completely off my scent. I was going strongly on method as it was, but I thought if I dragged him across the floor, like that maniac in New South Wales – what was his name? Crocodile Dundee or something.'

She stared innocently at Lisa, who replied, 'Slasher Harris, as you ought to know. I heard you talking to Harwell about him in the tea room and saying there were parallels.'

'Mm. Yes, I may have overdone that a bit, but you can well understand I didn't want people to go drawing the wrong conclusions after I'd nearly ruptured myself with the effort. Slasher

Harris! Crocodile Dundee! How these men dramatise themselves! Anyway, I got hold of his feet and just kept pulling; surprisingly easy really if you know how to brace yourself. Of course, I couldn't have guessed they were going to go for poor Sam. I thought the body would have been found by the caretaker. Silly me, of course the caretakers do stuff all on the weekends. Then of course, if I'd left him where I'd hit him, they could probably tell from his clothes that he'd been dragged there in the first place. Remember I didn't want them to think he'd been in the lab.'

'Just a minute,' said Lisa. 'I thought you said he was dead.'

'I did.'

'But you don't bleed when you're dead,' objected Lisa, remembering the long trail of blood with a shudder.

'Ten out of ten for practical biology,' replied Jacinta calmly. 'No more you do. Surprising how often they get that wrong in horror films, don't you think?'

Lisa gazed at her appalled.

'Look, for heaven's sake! It's one thing sitting discussing the ins and outs of all this by the fire, but it was quite another thing doing it, I can tell you. I didn't have time for the niceties of whether he was exactly dead at that moment. He certainly was not objecting and I definitely was not causing him pain. Try it yourself some time, it's different when you're half out of your mind with worry and thinking every creak is someone coming in to find you, bar in hand.'

'I don't suppose it would have made any difference to you if you had known about poor old Sam,' said Lisa crossly.

Jacinta smiled. 'No, I don't suppose it would,' she said. 'Selfish to the core. Anyway, it doesn't seem to be possible to predict what on earth is going to happen next in these situations. I mean, who could possibly have realised that me killing Johnston would have led to poor old Eddie going off his rocker and knocking off a student? I always thought his relationships with the students were outstanding for cordiality, closeness and intimacy.'

'You think there was a relationship between the two murders, then?'

'I don't know really, it did become obvious that Johnston was up to a lot more than anybody ever realised, so there may have been some sort of tenuous link, or it may have been just coincidental.'

'So then you went back into the lab, opened the safe, found your old notes, and left?' asked Lisa.

'It wasn't quite that easy, but that was about the strength of it. I knew I had to work fast because you or Seamus would be bound to get in sooner or later to start beavering away. Fascinating, some of the files that were in that safe. Interesting that I don't seem to have heard much about them since, but then I only had a brief look at them.'

'Why not take them away and read them at leisure?' asked Lisa, suddenly realising that the odds were Jacinta had done just that, but deciding it would be better not to say so.

'Because Johnston had made it too obvious that he had files on people, therefore files on people there had to be where others could find them. Besides, I already had the murder weapon and I didn't want too much more incriminating evidence floating about the happy home.'

Thin, Lisa thought, not to mention out of character, but she was beginning to think that reassurances or not, it would be nice to get home and think about all this calmly and alone.

'And the specifications on Civilein manufacture? You just left them there and didn't try to get a copy or anything? Perhaps you could make an antidote.'

'No. Well, sort of. I refiled them under "First-Year Statistics Notes" so the police wouldn't notice them. They were much too complicated. No-one could have copied them in the few minutes I had left after I'd got the safe open. You should know, you saw them youself.'

'But you could have just photocopied them and put them back, no one the wiser,' persisted Lisa. 'Anyway, was that the actual recipe I saw you working on? I thought you said nobody had seen it.'

'Come now,' said Jacinta, ignoring the question, 'you've heard a lovely fairy story. The burning question for me is, what are you going to do about it? Can you prove it? Is it true? Are you going to dob me in? For one thing, you might have the decency to let me know how it was you suspected me. It was quite obvious that you did, even before the bar nearly hit you on the head.'

'Well,' said Lisa, choosing her words carefully. She had a strong feeling that she was going to have to be very, very careful what she said. 'I had actually known it was you for quite some time. All this sudden interest in Johnston's work was a dead giveaway.'

'Oh, come on,' said Jacinta. 'That's not enough to suspect anybody on.'

'Well, it was out of character. Odd. And you were acting funny in other ways, I don't know, hard to describe, but uncharacteristic. For example, it was rather strange that the only Sunday in months that you supposedly stayed home, there just happened to be a rather nasty murder at work. The last time you had Sunday off, it was because your flu had turned into pleurisy. Then you turn round and say that you just felt like having a day pottering at home on your own? Possible, I grant you, but not very likely. And things you said, just little things, got me thinking.'

Jacinta looked triumphant, drained her glass, and waved the metal bar at Lisa, who flinched quite noticeably.

'So your only evidence is that I had a Sunday off once in a while and that you thought I was acting funny. The police will love that.'

'Don't get so het up,' replied Lisa. 'Who said anything about going to the police?'

Jacinta paused. 'Well, aren't you?'

'You obviously reckon you could ride it out if I do,' replied Lisa. 'Or are you planning on seeing I don't get there?'

'No, no, why confuse the issue? The police already have a perfectly nice suspect and I don't want to get them wondering about what really happened.'

'Well, that's a relief. No, I won't go to the police. Though I don't honestly see how you could explain away the fact that the murder weapon has been hanging around in your hall cupboard.'

'I was only waiting for the fuss to die down and then I was going to throw it in the Yarra; nobody need know it was ever here. I should have got rid of it on the way home that Sunday, but you'd be surprised how many people seem to be about when they're not wanted. But why not go to the police? I thought I'd have to talk you out of it.'

Lisa thought for a minute, trying to get her motivation clear to herself. Then she answered. 'Well, it seems to me as if you did the world a favour getting rid of the bastard. And anyway I'm not all that convinced that putting people in jail is a good idea.' She smiled at Jacinta. 'And besides, you're going to see to it that I get a well-paid, quiet job in the State Electricity Commission, aren't you?'

Lisa drained her glass in a silent toast to her lost innocence.